THE

UMBRELLA

MAKER'S

SON

THE UMBRELLA MAKER'S SON

A Novel of WWII

TOD LENDING

HARPER

NEW YORK • LONDON • TORONTO • SYDNEY

HARPER

Map on page vii: "Map I. The Invasion and Partition of Poland," from *A World at Arms: A Global History of World War II* by Gerhard L. Weinberg, 1126–54. Cambridge: Cambridge University Press, 2005. Reproduced with permission of Licensor through PLSClear.

HarperCollins books may be purchased for educational, business, or sales promotional use. For information, please email the Special Markets Department at SPsales@harpercollins.com.

FIRST EDITION

Designed by Jamie Lynn Kerner

Library of Congress Cataloging-in-Publication Data

Names: Lending, Tod S., 1959- author.
Title: The umbrella maker's son : a novel / Tod Lending.
Description: First edition. | New York, NY : Harper Paperbacks, 2025.
Identifiers: LCCN 2024012016 | ISBN 9780063413849 (trade paperback) | ISBN 9780063413863 (ebook)
Subjects: LCSH: Holocaust, Jewish (1939-1945)—Poland—Fiction. | World War, 1939-1945—Poland—Fiction. | Jews—Poland—Fiction. | LCGFT: Historical fiction. | Romance fiction. | Novels.
Classification: LCC PS3612.E526 U43 2025 |
DDC 813/.6—dc23/eng/20240528
LC record available at https://lccn.loc.gov/2024012016

ISBN 978-0-06-341384-9 (pbk.)

24 25 26 27 28 LBC 5 4 3 2 1

For my ancestors who perished in the
pogroms, ghettos, and camps.
And for my great-grandpa Raphael Lending,
1859–1914, the umbrella maker, who knew
to move his family out of Poland
before it was too late.

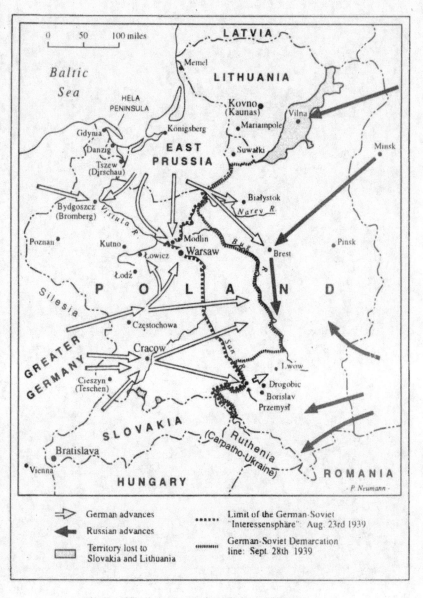

Map 1. The invasion and partition of Poland, 1939

THE
UMBRELLA
MAKER'S
SON

PART ONE

KRAKÓW

1

THE NIGHT BEFORE EVERYTHING CHANGED, I HAD A VISION.

Zelda gripped my hand, leading me through a pitch-dark forest with no path. The fall air was cool, the sky ink black and moonless. Our footsteps crushed dry leaves and snapped twigs and branches, breaking the haunted silence. Oaks and elms loomed over us with their long and knobby armlike limbs twisting and bending above. An eerie wind, heavy with the scent of damp soil, rustled the dying leaves. The dark wood, full of ghosts, reminded me of my family, making me long for them.

"Which way is it?" I whispered to Zelda.

"I'm not sure. Maybe this way." Still clasping my hand, she towed me toward the marshy scent of the Vistula River.

We crossed a small meadow of wet tallgrass and entered a tangled thicket that clawed at our arms and legs. The ground turned soft. Black clay sucked at our boots, the pungent river scent growing stronger. Shadows darted between trees. *Germans*, I thought. I wanted to run.

"What's wrong?" asked Zelda.

"Nothing." I didn't want her to think I was afraid.

We followed the rippling sounds of water running over rocks and logs to a clearing. The river revealed itself, its glassy waters shimmering in starlight, snaking between shores overgrown with dense bushes and brambles. Next to the river, several weeping willows dipped their stringy branches into the water. One of them was the same willow where I had kissed Zelda for the first time, hidden beneath its curtain of branches. We were twelve years old. She had initiated the kiss. I was shy. She was bold. Four years later, at that same willow, I got up the nerve to ask her to marry me. "I will," she said, "when we're older."

She led me to that willow. We sat beneath it, our eyes locked on the river, waiting for a boat to take us north, somewhere far away from the dark forest and shadows. As we watched for the boat, small black domes floated on the surface of the water, drifting toward us. When they got closer, I realized they were umbrellas.

2

MY ALARM ABRUPTLY ENDED THE VISION AT SIX IN THE MORNING. It was the first day of the new month, 1 September 1939. I'd turned seventeen three days earlier. As I lay there in bed, sheets moist with sweat, my mind drifted, disturbed by the vision, unsure of its meaning.

At the foot of my bed, the thin white window curtains fluttered and billowed in the unusually warm wind coming off the river. They reminded me of Zelda's sleeveless blue summer dress with yellow sunflowers. I liked that dress. It showed off her long slender arms, freckled and tanned by sun and wind. I was hoping she'd wear it that morning. We were to meet by the river soon to take our morning walk, a ritual of ours, before parting for work.

I got out of bed, threw open the curtains, and started for the bathroom when a heavy blast echoed in the distance, like a burst of thunder. But that couldn't be right—warm sunlight was pouring through my window. I scanned the morning sky above the three- and four-story apartment buildings lining our neighborhood, Kazimierz. The sky was cloudless, a seamless expanse of brilliant blue. Then another blast, closer this time, rattled the windows and doors. This was not thunder.

I yanked on my suit trousers, nearly ripping a seam, and ran to the sitting room hollering, "What the hell was that?"

"The *farshtunken* reporter knows nothing!" shouted Bubbe— my grandma. Planted in her plush, maroon velvet chair, she was listening to the radio, drinking black tea from a teacup and saucer with trembling hands, gnarled and arthritic from old age and decades of sewing clothes. She nervously set the teacup on the side table and grabbed the armrests to hoist her barrel-shaped body out of the chair.

Papa leaned out the French doors that opened to the street, searching the sky for clues. His left hand gripped the iron balustrade outside the window, a cigarette pinched between his thumb and index finger, a cup of coffee rocking in his other hand. Dressed in his chocolate-brown suit, he was ready to go to the umbrella shop. He was always ready to leave before me.

He nervously tapped the cigarette against the balustrade to get rid of an ash that wasn't there, took a deep inhalation from it before exhaling a stream of smoke. "Reuven, see over there." He pointed with the cigarette, dribbling a small amount of coffee on his trousers. He didn't notice, and I said nothing. "See what's coming from the airport?"

I leaned out the window and spotted an ominous column of black smoke churning and billowing in the sky. Several large twin-engine planes appeared from the west and circled the city. Something was so very wrong.

"Are those ours?" I asked.

"I think so. Those look like our Łoś warplanes."

"Oy—I don't think so," said Bubbe. She squeezed her stout, heavily perfumed body next to me. "Those are damn Germans." She breathed hard, her doughy arm jabbing me in the side.

"Bubbe, I'm sure they're ours," said Papa. "Maybe they're running drills." His voice sounded thin and uncertain.

"Bullshit," said Bubbe. "They're Germans." She spat out the window in disgust. "Such a *broch*!" She always spoke of curses.

"Why are there no air-raid sirens?" I asked.

"The mayor is an imbecile," said Bubbe.

Mama rushed into the sitting room, cinching the sash of her blue robe, her thick brown hair tousled. "What was that noise?" she asked.

Sara and Basha, my younger teenage sisters, trailed her.

"Thunder," said Sara, grabbing on to Mama's robe for security. She glanced around the room, her wide eyes darting about, searching for some kind of confirmation.

"No—something exploded," said Basha. She was thirteen, only a year younger than Sara. Confident and driven, Basha wore the intense, hardened look of a street fighter. "I think we're going to die," she said matter-of-factly.

"Don't be stupid!" said Sara.

"Don't you call me stupid! You're stupid!" Basha shoved Sara, who was taller, long-limbed, and thin, more delicate than her. Both, unlike myself, excelled in school and studied voraciously. Basha loved history and wanted to be a journalist, whereas Sara favored astronomy over all else. Most of the time, those two got along, spending hours studying together and reading their books. But Basha was competitive and acted as a thorn in Sara's side the moment she felt threatened.

Mama warned them to stop.

Bubbe waddled to the radio and turned up the volume. The news announcer's voice faded in and out of a storm of static. I adjusted the tuning knob in tiny increments and found a clear channel. The announcer was breathless. Stumbling on his words, he reported sightings of German warplanes bombing Warsaw and German troops and tanks crossing over the western border into Poland. But they hadn't confirmed anything.

Papa paced by the radio and stroked his thick black mustache, an annoying habit of his when agitated.

"Lev." Mama crossed her arms against her chest. "You and Reuven need to get to the shop and bring home the accounting books and everything in the safe in case the shop gets bombed."

Inside the safe was cash, ivory, and the precious gems and silver and gold bands we used for capping the umbrella handles.

Papa looked surprised. "I think we should stay together until we know the bombing is over, don't you?"

"It's quiet now. Maybe it's over. Just make it quick. Go there and come back immediately. We can't afford to lose those things."

Unlike Papa, Mama was unwavering. She would've made a good general in the army. She was mission driven. Once she made a decision, there was no turning back.

Bubbe shook her head. "No. They should wait."

"I agree with Mama. We should go," I said. However, I wasn't planning to go directly to the shop. I first needed to get to the river in case Zelda was there waiting for me. I wanted to be sure she was safe. But I knew if I said this in front of Mama, she'd say my place was with my family, and that Zelda would be with hers. It would be an argument I'd never win. So I kept quiet, a practice I was good at when dealing with Mama.

Mama and Bubbe argued, as they did often, with the fervor of a daughter and mother who had unfinished business from the past. We were used to it. Both were hardheaded, and it often took another family member to step in like a diplomat to help negotiate a resolution to their disagreements.

"Rachel does have a point," Papa said calmly to Bubbe. He usually took that role, always the mediator. "If we lose the books and all the valuables in the safe, it will set us back. There does seem to be a lull in the bombing."

"I agree," I chimed in.

"You're all *meshuga!* Crazy!" said Bubbe, plumping herself down into the plush folds of her chair. "You should stay right here until we know it's safe to go out."

Then Basha wanted to come with us. "Absolutely not!" said Mama, Bubbe, and Papa in unison.

"Oh, I think she should go," said Sara sardonically.

Basha raised her fist at her.

"Don't you dare," said Mama.

I went to my room to finish dressing while Papa retrieved a rucksack and valise from the front closet. We bolted from the apartment, rushing down the three flights of stairs to the street. People were cautiously emerging from their apartment buildings, gazing up at the sky and at one another, confused and terrified. There were only a few horse-drawn droskies on the street. Those that rushed past us, their drivers snapping the reins, had buggies already full of passengers. On the street, I told Papa we needed to stop at the river to make sure Zelda wasn't there waiting for me.

"I'm sure she won't be there at a time like this," he said while pacing anxiously, searching for an available drosky.

"But I have to be certain."

Finally, a drosky stopped. Papa stepped into the open buggy and motioned for me to get in. "Come on, let's go."

"I can't," I said, slowly backing away. "I need to check on her." I turned my back on him and started running toward the river. He immediately called after me and promised to first take me to the river.

That was Papa, always willing to compromise, always wanting to avoid confrontations and altercations. Although I'd been able to take advantage of this character flaw throughout much of my teenage years and enjoyed the freedoms his weakness provided me, I also resented it. I resented how Mama controlled him and how certain customers could see his kindness as an opportunity to exploit. They often persuaded him to sell an umbrella at a lower price, sometimes ten, fifteen, even twenty percent off the price tag. He was too accommodating.

It didn't help that he was slight in physical stature, humble in appearance. Average in height and narrow shouldered, he had deep-set eyes that appeared contemplative, and often uncertain. A thicket of unruly black hair that was tamed with oil and brushed straight back framed his broad forehead and bony cheekbones. His small wire-rimmed glasses, like those of an accountant or librarian, balanced on the bridge of his keel-shaped nose; beneath its overhang sprouted a thick black mustache, its edges always perfectly trimmed along the gentle curve of his upper lip. He was a kind man, good to his workers, soft-spoken. A man who sometimes was too emotional, too easily manipulated.

After I climbed in, the young driver steered his horse down Mostowa Street toward the river. From our open carriage, we witnessed swarms of people spilling out from the doorways of their apartment buildings, rushing frantically through the streets of Kazimierz.

Meyer the fishmonger and Naftoli the tailor next door frantically locked down their shops while Jakov the shoemaker across the street covered his shop window with an enormous piece of wood planking. Further down, Big Ziggy, his bearded face and hairy arms coated in coal dust, was hurriedly unloading the last of his coal boxes from the back of his long wagon when he dropped two of them, spilling a pile of the black rocks across the sidewalk where people were trying to pass. He looked up at the sky when another couple of planes soared overhead. The fierce, throaty sounds of their engines roared past as the menacing iron crosses beneath their wings glared down at us. Then the air-raid sirens blasted, causing even more of a commotion in the streets.

Old Schmuel, long-bearded and bent over like a fishhook, appeared oblivious to the mayhem. He continued sweeping the streets as people ran past him. Avrom the water carrier spun round a corner and almost knocked Old Schmuel to the ground with the wood beam stretched across his shoulders, the water buckets at each end of the beam splashing and spilling. A businessman dodged Avrom and Old Schmuel, tripping and falling over a curb, narrowly escaping being run over by Lipa's horse that was pulling the milk cart.

At the outdoor market on Gazowa Street, neighbors battled one another to fill their bags with food. Mrs. Baum, normally courteous and kind, shoved Mrs. Fischer out of the way to grab a loaf of bread.

"Thief!" an old man hollered, running after a boy weaving through the crowd with his pockets bulging with potatoes. A frantic mother used her pram, holding her baby and groceries, as a battering ram to push people out of the way. She nearly knocked down an elderly lady leaning forward on her cane as if battling a great headwind. She walked slowly amid the turmoil, taking one tiny, cautious step at a time.

Clogging the streets were delivery trucks and cars, anxious drivers banging on their horns, droskies jostling for position, bicyclists weaving in and out of the traffic. The horse-drawn carts from the local farms just outside of the city loaded down with gunnysacks of grains, cages stuffed with squawking chickens, wooden boxes of eggs packed in hay, and metal containers of milk had reduced the traffic to a crawl.

Our driver finally made it down to the Vistula River and turned on Podgórska Street, which ran alongside the river. At the bridge, I told him to stop.

"I'll be right back," I said to Papa.

"Hurry, and be careful," he said, scanning the sky.

While calling out for Zelda, I tore through the bushes and brambles to the path running parallel to the river. Red-winged blackbirds darted about as I frantically searched north and south for a flash of her curly copper-red hair. But not a human was in sight. Mama and Papa were right—she must've been home with her family. However, I needed to be certain.

I ran back to the drosky and told Papa she wasn't there and that I'd meet him at the shop after I checked on Zelda's apartment. It was only four streets away from the river.

"No, that's enough! You come with me now. We'll check on the way back." His hands gripped the seat railing, knuckles white. "Now get in, Reuven!" It was rare to see him so angry.

"I'm sorry, Papa, but I have to go." I took off toward Krakowska Street, where Zelda and her family lived. He called after me. I didn't stop. As I ran, a wave of guilt washed over me. Maybe it was a mistake, but I couldn't stop myself. I had to be certain Zelda was safe.

3

ABOVE, TWO TWIN-ENGINE GERMAN PLANES CIRCLED KRAKÓW like hawks searching for prey. Another bomb exploded somewhere in the distance, followed by the ominous howls of the air-raid sirens. Echoing across the city, their shrill pitch grew louder with a chilling intensity—a haunting primal wail slicing through the air. It was terrifying.

More trucks, cars, and droskies clogged the streets with people on foot scurrying between them as if being chased.

When I finally reached Zelda's building, there were frightened families loading mountains of luggage into two trucks, five cars, and three rickety horse carts that were parked in front. A driver nervously paced around a fourth horse cart, his dark beady eyes fixed on the sky, waiting impatiently for his customers.

Inside the building, the frantic voices of children screaming and crying and parents hollering directions to one another reverberated through the hallways. I ran up the stairs to the third floor, pushing past a barrage of people rushing down the stairs hauling luggage and furniture.

I pounded on Zelda's door. It swung open and there was her fourteen-year-old brother, Joshua, looking perplexed. "Reuven! What are you doing here?"

"I just wanted to check on Zelda."

"Come in. She's in her room packing."

Joshua was like a younger brother to me. Whenever I was at their apartment, he'd want to play a game of chess or go outside and kick a football around the yard. He was very adept at learning foreign languages and spoke fluent German and French and had a handle on English.

"We're leaving!" yelled his younger brother, Eli, as he ran past me down the hallway to his mother.

Mrs. Abramovitch didn't notice me enter the apartment as she dashed from room to room, packing clothes and kitchen items. "Hello, Mrs. Abramovitch," I said.

She looked up, startled. "Oh—hello, Reuven!" she said, tying a box closed. "What are you doing here? Why aren't you with your family?"

"I was worried about Zelda."

"Well, that was kind of you to come and check on her. But you should be with your family. Are they all right?"

"Yes. Everyone is fine."

"Good. You'll find Zelda in her room packing."

Zelda also hadn't heard me enter the apartment and was surprised to see me. I closed the door, threw my arms round her, squeezed her body against mine, and kissed her freckled lips. She caressed my face with her tender hands. Her green eyes, the color of oak leaves, were a shade darker from sorrow.

"Where are you going?" I asked.

"East. To my aunt and uncle's farmhouse outside Dębica. But I don't want to go."

"For how long?"

"I don't know. Papa says we'll come back when it's safe. I wish you could come with us."

"So do I."

"Is your family leaving?"

"I don't know yet. We have the shop to watch, and we don't have any family in the countryside. Let me help you pack." I handed her some clothes and felt such sadness as I looked around her small, sparsely furnished room containing a faded oriental rug, a dark wood dresser, a small bed, and a writing desk where she did her homework and read her books that lined the walls from floor to nearly the ceiling. Her papa had built the bookshelves from scraps of pine that he got from a friend of his who was a carpenter.

The room looked like a small corner of the Kraków library. Books helped feed her insatiable curiosity for stories about the world, and her spongelike brain absorbed knowledge effortlessly, devouring everything that piqued her interest. She was the smartest student in our high school, the most intelligent and sensitive person I'd ever known. Why she was with me, I never quite understood. When I asked her once, she said, "Besides being handsome, you have a kind heart, like your papa. And you're smart in your own way." I liked the handsome part, didn't like being compared to my papa, and wasn't sure what she meant about being smart "in my own way." I decided to never pursue the meaning of that comment.

On the one wall without books, a window looked out at the building sandwiched beside theirs. On the wall next to the window, Zelda had hung a framed print of a Matisse painting called *The Open Window*. It was so peaceful and beautiful that it completely overshadowed the dismal view from the real window.

I was with Zelda when we had discovered the print while garbage picking after school four years ago in the very wealthy section of Podgórze. This was a favorite activity of ours. The painting showed two French doors open to the Mediterranean Sea filled with sailboats. In the foreground were potted plants and greenery, perhaps vines, framing the view of the sailboats. The colors were bright and vibrant, with shades of turquoise, blues and greens, burnt oranges, and tomato reds, a wall that was a rich violet. These were Zelda's colors. She said this was her favorite painting in the world because the view filled her with inspiration, hopefulness, and a sense of serenity. When I looked at the picture, I felt similarly.

"Reuven, can you help me reach the books I want to pack? I told Mama I wanted to bring ten with us. She said five. We settled on eight." She selected *Boundary* by Zofia Nałkowska; Tolstoy's *Anna Karenina* and *War and Peace*; Dostoyevsky's *The Brothers Karamazov*; *The Great Gatsby* by Fitzgerald; the epic poem *Pan Tadeusz* by Adam Mickiewicz; a book on human biology; and *The Tree of Life*, written by Hayyim ben Joseph Vital in 1573, a book about the teachings of Kabbalah, the mystical and esoteric texts of Judaism. "Your parents won't like you bringing this one," I said as I handed it to her.

"Too bad. They know they can't stop me from reading it." Reading about Kabbalah was a huge source of tension between Zelda and her parents. The Orthodox believed it was forbidden for women to learn about Kabbalah and its teachings. But Zelda wasn't religious in the traditional Orthodox way that her parents were religious. She considered herself spiritual, not religious, and it was the mystical aspects of Judaism that fascinated her. She studied the teachings of Kabbalah through reading *The Tree of Life*, despite their concerns. There were times she shared with me what she learned, and I understood some parts of what she explained. But other times, it was as if she was speaking a foreign language. I once asked her why she was so interested in Kabbalah. She claimed that Kabbalah gave her a deeper sense of meaning and purpose in life, a more complex understanding of how everything on earth and throughout the universe was interconnected in ways we often didn't consciously perceive. "But you must live Kabbalah, Reuven. Not just read it," she'd say. "I promise, if you do, you'll see the world entirely differently."

Although she was aware of my resistance to anything considered religious or spiritual, she never gave up on trying to show me a new way of seeing and understanding the world.

"Reuven! Come and help me," beckoned Mr. Abramovitch's dry and gravelly voice from the sitting room.

Zelda drew me tight against her and kissed me. The warmth of her body, her steady breath, the scent of lavender on the gentle curve of her neck, her light blue cotton dress soft as silk in my hands, filled me with longing and deepened my gloom. I dreaded being separated from my brilliant, spiritual, incredibly sensitive Zelda. The longest time we'd ever been away from each other was for a mere ten days, when my family took a summer trip to the mountain resort in Zakopane. Those ten days seemed like a month. Daily, I wrote her postcards telling her how much I missed her, and how I longed to have her back in my arms the moment we returned.

As we embraced, troubling thoughts of something bad happening to her in the countryside consumed me. My heart felt heavy with foreboding. I feared she might vanish if I let her go.

"Reuven!" her papa yelled again. "I need you!"

"Go help him," whispered Zelda, followed by another kiss. "And don't worry. I don't think we'll be gone long."

In the small sitting room, hunched over and haggard, Mr. Abramovitch was stuffing an overpacked trunk with some more books and clothes. He carefully wrapped his sacred leather-bound Talmudic prayer book in his tallit—a white prayer shawl—along with his royal blue velvet bag containing his tefillin. These were two small leather boxes containing parchment scrolls that fit in the palm of a hand. Being Orthodox, Mr. Abramovitch dutifully wore the tefillin every time he prayed.

"Help me close this," he said while pushing down on the trunk's lid. I put all my weight on it and could barely latch it closed. Then he stiffly lifted one end of the trunk, groaning and complaining about its weight as I lifted the other end. We carried the trunk down the first flight of stairs and at the landing had to stop and put it down so he could catch his breath. The black velvet yarmulke capping the crown of his shiny bald head like an acorn was sliding off, revealing the last stray threads of gray hair clinging to his scalp firmly as weeds. Streams of sweat dripped down his dome-like forehead. "Oy gevalt," he grumbled while wiping away the sweat with his handkerchief and repositioning his yarmulke.

"Are you okay?" I asked.

"If I have a heart attack or stroke, you make sure my family gets out of here. Promise me that!"

"Of course, I promise. But please, don't have a heart attack or stroke, Mr. Abramovitch. Your family needs you."

"I should get a hernia for sure. My back is killing me!"

"Use your legs, Mr. Abramovitch, not your back."

"My *farshtunken* legs? The only thing they're good for is taking me to the kitchen table to eat and getting me to the toilet."

Mr. Abramovitch was a small, potbellied man, bespectacled and rabbinical looking with his long gray beard that blended with his curly sidelocks and tea-stained mustache that draped over his upper lip. He fervently studied Torah and went to synagogue daily, whereas my family, except for Bubbe, were socialists and culturally Jewish, but nonpracticing. The only time we attended synagogue was on the high holidays, for the sake of tradition, and on the anniversary of Grandpa Eliyohu's death, to honor Bubbe's wishes.

Mr. Abramovitch's dream had been to become a rabbi, a dream that had evaded him. Unable to make a living as a rabbi, instead he became an itinerant tailor, eking out a meager salary on an old Singer treadle machine that occupied a corner of the sitting room. Zelda told me that when she was little, she sometimes heard him praying at night, imploring God to tell him what he must do to make enough money to open his own shop. Sometimes he wept. Other times, he spoke in more angry tones, beckoning God to answer his prayers.

Mrs. Abramovitch earned most of the family income. Unlike her husband, she landed a steady job working as a mender for a very successful tailor, Mr. Fischler, on Józefińska Street. She learned the trade from her parents and started working at nine years old. She taught Zelda to sew, even though Zelda, from an early age, had planned on becoming a pediatrician. No matter that Zelda excelled in school and had skipped two grades, her mother still insisted she learn to sew. "Sewing is a trade people always need. And nobody can take it away from you!" she'd exclaim.

After finally loading the trunk, Mr. Abramovitch was too exhausted to do more heavy lifting. He climbed into the wagon with the help of the driver and sat down to rest his sore knees and back and catch his breath before returning to the apartment. In the meantime, I moved the rest of the luggage with the help of Zelda and Mrs. Abramovitch.

When we finished, the day had turned to dusk. Biala the lamplighter, a lonely figure bent over in black, raggedy clothes, limped down the street toward us, using his long wooden pole with a metal hook at the end to turn on the gas before lighting each streetlamp with a candle.

Zelda's parents sat on a bench behind the driver, their wagon stacked high with their valises, trunks, and satchels full of clothes. Joshua and Eli sat in the back where they had made a comfortable place to sit among the piles of luggage.

Before mounting the wagon, Zelda hugged me one last time.

"I love you and will miss you," I whispered into her ear.

"I love you and will miss you more," she whispered back.

"But I miss you already."

"And I already miss you." Her woeful voice was soft and airy, a gentle whisper, like the sound of the tallgrass by the river rustling in a warm breeze.

I wanted to give her something to remember me by but had nothing in my pockets except a few kopeks. I looked down at my clothes and tore off one of the large shiny black buttons on my trousers used for holding my suspenders.

"What are you doing?" she asked, looking confused.

I pressed it into her hand. "Hold on to this button for me and when you return, you can show me how to sew it back on." We kissed. I tasted salty tears running across her lips. Our beseeching smiles signaled to the other that we wanted to believe all would go well. And that we'd see each other soon. Yet in her deep green eyes, glistening in the flicker of the streetlamp's flame, there was anxiety, trepidation, and sadness. I'm sure she saw the same in my eyes.

Eli and Joshua were in the back of the wagon, sandwiched between the trunks and valises, passing the tattered football between them. Joshua looked over at me and waved excitedly. "Be prepared!" he said. "I'm going to beat you the next time we play chess!"

"I doubt it!"

"You'll see."

Zelda kissed me again, then climbed onto the wagon and sat down on the bench behind the driver, nestled between her mother and father.

"Watch for my letters," she said as their wagon slowly pulled away, heading eastward toward the bridge spanning the Vistula River.

"Don't lose my button!" I hollered back.

"Trust me," she replied.

As the horse towed their wagon through patches of darkness, Zelda appeared and disappeared in the warm glow of the streetlamps. Our eyes remained locked on each other as we blew one last kiss and waved desperately before she vanished into the obscurity of the night.

4

AFTER SAYING GOODBYE TO ZELDA, I REALIZED IT WAS TOO LATE to return to the shop. Papa would already be home, and I wasn't ready to go there to deal with the repercussions of my actions.

Meandering the gray cobblestones of Podgórska Street along the Vistula, I thought about how long it would be until I'd see Zelda again. Smoky clouds of dense gray fog climbed the riverbank and drifted across the road. Podgórska was crowded with droskies and horse-drawn wagons, pushcarts and trucks filled to the brim with families and their belongings. The steady stream of people fleeing the city flowed toward the bridge at Krakowska Street where they crossed the Vistula and headed eastward, away from the bombing, in the same direction Zelda had gone. I walked in the opposite direction, toward the train bridge.

At Starowiślna Street, I was about to turn left when I noticed, fading in and out of the fog, the blinking red lights of several ambulances parked near the train bridge. As I got closer, the misty outlines of people carrying shovels, wheelbarrows, and stretchers appeared in the field at the foot of the bridge where a bomb had dropped. The bomb had hit the tracks at the end of the bridge where the train crossed.

From the field, desperate voices called out for help; others cried out in pain. Polish soldiers directed civilians volunteering to help, showing them where to dig around the bomb site, and where they needed stretchers.

Emerging from the fog like a ghost, sauntering in my direction, came a tall lanky man with long wispy arms looking like willow branches, his face coated with specks of dirt and beads of sweat. He dragged one end of an empty stretcher through the grass, spotted me, and called out, "Come help. Take the other end."

We carried the stretcher through wet grass until we came across the bodies of wounded and dead soldiers strewn about the tangled tracks. The carcass of the nine-car military train on its side came into view. Black smoke and flames from the locomotive stirred with the fog and filled the air with the acrid stench of burning coal, oil, wood, and flesh. Half the train was still on the bridge with two of its cars blown wide open. Soldiers' bodies lay strewn across the wood floors and seats, their backpacks, canvas duffel bags, and clothes scattered across the tracks. Bloody body parts spread across the wet grass: a severed leg, bloody red bits of raw flesh, a severed finger with a silver ring on it.

Two soldiers supporting each other limped past us when the man carrying the other end of the stretcher stopped next to a soldier lying face down in the wet grass, motionless, blood pooling around his midsection. We set the stretcher on the ground and the tall man rolled the soldier over on his back to check if he was alive. His stomach was a bloody hole, ground meat and shiny pale intestines spilled out. I turned away. My legs went weak and my stomach churned. I vomited.

"He's gone," the man said plainly, as if what he'd just seen was something he'd seen many times before. "We'll come back to get him after we find the wounded." I nodded, trying to hold myself together. Yet the surrounding carnage was overwhelming, making me unsteady on my feet.

A dead horse lay on the tracks, head nearly severed, limp tongue hanging out of his mouth as if licking the ground. Another horse on its side struggled in the dirt, kicking its legs desperately, trying to stand up. Jagged white bone and sinew burst out at the knee of its right foreleg. A military officer walked up to the suffering horse, drew his pistol, and shot it between the eyes at close range. Blood spurted from its head in a stream as it hit the ground. I wretched again, thinking, I can't take this hellish place much longer. But to leave would've been cowardly, and so I forced myself to stay.

The man at the opposite end of the stretcher pointed to a wounded, barely conscious soldier in the wet grass. The young Polish soldier, maybe a few years older than me, moaned as blood from a deep head wound oozed into his blond hair and streaked down his face. His arm appeared broken, his foot nearly severed at the ankle; the repulsive bone tore through the flesh, the angles all wrong. The man beside me spoke calmly to the soldier, telling him everything would be okay. Acting without hesitation, he took the soldier's knife and sliced a strip of khaki-green wool from the soldier's pant leg and tied the ends of the cloth to make a tourniquet. He placed it around the bottom of the right leg and used a stick to twist the tourniquet and stop the bleeding.

I realized this man had seen war before. He was Papa's age and must've fought in the last war, like Papa. This man had smelled the blood and stench of burning flesh and had seen the wounded and the dead. And now, I had, too.

When we lifted the soldier onto the stretcher, he cried out in agony, a primal scream that sent chills through me. He then fell unconscious.

We carried him to the road where ambulances and droskies waited. The other man faced forward, holding the stretcher behind him with the soldier's upper body at his end. As we walked, I saw the mud and grass on the bottom of the soldier's black leather boots and the splintered white bone and tendons, like a mass of sliced white kite strings, protruding from the fleshy red meat of his ankle. At first, the sight repulsed me and I tried to avert my gaze. But then I forced myself to look at it. I wondered if it was possible to repair a wound like that.

We helped an ambulance driver load the soldier into the vehicle and immediately returned to the field where we repeated this task over and over, working late into the night.

When the field was finally clear of the dead and wounded, I told the man I needed to get home, that my family was waiting for me. He said goodbye and wished me luck. Grateful that I'd met him, I wished him the same and wondered if we'd ever meet again.

While walking home along the river, a barge carrying lumber emerged from the fog as it headed north. A man crossed over the logs near the bow, holding a kerosene lamp, its light small as a star floating in the mist. A map of the river appeared in my mind. It snaked through the heart of the country, connecting Kraków with Warsaw, Sandomierz, Bydgoszcz, and Gdańsk. I thought about how many other cities had been bombed, how many more dead and wounded lay scattered across the country.

In the late hours of night, fewer people were leaving the city. The skies were now quiet, the air still and humid. My mind fell into a state of numbness; a blanket of exhaustion swept over me. I should've been hungry, ravenous, in fact. I hadn't eaten all day, yet the thought of eating made me nauseous. Overwhelmed by the horror of what I'd witnessed, my mind was shutting down.

When I returned home, it was past midnight and Papa was on the couch in the sitting room reading a book. He put the book down on his lap when I walked in and gazed at me from head to toe, his face in shock. "My God, what happened to you?" he said. I looked down at my clothes and for the first time noticed bloodstains all over my shirt and pants with more dried blood staining my hands and arms.

Mama started yelling from the kitchen. "How dare you leave your father like that! You terrified us! What's wrong with you?!" She entered the sitting room with her hands flying over her head, her face peeled back in anger. "Where have you been all this—"

Her voice went quiet the moment she saw me.

"Oh my God, what did you do?" She gazed at me, clutching her hands.

I had little to say. I briefly told them about helping Zelda and her family pack and mentioned the bomb site. I was too exhausted to go into details, nor did I want to remember what I'd just seen.

"You should've never left your papa," said Mama. "He needed you more than Zelda's family needed you. And then to not come home afterward! To leave us here not knowing what's happened to you! How could you?"

Papa slammed his book down on the table. "That's enough, Rachel! Leave him alone."

There were only a few times in my life when I'd seen Papa suddenly snap and yell at Mama like that. Like a couple of years ago when Mama blamed him for not selling enough umbrellas in the months of April, May, and June—the rainy months. I appreciated Papa coming to my defense. He had never spoken about what he'd witnessed in the last war. But I knew he understood what I'd seen.

"I don't care!" said Mama. "He should've come home, Lev. He should've known better."

Mama always got the last word in.

Bubbe came out from her bedroom dressed in her long nightgown, ordering Mama to calm down and to lower her voice. She told me to run the bath, get cleaned up, and then try to eat something. She also seemed to understand what I'd witnessed because she, too, had lived through the last war, as did Mama. But that didn't seem to matter to Mama.

Before I headed to the bathroom, Bubbe whispered in my ear: "You did the right thing, honey. I'm proud of you."

That night, although I had not an ounce of energy left in me, I couldn't sleep. I lay in bed for hours, trying to rid my memory of all the bloody carnage at the bomb site. Staring up at the ceiling, I shifted my thoughts to Zelda. My heart was already aching for her, as if she'd been gone for months. The tears running down her face made me think of the river itself. How the water flowed from the mountains in the south to the Baltic Sea in the north with its tributaries branching out from its main artery like roots of a tree, feeding thick forests, farmlands, villages, small towns, and cities. Everything seemed interconnected by the river, just like what Zelda said the Kabbalah taught.

At this moment, I wanted Zelda curled up next to me, her arm draped across my chest, her hand cradled in mine. I missed the warmth of her skin pressed against me, my fingers combing through the long strands of her thick and curly copper-colored hair. I wanted her next to me talking about her day, or telling me stories, or describing what she learned about Kabbalah, or singing to me in her sweet raspy voice the Yiddish song "Belz, Mayn Shtetele Belz." I wanted her to hold me and to help me forget, if even for a moment, about the world crumbling around us.

5

OVER THE NEXT SEVERAL DAYS AND NIGHTS, THE TERRIFYING air-raid sirens sent us scrambling down the three flights of stairs to the dank, dirt-floored cellar. Bare bulbs hanging from a wire snaking along the low ceiling dimly illuminated our primitive cave crammed with families huddled together in trepidation.

Initially, panic quieted the people. But as the hours passed, a cacophony of sounds reverberated through the shelter. Conversations emerged, babies wailed, youngsters darted about playing tag and stumbling over people. Occasionally, there were arguments. And there were the elderly with their weak bladders who left quietly to relieve themselves despite their anxieties. Yet from the pungent scent of urine, clearly some were too afraid to leave.

Bubbe tired of going up and down the stairs every time the air-raid siren blared. She resisted leaving the apartment. But we refused to leave her behind. Then one day, the cellar lost its electricity. She panicked and grabbed my arm, gasping for air. I begged her to calm down, but she couldn't hear me. Her eyes glazed over, staring off into space. Her breath stopped for a moment, then her lungs gasped for air. I thought she was having a stroke. Mama started screaming. Papa helped me take her up the narrow, rickety wood staircase leading out of the cellar.

In the hallway, we gently laid her down on the white and black tile floor and I kept talking to her and patted the sides of her

face, trying to bring her back to life. Her inhalations turned
shallow, then barely perceivable. Papa and I told her to breathe,
keep breathing! Her eyes closed, and it seemed she was departing
for the next world.

Mama jumped up and down in the hallway, screaming at us to
do something. But I didn't know what else to do, and neither did
Papa. Then Bubbe's body jolted, followed by a deep inhale, then
an exhale, another inhale, and so on. "My God!" Mama cried
out. We all ordered Bubbe to keep breathing. With her eyes still
closed, she mumbled that she needed some fresh air. Then her
eyes opened, as if she'd just wakened from a deep sleep. "Take me
upstairs," she said. "Get me the hell out of here!"

The sirens continued to blare. Mama and my sisters hugged
Bubbe and begged her to come back to the cellar, but she refused.
"I want to go," she said. "I'd much rather die alone in the apartment
than inside that suffocating cellar with all those *meshuga* people."
Mama tried convincing her otherwise, but it was no use.

Mama, Papa, and the girls returned to the cellar while I assisted Bubbe up the staircase. With my arm strapped around her
barrel-shaped waist, we slowly made the ascent, plodding one stair
at a time, as if climbing a steep mountain. Her soft body pressed
against mine, her dress moist with sweat, her nervous body odor
a musty blend of sour lemons and sweet perfume. "Go faster,
honey," she said. "Go much faster. I need to pee!"

Tightening my grip on her waist, I pulled her up the stairs,
quickening our pace. "Keep going, honey. Faster, for God's sake!"

At the apartment, she threw open the door and scurried down
the hallway for the toilet with her legs pressed together, groaning
"Oy—oy—oy," the entire time. The moment she ducked inside
the bathroom there was a loud "Oyyyy veeeehhhhh!!" When she
came out the color had come back to her face and she smiled.
"That was a real close one, honey."

She went to the sitting room, plopped down in her cushy chair, and turned on the radio. The air-raid sirens fell silent. I adjusted the dial and found a station with some news. The announcer reported Polish troops were still holding their positions along the border but were suffering large casualties. Bubbe shook her head in resignation. "It's only a matter of time now before those Germans push our troops back."

"Why are you so sure?"

Bubbe explained how she'd seen it all before in the last war. She said in December 1914, first it was the Russians that invaded the country. She and Grandpa Eliyohu thought it would end there. But then in May of 1915, the Germans and Austro-Hungarian troops forced a Russian retreat and maintained control of the country until the end of the war. "Those damn Germans did what they wanted!" she said. "But now it's different. Now they have it out for the Jews. In Russia there were the pogroms, and those were horrific. But these Germans . . . what they want to do to us is just as bad, or even worse. Hitler and his Aryan race . . . Damn *mamzer* sonofabitch. He and his followers called us a subspecies of human beings. Who could think such a thing?!"

"What do you believe will happen if they occupy our country?"

"I can't imagine. I saw such terrible things when they occupied Kraków in the last war. Food was hard to come by, people went hungry, the women . . ." She paused for a long moment. Tears welled in her eyes and she shook her head from side to side, as if trying to suppress a painful memory that had just surfaced. "I worry about your mama and sisters. You and your papa must make sure you hide them from those Nazi soldiers if they come here. You promise me that!"

"Of course."

She switched off the radio and gently closed her eyes. "I'm so tired, my dear. So tired of this world." She took a full breath and sighed. The deep lines of history etched in her forehead and carved round the corners of her eyes made me think about what it must be like to experience yet another war at her age. It was confounding and filled me with a profound sadness. She was such a good person, so naturally loving, kind, and generous. A person like her having to endure so much suffering—it made no sense.

"Can you make me a cup of tea, honey?" she asked with her eyes still closed.

"Of course, Bubbe."

6

IN THE DAYS THAT FOLLOWED, A RELENTLESS WHIRLWIND OF events unfolded, stealing our sleep and fraying our nerves as tensions escalated by the hour. Britain and France had declared war on Germany, providing us with a sliver of hope. Yet that hope slipped away as parts of our nation swiftly fell under German control. While Warsaw tenaciously clung to resistance, Kraków, for some unknown reason, had quickly hoisted its white flags of surrender, shamefully handing over control of our city to the German authorities without hardly a fight. Why Klimecki, the mayor of our city, had surrendered so quickly to the Germans was baffling. Some said it was to save lives, others said he was simply a coward.

Everyone in my family felt the prospect of beating back the German forces was evaporating. Even Papa, the eternal optimist, succumbed to a melancholy whenever he picked up the newspaper and read about another defeat.

To make matters worse, paranoia was infecting our community. Some neighbors and people in the markets and shops claimed a "Fifth Column" of Poles were working for the Germans. They accused others of spying, planting bombs, and even poisoning the water. Some said they were falling ill from the poisoned water; others said they saw assassins hiding on the rooftops.

Deciding which rumors were true and false was a confounding task. No one knew whom to trust. Mama and Bubbe were certain there were already large numbers of Poles siding with the Germans. They warned my sisters and me to be careful with whom we spoke, including our goyim friends. But Papa thought they were over-reacting, and I agreed with him.

As depressed as he was about the German offensive, Papa still wanted to believe in the allegiance of the Poles, as did I. He told Mama and Bubbe that until proven otherwise by facts, and not rumors, he still considered our Polish customers as trustworthy as our Jewish ones, and he'd treat them the same. Mama and Bubbe argued with him, working as a team to try to convince him otherwise. But Papa refused to debate the issue. He stated his opinion, and this time he held his ground. He had no patience for long-drawn-out arguments.

During this chaotic period of upheaval and uncertainty, Papa and I went to work every day, trying to maintain a sense of normalcy, even if it was only for a few hours. Mama and Bubbe made quick runs to the market for food and managed the household while Sara and Basha continued studying for school, hoping it would open again someday soon.

Unfortunately, few customers visited the shop. With people feeling so insecure about their finances and the economy in danger, I suppose buying a custom-made umbrella was one of the last things a person wanted to spend their money on.

The men working for us, Khone, Icek, Pinie, and Hersch, appreciated whatever hours we could give them. They all had families with hungry mouths to feed, except for Khone, our master wood and ivory carver.

At eighty-two years old, Khone lived alone with his cat, Nes—which meant "miracle" in Yiddish. An aggressive cancer had taken his wife, long gone. He had only one child, a son, married and living with his family in Gdańsk. Khone had worked for Papa from the time he opened the shop eleven years ago and was more of a family member than an employee. He and Papa were best friends, and he was like a grandpa to me. He often joined us for Shabbos dinner and was always with us on the holidays.

Khone was the most cheerful person I'd ever known, content with his sense of purpose and place on earth. He was solid as the cornerstone of a building. Nothing seemed to rattle him. In situations of tragedy and loss, he'd always point out the places where shiny gems of hope still existed. His oval, thickly bearded face was always welcoming, beaming an intelligence and wisdom about the world that I could always learn from. Yet now his smile was fading from day to day. The wrinkles framing his eyes from laughter had transformed into furrows of anguish. His broad shoulders had rounded and turned inward.

EARLY MORNING ON 6 SEPTEMBER, JUST FIVE DAYS AFTER THE bombing started, while everyone slept, I tiptoed in my pajamas to the open window in the sitting room where I peered three floors down to the gray cobblestone street below. The neighborhood was silent and peaceful. In the purple darkness of dawn, pools of golden light circled beneath the streetlamps. From around the corner, Biala the lamplighter slowly limped down the street toward my building, using his long wooden pole to shut off the gas valves and extinguish the flames.

At the end of the street, I imagined the image of Zelda on the horse cart gazing back at me, looking forlorn before disappearing round the corner. I pondered how she was surviving and if she was safe. It was frustrating and worrying to not hear from her. Yet she'd only been gone five days, just five days! Five days that felt like a year.

With the war throwing everything into turmoil, I figured it would take time for the postal service to deliver her letters to me. But I longed for that first letter. I couldn't wait to hold the envelope in my hand and smell the lavender scent on it before unsealing the flap that her sweet tongue had licked. Inside would be her letter with the fine lines of her ink-black words sweeping across the page in a seamless stream of curves, dashes, and dots. I hungered to hear her thoughts, absorb her words, and sense once again the beat of her heart pulsing inside me.

From my perch, I spotted Ziggy traveling down the street with his coal cart, the horse's hooves clip-clopping steady as a metronome on the cobblestones. He stopped in front of our building and unloaded several boxes of coal before climbing back into his cart and moving on to the next block. Avrom walked past Ziggy carrying buckets of water on the wood beam balanced across his shoulders, his arms stretched wide like Jesus on the cross. He was young, in his late teens, thin as a broomstick and astonishingly strong for his slight build. No one in the neighborhood understood where his strength came from. People joked that were it not for the buckets of water holding him down, it would take only a light breeze to lift him in the air and carry him all the way to Jerusalem.

Avrom passed beneath my window when suddenly the deep thunderous rumble of truck and tank engines echoed through the streets. The sound gradually grew into an ominous roar as they approached. Our building trembled, the windows rattled, dust filled the air. Across the street, people gazed nervously out their windows, fear contorting their faces, searching for the menacing source of the rumbling sounds. Mama, Papa, and my sisters entered the room and stood at the windows next to me, looking down in a horrified silence.

A line of three camouflage trucks rounded the corner followed by three tanks. "No," said Basha, clutching a book against her chest. Papa put his arm round Mama's shoulders and pulled her close. Her pale blue eyes were now dull, void of their usual vibrant spirit. Her index finger nervously picked at the cuticles and raw corners of her thumbs.

The vehicles quickly approached Avrom. We all yelled for him to move. He jumped to the sidewalk and pinned himself against the wall of a building, dropping his buckets of water, and narrowly escaped being hit by the truck.

Inside the camouflaged trucks, German troops dressed in drab green uniforms and helmets held their rifles with bayonets pointing skyward, at us. Then came the massive wave of soldiers' boots pounding the cobblestones in perfect unison, a terrifying drumbeat that echoed through the corridor of the buildings lining the streets. From behind the trucks and tanks, soldiers fanned out around the corner onto our street, row after row of seven across, pouring down the street like a river that had broken its dam. Behind the marching German soldiers were rows of defeated Polish soldiers, their heads hanging in shame, hands tied behind their backs, some of them limping. Others lay in horse carts, their wounded bodies bloodied and wrapped in bandages. Piled next to them were the corpses of their comrades .

I felt a sinking sensation in my chest. Tears filled my eyes and spilled down my cheeks as the long lines of German trucks and tanks, soldiers, jeeps, horses, supply carts, and antiaircraft artillery overran our neighborhood, Kazimierz. Mama made some murmuring sounds as she leaned against Papa. He handed her his handkerchief so she could wipe her eyes, then used it to wipe his own. Sara cried silently with her arm wrapped around Mama's waist. Basha was stern and silent with her arms defiantly folded across her chest, her hands balled into fists. She gazed down at the street in disgust.

I went to Bubbe's room to check on her and found her lying awake in bed, staring at the ceiling, eyes filled with tears. She pulled the sheet up to her chin and closed her eyes.

"Are you okay, Bubbe?" I asked.

"I miss Eliyohu," she whispered. "Why go through this? I'm tired. I don't want to see my family suffer. I've seen enough suffering. Tomorrow will only bring more."

I went to the side of her bed, sat down next to her, kissed her soft, wrinkled cheek, and held her gnarled hands. "Please, Bubbe. Don't give up. As you always say: *Far morgn, vet Got zorgn*—Let God worry about tomorrow."

She curled her thick, arthritic fingers round mine and kissed my cheek.

That night I lay in bed unable to sleep, thinking about Zelda and her family, wondering if they were safe, and where exactly they were living in the countryside. Being cut off from her was maddening. I started imagining Zelda and her family captured by German soldiers, held as prisoners and then killed. I'd tell myself to stop thinking such things, but the dark thoughts ignored my commands and kept plaguing me. After all, we'd heard what the Germans had done to the Jews in Germany the year before— how one night in November they had burned down more than a thousand synagogues, ransacked hundreds of Jewish homes and hospitals and schools, destroyed and damaged thousands of Jewish businesses, arrested tens of thousands of Jewish men, and killed ninety-one Jews. Our lives were disintegrating rapidly, as if they had never been real to begin with. I lay there wondering. What will happen now? What should we do? What should we plan for?

7

IN THE DAYS AFTER KRAKÓW SURRENDERED TO THE GERMAN army, droves of people who had left for the countryside to escape the bombings began returning to the city. However, Warsaw still resisted as the German army continued marching east across Poland. To make matters worse, we learned the Russians had invaded from the east. By the middle of September, our country split in two. The newspaper reported that the border between eastern Poland, controlled by the Russians, and western Poland, controlled by the Germans, ran along the Bug River in the north and the San River in the south.

With so many people returning to their homes, I was certain I'd see Zelda soon. I checked on her apartment almost daily, but it remained empty. I couldn't understand why her family hadn't returned when so many others had. None of the neighbors had answers. I prayed for at least a letter. But nothing came.

To ease my worries, I reasoned there were no letters because she was out in the farm country where mail service was sparse at best. And now, because of the war, mail service had possibly ceased altogether. If I had known exactly where her uncle's farm was located, I would've begged Mama and Papa to allow me to go look for her. But I knew Mama and Papa would never hear of it. Mama would've broken my kneecaps before letting me leave to go search for Zelda during this time of war.

* * *

PAPA AND I RETURNED TO WORK FULL-TIME, WHICH GAVE US something to do. Yet sales were abysmal. Now we mostly repaired old umbrellas. Khone, Pinie, Icek, and Hersch had so little to do that we had to send them home early each day and reduce their pay. The guilt from cutting their pay weighed heavily on Papa and me because they badly needed the money. But we had no choice.

On our morning drosky rides from Kazimierz to the shop in Podgórze, some aspects of life in the city appeared to return to a sense of normalcy. The trains and trams were running on time, shops were opening, the markets filled again with people buying and selling food; Biala lit the streetlamps. Avrom delivered water. Old Schmuel swept the streets, and Ziggy delivered the coal.

Yet other aspects of our lives were far from normal. German soldiers and policemen now patrolled the streets on foot and in cars. Men wearing SS uniforms ate and drank in cafés, bars, and restaurants. A Gestapo headquarters had opened at 2 Pomorska Street. Every day more Nazi flags replaced our Polish flags in front of government buildings, schools, and offices, in parks and squares. On the radio, we learned Kraków had become the "General Government" for the Third Reich, and that Hitler's personal legal advisor, Hans Frank, was now governor of the German-occupied territories.

Our reality shifted so quickly it was difficult to comprehend. Mama and Papa were more agitated than normal. Mama would bark at Papa for small things, like leaving the butter out. Papa would yell at Mama for not fixing the button on his shirt that he'd asked her to fix a week ago. Bubbe alternated between being angry at the world and a quiet melancholy. She kept to herself more than I'd seen before, preferring to read and knit in her room than spend a lot of time in the sitting room sipping her tea and listening to the radio. Sara and Basha buried themselves in their books. I felt numb inside, complacent, lost without a compass. I hated not knowing if Zelda was safe, or where she was, or when she'd return. The weakness of our Polish army disgusted me. And an anger at the so-called Allied forces, Britain and France, for not attacking the Germans by now, burned inside me. We needed their help badly. Where were they? Nobody had any answers.

8

ON YOM KIPPUR, THE HIGH HOLIDAY, PAPA AND I HAD ALREADY locked the door, preparing to close early, when an SS officer with two soldiers pounded sharply on the shop door, demanding we open it. Through the windows, they could see me at my desk where I was filing papers. With my back to the door, I pretended not to hear their knocking as I considered what to do. Then Papa ran in from the workshop, obediently unlocked the door, and welcomed them inside with an obsequious smile. "Come in," he said with a generous sweep of his hand, followed by a subtle bow. While inviting the wolves into the henhouse, he showed them a respect and deference that was shameful. It was so nauseating I wanted to leave.

On the front of the SS officer's gray hat, just above the shiny black visor and gold braided rope, was an ominous silver skull and crossbones pin. Above that was another pin, a gallant silver eagle with the swastika clenched in its talons. The pins were repulsive and intimidating.

"How can I help you?" Papa asked the SS officer, his voice thin and wavering. One soldier, thick-necked and burly, a rifle slung over his shoulder, translated from Polish to German. His German was raw, coming from the back of the throat in growling, barking sounds.

The SS officer casually removed his hat and placed it on the cherrywood handle of a black umbrella displayed in the window.

He was tall and sinewy, with an odd little hump, like a turtle shell, bulging from his right shoulder blade. I wondered if this was a birth defect, or the result of a war wound. He had fine, receding blond hair combed to the side, intelligent brown eyes set deep in the sockets of his high cheekbones; a long and narrow clean-shaven face. He could've been in his thirties, possibly forties. It was hard to tell his age. His sidearm, a black Luger with a walnut handle, rested on his right hip in a polished chestnut-brown leather holster.

He introduced himself as Captain Schlöndorff as he strolled slowly and purposefully, appearing to glide through the shop as if skating across ice. When he stopped to look at an umbrella, the way he examined it reminded me of how the blue herons studied the water along the river's edge when they were hunting fish. He took his time examining each part of the umbrella, holding it up to the light, scrutinizing every detail as if looking at a precious artifact. "Is there something specific you're looking for?" asked Papa. Schlöndorff carefully continued to assess each umbrella, ignoring the question. Then, after an uncomfortable stretch of time passed, he finally spoke.

"How long have you had this store?" he asked, opening and closing one umbrella. He examined the runner on the shaft and the stretchers inside the canopy. His German was more fluid, less guttural. The edges around the hard vowels were softer and smoother, making him sound intelligent and well read. The soldier translated from German to Polish, although we understood the question since we spoke Yiddish.

"Eleven years now," Papa said.

"And do you have shops in other cities?"

"Not yet. Although my son plans to open one in Warsaw. Right, Reuven?"

Papa's pathetic face struggled to maintain a manufactured smile. I wished he hadn't given the SS officer my name. How stupid could he be? I turned my back on them, returning to my desk to do some paperwork. I wanted to leave, but realized it was more important to stay and monitor what else he might tell Schlöndorff. Would he tell him where we live? How many we were? The names of everyone else in the family?

"Well, I think it's too late for opening a shop in Warsaw," said Schlöndorff sardonically, gazing at me with his cavernous eyes. He picked up an umbrella with a bear's head carved into the cherry-wood handle and cradled it in his large hands. "I don't think I've ever seen such unique and finely crafted umbrellas before."

Papa plucked one umbrella from the display window. Holding it in his long, slender fingers, he spoke slowly, so the soldier accompanying Schlöndorff had time to interpret. His tone was calm and confident sounding, as if he was trying to reclaim his dignity. "Each one of our custom umbrellas is handcrafted and made to order," he said, cradling the umbrella. "Customers can choose from oak, walnut, cherry, mahogany, or ivory for the handle. They can give us a design for the handle or choose from many others that we suggest. Women tend to order handles with delicate floral patterns or intricate geometric designs while the men lean toward animals of prey—a wolf, bear, hawk, eagle, and so on. We've even had some customers order jewels, such as ruby, emerald, sapphire, garnet, and diamond, used in decorating the handle. They can select the wood they want for the shaft, bamboo or birch, the shade of the stain, and the design and color of the canopy. For additional fees, the customer can have their initials engraved on the handle ring. The ring can be ordered in brass, sterling silver, or even fourteen-, eighteen-, or twenty-four-karat gold. The same goes for the handle cap, should they choose to have one."

Papa's incessant talking was getting on my nerves. "I think he understands," I said.

"I'm sure you must have a special umbrella for yourself," said Schlöndorff.

"Yes. Mine has an ivory handle with the three wise monkeys carved into the ivory. Hear no evil, see no evil, speak no evil. The handle is capped with eighteen-karat gold and the handle ring, also eighteen karats, has my initials etched into it."

"And the shaft?"

"Birch."

"May I see it?"

"I would show it to you, but it's not here."

Papa deliberately did not mention the six-inch letter opener attached to the handle, sharp as a dagger, that slides in and out of the umbrella shaft once the small nickel-spring clip on the shaft is depressed. Khone made that umbrella special for Papa five years ago, for his fortieth birthday.

"My father was a woodcarver," said Schlöndorff, holding the bear-head handle up to the window light, noting the finely carved details. "I never had a talent for it. But I know fine craftsmanship when I see it, and this is superb. Who did it?"

"A man who has been with me for many years."

"Is he here? I want to meet him."

Papa led Schlöndorff through the doorway to the workshop where Khone, Pinie, Icek, and Hersch were at their benches finishing their work, preparing to leave for Yom Kippur services, the most sacred Jewish holiday. I stood at the door, watching as Papa and Schlöndorff circled the benches with his interpreter right behind them.

"This is where we make our umbrellas, and repair them," said Papa.

Schlöndorff slowly walked past the workbenches, carefully noting all the tools and parts that were spread across them. For making the umbrella canopies, Pinie's and Icek's benches had sewing machines, rolls of nylon material in various colors and patterns, and large spools of rainbow-colored thread stacked on spindles next to containers holding the tiny steel tips, shaped like pointy hats, that were used for securing the edge of the canopy to the stretchers. Hersch's bench had piles of bamboo and birch used for constructing the shafts along with springs, clips, brass and nickel bands, and stacks of long and thin metal stems used for constructing the umbrella's ribs and stretchers. They reminded me of the bird bones I sometimes found on the river's edge. The last bench, Khone's, our master woodcarver, was covered with clamps; various grades of sandpaper; wood blocks of oak, black mahogany, cherry, and walnut. There were ivory horns, cans and bottles of stains and lacquers; his precious carving tools were various small blade saws, knives, awls, a bone groover, and files for wood and bone.

Schlöndorff seemed fascinated by it all. He stopped at Khone's bench and picked his way through all the tools, wood blocks, and ivory, and then came across the umbrella handle Khone had been working on all day. It was a beautifully carved ivory handle with a finely detailed scene of three white cranes flying over a river. Schlöndorff rubbed his fingers across the ivory handle, feeling the ripples in the river, the clouds in the sky, the cranes' feathers, beaks, long necks, and stick legs.

"This is the man who carves all our handles," said Papa, this time being careful to not mention names.

"How old is he?" asked Schlöndorff.

"I'm eighty-two," Khone said in German, not looking up. He responded before the interpreter could translate the question. Khone spoke perfect German since he had been born in Berlin and had lived there until his family moved to Kraków after the last war.

"What is your name?" asked Schlöndorff.

"Khone."

Schlöndorff crossed his arms and narrowed his eyes at Papa. His mood suddenly shifted. "I want an umbrella with a wolf baring its teeth carved into an ivory handle, rubies for eyes, and my initials, V. S., engraved on a twenty-four-karat gold band that caps the handle. And on the opposite side of the gold band, I want 'SS' engraved. I want the shaft to be made of birch with a dark, chestnut-brown stain, the canopy black, and I want a thin gold band around the tip of the umbrella with the swastika etched into it. Understand?"

Papa dutifully wrote the details down and then read them back to Schlöndorff.

"How soon will it be ready?"

"I can have it ready in two weeks."

"That's too long. I need it by Wednesday."

"But today is Friday, that gives us only four days to finish it. Plus, it's . . ." Papa's voice quickly trailed off. He was about to mention Shabbos and Yom Kippur but realized saying that would mean nothing to Schlöndorff, or worse, possibly enrage him. Papa stroked his black mustache with his index finger, something he always did when agitated or upset. "We'll need more time, given how long it will take to carve the handle properly." He shot Khone a glance to search for a sign of confirmation. Khone didn't look at Papa. He just stared at Schlöndorff, as if he were assessing the dangers this man posed to us.

Schlöndorff smiled at his men, as if Papa had just made a joke. "Wednesday it is. You will make it possible. I have confidence in you." He tapped Papa on the shoulder with the umbrella he'd been holding, as if they were longtime friends, then tossed it to him. Papa caught it and remained silent as Schlöndorff abruptly turned and headed out the door.

Papa gripped the umbrella in both hands, staring after him. Khone stood up and patted Papa on the back. "Don't worry, Lev," he said. "We'll do whatever it takes to finish the umbrella for that schmuck."

Papa thanked him, then turned to address Pinie, Icek, and Hersch, who were at their workbenches, unpacking their bags and removing their jackets, preparing to return to work.

"I apologize, my friends, but we must—"

"No need to apologize, Mr. Berkovitz," said Pinie, a little man in oversized clothes who cut and sewed the canopies. "We understand."

"Don't worry, Mr. Berkovitz," said Icek. "In all our years of working here, this has never happened. God will understand and forgive us for not making it to synagogue this one time. We'll take care of this."

"Did you notice he didn't even ask what the umbrella would cost?" asked Khone.

"We should charge the *mamzer* extra," said Hersch, who cut and assembled the shafts, stretchers, ribs, and runners. Icek nodded in agreement.

"Maybe he expects it for free, as a gift of appreciation for invading our country?" said Khone.

"God help us," said Papa.

"He will," said Khone. "You'll see. And then maybe you'll start to believe in him!"

I TELEPHONED MAMA TO LET HER KNOW WHAT HAD HAPPENED and that we'd be home too late for Shabbos dinner and to attend synagogue for Yom Kippur service. She was angry at first and ordered us to come home, then was terrified. She cried and asked to speak to Papa. He tried consoling her before Bubbe took the phone from Mama. She told Papa not to worry about Mama and to do whatever work needed to be done.

We labored late into the evening. Khone and Icek worked on Schlöndorff's umbrella while Papa and I helped Pinie and Hersch with cutting and sewing the canopies for the umbrellas that were already on order and had firm delivery dates.

Around midnight, Papa and I took a drosky home. The evening air was cool and the fall leaves tumbled across the road in the light breeze. Papa tried making small talk, but I was in no mood to engage in conversation. I just wanted to be left alone to stew in my thoughts.

"What's wrong?" he asked.

"Nothing," I said.

"You thought I was too nice to the man?"

"Yes. It makes you look weak."

"So, let him think I'm weak. What do I care? All that matters is that we're safe. You understand? When your enemy has all the power, you try to make friends with them."

"But then he'll take even more advantage of you if he thinks you have no backbone."

"Let him think he's all-powerful so he doesn't think he has to prove anything. The moment he feels he must prove something, then we're in trouble."

"I disagree. The moment he sees you're weak, he has no respect for you. And then he'll crush you."

"You don't know what we're dealing with here."

"Neither do you."

"Don't be disrespectful!" Papa wagged his finger at me and then turned away.

We rode the rest of the way home in silence. As we crossed the bridge spanning the Vistula, German jeeps, tanks, and transport trucks passed us, a grim reminder that we no longer controlled our country, nor our lives.

* * *

WEDNESDAY WAS GLOOMY WITH A COLD AUTUMN RAIN. IT WAS almost closing time, and I had just finished helping Pinie, Icek, and Hersch clean the shop. Papa was putting papers away. I leaned against the display window sipping a hot cup of tea, gazing across the square through the rivulets of rainwater running down the glass, waiting for Schlöndorff to arrive. The water distorted the branches on the trees lining the square, making them melt as they bent and twisted in the wet wind.

Schlöndorff's shiny black sedan finally showed and parked in front. His driver opened the door for him and they entered the shop. Papa greeted him warmly, offering a handshake.

"So let us see what you've made for me," he said, walking past Papa's open hand, as if oblivious to it, and entering the workshop.

Hunched over his workbench was Khone, putting the last touches on the handle, shining the finely carved ivory with a polishing cloth. Schlöndorff stood next to Khone, intently watching him, his hump protruding more when he bent forward. Khone handed the umbrella to Schlöndorff. He carefully examined the finely carved ivory handle, rubbing his finger over every inch of the wolf's head, holding it up to the soft gray light filtering through the window, noting the precisely etched detailed lines of the fur. The wolf's ears were back and its jaw wide open in a fierce growl, each of its sharp fangs individually carved; its ruby eyes were ghostly. He examined the twenty-four-karat gold band with his engraved initials and the double "SS" shaped like twin lightning bolts.

"Well done." His dark eyes gleamed. "My father would have approved. What is the cost?"

"One hundred and forty zloty," said Papa, stroking his mustache.

Schlöndorff raised an eyebrow and turned to the soldier, who shook his head disapprovingly. Schlöndorff looked back at Papa. "Is this the Jew price or the German price?"

Papa did not answer. His mind was churning, trying to figure out how to respond without offending the Nazi. He finally took a deep breath to steady his voice. "The price is the same for every customer," he said while stroking his mustache. "It's based on time for labor and cost of materials. For instance, the handle you ordered is a bit more expensive because you selected rubies for the eyes, an expensive stone, and twenty-four-karat gold for the bands, rather than eighteen or even fourteen karats."

There was a long silence as Schlöndorff studied the umbrella, opening and closing it, carefully examining the shaft, canopy, and stretchers. "But pay whatever you like," said Papa, suddenly giving up his ground and surrendering to the Nazi.

"I'll pay the one hundred and forty zloty so long as I know you're not overcharging me. Can I trust you?" Schlöndorff's tone was belittling.

"We're fair to all our customers," said Papa.

"You didn't answer my question. I asked if I can trust you. You're a Jew, after all."

Papa looked away and nodded. "Yes. You can trust me."

"Pay him," Schlöndorff said to his soldier as he turned to leave. The soldier handed Papa the money and exited the shop.

Papa went to his desk, not looking at me, nor saying a word, and recorded the one hundred and forty zloty in the accounting book that Mama would reconcile later.

9

BY DECEMBER, WE WOKE EVERY MORNING HUDDLED BENEATH thick layers of wool blankets, fighting off the cold. The Germans had placed restrictions on coal consumption for the Jews. Our windows, glazed over with frost and ice, appeared as topographical maps. Some of the water pipes had frozen and broke—the vapors of our breaths hung in the air before vanishing. Like everyone else, we relied on the woodburning stove in the kitchen to heat our entire apartment.

Sara and Mama were sick off and on. For some reason, Bubbe never had more than a runny nose. It was the same for Basha and me. And Papa appeared to be retreating from the world. He'd become extremely quiet; his head hung low with shades of gray beneath his eyes. Sometimes he went days barely saying a word.

Like Papa, I, too, wanted to escape the world, for it was a place we no longer knew or understood. The chaos of German occupation had crushed the rhythms of the daily life we once enjoyed. Week after week, month after month, the Germans created laws that butchered our rights—the right to engage in politics, to go to school, to have a bank account, to own real estate, to own a car, to even own a radio! They tagged us like livestock, forcing us to wear the Star of David armbands and patches on our clothes and carry special IDs that identified us as Jews. They crudely painted the word *Jude* on our shop windows, doors, and signs. One by one, they shut down our businesses, or took them over. Meyer's fish shop, Moishe's bakery, and Jakov's shoe store were now run by Poles working for the Germans. Saul, our downstairs neighbor, had lost his clockmaker business, as did Zisl the butcher. I figured it was only a matter of time before they'd take our shop. But Mama and Papa continued to naïvely believe they'd leave our shop alone since Schlöndorff liked our umbrellas and had purchased one from us.

I let them believe what they wanted to believe by keeping my mouth shut until one day I'd had enough. I called them naïve fools to believe in such nonsense. Papa said my arrogance had gotten the best of me and that in fact I was the naïve fool, not them.

"What do you know about the world at seventeen?" he said as he threw on his winter coat. "Nothing!" he answered as he abruptly left the apartment to go to the shop alone. But Mama continued heatedly engaging with me. We went round and round in a circular argument, accusing each other of being ignorant and living in denial. Mama's ire grew out of control as I kept hammering my opinion, as if in a court of law, trying to force her to admit that we will, in fact, lose our business at some point.

Bubbe emerged from her room with a pair of crimson wool socks she was mending and tried to neutralize the argument. But Mama and I were too far gone, sucked inside our eddies of anger and frustration with the world and each other. The harsh sounds of our fuming voices built to a crescendo of personal attacks and accusations. I called her a depressive moron, something I'd never imagined saying. She grabbed a pan and threw it at me, something she'd never done before, missing me by centimeters, then broke down screaming and crying, calling me a monster and ordering me out of the apartment. Bubbe hollered, demanding we calm down. I grabbed my hat and coat and quickly left.

The street was cold and covered in snow and ice. A group of Jews were shoveling snow off the sidewalks and streets. German soldiers commanded them on where to shovel next. Sickened by the argument I had with Mama, my hands trembled. I regretted what I had said.

I couldn't face Papa at work and went to Zelda's apartment to see if they had finally returned.

I climbed the three flights of stairs to their floor and put my ear to their door. There was a woman's voice. It sounded like Mrs. Abramovitch. My heart jumped, and I pounded on the door in disbelief that I'd finally see my Zelda.

The woman spoke from behind the door. "Yes?"

My breath quickened. "Mrs. Abramovitch! It's me, Reuven!"

She opened the door and standing before me was a lady my height, blond-haired and blue-eyed, her hair wrapped in a white babushka. She was clearly a Pole. "Pardon me," I said, trying to control my fluster. "I'm looking for the Abramovitch family. They used to live here. Do you know where they are?"

"No. We don't know anything about them."

"But this was their apartment."

"We moved here a week ago. I'm sorry, I can't help you." She closed the door.

I trudged back down the stairs one step at a time, terrified that something horrible had happened to Zelda and her family. Many families had returned to Kraków from the countryside. Why hadn't they?

From Zelda's place I went down to the river, being careful to avoid the German police and soldiers, and found an isolated spot beneath a willow. The frozen river was silent and pure white. In the ground next to me was a flat sheet of ice the size of a large frying pan. I used the sharp tip of a rock to etch into the ice a map of the Vistula River and the woods where Zelda and I used to go cross-country skiing together.

When there was fresh snow, like now, we'd ski across the river to a small winding trail leading through the woods to a bluff that overlooked the woods and the river. The bluff was our special place where we'd clear a small snowy area and spread a wool blanket across the frozen ground and sit there pressed against each other eating jelly and butter sandwiches, apples or oranges. Afterward, we'd kiss and explore each other's bodies beneath the thick layers of our clothing and sometimes make forbidden love inside the folds of the heavy wool blanket. Zelda was precocious, while I was timid. We'd both jump and laugh at first when our icy hands would touch the other's skin. But they'd warm quickly as our fingers began exploring the most intimate places of each other's bodies.

Nothing compared to making love to Zelda. My entire body would melt into hers as we embraced, our lips playfully exchanging soft, lingering kisses, Zelda's lavender scent making me delirious with desire. The world would fade away. Pure joy enveloped us. Nothing else mattered. All that existed in those moments was us, wrapped in the warmth of each other's bodies, our breaths and heartbeats falling into a perfect rhythm, our limbs intertwined like the willows' roots growing along the surface of the riverbank. We knew we had each found that one person in the world whom we were meant to spend the rest of our lives with, that person whose spirit we shared. We were each other's firsts, and so we knew nothing other than what we had—a love for each other that astonished us, and consumed us.

IN THE LATE AFTERNOON, I WENT TO THE SHOP AND APOLOGIZED to Papa for what I'd said earlier in the day. He accepted my apology and said we needed to be more kind to one another during these difficult times. I agreed.

On the way home, we stopped at the market where I bought Mama a piece of her favorite hard cheese. At home I gave it to her and apologized for all the terrible things that were said. She accepted my apology and gave me a hug.

10

A FEW DAYS LATER, ON A COLD SABBATH MORNING, A LOUD pounding on our front door jarred us awake. I reached the door first and opened it. There stood Schlöndorff, tall and arrogant, with three soldiers and two Polish police officers behind him. A wretched grin spanned his face, both hands resting firmly on the umbrella we had made for him, the growling wolf's head with its piercing ruby eyes peering out the side of his palm, his black boots shiny and speckled with melting snow, his cavernous eyes exuding disdain.

One of the Polish policemen announced they had an order to search our apartment for weapons. I asked why they thought we had weapons. They said the search was mandatory and shoved me to the side as they entered the apartment. Papa asked if they'd give us a moment to get dressed. They refused. Instead, they forced us into the sitting room in our nightclothes and made us wait as they marched from room to room ransacking the apartment.

Sara and Basha huddled next to each other on one end of the couch. Basha steadied Sara, who shivered uncontrollably. Mama and Bubbe sat next to them, their arms tightly interlocked. No one said a word. Mama picked incessantly at the raw skin around her thumbnails. Papa stood behind her, his hands quivering as he squeezed her shoulders, his eyes cast down, timid and afraid. It angered me. I wanted him to do something. Yet what could he do? What could any of us do to stop these armed *mamzers* from treating us as though we were their prisoners?

Schlöndorff proudly strolled through the apartment, using his umbrella as a walking cane, as if our apartment now belonged to him. His crisp gray uniform, perfectly pressed, smelled of damp wool from the melting snow. The turtle shell hump on his upper back was obscured by the black cloak draped over his shoulders, the brass buckle on his belt impeccably polished, and his black Luger, with its dark walnut grip, holstered on his right hip with a brown leather strap snapped across it. When his back was to us, I fantasized about lunging for the gun, swiftly unstrapping it, and using it to shoot him and his men. It seemed so possible, so tempting.

As if shopping in a store, he opened every drawer in the dining room bureau and examined with intense curiosity the silverware and china in the cabinets and silver candelabras. He noted the paintings and went through the titles of Papa's books. He began reading the authors out loud: "Kant, Hegel, Spinoza—Jew; Aristotle, Plato, Schopenhauer, Isaac Babel—a Bolshevik Jew. Yes? Nietzsche, Erich Maria Remarque. You have an impressive library and seem to favor philosophy over all else. Is that true?"

"I'm no expert," said Papa. "I just read for guidance and learning. I'm a businessman, not a philosopher."

"But you're a thinker, like myself."

"I suppose so."

"What do you think of Kant?"

"I appreciate what Kant had to say about individual rights and liberty."

"Such as?"

Papa paused, considering his words carefully, sensing a trap. "It's been a while since I've read him. But if I remember correctly, he argued that all human beings possess an inherent dignity and that we should treat them as ends in themselves, rather than as a means to an end. He argued every person has a right to be treated with respect and to live free from coercion or persecution."

"I see," said Schlöndorff as he continued to study Papa's library. "And what would Kant have thought about this book had he been alive when it was published? *The Communist Manifesto* by Marx and Engels. Does communism provide people with freedom? Are you a Communist? Are you a Bolshevist Jew?" He walked up to Papa and looked him square in the face, just inches away. Mama sat on the couch between them with her head down, the intimidating wolf's head on his umbrella handle at her eye level. Papa's hands still gripped her shoulders, his head angled downward, like a timid dog, his frightened eyes cast toward the floor. "Is that what you are?" Schlöndorff placed his umbrella handle beneath Papa's chin and used the shaft as a lever to lift his face up so they were eye to eye.

"I'm a Jew," said Papa, his gaze slowly coming up from the floor to meet Schlöndorff's cold, expressionless face. "I'm just a Jew."

Schlöndorff handed the book to one of his soldiers and told him to burn it. Then he saw the yahrzeit candle on the dining room table that was lit to honor the anniversary of Grandpa Eliyohu's death—he died three years earlier. We also called him Zayde. Without warning, Schlöndorff casually extinguished the flame with his thumb. Bubbe gasped. Mama moaned.

"He can't do that to Zayde!" yelled Basha.

"Basha, be quiet," said Papa.

Schlöndorff turned round and slowly walked back toward the couch and picked up Bubbe's prized radio from the small side table, ripping the cord from the wall. "I could arrest you for having this radio," he said to Papa as he handed it to one of the policemen. "But you made me a beautiful umbrella, so I'll let this one go, along with the book." He walked up to Basha, removed his black leather gloves, reached into his pocket, and offered her a hard candy wrapped in brown waxed paper. She looked at it in the middle of his open palm and did not move.

"Take it," he said, moving his hand closer to her face.

Basha reached for the candy. His hand snapped around hers. "Got you!" he said with a sickly grin. The two policemen laughed. She looked up in shock as he continued holding on to her hand, tormenting her. Ugly burn scars marred his hands and wrist, perhaps from the last war, or this war, or an accident. When he finally let go, Basha held the candy in her hand and looked askance, avoiding his gaze. "Eat it," he ordered.

Basha stared at the floor, then said under her breath, "I'm not hungry."

I admired her rebellious rejection of his order but worried about what he'd do next. He looked down at her with a dark glare, making me think he might strike her. "Well then," he said, "maybe you'll eat it later. I have a little girl at home your age, and she loves this candy. I think you and her would get along."

He casually walked back to the door, where his soldiers waited. Before leaving, Schlöndorff turned to face us, tipping his hat with the umbrella. "I'm glad we didn't find any weapons here. It would've been a shame to arrest you."

The door shut, and we stared at one another in stunned silence. Basha jumped up and threw her candy across the room and hollered, "I want to kill that man! I hate him!" She went to her room and screamed. Everything inside her room had been turned upside down. Drawers were pulled out of the dressers, their contents dumped on the ground; her bed was flipped over, the closet emptied, pictures torn off the walls. All our rooms suffered equal destruction. Bubbe and Mama discovered some of their jewelry was missing, as well as an envelope of emergency cash that Papa had stored inside a shirt in his bottom drawer. Fortunately,

Mama and Bubbe had hidden most of their jewelry inside a secret compartment in the floor of Bubbe's closet. Papa had hidden more cash there as well.

Before cleaning up all the damage, we sat with Bubbe at the dining room table and held hands as she relit the yahrzeit candle for Zayde and said a prayer. She spoke to Zayde, telling him he was smart to leave this earth when he did, and said she looked forward to being with him soon. "May these Nazis rot in hell and their bones be drained of marrow," she said to him. "*Di beyner zolen im oysrinen!*"

11

A WEEK LATER, IN THE MORNING BEFORE GOING TO WORK, I washed and shaved with ice-cold water. The hot water had been out for several days. Once I finished, I went to the kitchen for a cup of coffee and some food. I found Papa sitting there alone in a wrinkled suit that hadn't been cleaned or pressed in a month. Even the threads holding the top button of his jacket were coming undone. A few days of black beard stubble cast a dark shadow across his face. He sipped his coffee and mindlessly ate a piece of challah with some butter and jam on it and stared off, lost in his own ruminations. The jam slid off his bread and dripped on the table. He was retreating further into himself, withdrawing from a world that was perhaps becoming too overwhelming for him to cope with. His deepening melancholy disturbed me. But when I spoke to Mama and Bubbe about it, they told me not to worry, that it was a phase of behavior that he simply needed to work through. I didn't find their words convincing, or consoling.

I poured myself some coffee and sat down with him while the rest of the family slept. He looked gaunt, his cheekbones and chin protruding sharply; his pale gray skin emphasized the heavy black eyebrows framing his sunken eyes. His unkempt mustache, a bushy hedge, had jagged edges and drooped too far over his upper lip.

"Are you okay?" I asked. He didn't respond. "What are you thinking?"

"I don't know what to do." He gingerly set his cup of coffee down and wiped the jam off the table with his finger and licked it.

"About what?"

"Nothing."

"Tell me."

He continued staring off, lost in some internal dialogue he must've been having about the hopelessness of our situation. His head shook disapprovingly. "No one is buying our umbrellas, and we can't make a living from doing only repairs. We've had to let go of Pinie, Icek, and Hersch when they have no other income. The goyim customers don't want to buy from us, and our Jewish customers are trying to save every kopek they have."

"A least we've kept Khone working."

"Barely part-time."

"Maybe we should try to advertise?"

"How? There's no money for that. And it wouldn't make a difference."

"What if we try selling our umbrellas to some stores in Warsaw?"

"Don't be ridiculous. They're in the same shape we're in."

"What if we try going outside the country? Could we sell in Britain or Scandinavia? Maybe we change the name of our company so they don't know we're Jewish?"

"You know, we once had a customer who did business in England. Poznanski. Remember him?"

"I do."

"He had lots of connections and a good business."

"He was quite wealthy."

"Yes. And Albert Beitz, the same."

"I remember him, too."

"Do you know where they are now?"

"No."

"They're both broke and shoveling snow for the Germans."

"So, what do you suggest?"

Papa slowly picked up his cup of coffee, gazed across the room listlessly, and took a sip, leaving beads of coffee clinging to the ends of his raggedy mustache. "I don't know," he said wearily. "I don't know what to do."

ON THE SNOWY STREET WE WALKED TO THE SHOP WEARING layers of clothing beneath our heavy wool coats, our Star of David armbands pinned to our sleeves. Despite all the layers, the wind cut through my coat, making me damp and chilled. Snow coated my cap and shoulders; the heavy gray sky bore down upon us. Papa opened the umbrella to shield us from the pelting snow. I desperately wanted to take a drosky to avoid walking in the cold slush that clung to our ankles and melted inside my shoes. But we could no longer afford one. Instead, we walked the entire route on streets we knew were less frequently patrolled by the German soldiers, SS, and Polish and German police. They were the ones, along with the Jewish police, who would harass us for money, or worse, snatch us off the street and transport us to forced-labor worksites to do things like shovel snow, empty garbage, dig trenches, chop wood, and so on. Up to this point, Papa and I had been lucky to avoid forced labor assignments.

We crossed the snowy bridge spanning the Vistula. Beneath us, a barge loaded with huge logs chugged north with the current toward Gdańsk, black smoke billowing from its stack. I wondered if the wood was for building boats in Gdańsk or constructing barracks for the Germans. Then the barge vanished behind the white curtain of snowfall as if it were an apparition.

Papa and I reached the end of the bridge, crossed Zgody Square, and approached our shop, which now had a white Jewish star crudely painted on the display window. Paint dripped from its points, like tears.

Inside, we found Khone sitting alone in the dimly lit workshop repairing an umbrella that belonged to Mr. Malinowski, the pharmacist at the opposite end of the square. Hunched over his workbench, he examined a thin metal stretcher used for supporting the umbrella canopy. For closer inspection, he held in his meaty hands the delicate metal twig up to the gray light spilling through the window, his small wire-rimmed glasses resting at the tip of his long hawklike nose as he focused on the bend in the metal to determine if it was reparable.

Beneath his black fisherman's cap, the edges of his yarmulke were visible. The yarmulke and his long gray beard framed by curly gray sidelocks, always well groomed, spoke to how serious he was about his religion, a subject he never addressed with Papa and me since he knew we weren't devout. Every now and again during a tea break, when he didn't feel like talking, he'd remove a Hebrew prayerbook from the inside pocket of his black coat and read a few passages before returning to work. The pages, wrinkled and tattered, had sections underlined with pencil. Through prayers and readings, he found solace and a way to comprehend the unexplainable. When I asked him one day why he thought God would allow the Germans to oppress and abuse the Jews, he replied, "Who said that God allows it? You think just because something bad happens, it's because God allows it? Nonsense. Rather than question God, I question man. Why are people so cruel to one another? This is not the fault of God, but of man himself. It is man alone who is responsible for behaving in such stupid, evil ways. God is good and just. When we suffer, he's there. Believe me. You just need to believe in him to know that. No—I've not lost faith in God, only in man."

Although I thought the concept of God was nothing more than a biblical folktale, I sometimes envied Khone's deeply held belief and commitment to a force much greater than ourselves. His faith seemed to provide him with a compass for navigating the dangerous world we were now living in and gave him a deep sense of hope to use as a shield against the mayhem of evil.

Papa made some tea and I went to work reviewing what few orders we had, and then tended to a customer, a middle-aged Polish businessman who was looking for an umbrella to give to his wife as a birthday gift. He found one he liked, an emerald-green canopy decorated with blue and white irises. The lacquered cherrywood handle glistened in the cool light. When he asked the price, I told him seventy-five zloty. He said it was too expensive. I told him I could come down ten percent. He said that was not enough and started to leave when Papa appeared from the workshop. "Then how much will you pay?" asked Papa.

"Half," said the man.

"That's ridiculous," I said to Papa.

"I'll sell it to you for forty. Give the money to my son." He turned his back on the man and walked away. I couldn't believe he agreed to sell it for so little without even trying to negotiate. I started to protest, but Papa held up his hand to stop me. The man handed me the forty zloty, took the umbrella, and left.

"Why did you do that?" I asked, following Papa into the workshop. "That amount doesn't even cover the cost of materials and labor!"

"Why do you think?" He sat down at Pinie's workbench and worked on repairing a broken shaft. I was about to continue pressing the issue when Khone caught my eye from his workbench and shook his head, indicating I should let it go.

An hour later, I was taking inventory of our supplies when Schlöndorff's black sedan parked in front of the shop. He exited the car wearing a long black trench coat over his gray uniform, the top of his black visor beaded with melted snow, his turtle shell hump barely visible beneath his coat, his umbrella in hand. He entered our shop followed by two soldiers and a short, round, middle-aged man with a ruddy face wearing a camel hair overcoat and black derby. His rectangular wire-framed glasses clung to his stubby nose. A slim handlebar mustache lined his upper lip, with the waxed ends curling up like little rat tails.

"Where's your father?" asked Schlöndorff as he removed his black leather gloves, revealing scarred hands that looked like old parchment. I pointed to the workshop.

Schlöndorff entered the workshop, followed by his soldiers and the round man. From the doorway I watched as he walked over to Khone's workbench and picked up the awl and fiddled with it before approaching Papa's bench where he worked on replacing the broken shaft.

"Today is a new day for your shop," said Schlöndorff in a cheery tone. His soldier translated. "As I'm sure you know, regulations are in place stating Jews are forbidden to own businesses. You managed to keep yours longer than most. But today it ends. Today you will voluntarily assign ownership of your shop to Mr. Witek." Schlöndorff motioned for the round man to step forward.

Removing his derby, bowing courteously, Witek revealed a bald dome decorated by a fringe of dyed black hair draping the sides, a few lonely oily strands pulled across his pate. He flashed a sheepish smile and waved to Papa and Khone. "Mr. Witek had his own shop in Warsaw, so he knows how to run the business. You," he said, pointing to Khone, "will continue working here while you"— pointing to Papa—"will start working tomorrow on repairing the railroad tracks along with your son." Schlöndorff motioned for his two soldiers to stand next to Khone. "You will need to cut your beard now," he instructed Khone. One soldier offered him a pair of scissors.

"Please," said Khone in German. "It's against the laws of my religion."

Without hesitating, Schlöndorff motioned for the two soldiers to proceed. One stood behind Khone, first throwing his hat and yarmulke to the ground, then tightly gripping his head with both arms and restraining him in a headlock while the other forcefully cut off his beard and sidelocks from ear to ear. Khone didn't resist. He knew there'd be no point. He sat still with his eyes squeezed shut, his lips moving as he must have been whispering Hebrew prayers to his God.

I felt a pit in my stomach and averted my eyes from witnessing such a defiling deed. The metallic clipping sounds of the scissor blades brutally cutting Khone's beard haunted the room. Papa stood in the shadows at the back of the workshop, his face buried in his hands. He removed a handkerchief from his back pocket and wiped his eyes.

"Now you'll be able to see better what you're carving without that beard in your way," said Schlöndorff. The soldiers laughed, but Schlöndorff's revolting face was indecipherable, cruelly distant.

Schlöndorff motioned with his index finger for Papa to follow him into the shop. When Papa passed by Khone, he reached out to grab his arm and they squeezed each other's hands. Papa handed him his handkerchief to wipe away the blood streaming from the cuts on his chin and cheeks and below his nostrils.

Inside the store, Schlöndorff forced Papa to sign and date several papers that made Witek the new owner. Then he demanded the keys. As if in a trance, Papa slowly reached into his right front pocket and surrendered the keys by dropping them on the desk.

A soldier outside the shop scrubbed the Star of David off the window while the other soldier was on a ladder taking down our sign, BERKOVITZ CUSTOM UMBRELLAS, and replacing it with the new sign: VISTULA RIVER UMBRELLAS.

Before leaving, Schlöndorff handed Papa another document that instructed us to report to the train station the next morning at seven o'clock for our work assignment on the tracks.

"Good luck to you, Mr. Witek," said Schlöndorff as he exited the shop.

Papa and I stared at Witek, who was now removing his overcoat and hanging it on the standing coatrack next to Papa's coat, avoiding our gaze.

We went back to the workshop and sat next to Khone at his workbench. He was in a daze, unaware of the small cuts on his cheeks and chin that were still trickling blood. I retrieved a towel from the bathroom and dabbed the cuts on his face.

"Are you okay?" asked Papa.

Khone nodded and drank his tea. "I lost my beard and sidelocks while you lost your entire business. Are you okay?"

Papa nodded. "I never wanted to admit it, but deep down, I knew this was bound to happen."

Then Khone leaned in close to Papa and whispered in his ear in case Witek, who now was in the shop organizing the display and unpacking his files, was listening. "You need to get your family out of here, now. This Schlöndorff fellow has it out for you."

"But where should we go?" whispered Papa.

"East, into Russian-occupied Poland. Go to Przemyśl. You should be safe there."

"And how would we get there?"

"By train."

"But we're forbidden to ride the trains."

"My neighbor took his family by train and came back to bring even more family east. He said it's all about paying off the right people."

"You must come with us."

"I'm meant to stay here."

"Think about it. Please," said Papa, patting Khone on the back.

Before we left, I emptied the safe without Witek knowing it. Only a few items remained: gold and silver bands, some cash, useless ownership titles for the shop. Witek kept himself busy with organizing and dusting the umbrellas on the other side of the store while Papa packed his briefcase with the ownership titles, accounting books, and a few other files. When I asked him why he was keeping these useless items, he told me, "In case one day things change. Which I believe they will." I thought he was deluding himself but said nothing.

From the sidewalk, we glanced up at the fresh sign above the store, VISTULA RIVER UMBRELLAS. Our business had disappeared, as if it had never existed.

Suddenly, Papa and I were no longer umbrella makers. We were nothing.

12

THE FOLLOWING MORNING, PAPA AND I WOKE BEFORE FIRST light and quickly prepared to leave. To protect ourselves from the cold, we each wore two pairs of wool socks and long underwear beneath our thick wool pants, extra sweaters over our shirts, our wool coats, and the heavy rubber boots we used for fishing. Papa packed a rucksack with a couple of chicken liver sandwiches, apples and carrots, and two bottles of water.

Under the dim glow of the streetlamps, we trudged through a half foot of snow to the train station where we reported for work.

A group of weary men tagged with Star of David armbands, about twenty, huddled together in front of the station doors. The doors remained locked. Papa pulled one man to the side and showed him our papers and asked if this was our group. The small unshaven man with a swollen runny nose, thin and wearing round black-framed glasses with lenses thick as the bottom of a water glass, had friendly, intelligent eyes. He glanced at the papers. "Yes, you're with us." He put out his hand. "My name is Chaim."

Papa shook his hand. "I'm Lev and this is my son, Reuven."

"Pleasure to meet you both. I would've never guessed you're related."

"He takes after his mom's side."

Unlike Papa's and my sisters' darker, Semitic looks, I shared Mama's light brown hair and gray-blue eyes. We could easily pass for goyim.

When the army transport truck pulled up, a soldier jumped out, ordering us to load into the back of a truck covered by a tattered green canvas canopy. Chaim took a seat on the cold steel floor next to Papa. He told us he'd been the chief loan officer at the Bank of Poland before the Germans removed him from his job a month ago, assigning him to shovel sand at the brick factory and sweep the streets. Two weeks ago, they moved him to work on the railroad tracks. "I'm not used to doing all this manual labor," he said. "It's making me sick." He asked Papa what his profession was, and when he learned Papa had been the owner of our umbrella shop, his face lit up. "My wife bought me one of your umbrellas seven years ago for my fiftieth birthday. I still have it! I must say, it's a piece of art."

"Describe the handle," said Papa.

"It's ivory with two deer carved into it, I suppose representing my wife and me, and it has a sterling silver band at the end of the handle with my initials. I carried that umbrella to work with me almost every day, rain or shine. When not using it as an umbrella, it was my walking cane. I must say, it made me look quite dapper." He laughed and patted Papa on the leg.

Chaim took out a pack of cigarettes and offered it to us. It had been months since I'd had a smoke. I plucked a cigarette from the pack, smelled the tobacco, and savored its bittersweet aroma. Chaim lit a match and cupped the flame in his small hands. The bite of the tobacco on my tongue brought back memories of the days when I'd smoke with Papa, Khone, Icek, Pinie, and Hersch in the workshop after lunch with a cup of hot black tea. We'd discuss the news and debate politics and sometimes place bets on which football team would win and by how many goals. I wondered if I might find myself on a work crew someday with either Pinie, Icek, or Hersch. I hoped Khone would never lose his job.

For an hour we bounced around on the cold steel floor, huddling together for protection against the biting wind slicing through the tattered canopy. The truck pulled up to a snowy field some forty kilometers west of Kraków. It turned left down a dirt road and went another kilometer where it met the railroad tracks. We all jumped out of the back of the truck and carried tools to the worksite—sledgehammers, iron spikes, pry bars, shovels, wheelbarrows, and pickaxes.

We met five German soldiers at a spot where the tracks had been sabotaged by an explosive device. The twisted tracks and crater looked like the bomb site I worked at next to the bridge in Kraków on the first day of the war.

The soldiers casually smoked cigarettes while drinking hot coffee, their rifles slung over their shoulders. One soldier gave directions to a man in the group who had taken the role of supervisor since he spoke German and appeared to have some understanding of track work. Six rails had to be replaced and the ground needed to be filled and leveled. He divided us into two groups. One group would fill the wheelbarrows with dirt from the field and transport it to the track to fill the bomb crater. The other group would pull spikes out of the railroad ties and remove the damaged tracks.

They assigned Papa and me to the group responsible for digging and transporting dirt. The men paired off and shared a wheelbarrow, shovel, and pickax. Papa and I found a spot to dig and discovered the frozen ground was like rock. Before shoveling it into the wheelbarrow, we had to break it with a pickax. We agreed to take turns using the pickax and running the dirt-loaded wheelbarrow to the tracks. Chaim and another man worked just a few meters away from us and Chaim had difficulties swinging the pickax and pushing the heavy wheelbarrows.

The ruthless icy wind blasted across the fields, stinging our exposed skin and making our faces ache. Looming over us, the sky was a gray void. I ran the full wheelbarrow to the tracks, dumped the dirt into the hole, then ran the wheelbarrow back and took my turn swinging the pickax as Papa shoveled the broken dirt into the wheelbarrow, then hauled it to the tracks. But like Chaim, he had trouble balancing and managing the weight of the wheelbarrow on the frozen, uneven ground. I insisted that I be the one to run the wheelbarrow to the tracks, but his pride wouldn't allow it. I was about to argue with him when we saw a guard give a rifle butt to the head of a man caught talking. From that point on, we remained silent and communicated only through looks and body gestures.

The soldiers watched us from their trucks while staying warm, smoking cigarettes, drinking tea, and eating bread, cheese, sausage, and whatever else they had.

After three hours of backbreaking work, the soldiers gave us a fifteen-minute break to go relieve ourselves in the fields, have some water, and eat the food we brought. Papa and I sat next to our wheelbarrow and ate our chicken liver sandwiches and drank our water. We saved the apples and carrots for later.

When they ordered us back to work, three trucks arrived, one loaded with small crushed stones, the other carrying slightly larger stones, the third stacked high with thick wooden railroad ties.

A soldier announced that once we filled the hole, we would construct a track bed by building a layer of small stones as sub-ballast, followed by a layer of larger stones as ballast. Then we would set and level the ties in the ballast and lay new iron rails across them.

As the day wore on, both Chaim and Papa were losing strength. Each trek to the tracks became slower and more agonizing. Chaim's partner and I, both of us around the same age, took extra loads of the dirt to the tracks to give Chaim and Papa more time to recuperate. By this time, Papa no longer argued with me.

In the late afternoon, Chaim insisted on taking a turn with the wheelbarrow. He was struggling to push it up the embankment when he tripped over a tree root, spilling the entire load of dirt before reaching the tracks. One of the younger soldiers with a cigarette dangling from his thin bluish lips, maybe a couple of years older than me, came over and yelled at Chaim to get up. Chaim, exhausted and in pain, kept apologizing to the soldier as he struggled to get to his knees. The soldier called him a *schwein* and rammed his rifle butt three times into Chaim's head. Chaim fell unconscious. The soldier called him a useless *Jude* rat, kicked him, and then ordered me to pick him up and throw him in the back of the truck.

I gathered Chaim in my arms as he came back to consciousness. Blood streamed from his swollen nose and a deep gash on the forehead. I draped his arm over my shoulder and supported him by the waist as we lumbered back to the truck. "Are you okay?" I whispered.

Chaim mumbled and groaned, "I'm sorry. . . . I'm just too weak for this work. . . ."

I tore out a piece of lining from inside my coat and gave it to Chaim to press against his head cut, something the man at the bomb site in Kraków had shown me how to do. "Keep pressure on the cut," I told him.

Chaim lay on his back in the truck and pressed the cloth against his forehead. Blood pooled around his head and streamed from his nose. I didn't know what else to do and felt guilty leaving him, but I also worried about Papa tripping and falling and then suffering the same consequences as Chaim. I told Chaim to keep putting pressure on the wound and that he'd be okay, although I had my doubts.

When I returned, Papa was struggling to push the wheelbarrow up the embankment. I took over before he stumbled. He went back to breaking up dirt as I ran the wheelbarrow and filled it so he could rest while pretending to work. The new blisters on my palms stung and bled, my legs and lower back ached. I knew the young soldier wanted to break us so he could do to us what he'd just done to Chaim—or worse, just shoot us. Working under this fear gave me the strength and determination to keep going.

AT DUSK, FOUR NEW GERMAN GUARDS REPLACED THE ONES WHO had worked us since the morning. The fresh guards continued working us into the early evening as our bodies, damp with sweat, became frozen to the bones once we stopped moving.

Papa was steadily losing his strength, and I did my best to continue carrying his load so he wouldn't get beaten. It was a responsibility, I'm ashamed to say, that I resented. I wanted him to be stronger than he was, more determined, more reliable. His physical weakness became a liability and a burden that weighed me down with constant worry. I knew if something terrible happened to him, like what happened to Chaim, Mama would blame me for it. Maybe Bubbe and my sisters would, too. But Mama for certain. "How could you have let this happen?" I could hear her shrieking. "Why couldn't you have protected him?" And I'd be asking myself the same questions while overwhelmed with guilt and angry with resentment.

13

AROUND NINE O'CLOCK WE HAD FINISHED BUILDING THE
track bed, laying ties, setting rails, and pounding the remaining spikes. I climbed into the back of the truck last, my body
completely depleted from the brutal day of labor in the freezing
cold. The blisters on my palms burned; some bled, others were
filled with fluid. I pinched a few of them with my nails, making
a small hole for the clear liquid to drain. Leaning against me, a
man appeared to be asleep with his head drooping forward.
Papa sat on the other side of him. I closed my eyes for a moment.
We all needed sleep. Then I remembered Chaim. Where was
Chaim? I looked around the truck. In the cold darkness, it was
hard to see anyone's face. I reached across the sleeping man next
to me to tap Papa's leg and get his attention. "Where's Chaim?"
I quietly asked.

"Chaim is dead," said Papa in a whisper. "But the Germans
don't know."

"Dead?"

"Yes."

"Where is he?"

Papa pointed to the man between us. I looked more closely. Dried
blood caked his clothes and covered parts of his head and face like a
mask of mud. On the cold steel floor, near his shoes, was a pool of
frozen blood. The arm pressing against my side was stiff. The torn

cloth I'd given him was clenched in his hand. I didn't know he was that badly injured. I felt guilty and wondered if there was anything else I could've done to save him from dying. Then I realized this easily could've been Papa. It scared me to think about how he'd survive more days of this type of work. What would occur if he was paired with someone else? Someone who was unable or unwilling to help him? What then?

Papa leaned forward. "We can't leave him here. He has a wife and child and if the Germans find out he's dead, they'll bury him in a ditch God knows where. When they drop us at the train station, we'll put his arms around our shoulders and walk him home as if he's very ill. The man next to me gave me his address. It's only two blocks from where we unload."

Papa's idea took me completely by surprise. It was dangerous and none of us knew what the guards would do if they discovered us taking a person they'd killed back to their home for a proper burial. Plus, Papa was dog-tired. He barely made it through the day. Yet here he was, wanting to protect Chaim's dignity by not allowing the Germans to desecrate his body by tossing it like a piece of garbage into some field or hole in the ground. I realized this was his form of resistance. His way of battling the almighty Germans. His way of retaining some shred of his own self-worth. Papa was a mensch in this situation, making me proud of him in a way I'd not felt before.

Our truck pulled into the *Arbeitsamt*. Before we unloaded, Papa tore off a piece of Chaim's undershirt and used it to wipe some of the blood off his face that appeared frozen. We climbed out of the back of the truck as one guard kept watch. The other men circled around us so that Papa and I could slide Chaim out the back without the guard noticing he wasn't moving. I put my cap on Chaim's head to cover the blood. Papa and I placed his rigid arms over our shoulders and held his waist to support him as we walked away with several of the men still surrounding us. We had to move fast because it was past the nine o'clock curfew for Jews.

Papa was breathing hard with Chaim's dead body weight bearing down on him. He seemed about to collapse when another man stepped in to take his place.

We had one more block to go when a Polish police officer rounded a corner and stopped us. He demanded to see our *kennkartes*—Jewish identification cards. I found Chaim's ID in his pocket and gave it to the police officer, along with mine. He asked what was wrong with Chaim and I explained he was very sick and needed to see a doctor. The policeman threatened to arrest us for being out past the curfew. Papa explained the Germans had just brought us back from a worksite. He showed him his bloody blisters, as did I and the other man helping us. Then Papa offered to buy the policeman dinner as he handed him seven zloty, the only money he had on him. The policeman took it and warned us to not be out past curfew again. He shoved our *kennkartes* into Papa's chest and strolled away.

At Chaim's apartment, his wife gasped the moment she laid her eyes upon him. She tried saying his name, but nothing came out. Stumbling backward, she knocked over a vase of flowers. Papa helped her to the couch as the other man and I gently laid Chaim down on the floor in the sitting room. Chaim's teenage daughter came into the room, saw her father on the floor, grabbed her hair and hollered a piercing screech that sent chills through me. She collapsed on the couch, sobbing, burying her head in her mother's bosom.

Papa waited a moment before guiding the grieving wife and daughter into the next room. He sat them down on the bed and asked them to give us a little time to clean Chaim's face and hands. He seemed knowledgeable about how to handle the situation.

His gentleness helped calm them. I'd always seen his gentleness as a weakness. Now I witnessed its power.

In the kitchen, he found towels and filled a pot with water. He removed my hat, which had concealed Chaim's injuries, and gently wiped his face and neck with a damp towel. The fringe of hair on the back of Chaim's head where the rifle butt hit him was indented and caked with blood and mud. His face was gray as the clay we had dug from the ground. The cut on his forehead, the size of a plum, swelled with a long crimson slit running across it. Through the half-open bedroom door, I watched Chaim's wife and daughter sitting on the bed, staring at us in shock, their bodies trembling as they grasped each other.

After cleaning Chaim, we wrapped his body in a white sheet like a cocoon.

The wife and daughter returned to the sitting room and knelt next to Chaim's body. The wife lifted the sheet so she could see his face. She and her daughter, sobbing, placed their hands over his heart and talked to him as if he'd hear their loving words and somehow speak back to them.

Word of Chaim's death quickly spread through the building and soon the neighbors and some of his extended family appeared. They sat with Chaim's wife and daughter, trying to console them. Papa and I were no longer needed and so we returned home.

SOMEHOW, PAPA ENDURED THE LONG DAYS OF MANUAL LABOR IN the unforgiving winter cold. His body had adjusted to the toil of moving wheelbarrows full of stone and clay and the endless hours of swinging sledgehammers and pickaxes into frozen dirt. As if he'd been a laborer his entire life, the palms of his long and slender hands were now calloused and thick as cowhide, his knuckles scarred and wrinkled.

Mama and Bubbe helped us survive by keeping us relatively well fed despite the food rationing. Since we still had some money, Mama found the ingredients she needed for making her delicious chicken soup packed with tender pieces of chicken, potatoes, celery, carrots, onions, and garlic. Bubbe's thick cabbage borscht helped give Papa and me the energy to work through those days of cold that stung our skin, fingers, and toes, and numbed our minds.

14

WHEN SPRING ARRIVED, THE SNOWY FROZEN FIELDS MELTED, turning the hardened earth back into soft soil. Papa and I continued to work whatever jobs the Germans forced on us for as many hours as they demanded, and always without pay. Besides repairing the railroad tracks, they had us shovel sand, dig trenches, clean latrines, repair the cobblestone streets, load bricks, fill trucks with coal and wagons with gravel, cut trees, and carry lumber.

The Germans now required every Jew in Kraków to register all their property and assets. Jews unable to work were moved out of the city and into the surrounding countryside.

In April, we learned the Germans were continuing their expansion across Europe as they invaded Denmark and Norway. It was becoming clear there was no country capable of stopping them.

Mama and Bubbe tried to keep us all well fed, but I noticed less chicken meat in Mama's soups and fewer pieces of beef in Bubbe's cabbage borscht. The cost of food was rising, and there was less of it. The money we had saved was steadily dwindling away.

Sara, Basha, and Mama searched for various ways to bring in money, no matter how little. But work was scarce since everyone was hurting for money. They found temporary jobs cleaning homes and businesses, washing clothes, running errands, mending clothes. Sara eventually landed part-time work, assisting a tailor on the other side of Kazimierz.

Exhausted by the physical labor, Papa had no energy to take on additional work that would pay. But I eventually found some paying work on the weekends at the Podgórze Pharmacy on the corner of Zgody Square, at the opposite end of where our umbrella shop was located. Although the pay was meager, I was very fortunate Mr. Malinowski, the pharmacist and owner, had hired me. Papa knew him well and I'm certain that's why he gave me some work.

Mr. Malinowski was a tall, handsome man with a meticulously groomed light brown mustache accenting his rugged cheekbones. He always stood soldier straight, his face tanned from mountain climbing, skiing, fly-fishing, and hunting. He was Papa's age but looked much younger, single, and never married, which was surprising. I saw many women flirt with him while he wrote their prescription order or provided them with medical advice. He had a natural ability to set people at ease by the way he looked at them and listened. He was easy to trust.

He was also a devout Catholic and a good friend to the Jewish community. While working there, I witnessed how Mr. Malinowski would lower the price of medications when a Jewish customer couldn't afford the full price and would allow them to purchase items on credit. He even gave money from his pocket to the most desperate customers. Why he cared about the Jews when so many Poles didn't was a mystery to me. Then one day I asked him. He replied, "My purpose is to help relieve people from their suffering, no matter who they are, what they have, or where they come from. It's that simple." Mr. Malinowski was a true mensch, and a very courageous man to be helping the Jews during the occupation. To know him helped encourage me to not give up hope in humanity.

I'd show up at the pharmacy whenever I was free from working for the Germans and do any job Mr. Malinowski gave me. I stocked the shelves with medications and supplies; swept and mopped the floors; dusted and polished the white marble counter-tops, brass doorknobs, and wood and glass cabinets; and mostly ran deliveries to people across the city who couldn't make it to the pharmacy. Mr. Malinowski gave me a shiny black bicycle with wire baskets mounted on the back to use for deliveries, so I didn't have to spend any of his money on droskies or trams. He was a prudent man who saved every grosz. He once told me that every grosz saved was a grosz for helping others.

As money trickled into our home, we regained a sense of stability and control over our situation. The money helped ease the constant fear for our survival that we confronted on a daily basis. But then life suddenly shifted again on the evening of 14 May, just past curfew.

After making my last delivery for Mr. Malinowski in Podgórze I returned home late that evening, just as curfew started. I flung open the door to our apartment and was startled to discover my family busy packing boxes with all our belongings. "What's going on?" I asked.

"That SS officer came here and ordered us to move," said Bubbe. "*A kholerye oyf im!*—The cholera on him!"

"Schlöndorff?" I asked.

"Yes," said Papa, rolling up the oriental carpet in the sitting room. "I found a small apartment a few blocks away. We'll move there temporarily until we can find something larger."

"A Polish family is moving in," said Basha, packing a box with bedding. "The man is a police officer. They ordered us to be out of here by tomorrow morning."

Mama sat on the couch in a stupor, her index fingers picking at the raw skin around her thumbs, the rim of her eyes red from crying. Sara sat on one side of Mama, rubbing her back and stroking her arm as Mama trembled while staring down at the carpet disturbingly. I sat on the other side of Mama and held her right hand so she'd stop picking at her thumb. "It's going to be okay, Mama. We'll get through this," I said.

"No," she said. "No, I won't leave here. They can't take my home away from me. It's my home. They'll have to carry me out of here!"

It was frightening to see our strong Mama so distraught. I'd never seen this side of her before. We all loved our home, but none of us loved it more than her. It was the only home she'd ever had. She grew up here with Bubbe, Zayde, and her brother, Uncle Zel, who died in the last war, then married Papa and raised us here. Her memories and stories, her sense of safety and security were rooted in this apartment. After everything had been taken, the apartment was the last thing she had, the last thing any of us had, besides the clothes on our backs, our furniture and belongings, and our lives.

"For God's sake, Rachel," pleaded Papa. "We have no choice here. We must move. If you try to stay, they'll throw you in jail. Is that what you want?"

I handed Mama some tissue for her to wipe her eyes and blow her nose. Sara and I sat with her, hoping to calm her nerves so she could come to terms with our situation and start packing. I offered to make her some tea, but she declined. In her beautiful steel-blue eyes, I could see her wrestling with the sad reality of our situation. "Wherever we land, we'll make a new home," said Sara in a soft tone. "And once the war ends, we can reclaim our home. You need to have hope, Mama. You can't give up. We need you." I watched Mama's face carefully as Sara spoke. Her words seemed to reach Mama. Or maybe it was her tone. Mama's grip relaxed in in my hand as she turned to kiss Sara, and then me, and then rose from the couch in silence and began packing.

"The *farshtunken* Poles and Germans do what they want to us!" yelled Bubbe from her bedroom. "To hell with these *mamzers!* *Di beyner zolen zeyer oysrinen!*"

Bubbe was right—*Di beyner zolen zeyer oysrinen*—May their bones be drained of marrow. But most of all, it was Schlöndorff's bones I wanted drained of their marrow. For he was intent on destroying our lives. Though the Jews in Kraków were all experiencing the same hardships, Schlöndorff appeared to derive a sadistic pleasure from our suffering. As though we were a special project for him. Maybe a social experiment where he could dismantle our lives piece by piece and then observe at what point each person crumbled until the entire family collapsed. He was a sick *mamzer*. I decided right then that I wanted to kill him. I knew it was pure fantasy. But it was a relief to imagine ways of murdering him without getting caught.

I went to my room and changed into dry clothes and started packing. I first removed from the wall the framed Benny Goodman poster Papa had given me when I started playing clarinet back in third grade. I wrapped it in a sheet and then packed a trunk with my old clarinet, which I hadn't played in several years, along with clothes, an alarm clock, detective novels stored on my bookshelf, fishing gear, clothes and bedding, shoes, coats and hats.

When I finished with my room, I went through the house and helped pack our other belongings including the decorative bowls and dishes; oriental rugs; sterling silver candelabras; lamps and books; the small wood-carved figurines of a mermaid, a fisherman, a shoemaker, a dancer—all of them carved by Khone's remarkable hands. We packed the sterling silver menorah that belonged to my paternal great-grandfather, an Orthodox shoemaker from Warsaw, and the sterling silver Seder plate belonging to Bubbe's mother; we packed the photographic portraits of my family along with portraits of my mother's and father's families, the painting of a rolling golden wheatfield at dusk with a flock of crows flying toward a setting sun, the painting of a sailboat crossing a violent sea, and the ink drawing of a rabbi in prayer with a tallit, his prayer shawl, draped over his head, the ancient lines in his face carved by shadows. Mama's great-grandfather, a rabbi himself, originally owned this drawing, and the family has passed it down for generations.

I thought of Zelda and her family packing the last time I saw her. Now their apartment, along with all the things they left behind, including Zelda's books, belonged to the Polish family living there. How my dear Zelda must miss her books more than anything else. At least we could take everything we own with us. I wondered where Zelda and her family would find a place to live should they ever return to Kraków.

THE NEXT DAY, SHIPPING TRUNKS AND VALISES LINED THE hallway, carpets rolled and tied, sheets and blankets were used to protect the furniture. Except for Bubbe, all of us spent the morning carrying our belongings down to the street where Papa had hired two horse-drawn carts to transport our belongings to the new apartment several blocks away. It was at the edge of Kazimierz. Saul, the downstairs neighbor, and his brother-in-law helped us move the heavy furniture.

A light rain began falling as we loaded the carts. Mama wanted us to delay the move because she was afraid the rain would ruin the artwork and furniture. Her eyes were bloodshot from stress and sleeplessness, her voice quivering, her index fingers obsessively picking at the corners of her thumbs. Papa reminded her that Schlöndorff had ordered us out by noon. Our only choice was to move now.

I rode in a cart next to the driver, a young Jewish fellow in his twenties, the edges of his sleeves and coat hem tattered and dirty, dark beard stubble covering his thin face. He pulled a small black canopy over our heads to protect us from the rain that was now coming down harder. All our belongings were getting soaked. I asked if he had a tarp. He said he didn't have one. Then he told me we were the eleventh Jewish family he moved in the past few days, all in Kazimierz. He said the Germans and Poles wanted to move here because the apartments were larger and well kept.

At the new building on Gazowa Street, everyone quickly unloaded the carts to save what we could from water damage. Fortunately for Bubbe, our apartment was on the first floor, so she wouldn't have to climb three flights of stairs anymore. But once inside, we were all stunned by its tight quarters. None of us ever imagined living in such a small space. Sara and Basha held hands and struggled to hold back tears while Bubbe and Mama wandered around in a state of utter disbelief. The apartment did not have a bathroom, only a toilet in the hallway. The other rooms were half the size of the rooms in our other apartment. Instead of four bedrooms, we now had two tiny bedrooms, plus a small sitting room and a stand-up kitchen with a stove, a sink, and a few cabinets. To make matters worse, the apartment was filthy and smelled of something decaying. I searched the place and found a dead rat beneath the kitchen sink. After wrapping it in a piece of old newspaper, I took it outside to dispose of it.

When we got everything inside, we could barely move around our piles of boxes and furniture. My Benny Goodman poster got damaged from the rain, as did the print of the rabbi and the painting of the ship on the sea.

Mama grabbed Papa by the lapels, her pale hands clenching his coat and shaking. "We need to leave here immediately," she said. Papa tried to embrace her, but she pushed him away. "My love," he whispered, trying to get closer to her, "this is temporary."

"No, no, no . . . I won't stay here one night. We can't live here." She backed away from him, pacing and trembling. "This place is a curse—a *broch*!"

Bubbe stepped in and put her arms around her. "My *bubeleh*, we have no choice right now. We'll make do. You need to be strong now."

"But I can't breathe here—the stench. No bathroom, not even a toilet!"

"There's one in the hall," said Bubbe as she rubbed Mama's arms and tried to soothe her.

"The one that everyone else in the building uses. I'm sure it's filthy!"

"It's temporary," said Bubbe. "You need to calm down."

"I'm suffocating in here. We must leave."

"And go where?" asked Papa.

"Anywhere but here."

"We will move, my sweetheart. I told you this is just temporary."

"Our dining room table and bureau at the apartment—you need to go back and get them."

"But they won't fit inside here."

"I'll find a place for them."

"Where?"

"Right here!" She was frantically pacing in small circles, pulling at her hair.

"In the middle of the room?"

"Yes! Right here."

"But we won't be able to move. We'll have to climb over the furniture to get anywhere. There'll be no place to sit."

"I don't care. Those two pieces came from my grandparents!"

"Rachel, be reasonable. We can't live like that. Trust me, we'll sell the furniture to the new renters. We need the money."

"Lev is right, my darling," said Bubbe. "We need the money. And if I can let go of those two pieces that belonged to my parents, then you can let them go, too."

"No, Mama! I won't sell anything. Do you know how valuable that furniture is?"

"You need to let it go, Mama," I said.

"I don't need to let go of anything. Look around you. This is all we have! This is it!"

She broke down, crying hysterically. Papa didn't know what to do. Bubbe stepped in and sat Mama down on the couch, consoling her in the way only she could do. Sara and Basha sat next to Mama and held her hands. Papa and I couldn't watch any more of her suffering and went outside to join Saul and the drivers for a smoke. The rain had stopped and the sun was trying to burn through the clouds.

We went back to the old apartment and picked up the last piece of furniture that we'd somehow squeeze into the new place—Bubbe's red velvet reading chair. Papa asked Saul if he wanted to trade his smaller dining room table set for our larger one, including the bureau.

"Your dining room set is much more beautiful and more valuable than ours," Saul said. "Is that ebony?"

"Yes."

"It's gorgeous, and I'd love to take that bureau. But I think it's only a matter of time before we're forced out, too. Then I'll have the same problem as you."

"That's probably true," said Papa. "I guess we'll leave it here for the moment and hopefully the people moving in will buy the set from us. If they don't, then I'll sell it on the street."

"I think that's your best option," said Saul. "I know of no other place to store it. And like you said, you need the money."

* * *

TWO DAYS LATER, PAPA AND BUBBE PERSUADED MAMA TO SELL
the furniture. That evening Papa and I returned to the old apartment after working a long grueling day laying rail track. Our
muddy boots left a trail of dirt clumps as we climbed the creaky
stairs. I already felt like a stranger in the building I'd grown
up in.

Papa knocked on the door.

"What?!" came a man's gruff voice from behind the door.

"Yes—my name is Lev Berkovitz. We had lived here and left
some furniture behind."

There was silence.

"Hello?" said Papa.

"What?!"

Papa frowned and glanced over at me. I shook my head in
disgust. "Can you open the door, please? May I have a moment to
speak to you?" said Papa politely.

The door opened and before us stood a heavyset man built like
a truck with a potbelly stretching the seams on his tobacco-stained
undershirt. Behind him, we saw our apartment in disarray, with
trunks, suitcases, carpets, dressers, chairs, and bureaus scattered
about. "We're eating," the man said through his bristly brown mustache, its whiskers stained with tomato sauce. "What do you want?"

"I'm sorry to interrupt, but we left our dining room table
and bureau here and we're wondering if you might be interested
in buying them from us."

The man laughed. "Ha! That's a good joke!" He turned and
yelled to his wife and four children eating at the dining room table.
"The Żyd wants us to buy the table and bureau!"

"Tell him to go to hell," his wife yelled back. "The building
manager said they're ours."

The man looked at Papa, grinning derisively. "You heard my wife. Go to hell, Żyd. The furniture came with the apartment." He slammed the door shut in Papa's face before he could reply. My chest and throat tightened. Papa flushed and his dirt-covered hands curled into fists quivering with rage as they opened and closed, as if they were searching for something to grab on to. He seethed with an anger I'd not seen before. "He has no right," he muttered, eyes fixed on the door. "No right."

"We can't let him get away with this," I shouted.

"Lower your voice. He's a police officer," he said under his breath. "Do you want him to throw us in jail? Then Bubbe, Mama, and your sisters will be alone. Is that what you want?"

I didn't care at that moment. I swung my fist against the door and was about to pound again when Papa grabbed my arm. "Don't you dare," he said. His grip was like a clamp as he pulled me down the stairs alongside him with a force that surprised me. The man's voice boomed from the top of the stairs: "Don't come back, Żyd! If I see you again, I'll lock you up and beat you!"

When we reached the street, we ran a block and disappeared round the corner. We found a small park and sat down on a bench to catch our breath. Papa took out two cigarettes and handed one to me. He cupped his hands and lit the end of my cigarette, then his. We smoked in silence for a long time, sucking down the rage ignited by yet another humiliation.

Papa finally broke the silence. "Your mama will go crazy if we tell her the truth of what happened. We need to come up with a story." He stubbed his cigarette butt out in the dirt. He was right. So we agreed to lie and tell her the police officer was going to purchase the furniture from us for three hundred fifty zloty and would pay for it over the next four months. We agreed that every two weeks Papa would show Mama some of the money I'd made at the pharmacy, and money he had hidden, and claim it had come from the police officer.

I finished my cigarette as we started walking home. My anger gradually dissipated as a deep sadness enveloped me. Everything seemed so futile—so utterly bleak. The future I once imagined had disintegrated into dust. Within nine months, the Germans had stolen our business, belongings, and identities. Zelda had disappeared. The safety, comfort, stability, and normalcy of our past lives had evaporated and were now too painful to remember. It was best to forget.

We were now living in the timeless void of the present. All we could do now was merely survive from one fleeting moment to the next.

I began asking myself: If this is living, then why live? What's the point? I thought of Khone, his beard sheared off, degraded. Yet he still held fast to his belief in God. Yes, his beliefs and work provided him purpose. But I didn't believe in God, so what did I have? I had my family and Zelda to live for. I realized protecting my family and finding Zelda was now my sole purpose for living.

15

A FEW DAYS LATER, THEY TRANSPORTED PAPA, ME, AND TWELVE other men twenty-five kilometers north along the Vistula River. We unloaded where the Germans were constructing a bridge, presumably for German military transports. They strapped wood frames to our backs and ordered us to move the bricks piled on the road down to the river. There, they used them for constructing the bridge footings.

The spring morning was unusually hot, the air heavy with humidity. By noon, the burning sun loomed over us in the cloudless sky. We carried the bricks on our backs down a narrow, rocky dirt trail to the river. Swarms of hungry black flies buzzed about feasting on our faces, necks, and hands.

I kept my eye on a stout German commander, potbellied and clean shaven and sweaty with puffy, red-rimmed piglike eyes. He casually strolled through the worksite, shading his pale skin from the stark sunlight with a black umbrella. With his other hand, he swatted away the flies and cooled himself with a small gold-and-red oriental fan. Hanging from his belt was a leather riding crop that tapped on the side of his boot as he waddled through the worksite. When seeing a man working too slowly, he'd stop, fold the fan, stick it into his rear pocket, then use the riding crop to whip the man's legs with a gleeful grin.

Papa and I avoided the whippings until midday when the heat was getting to Papa. After only two brief breaks, Papa was dragging himself. With the bricks stacked on his back, every step took tremendous effort, as though each of his shoes weighed twenty kilos. Sweat mixed with red clay caked his clothes and coated his anguished face like a mask. His weary eyes strained beneath his thick, red-dusted eyebrows. Bent almost in half under the weight of the bricks, he kept his eyes glued to the ground to avoid twisting an ankle on a rock or tripping on a tree root. The mud at the bottom of the trail swallowed our feet as we trudged through it.

The commander caught sight of Papa's exhaustion and I knew something bad was about to happen. Sneaking up from behind Papa, the commander yelled at him to move faster. Papa couldn't follow the orders, so the commander whipped his legs with the leather crop until he dropped to the ground. Chaim flashed before me. I was terrified and moved toward the commander, angling to get between him and Papa, but Papa saw me and waved me away. Papa pleaded with the commander to stop. But the beating continued until the commander ran out of breath. He then spat on Papa in disgust, calling him a dirty *schweinhund Jude*, before continuing his afternoon stroll among the other laborers, searching for more victims.

Papa somehow recovered and made it through the work shift. When we arrived at the apartment that evening, the bloody welts and bruises marking his legs, arms, neck, and back horrified Mama, Bubbe, and my sisters. Papa rarely drank, but on that night, he poured a tall glass of vodka and guzzled it before washing himself by the kitchen sink. Bubbe had strung a rope from one end of the kitchen to the other and hung a sheet so we each could wash ourselves in privacy.

After Papa and I finished washing and putting on a fresh set of clothes, we sat down at the table for dinner. Papa poured himself another vodka, something I'd never seen him do.

Basha and Sara chatted about their new jobs working in the textile factory repairing German army uniforms. "A lot of the uniforms have bullet and shrapnel holes with dried blood all over them," said Sara.

"I even had one uniform with pieces of flesh on it," said Basha.

"I hope that soldier was killed!" said Bubbe.

"Enough!" said Papa. "Not another word about those *mamzers* while we're eating." He was already slurring his words. Mama suggested he slow down on the vodka. He slammed his fist on the table and yelled at her to mind her own goddamned business. Bubbe grabbed my arm and pulled it toward her. Tears flowed down Sara's face. Basha and Mama gazed at him in silence, their faces taut with fear. No one said a word as he took another swig from his glass before defiantly refilling it. By his temples, flecks of mud clung to his hairline. Welts from the black fly bites speckled his neck and the backs of his hands. His eyes shifted, appearing glassy and unfocused, listless. He seemed lost in some dark corner of his mind.

From outside our small windows came the distant low rumble of thunder approaching, then the light patter of rain hitting the sidewalk and street. Papa finished his glass of vodka and rose from the table on shaky legs. He headed toward the door, balancing himself against the furniture and walls, as if walking the aisle of a train rocking from side to side.

"Where are you going?" asked Mama.

"Out."

"Don't. It's only forty-five minutes before curfew and you're drunk. It's pouring rain outside. Stay here." She started picking at her thumbs again.

"No. I'm going out." He wobbled out the door and slammed it behind him.

Mama yelled after him to take his umbrella, but it was too late; he was already gone.

Bubbe grabbed my arm and told me to go with him to make sure he'd return home before curfew and wouldn't get into trouble.

Mama demanded I go as well and Basha wanted to join me. But everyone told her she needed to stay at home. Although Papa's behavior was disturbing, I understood it. The mind can handle only so much abuse and humiliation before it breaks. Given his unstable mental state, I, too, was extremely worried. I grabbed my raincoat and his umbrella and chased after him.

The rain was falling hard. Water gushed out of the buildings' drainpipes onto the sidewalks and streets, washing away the dirt and scattered piles of horse manure. Jagged lines of white lightning cut across the black sky, followed by loud cracks of thunder. When I caught up to him, Papa was mumbling to himself, his clothes drenched. "Where are you going?" I asked. He didn't answer. He seemed to wander aimlessly with no destination in mind, swimming in drunken thoughts.

I opened his umbrella and handed it to him as we walked across the bridge spanning the river toward Zgody Square. After twenty minutes of walking, the heavy rain shifted to a light drizzle for a time and then stopped. He closed his umbrella and used it as a walking cane for balance. When we passed the Podgórze Pharmacy, I wished it was open. I would've considered asking Mr. Malinowski to help me get Papa home. Then Papa started to cross the square, but I grabbed him. "What are you doing?"

"I want to see our shop," he said, trying to pull away from me.

"But it's illegal for us to be in the square. You want them to arrest you?" I pointed to a small group of SS officers halfway down the other side of the square sitting outside at a café smoking cigars and drinking beneath a wet canopy. "They'll see you," I said.

"To hell with them." He continued stumbling in their direction.

I snatched his arm. "Let's go this way." He allowed me to lead him down the sidewalk bordering the square toward the umbrella shop.

From a short distance, we saw the bright red Nazi flag with its bold black swastika waving proudly from a pole mounted on the front of what used to be our umbrella shop, a foot above our display window. The Vistula River Umbrellas sign that had replaced ours was now gone. The new sign below the flag had thick black letters on a bloodred background reading: LSSAH OFFICE LEIBSTANDARTE SS ADOLF HITLER, A DIVISION OF THE SS.

Papa and I peered inside through the half-closed blinds and saw three large desks, each with a typewriter, telephone, lamp, stacks of papers, and piles of manuals. Large oak filing cabinets lined the walls. On one wall above the cabinets was a map of Poland with a bright red piece of yarn dividing Nazi-occupied west Poland from the Russian-controlled east. Through the doorway to the workshop, we saw more desks, filing cabinets, and uniforms.

We stood there staring through the window, speechless. The memory of having once owned a successful umbrella business here, of having a display window filled with our beautifully handmade umbrellas, of having a workshop where Khone, Pinie, Icek, and Hersch made new umbrellas and repaired old ones, now seemed nothing more than an imaginary fairy tale. To lose everything and end up with nothing? It just didn't seem possible.

The rain stopped. "Looks like the Pole—what was his name?" asked Papa, folding his umbrella.

"Witek."

"Yes, that Witek *mamzer*. Looks like he lost the business to his best friends." He laughed with a drunken bitterness.

"Let's go," I said. "I can't look at this anymore."

Papa continued staring through the window, his weary eyes glazed over by intoxicated thoughts. I worried he'd draw attention to us by doing something stupid in his distressed, inebriated state.

"It's almost curfew, Papa. We must go." I tried pulling him away from the window, but he remained rooted to the ground. His body trembled slightly as I tugged on him, his arm rigid and right hand clenching the handle of his umbrella. I feared he was getting close to having a mental breakdown.

"Please, Papa. Let's go." I tugged again, but he didn't budge.

"This was ours," he said in a slur of words. "He had no right to take it away from us. It was ours. I built it from nothing! He had no right . . ."

"Yes, you're right, Papa. But we must go now. We have five minutes until curfew." After he repeated himself a few more times, I was able to lead him away from the shop.

We hurried along the perimeter of the square, avoiding the sight lines of the SS officers in the café, who sang and laughed while filling themselves with drink. Papa kept looking behind us, as if he wanted to return to the shop. I clenched his arm, pulling him toward home.

We picked up our pace across the bridge and took the narrow side streets to avoid the German and Polish patrols. A man nearby called out for help. As we rounded the next corner, we spotted a tall figure about thirty meters away swinging his club against the back of an elderly man dressed in black, bearded, and wearing the same fisherman's cap that Khone wore. The assailant had on the long trench coat of the SS.

"My God, that's Khone," said Papa.

"I don't know," I said.

"Yes—yes, that's Khone." Papa suddenly took off running toward the scene. I yelled at him to stop, but he kept going. The old man curled himself into the fetal position on the street. The officer's club made a loud thud each time it bashed against the old man's back, arms, and legs. Papa broke into a sprint. "Stop!" he hollered at the officer.

"Papa!" I called out again while running after him. I feared he'd get arrested, or beaten, or even killed. But he kept running wildly while calling out Khone's name.

The old man tried getting to his feet to escape, but every time he stood up, the officer let him take a step or two before thrashing him with his club, punching and kicking him, and knocking him back down to his knees.

The old man, now a crumpled heap lying in a dim yellow pool of streetlight, pleaded for his life. "Stop it!" Papa yelled again. The third time the old man got up, the officer kicked him in the ribs with his shiny black boots, making him collapse. His head hit the street and blood streamed down his face. The old man wept and moaned as the officer prodded and poked him in the sides with his club, taunting him, ordering him to get up as if he were a dog. But the old man was semiconscious, groaning, gasping for breath, unable to move. The officer, possessed by his power, kicked the old man in the stomach and smashed the club against the old man's head, producing a loud "crack!" The old man went silent.

Papa threw his body into the officer, knocking him down, and then knelt next to the old man to try to help him. "Khone," he kept saying. "Khone, are you okay?" I stood next to Papa watching the officer, who was now slowly rising to his feet after having landed on his stomach. That's when I noticed the hump on his shoulder and the broken umbrella lying on the ground with the ivory handle carved into a wolf's head with ruby eyes. Beneath the trench coat appeared his SS uniform. I figured Schlöndorff must've broken the umbrella while beating the old man. Schlöndorff stood up and faced us; the flickering yellow flame of the streetlamp contorting his vicious face; his eyes dark, hollow caves. He recognized us.

Pointing his club at me, he yelled, "On your knees, *Jude schwein.*" I stood still, holding my ground, my mind blank, waiting for what would come next. He smashed the club into my thigh, sending a bolt of pain through the bone and muscle, buckling my leg. Then he raised his club high in the air and was about to crack me on the head when suddenly he arched backward and gasped, his eyelids pulled back, his

mouth agape. Papa had plunged the long blade of his umbrella handle into his back. Schlöndorff spun round and swung his club against
Papa's arm, knocking the dagger out of his hand, then swung again,
smashing the club into Papa's chest, sending him sprawling to the
ground. He leaned over Papa and was about to continue beating him
when I snatched the dagger off the street and stabbed Schlöndorff
in the back repeatedly, each thrust of the blade puncturing his coat
and uniform, skin and muscle, hitting and sliding past bone. Repeatedly, the blade went through him. I wanted him dead. He collapsed
face down on the street, wheezing and gurgling as blood flowed from
his mouth and pooled on the street and more blood seeped from the
gashes in his trench coat where the blade had punctured his body.

I wiped the blood off the blade on Schlöndorff's pant leg before sliding it back into the umbrella shaft. Papa looked at me as if
in a trance. I wasn't sure what had just happened.

"Let's go," I said, tugging on his sleeve. "Before someone sees us."

Papa pulled his arm away from me and rolled the old man onto
his back. He was not Khone after all. And the man was dead.

"Please, let's go," I said again. Papa stared in disbelief at
Schlöndorff's body splayed on the street, still wheezing, sounding
like a bellows with holes in it. We didn't know if he'd live or die. If
he lived, he'd be able to identify Papa and me, and that would be
the end of our family. But even if he died before he could speak to
anyone, we feared there may have been witnesses watching from
their windows who could identify us. Some would be eager to help
the Germans find us. But others, mainly Jews, might be coerced
to identify us through threats of beatings, torture, and arrests.
Papa and I were certain about one thing. Our family had to leave
Kraków immediately.

WHEN WE RETURNED TO THE APARTMENT, PAPA WAS MORE SO-
ber, yet we were both still in shock. He gathered everyone in the

sitting room and told the story of what had happened. When he finished, there was a long silence. Mama gazed down at her cup of tea in disbelief; my sisters, with their books on their laps, stared at Papa and me as if we were strangers. From the apartment above, the floorboards kept creaking as someone paced methodically back and forth. I feared they were listening.

Bubbe set down the navy blue scarf she'd been knitting and climbed out of her chair and kissed Papa on the cheeks. "Thanks to God you're both alive." Then she came to me and kissed both my cheeks and forehead. "You and your papa did the right thing. That Nazi *mamzer* got what he deserved."

"So, what do we do now?" asked Mama in a mere whisper, as if she were speaking to herself.

"We leave right now," said Papa. "We go east to Przemyśl. It's a small town on the other side of the San River that's protected by the Russians."

"Who told you we should go there?" Mama shook as if she was suddenly cold, and she kept picking at her thumbs. I asked her to stop; she ignored me.

"Khone, and a man I worked with on the tracks, Moishe. His neighbor took his family there for safety."

"Are there any Jews in Przemyśl?" asked Basha.

"Yes. A small Jewish community exists there, including Jews from Kraków who fled deportations."

I wondered if Zelda and her family had left Dębica and were now in Przemyśl. It would make sense because in Przemyśl, they could find safety until the war ended. The strong possibility of finding Zelda there subtly lifted my spirits.

"But how will we get there?" asked Sara.

"There's a midnight train we can catch tonight. When we get to the border, we go through a forest and down to the river where a boat will take us across. This is what Khone told me."

"But it's illegal for us to travel by train," said Mama. "We should go by carriage or find a truck."

"We can't. Germans patrol all the roads to Przemyśl. It's too dangerous."

"So how do we get on the trains?" asked Mama.

"We bribe whomever we need to. That's how Moishe did it."

"And what will we do when we get there? Where will we live? How will we survive?" Mama's face was pale, and she continued shaking.

"Enough!" said Bubbe, sitting next to Mama on the couch and putting a blanket around her shoulders. "No more questions. We should've left months ago, like those other families. We will survive this, just as we survived the last war. Have faith—Eliyohu is watching over us. Now let's pack what we can carry and go."

Mama said nothing as she stared down into her cup of tea, as if she was trying to read the tea leaves to see what the future held for us. Then something came over her. She stopped shaking, and the color came back to her face. Her gray-blue eyes became clear and focused; her body moved from a slump to standing erect. She displayed a sense of resolve. "Lev, be sure to give a small amount of cash to each of us in case we get separated. Sara and Basha, I want you to hide cash inside the linings of your suitcases. Bubbe, we'll sew the jewelry we have left inside the linings of our coats. Lev, you do the same with the tiny amount of gold and silver we have left from the shop."

As I packed my valise with clothes, I watched Mama go to work taking down from the walls the painting of the rolling wheat fields at dusk that had belonged to my great-grandparents, and the water-stained ink drawing of the rabbi in prayer belonging to my great-great-grandfather. In the kitchen, she used a knife to cut them from their frames, rolled them together, and tied them with a piece of string. She packed the sterling silver menorah belonging to Papa's grandfather and the Seder plate that had been her grandmother's. She removed a few family portraits from their frames and packed them as well. The chinaware, oriental carpets, furniture, books—objects that her family had passed down for generations—were left behind.

Unlike her reaction to when we lost our apartment, Mama now let go of everything without saying a word or shedding a tear. She moved about the room stoically, packing what would fit into a small valise, and leaving everything else behind.

16

WHEN WE LEFT THE APARTMENT, WE HAD ONLY TWENTY MIN-utes to make it to the train. Fog shrouded the city. Papa flagged down a drosky that was about to pass by us. The driver pulled up to our building, and we prepared to load our luggage when he stopped us. "You're Jews?" he asked. We were silent, unsure of what to say. He knew what we were. "It's past curfew. I can't take you." He grabbed the reins, ready to leave.

"Wait!" said Papa, reaching into the breast pocket of his jacket. He offered the driver fifteen zloty, at least four times the normal cost of the ride. "Please," said Papa. "We're going to the train station."

Taking the money, the driver signaled for us to board. He snapped the leather reins against the horse's scarred flanks. The old horse broke into a trot. We all prayed we'd make it to the train station without being stopped. In fear of being identified, Papa tilted his chestnut-brown fedora forward to obscure his face. I angled my cap so the brim shielded my eyes.

Next to me, Sara wept quietly as she held Basha's hand, wondering out loud what was going to happen to us in Przemyśl. I pointed at the driver and motioned for her to be quiet. "No one should know where we are going," I whispered in her ear. Mama, Bubbe, and Papa sat behind us, silent.

We crossed the river and entered Podgórze. It was just ten more minutes to the train station. At Zgody Square we rode by the pharmacy, and I thought of Mr. Malinowski and regretted not being able to say goodbye to him. I doubted I'd ever see him again. It seemed we were leaving Kraków for good, never to return. I worried if I didn't find Zelda in Przemyśl, then where would I find her? But then I figured there'd be other Jews in Przemyśl who had escaped the German-occupied countryside, and maybe some of them might know the whereabouts of her family.

We rounded a corner and a German army jeep seemed to appear from nowhere. It cut in front of our drosky, forcing us to an abrupt stop. My heart quickened.

Two soldiers jumped out of the jeep with rifles in their hands. One was tall and older with half-open eyelids; the other was medium height, awkward and young with pimples dotting his small chin and chubby cheeks. The pimpled soldier demanded our *kennkartes*. We handed them to him and he took his time looking them over, appearing to enjoy his sense of power over us. Sara clenched my hand and shook. I thought it was over. Surely they would take Papa and me in for questioning, and that would be the end of us.

"It's past curfew," said the older soldier, his sour breath stinking of beer and onions. "Where do you think you're going?"

"My wife's brother is very sick in Rzeszów. We're going to help him." Papa knew that mentioning Przemyśl could've caused suspicion.

The soldier looked at Papa and smiled sardonically. "We could arrest you right now."

"Please don't. Let me buy both of you dinner," said Papa as he offered the older soldier twenty zloty, more than a month's pay.

He gazed at Papa with his blank, half-open eyes. "That's good for me, *Jude*, but what about my partner here? He's hungry, too."

Papa dug into his pockets, retrieved another twenty zloty, and handed it to the younger soldier. He took the money and offered Papa his *kennkarte*. Papa reached for it but the soldier quickly withdrew it, smiling like a malicious child, toying with Papa and drawing a chuckle from the older soldier. "If I were you, *Jüdischer parasit*," said the older soldier, "I wouldn't ever come back here."

The soldiers returned to their jeep and drove off into the heavy fog, disappearing as fast as they had appeared. Mama and Papa yelled at the driver to get us to the train station quickly. We had only thirteen minutes left before the train was to leave. The driver snapped the reins and used the riding crop to drive his old horse into a fast canter. Upon arriving, I grabbed Bubbe's valise and ran with Papa inside the station. At the ticket counter, we encountered a sparrowlike, small-boned man with oily black hair and a shiny, clean-shaven face. Leaning back in his small wooden chair, he slowly turned the page of a book, ignoring us. "Sir?" said Papa. The small-boned ticket man looked over his spectacles, appearing irritated by the interruption. "Yes?"

"We need six tickets to Przemyśl."

"Przemyśl?"

"Yes, sir. Przemyśl, please."

The ticket man carefully put down his book on the table and glanced at his watch. "That train leaves in four minutes."

"Yes, sir. That's why we're in a bit of a hurry." Papa was trying to be polite and sound calm. He used his handkerchief to wipe the sweat from his forehead. His long fingers anxiously tapped the counter. The ticket man asked Papa for his *kennkarte* and took his time examining it, just as the soldiers had done. Bubbe, Mama, and my sisters stood behind me, pacing nervously. I looked up at the station clock—a minute had passed. Bubbe quietly warned Mama: "This is not good. We need to get out of here." Mama whispered into Papa's ear, ordering him to hurry the man. Papa motioned for her to stay calm.

I glanced around the station for police officers, SS, and Gestapo. A Polish police officer strolled aimlessly at the back of the station while a German soldier slept on a bench. "I'm taking Bubbe and your sisters to track five," said Mama. "We'll try to delay the conductor from closing the doors so you and Papa can get there." They left.

"Sorry. But no Jews allowed on the train," said the ticket man matter-of-factly, looking down at Papa's *kennkarte*.

Papa looked around, making sure no one was watching, and slipped the ticket man forty zloty—a large sum. I prayed for the man to quietly accept the bribe and not report us. The ticket man quickly stuffed the money into his pocket, his eyes on Papa's *kennkarte*, never making eye contact with either of us. His slender index finger, the nail perfectly trimmed and polished, tapped the counter, signaling he wanted more. Papa anxiously glanced around the station again, then added another twenty-five zloty. The ticket man tapped the counter a third time. I worried he'd squeeze us dry. Papa continued wiping the sweat off his forehead and leaned forward and whispered to the ticket man, "Please, let us go," as he slipped him another twenty zloty. I now didn't care if Papa gave him all our money. We needed to get on the train.

The ticket man charged Papa another fifteen zloty for six tickets and, when he handed them to him, said under his breath, "If you ever mention what occurred here, I'll deny it and make sure your entire *Żyd* family never sees daylight ever again. Understand?" Papa nodded and handed me the tickets before we grabbed our luggage and bolted out the train station door just as the train whistle sounded, signaling the train was about to leave.

We spotted Mama, Bubbe, and my sisters thirty meters down the platform on track five. Kneeling on the ground before the conductor, they pleaded with him to hold the train. He was on the doorstep with Bubbe waving her arms in front of him and pointing at us as he prepared to blow his whistle to signal the engineer to depart. "Stop!" I yelled, running as fast as my legs could carry me. Papa was close behind, also calling out to the conductor. He clenched the whistle between his teeth, about to blow it, when I reached him, thrusting the tickets into his hands. Papa came up behind me, breathless. Without saying a word, he slipped twenty zloty into the conductor's hands. The conductor waved us onto the train, then blew his whistle for the train to leave.

I was last to get on, carrying my valise and Bubbe's through the narrow corridor running through the train car. I glanced through the windows of each compartment, searching for one that was empty. Maybe it was my imagination, but I thought the passengers' faces were looking at me suspiciously. I tried shielding my face even more by tilting my hat farther forward as I moved awkwardly through the tight corridor.

At the center of the train car, we found an empty compartment and loaded our valises in the wood rack above the two bench seats facing each other. I sat beside Bubbe and felt the familiar comfort of her warm, plump body pressed against mine. The fragrance of her floral perfume was comforting and made me drowsy.

The train jolted when it kicked into gear and there was the loud "clunk" of the cars' couplers. The station slowly moved past our window as the train's iron wheels ground and squealed on the iron tracks, making a slow clacking sound as they rolled over the track seams, each one marking the beginning and end of a rail track. I thought about all that track we laid through the winter, the cold burrowing into our bodies, freezing our fingers and toes. As the train picked up speed, the slow rhythm of the clacking steadily increased, and the memories started speeding past me, dissolving into a blur of nothingness.

As I gazed out the window into the night, the ghostlike image of Zelda's face appeared reflected next to mine. Her sad eyes, full of longing, made my heart ache. I wondered where she could be, and if I'd ever see her again. I feared the terrible things that could have happened to her and her family in the countryside, horrific things that I didn't want to think about.

Nestled next to Bubbe, I shifted my focus to watching the fields and forests, small villages and little towns speckling the countryside sail past us. We chugged past streams and rivers fed by the Vistula, glimmering in the silver moonlight. German army camps dotted the roads with garrisons of jeeps, tents, tanks, anti-aircraft artillery, and convoys of supply trucks. As the train made its way toward Przemyśl, it stopped at Bochnia, Brzesko, Okocim, Tarnów, Ropczyce, Rzeszów, Łańcut, Przeworsk, and Jarosław. At every stop, we worried that German or Polish police or military would search our train for Jews and resistance fighters.

Then at Radymno, the last stop before Przemyśl, at four o'clock in the morning, three Gestapo officers carrying briefcases boarded the train car next to ours. We pretended to be asleep, hoping the Gestapo would leave us alone. Papa angled his fedora so it covered his entire face, and I tilted my cap down while watching the door to the compartment. Sara began crying in a soft whimper. Bubbe took her hand and whispered some words that seemed to console her. Basha ordered Sara to pull it together and Mama told Basha to mind her own business. Then we heard the door to our train car open and the sounds of the Gestapo laughing as they went through the car looking for a compartment to occupy. They stopped by our compartment and peered inside, and I prayed they'd keep moving past. They paused for a long moment, silent, then moved on, finding seats in an empty compartment next to ours.

The rest of the train ride we all remained quiet, fearing if the Gestapo next door heard us talking, they'd become interested in us.

At 5:12 a.m. we finally arrived at the Przemyśl station, the last stop at the Polish border dividing German-occupied western Przemyśl from Russian-occupied eastern Przemyśl. Similar to Kraków, a river, in this case the San River, divided the town in two. We needed to cross that river to get to safety in eastern Przemyśl.

We waited for the Gestapo to leave the train before we gathered our belongings. I looked out our window to make sure they were gone, then helped Papa bring down the luggage from the overhead racks.

When we finally departed, we were the last to leave the train before it reversed its direction and returned to Kraków.

17

THE VACANT, EERILY QUIET PLATFORM FELT ABANDONED, CUT off from the rest of the world. Only the lonely drone of crickets permeated the night air that was cool and damp, and perfectly still. Not even a leaf moved on the tree across from us.

Bubbe sat down on a bench to rest her arthritic legs, releasing a long sigh of relief that we had made it this far.

Basha paced back and forth, then picked up a small rock and started kicking it from one end of the platform to the other. "Where do we go now, Papa?" she asked.

"We wait here for a man driving a cart that will take us to a path leading down to the river."

"And then what?"

"And then a boat will come to transport us to the other side."

"Who told you all this?" asked Sara, placing her valise on the ground and then sitting on top of it.

"Khone. I wish he had come with us."

"But how will we know that we can we trust this person who picks us up?" asked Sara.

"Khone said the driver will tip his cap, revealing a yarmulke."

"Is there a Jewish resistance here?" asked Basha.

"Yes. But Khone told me nothing about it other than they help Jews safely cross the river to the Russian side."

"I don't see any carts," said Sara.

"Be patient," said Mama, taking a seat next to Bubbe. "And stop asking so many questions. You're giving me a headache."

"We just want to know," said Basha.

"So now you know," said Mama. "Now let's be quiet and watch for this cart."

I paced from one end of the platform to the other, watching out for the Germans, afraid they may appear at any moment and arrest us for being Jews who had traveled by train. They'd want to know why we left Kraków and I feared their questioning could lead to making Papa and me suspects in the stabbing of Schlöndorff. Mostly, I worried Schlöndorff was still alive. I walked up to Papa, who stood near the bench where Mama and Bubbe sat. "Papa, please get rid of the umbrella," I whispered in his ear so no one else would hear.

"No."

"Why?"

"Because Khone made this for me. And I told you before, it's the only protection we have."

"But if we're caught and questioned and Schlöndorff is still alive, your umbrella could confirm our guilt. He saw the dagger come out of it."

"That won't happen. And I'm sure he's dead, anyway."

"You should get rid of it," said Mama in a harsh whisper. "It's a *broch* to carry it with us."

Papa ignored her and walked away to the far end of the platform.

Frustrated with Papa, I went to sit next to Bubbe on the bench. She patted my knee. "Let it go," she said. "No sense in fighting. We need to get to the river. That's all that matters now." She took out her navy blue scarf and began knitting again, the metal needles clicking like the seconds on a clock, weaving the thick wool yarn, making a seamless chain of interlocking loops.

I leaned into her and whispered in her ear, "Who's that for, Bubbe?"

"I can't say," she whispered back.

"Please, tell me."

She looked at me and smiled. "You'll soon find out."

Mama was on the other side of Bubbe, pressed against her and fidgeting with a button on her dress that had frayed threads. I ran my finger across the broken threads on the top of my pants where I'd torn off the button to give to my Zelda. Not hearing from her, or knowing where she was, had left a void inside me. I could easily fall into it and get lost in the sadness of missing her. So I tried shifting my thoughts to ones that were more hopeful. I decided Zelda had to be in Przemyśl, since her uncle's farm wasn't that far away. I imagined our families living in the same apartment building there, having dinners together and helping one another survive. I even thought about Zelda and I having children one day. She wanted two at the most. I wanted three, two boys and a girl, but told her I'd be fine with two. Seeing what a good sister she was to her younger brothers, there was no doubt in my mind she'd be a wonderful mother.

I stood up and walked past Sara and Basha sitting on their valises side by side, their knees cinched to their chests, both using the sharp edges of the rocks they found by the rails to carve out a game of tic-tac-toe into the wood planks of the platform.

Papa continued to pace while searching the pockets of his coat and trousers for a cigarette he thought he had but couldn't find. I was hoping Papa would find at least one cigarette for us to share. But he came up empty.

Another twenty minutes, feeling like hours, slowly ticked by. The air was stagnant and damp, the crickets' drone still echoing all around us, the stars inching their way across the night sky, the half-moon descending; Papa paced, Bubbe's knitting needles clicked, and the corner of Mama's right thumb near the nail was more raw from her picking at it.

No one came.

I peered down the road leading into the blackness, searching for some sign of life. "We should get to the forest before daylight," I said impatiently. "It's too dangerous to keep waiting here."

Everyone agreed except Bubbe. She wanted to wait a little longer. But Mama and Papa persuaded her otherwise.

Bubbe reluctantly packed away the unfinished scarf. I picked up her valise in one hand and carried my own in the other. We walked cautiously down the dirt road next to the forest on our left. Our eyes searched through the darkness for a path leading down to the river. None of us spoke. Pebbles and sand crunched beneath our feet, breaking the tense silence.

Suddenly, some leaves rustled and branches snapped inside the woods near us. Bubbe grabbed my arm and Sara gasped. We stopped and listened, holding our breaths, our eyes straining to see what was possibly moving in the shadows of the woods. We saw nothing, and the woods were silent. "Maybe that was a deer," I said. "Let's keep going."

We walked about another fifty meters when, in the distance, coming toward us, a small kerosene lamp flickering like starlight illuminated the vague outline of a horse-drawn cart and its driver. Nervously, we stepped to the side of the road. Bubbe grabbed my arm again, this time squeezing it more tightly than before. My hands grew sweaty as they clenched the valises' leather handles. Mama, Papa, and my sisters pressed together, shoulder to shoulder. Sara's legs trembled.

The driver slowed down and stopped before us. He was a young man, perhaps my age, but looking older than his years. He wore a black short-brimmed cap and had a patchy dark beard. Uneven, hand-stitched threads held his tattered clothes together.

Soil stained his hands and blackened his fingernails, as if he'd been digging in the dirt.

He blew out the lamp and anxiously glanced in every direction, clearly worried about being followed. From his looks, I knew he was one of us before he tipped his hat, revealing his yarmulke. "Where are you going?" he asked in Yiddish.

"You know," said Papa, answering in Yiddish.

"Tell me."

"We need to cross the river."

The young driver jumped down from the cart and quickly loaded our luggage. He exuded a strong acidic odor of sweat and vinegar. "How far is it to the crossing?" I asked.

"Just up the road," he said. "Everybody in. We need to move."

"What happens when we get to the river?" asked Mama.

"A boat will pick you up. There are several other families down there already waiting. You'll go with them."

"And what happens when we get to the other side?"

"Another driver will take you to an apartment where you'll get settled."

"Are you with the resistance?" I asked.

He looked at me as if I'd just asked a most foolish question. "Hurry up," he said, climbing back onto the cart. "We need to move quickly."

Papa and I hoisted Bubbe into the back of the cart, where dirt and straw covered the wood floor. We sat on our luggage as the driver turned the cart around and headed back east.

The bumpy road jostled us from side to side as we kept watch for German vehicles coming from either direction. The driver told us to be prepared to grab our luggage and run into the woods if we saw any Germans.

After fifteen to twenty minutes, the driver slowed down and pulled over. "You see that path?" He pointed into the woods.

In the dark, nobody could see anything. Papa and I jumped down from the cart and went to the edge of the woods, where we spotted a very narrow dirt path, barely perceptible, snaking between the trees and shrubs. A cool breeze from the north rustled the young leaves on the elms and oaks. The relentless drone of the crickets had fallen silent.

The driver dismounted the cart, pointed into the woods, and whispered to us, "You follow this path down to the river and there you'll find three other families like yourselves waiting to cross. You wait there with them. I'll be back. Understand?"

"When will the boat come to take us across the river?" asked Mama. Her voice was tense and full of suspicion.

"You'll wait by the river today and it will come at night."

"When?"

"A few hours after sundown."

"Thank you," said Papa, offering the driver twenty zloty.

The young driver waved him off. "Keep your money. You'll need it."

"I insist," said Papa. "For the resistance." He stuffed the money into the young driver's pocket. "What's your name?"

"It doesn't matter," said the young driver, climbing back into the cart and taking his seat. He relit the small kerosene lamp mounted to the side of the carriage, snapped the reins, and drove away.

18

WALKING IN SINGLE FILE, WE FOLLOWED THE TWISTING MUDDY
trail through the trees and thickets. A web of tree roots crisscrossed the path, making it treacherous for tripping and falling,
especially for Bubbe. Our progress was painfully slow.

Papa led the way, followed by Mama, who held Bubbe's hand
behind her. Bubbe's black square-heeled shoes kept sliding on
the mud. She struggled to keep her balance while stumbling over
the roots and rocks poking up from the ground. "Oy veh—they
couldn't widen this trail? Is that asking too much?" she grumbled. I worried if she fell and injured herself that we'd have to
carry her the rest of the way, and we did not know how long the
distance was.

"Go slow, Bubbe," I said, while dodging the knobby branches
and prickly shrubs reaching across the path.

Basha suddenly let out a yelp as she tripped on a root that sent
her sprawling face down into the dirt. "Shhhhhhh!" said Sara. I
dropped my two valises and helped her stand up. She fought back
tears while holding her right knee that bled from landing on a rock.

"Can you walk?"

"I think so. But it really hurts."

Everyone stopped and waited as I looked at her knee. The
gash wasn't too deep. They all asked if she was all right. "She'll be
okay," I said. From my valise, I grabbed a sock and tied it around
her knee. "When we get to the river, we'll clean it there."

She picked up her valise and continued limping down the path. As we got closer to the river, the path became increasingly wet and muddy. Bubbe kept struggling to keep her balance as the mud sucked at her heels. Sara grasped her forearm and helped guide her along the outer edges of the path where it was slightly less muddy. "Where is this *farshtunken* river? I feel like we've been walking for days," said Bubbe. She swatted away the pesky mosquitoes that now buzzed by our ears and stung our necks and arms. "That driver said it was a short way."

"We must be getting close," said Papa.

To the east, the night sky transformed from black to a deep, vibrant blue as the first light emerged. The air became pungent with the scent of marsh grass and wet soil. Then the river appeared, with the streetlamps of Przemyśl on the opposite side glinting across the water's surface like beads of mercury.

I saw the silhouetted outlines of people gathered near the edge of the forest where it met the riverbank. A swath of open grass, bushes, and brambles led up to the riverbank lined with willows and oaks. It was a relief to know we were no longer completely alone.

I took Basha to the edge of the river and washed her knee with the sock. We then returned to the shore and sat down on a log beneath a willow where I took a dry sock from my valise and wrapped it around the gash again. "Is that better?"

"Yes. Thanks, Reuven. You know, sometimes you can be a nice brother."

"Just sometimes?"

"Yeah. Just sometimes." Basha looked at me and smiled, then turned her gaze across the river. Her smile faded as she became more serious. It was uncanny how similar her face was to Papa's. The same long prominent nose; the same wiry, thick black hair, arching eyebrows, and olive skin. "What do you think life will be like over there?" she asked, staring intensely across the river.

"Will Papa find work? And what will school be like there? Where will we live? Will I make new friends there?"

"We'll figure it out. And when we defeat the German *mamzers*, we'll go back to Kraków and resume our lives there," I said, trying to sound confident, yet completely unsure myself of what lay ahead.

"But what if we don't defeat the Germans, then what?"

"Then we'll stay in Przemyśl and rebuild our lives here. Papa and I will open a new umbrella shop and we'll find an apartment we can afford. And you and Sara will finish school here and hopefully go to university so you can become a journalist and Sara can study the stars."

Basha continued staring across the water. From her stern appearance, I knew her sharp and inquisitive mind was unconvinced by my attempt to sound optimistic.

"I just hope the Allies destroy the Germans," said Basha. "I want to go back home to the life we had in Kraków before the war. I miss it terribly."

"I do, too," I said. I took her hand and helped her get to her feet. "How's your knee?"

"It's okay," she said, limping slightly. "Let's go back." She held my hand as we trudged up the embankment and returned to the group.

I found Papa conversing with the three other fathers. "Counting your family, now there are twenty-four of us," said one father, a bear of a man, big and hairy-knuckled, sweat beading on his forehead. He wore a fedora like Papa's and breathed heavily through his mouth while pacing impatiently. "It's too dangerous to have so many families in one spot," he continued. "We need to cross that damn river before more families get here."

"How long have you been waiting?" asked Papa.

"Since yesterday, early evening," the man grunted.

"Where did you come from?"

"We took the train from Kraków. The kid driving the cart told us a boat would come by midnight. But there was no boat. No explanation. How do we know this isn't a setup?" The bearlike man removed his hat and with his sleeve wiped away the streams of sweat running down his meaty forehead.

"The driver reassured us the boat would come tonight, a few hours after sundown," said Papa.

"I don't trust him."

"I do."

"Why?"

"Because he's a poor Jew who's in the resistance and trying to help us."

"How do you know he's part of the resistance?"

"When I offered him some money for bringing us here, he turned it down. And there was this look in his eyes. I trusted him."

The big man shook his head in befuddlement. "Well, he's a fool to turn down money. And this is a disaster." The big man turned and lumbered back to his family.

We all watched him for a moment before another man leaned toward Papa and spoke under his breath. "Don't let Max bother you. I've known that *mamzer* since cheder and he's always been a *bulvan*." Then the man introduced himself. "My name's Raphael. Come and join my family."

He led us to where his family rested on an elevated and dry patch of ground hidden behind the willows lining the river. His wife and six children were asleep on clothes they had laid over a bed of oak leaves. We all sat on our coats and ate some apples, cheeses, and breads we had brought with us. Across the river, the sun's red glow stained the edges of orange and pink clouds suspended along the eastern horizon behind the one- and two-story brick buildings of Przemyśl. They seemed so within reach you could almost touch them. I wondered if we might find an apartment in one of those buildings.

Bubbe laid down on her coat next to me and propped her head against her valise, closed her weary eyes, and fell asleep. Mud spattered her shoes and clusters of burs clung to her thick black stockings. The edge of her skirt reaching below her arthritic knees was wet and dirty. I watched her sleep and wondered what it must be like for a woman her age to be displaced again, to have lost her home and belongings and security, to be wandering through the woods on a muddy path riddled with roots in search of a river to cross.

During the last war, she fled to the countryside with her husband, Grandpa Eliyohu, and Mama, four years old at the time. They found safety with Bubbe's uncle, who was a blacksmith. But within a few months, once the fighting ceased in Kraków, they could return to our apartment and resume living there through the duration of the war, and afterward. However, what she lost in that war was devastating. Her son, Mama's older brother by twelve years, was killed in battle, along with two nephews. Bubbe said the loss of her son, my uncle Zel, was something she never got over. Mama said she barely knew her older brother because she was so much younger than him. But she remembered him always being kind and entertaining, performing magic tricks and telling her stories while she lay in bed getting ready for sleep. Some stories he made up, others he read from books and newspapers.

When the war was over, Bubbe never thought it possible to go through such terrible upheaval again, certainly not during her lifetime. Yet here she was running again, this time from a situation more dire than the last. Poor Bubbe, I thought. No person should have to go through so much loss in their life. Yet the way she kept going, her tenacious desire to live, her ability to adapt, her resilience, always astounded me.

I turned to Basha next to me. "How is your knee?"

"It's hurting, but it's okay."

"You should get some sleep."

"I'm not tired."

"Well, I am." I lay down and covered my face with my cap and immediately drifted off.

In the late afternoon, I wakened to the sounds of Bubbe's knitting needles clicking again. She had almost finished the scarf. I begged her to tell me who it was for, but she still wouldn't say. I offered to buy it from her. "With what?" she said. "You don't have two groszy to rub together."

"I have the money Papa gave me."

"Forget it. That's not your money. And it's not for sale. It's a gift."

"But for who? There are no birthdays coming up."

"You'll find out when I'm finished. Now drop it."

"I can't." I moved in closer and whispered in her ear: "I need to know, Bubbe. Please, just tell me. . . . Please?" She looked at me, her beguiling eyes twinkling devilishly in the warm light, the scent of her sweet perfume succumbing to the fertile odors of the woods. She smiled and nodded, confirming it was for me. I kissed her soft, wrinkly cheek and said, "I love you, Bubbe." How lucky I was to have her as my grandma.

Basha and Sara were still asleep near me, both on their sides curled up next to each other like cats, their heads resting on pillows made of rolled-up clothes. Papa and Mama sat on a log a short distance away holding hands and engaged in what looked like a very serious conversation. She rested her head on his shoulder, and they kissed. It had been a long time since I'd seen that kind of affection between them. I supposed that was what happened when everyone was just trying to survive.

Before the war, they were often playful and very physical, to the point of embarrassment. Sometimes they'd jokingly grab each other in places I didn't want to see. I'd yell at them to stop and they'd laugh and tell me it was my fault that I was watching them.

I missed our Shabbos dinners when Papa always came home with flowers after he and I took our baths at the mikvah. And Mama, with the help of Bubbe, would have a beautiful meal prepared. Sometimes it was brisket, or whitefish with pickled herring, or roasted chicken, or baked lamb. And she made the best chicken soup I ever tasted. There was always a vegetable dish of either carrots, spinach, cabbage, green beans, or whatever was in season, along with salad, and often homemade kugel or rugelach for dessert. Best of all was Mama's freshly made challah, the rich honeyed scent of it filling every corner of the apartment—even the stairwell. I'd slather it with butter that would melt into it, adding a touch of salt to the sweetness. We always had more than enough food to eat, and so I would stuff myself.

Afterward, we'd often sit by the radio listening to a show where they played jazz and interviewed all types of people, from politicians to scientists to artists, writers, actors, philosophers, and historians. Mama was most interested in the artists and writers while Papa preferred the politicians, journalists, philosophers, and historians.

Whether it was warm or cold out, after Shabbos dinner we'd take an evening walk by the river before getting ready for bed. There were a few times, late at night, when everyone was supposed to be asleep, when I heard noises coming from their bedroom that I didn't want to hear. Papa was so in love with Mama that he would've rowed across the Atlantic Ocean to be with her, and give her the stars and moon if he could.

RAPHAEL CAME OVER TO MAMA AND PAPA AND SAID SOMETHING to them. Then Papa followed Raphael down to the river where they stood in the cover of the willows. I got up and joined them. Raphael took out a pack of cigarettes from his breast pocket and shared the last of them with us.

From our vantage point, looking north, a train bridge crossed the river about a kilometer downstream. There appeared to be Russian troops guarding the east end of the bridge, while Germans guarded the west end.

"The river is the only way across," whispered Papa. "Where is that damn driver?"

"If a boat doesn't come tonight," said Raphael beneath his breath, "what do you think we should do?"

"I don't know," said Papa.

The river was high and the current swift. We knew that to swim across would be extremely difficult and dangerous, even for the best swimmers. I suggested we walk south along the river, upstream, to see what other bridges there were for crossing. But Papa and Raphael worried they'd also be guarded, plus there was the risk of being seen by German patrols along the roads and near the woods. If someone spotted one of us, it would put everyone in jeopardy. Both wanted to wait for the driver to return with additional information.

"If he doesn't show," said Papa, "then let's agree to wait until at least midnight for the boat. And if it doesn't come, then we follow the river south and search for another way to cross."

"But we're wasting valuable time by waiting and doing nothing," I argued. "I can head south now and at least see what's there."

"No, let's wait," said Papa. "We need to be patient."

"Your papa is right," said Raphael. "We'll give the boat one more chance to get here before we risk searching for another way to cross."

19

NIGHT FELL, AND THE DRIVER STILL HADN'T SHOWN. PAPA AND I took turns sitting by the river, keeping watch for the boat. We decided one of us should always be with the rest of the family in case the Germans discovered us in the woods. Should such a tragedy occur, we made plans to run south, upriver, away from the bridge. However, with Bubbe and other elderly with us, it would be extremely difficult to make an escape.

Sara had accompanied Papa on watch, and now Basha wanted to go with me. I was happy to have her join me. She limped through the tallgrass to the riverbank where we found Max anxiously pacing around a tree, breathing heavily and talking incessantly about the boat not being there and the driver disappearing. He used a white handkerchief to wipe the sweat off his neck and forehead as he nervously fanned himself with his fedora. Leaning against a tree, Raphael patiently listened to Max's rant, then put his arm around him, trying to ease his frustrations.

"Don't tell me to calm down!" yelled Max, throwing Raphael's arm off his shoulder.

"If you don't calm down, you'll have a heart attack," said Raphael. "And keep your voice down if you don't want the Germans to find us."

"Something is very wrong here. You know something is wrong."

"There's no point in panicking, Max. We all need you to be calm, especially your family." He put his arm around Max's huge shoulders again and led him away from the river. "Come with me. You need to be with your family." As they passed us, Raphael told us he'd be back.

Lost in the currents of our confused thoughts, we sat on a log side by side and watched the river as it silently flowed past. The oak leaves rustled in the light breeze. From the depths of the woods, dark and desolate, echoed the lonesome hoot of an owl.

"I love owls," said Basha.

"Really? I didn't know that. I love them, too."

"I love the way they look, with their big heads and huge eyes and pointy ears. And the way they can see in the darkness to hunt at night, soaring on wings specially shaped to make them totally silent."

"They are built to hunt."

"And they're mythical creatures. Did you know that?"

"What do you mean?"

"I read the Egyptians saw owls as protectors of the dead. That's why they carved and painted them on coffins and made amulets in the shape of them. They believed owls could communicate with the spirit world, the world of the unknown."

"Why?"

"Because they're creatures of the night."

"You know a lot more about owls than me."

"I wrote a paper about them in school."

"Did you get a good grade?"

"I got an A." She smiled and looped her arm through mine.

I felt the closest I'd ever felt to Basha just then. It made me regret not showing more interest in her while growing up in Kraków. I'd been an absent older brother, always busy with my own friends, rarely spending time with her, or Sara, for that matter. Sitting next to her with our arms linked, I made a promise to myself to spend more time with her and be a better brother from now on.

"How's your knee?" I asked.

"It hurts, but it's okay."

We sat quietly for a stretch while keeping a close watch on the river. Then Max's yelling echoed through the trees. We jumped up and ran back to our family to see what was wrong.

In the darkness of the woods, we found Papa and another father on the path trying to pull Max off the driver. He had grabbed the scrawny young man by his tattered coat and was shaking him in a rage, demanding to know where he'd been and when the boat was coming.

"Get your fucking hands off me!" warned the driver. His hands curled into fists, trembling with rage.

Raphael and I wedged ourselves between the two, finally separating them.

For some reason, the young driver looked more impoverished and bedraggled than when I first saw him. I noticed a scabby sore on his neck, the ragged holes in his shoes and pants.

"The road was too dangerous for travel," the driver continued. "And we don't know why the boat is delayed. It happens. But they told us it's coming in the next hour."

"Who's they? Who told you this?!" hollered Max.

The driver had had it with Max and turned to leave.

"Stop!" Max dropped his meaty hand on the driver's shoulder and spun him around. "How do we know this isn't more *shmontses*?!"

The driver swiped Max's hand off his shoulder. "I told you not to touch me!"

Raphael and I got between the two of them again as Papa and the other father grabbed hold of Max's arms and pulled him farther away from the driver.

The driver glared at Max. "Why do you think we're risking our lives helping you? Me, the boatman, the other partisans who you don't even see or know about. We're the only ones doing this work. You do not know how many families we've helped cross the river to safety. You should be grateful, you stupid *mamzer*." That set Max off again, making him lunge after the driver like a bull. But we all held Max back.

The driver angrily pointed his finger at Max. "You'll just have to trust me. The boat will come tonight."

He turned and started up the path. I ran after him to ask about other places where we could cross the river in case the boat never shows. "This is the safest place to cross," he said. "There are no other places to cross from here."

As I followed him up the path, we suddenly heard the low rumble of truck engines emerge from the road beyond the woods. We stopped and listened. Ominous yellow light beams appeared at the top of the path, carving silhouettes out of the trees and branches. We maintained our stance, still as stone, watching and listening for whatever was coming next.

The trucks abruptly stopped.

I thought there were two of them from the number of lights shining and the low growling drone of their engines.

The driver and I stayed bolted to the ground; my muscles clenched, breath quickened, and heart pounded with terrifying uncertainty. The driver stared at me with his index finger pressed tightly against his lips.

The truck engines shut off, but their yellow lights stayed on, flooding through the woods.

A haunting silence enshrouded us, save for the din of the crickets.

Then the wind unfortunately shifted, carrying on its back the soft murmuring voices of our group waiting near the river.

The driver's horse at the top of the path must have caught his owner's scent and whinnied. A group of dogs barked and growled viciously in response—sounding large and dangerous like the German attack dogs I'd seen in Kraków.

It was clear they'd found his horse cart parked off to the side of the road.

The metal doors and rear gates of the truck slammed open. A commanding German officer shouted orders to search the forest.

"Go!" said the driver beneath his breath. He sprinted toward the riverbank. Gunfire erupted in sharp cracks. His hands jolted skyward, as if lightning struck him. A spray of blood burst from the back of his head as he fell to the ground.

I sprinted the path to the riverbank and first spotted Raphael and Max. "Germans are coming, run!" They must've heard the gunfire and seen the lights, yet at first, they just stared at me with looks of disbelief and anguish, as if none of this could be true. More gunfire blasted, shocking them into action. They took off through the woods, calling out desperately for their wives and children.

Spinning round, I caught sight of the soldiers' torchlights piercing the darkness, the savage barking of their dogs rapidly encroaching.

Amid the pandemonium, shrieks of anguish penetrated the air as people cried out for their loved ones. As they raced frantically through the woods and thickets, their paths crisscrossed in chaos, like startled bees fleeing their hives in a panic.

I hollered for my family while sprinting to the willow where we had last gathered. When I arrived, their valises were there, but they were gone.

I bolted through the darkness toward the river, scrambling through the maze of trees while dodging the other people fleeing, screaming for my family at the top of my lungs, but no one answered my calls.

Then Basha's voice came from behind. "Reuven!" I spun round and she suddenly appeared from nowhere, her eyes wide with terror. I grabbed her. "Where is everyone?"

"I don't know," she said, panting, tears streaming down her face. "I wasn't with them when they attacked and I ran to the willow where I thought they'd be and they were gone. I'm scared, Reuven."

I grabbed her hand and we ran past the willows through the thicket along the riverbank. Gunfire continued cracking around us. Through the darkness we saw the outlines of people running and getting shot. We kept crying out for Mama, Papa, Bubbe, and Sara, but they never answered.

I pulled Basha down to the ground behind a tree on the riverbank and we hid in the tallgrass and were quiet. Scanning the terrain, I caught sight of the soldiers moving in a line from the woods toward the riverbank led by their dogs. There was no sight of our family.

"Where could they be?" whispered Basha, her hand squeezing down on mine.

"I don't know."

Peering through the thicket, we saw more people shot. One person after another—children, men, women, old people—collapsed to the ground when the bullets struck. The hulking figure of Max went down, as did Raphael, along with his wife and children.

The soldiers kept moving toward us. We were upwind from the dogs, so I knew they'd already caught our scent.

"We need to move!" I whispered to Basha.

She hesitated, paralyzed by fear. "I don't want to leave here until we find them."

"We can't wait here any longer. Look, they're coming this way."

They were maybe twenty-five meters away, their attack dogs straining against their leashes. If the soldiers released them, they would finish us.

I tugged on Basha's hand. She resisted at first. "Basha, let's go!"

We ran farther north along the riverbank, downstream, toward the bridge. Still clenching her hand, I pulled her through the brush. She limped from her wounded knee and stumbled over rocks and roots but kept pace with me as we tore through the bushes and brambles.

Several more gunshots cracked past our ears. Basha tripped and fell again and this time was slow to rise. "Come on! Get up!" I ordered under my breath. But she didn't respond. Her hand no longer gripped mine. She lay motionless on the ground, her face planted in the dirt, her arms slack and body limp. I dove on top of her as more bullets sizzled past. "Stay still," I whispered in her ear. She didn't respond. "Basha? Are you okay?" I thought she'd passed out.

Turning her over, my eyes followed a large bloodstain flooding across her dress. The blood flowed from a small black hole at the top of her rib cage. I covered the hole with my hand and pressed down to stop the bleeding. But the warm blood kept leaking through my fingers. "Basha," I repeated. "Basha, wake up!" I realized she wasn't breathing. Grabbing her shoulders and shaking her, I ordered her to breathe, then pressed my ear to her chest and strained to find a beat. Her heart was silent.

This couldn't be true, I thought. Opening her mouth, I sealed my lips against hers and breathed into her. One breath, two, three, four . . . She didn't respond. I gave more breaths while keeping pressure on the bullet wound with my right hand. Glancing up to take another breath, I caught sight of several soldiers with torch lamps searching through the thicket near us. My left hand squeezed her shoulder. I pleaded with her to breathe, begged her to come back, to not leave me.

Her intense brown eyes—always curious and mischievous, intelligent, and so dear to me—stared off into the night, despondent, lifeless. Her spirit had departed.

Leaning over her, our faces within inches, my bloody fingertips gently closed her eyelids.

I cradled her head against my chest, heavy in my bloody hands, and kissed her forehead where her thick raven hair parted. I was too stunned to cry, too completely overwhelmed by a loss that was impossible to comprehend.

Time stopped.

The world fell silent for I don't know how long—maybe seconds, maybe minutes. Then an earsplitting gunshot snapped me out of it. The dogs were close, somewhere in the shadows and barking in a rage. I had to leave Basha.

I cut through a small marsh and moved into a covered position behind a low-rising knoll, now downwind from the dogs and soldiers.

The German commander's harsh, merciless voice ordered his soldiers to kill the wounded. They obviously had no interest in taking prisoners.

Peering above the tallgrass again, I caught sight of the position of the soldiers and their dogs. Their dark shadows moved furtively in and out of the trees surrounding me. There was no sign of my family. I wanted to call out to them, but that would give the soldiers my position. I wasn't sure what to do.

Another gunshot drew my attention to the south where in the distance there were two soldiers shoving four people from the tree line down to the river. The man wore a fedora looking exactly like Papa's hat, and the old woman limping was Bubbe. Mama held Bubbe's hand while Sara clasped Mama's other hand. The dogs on their leashes nipped at their legs. Mama's desperate voice, pleading for their lives, cut across the riverbank. One dog lunged at Bubbe, who was still holding the navy blue scarf she'd been knitting. Papa kicked the dog back. His umbrella had disappeared.

Paralyzed by my terror, I didn't know what to do. A soldier raised his pistol and pointed it at Mama's head. She waved her hands before him, begging for mercy. He ignored her pleas and shot her. She dropped to the ground in a heap. Three more shots cracked the air in quick succession, killing Papa, Bubbe, and Sara. I screamed but only wisps of air came out, as if my vocal cords had been cut.

Trapped inside a cage of terror and grief, I froze. It felt like my guts had been ripped out, my heart pulverized. I watched in horror as they used their knives to slice open the seams of Papa's jacket where they found some jewelry and cash. The soldiers went from Sara to Bubbe to Mama, cutting their clothes to shreds in search of more valuables.

When they finished, they dragged their half-naked bodies to the river's edge and tossed them into the churning waters.

Straining to see the river through the darkness, my eyes caught sight of the outlines of their discarded bodies floating past, face down in the water, abandoned, drifting aimlessly to wherever the river was taking them.

Papa's brown fedora floated past, followed by a shape that looked like Bubbe's blue scarf.

It was impossible to absorb what had just happened. For a moment, I considered it a terrifying nightmare that my broken mind had concocted. It just simply couldn't be true. But then a soldier's torch beam scanning the thicket along the knoll where I hid caught my eye. He emerged from the tree line close to me with his big black attack dog pulling against the leash, barking and baring nasty white fangs, towing the soldier in my direction. The dog was downwind from me and had caught my scent.

The commander's torchlight flashed across me once, then returned, capturing me in its dagger of light. He pointed at me, released his dog, and blew his whistle.

Jumping to my feet, I sprinted north along the riverbank, weaving through the thicket and tallgrass like a scared jackrabbit. Glancing back, I saw the dog tearing after me with two more dogs and several soldiers in the rear.

I bolted down the riverbank, my lungs straining to suck in air. Shots rang out, bullets sizzled past my ears, cracking into trees, bits of wood exploding off the trunks.

At the river's edge, I tore through the shallows as the dogs closed in. Soldiers hollered commands; the gunshots grew louder. Bullets pelted the surrounding water. A sharp burning sensation penetrated my right thigh—like a knife stab.

The dogs were almost on me, their relentless barking piercing my eardrums. I rushed deeper into the cold water, up to my chest. Drawing a deep breath, I plunged beneath the waters and swam on that one breath for as long as possible. I kept pulling myself through the water until my lungs emptied and burned and begged for air. Depleted of oxygen, I saw white dots floated inside my eyelids; my arms and legs began cramping. I surfaced, gasped, caught another breath, dove again. The muted sounds of more bullets punctured the water near me. Up again for air, then down again beneath the cold waters, I kicked and clawed with all my strength.

When I surfaced again, the barrage of gunfire had stopped. I paused for a moment and caught my breath and surveyed the soldiers' positions. They had receded into the distance. Now far away upstream, their torch lamps cast mere pinpricks of light as they scanned the river. Gradually, the tiny lights dwindled, then vanished entirely inside the black shroud of night.

20

I BATTLED THE RIVER FOR A WHILE BEFORE REACHING THE other side where I crawled along the shore through a thicket that led to the forest. My right thigh burned as if hot coals were buried inside it.

At some point, I entered a small grassy area protected by oak and birch trees where I lay down to catch my breath and have a look at the leg. I pulled down my bloodstained pants and found a bullet wound that went through the flesh and muscle of my right thigh, perhaps missing the bone before the bullet exited. I tore off the right sleeve of my shirt and wrapped it tight around my bloody leg wound, just like the man had shown me at the bombing site in Kraków. After tying off the bandage, I pulled on my wet pants and stood up, using a broken oak branch as a cane. Limping away from the river, I continued heading east, as best I could tell. Although it seemed I was now in Russian-occupied Poland, I wanted to keep moving as far away from the Germans as possible. Even farther east than Przemyśl.

I hobbled aimlessly through the dense woods for some time. My mind was void of any feelings or thoughts, stunned and obliterated by what had just happened. The only thing I felt was the throbbing burn in my thigh. The searing pain surged in waves, as if a red-hot poker was being thrust into it.

I wanted to stop and rest, but the thought of being pursued by the Germans haunted me. Although I had assumed that I must now be on the Russian side since I'd crossed the river, I started to question if it really was the east side of the river I landed on. Maybe I got turned around in the water and exited the west side of the river. Maybe I was heading back toward Kraków, deeper into German territory. I couldn't differentiate anymore between what was real and what was imagined.

I came to an area where granite slabs and large rocks jutted out from the forest floor like broken ancient bones. One gray slab formed a roof over the ground with enough space beneath it for me to hide. I gathered some fallen branches and brush and vines along the ground to form a wall around me that served as camouflage. Exhausted, I curled into the fetal position beneath the rock slab and plunged into an unsettling sleep filled with terrifying dreams.

Some hours later, a loud clap of thunder jolted me awake. Buckets of rain pummeled the forest floor; lightning split the sky. I staggered out of my hiding place to urinate. The winds thrashed the trees, snapping the frail branches, sending them crashing to the ground. I burrowed beneath the rock slab again and was thirsty. Rivulets of rainwater fell from the edges of the jagged rock. Lying on my back with my mouth open, I drank until I had my fill of water.

By evening, the storm ended and the air turned cool and clean, smelling of wet leaves and damp soil. There were small snails the size of brass buttons crawling across the dirt and along the bark of fallen trees.

I traveled by night, still uncertain if I was on the Russian or German side of the river. Leaning heavily on my walking stick, I hobbled through the woods disorientated, hoping to still be heading east toward a village where I'd find safety.

I'm not sure how many days I wandered, maybe three, four, five. I continued to find shelter beneath rocks and fallen trees and drank water from small streams snaking through ravines. My wound continued to throb and ache, as if someone were pounding it with a sledgehammer. The bandage stunk of old blood.

My belly hurt from pangs of hunger. I found more button-sized snails beneath a rotting log, crushed one of them with a rock, separated its slimy body from its shell, and swallowed it whole. It had a bitter taste that turned my stomach. I tried eating a few more but almost brought them back up. I turned to ants and beetles, crushing them and swallowing them whole. They were more tolerable. But they did little to satisfy my hunger.

One day, in a dizzying, feverish state, I discovered a small stream in a ravine where I unwrapped the bandage to clean the wound. It was red and swollen, with pus oozing out of the bullet hole. I washed the bandage in the stream, turning the clear water into the color of red wine. Then I wrapped it around my wound again and tied it off, hoping it would stop the infection from progressing.

That night I became more feverish and went in and out of nightmares where cracks of gunfire and bullets thudded against earth and trees. Attack dogs barked madly, baring bloody teeth, the fierce whites of their eyes glaring, chasing me down through woods and river, riding my back, sinking long, razor-sharp claws into my shoulders. The entire murderous scene by the river played out repeatedly, ravaging my thoughts like a wildfire out of control. I kept seeing their bodies floating face down in the river, Papa's hat and Bubbe's scarf getting sucked beneath the surface in swirling eddies. Why? I kept asking myself. Why didn't the boat come? Why did the Germans find us? Why was Basha killed and not me? Why couldn't I stop my family from being killed? Why had my voice vanished? Why was I silent? Why was I alive and not them?

In the forest, I felt I was going insane. I sweated and trembled from chills. My leg continued swelling and sizzling as if scalding water were being poured on it. I'd reached a point where I was too weak to go on. Dawn was dusk and dusk was dawn. I fell into a whirlpool of delirium. There were ghostly German soldiers hiding behind the trees and attack dogs lurking in the shadows of the rocks and bushes. I dragged myself through the dense forest for what seemed like an eternity before I passed out.

When I woke, sweat covered my body, my bones were cold, I ached all over. Overwhelming odors of rotting wood and wet moss permeated the air. Standing up with the help of my walking stick, I hobbled through the woods some more, directionless, until I spotted in the distance a long-horned buck in the blue light of dusk. He saw me and took off, knitting his way through trees and dense thicket, disappearing and reappearing like an apparition. I hobbled in his direction. The forest abruptly opened. Before me lay a dirt road running straight as a plumb line in either direction, dividing the forest in two. I hesitated, unsure of which way to go— left or right. The sweet aromas of Mama's challah baking in the oven came from the right. I limped in that direction. Then Zelda's silhouette in the distance appeared down the road. She glided toward me. Where had she come from? Was it really her, or another apparition? I hobbled several more painful steps toward her shadow, then fell unconscious on the road.

PART TWO

THE FARM

21

IT WAS DARK WHEN I WAKENED IN A COLD SWEAT, THE DIRT ROAD rocking drunkenly from side to side. I don't know how long I'd been lying there. Feverish chills ran through my neck and back. My head pounded. A strange wind rustled the trees eerily spinning above me—their leaves murmuring indecipherable messages. I didn't know where I was, nor how I got there.

Pungent odors of horse sweat and wet hay filled the air. A horse appeared, leaning over me, her coat forming a white diamond between her black marble eyes. Her muzzle, soft and velvety, brushed against my cheek and ear, exhaling humid puffs of air as she sniffed curiously. Her hooves stamped the earth. Near her flanks loomed the vague shape of a broad-shouldered man towering over me. He drew back the horse. Stars peppered the night sky behind him, the woods bathed in pale moonlight.

The man wore a gray wool cap accentuating his muscular face and piercingly bright blue eyes. Pieces of hay and leaves and dirt clung to his shirt, his dark pants tucked inside mud-splattered leather boots that reached his knees. He knelt next to me and unzipped my pants and looked at my privates. "*Ach, Żyd!*" he said. His breath stunk of garlic, pickled herring, vodka. He walked back to a cart. "*Żyd*—get up!"

I wanted to stand up but couldn't move. My right leg burned and throbbed as if it had been branded. I was nauseous and chilled, my clothes soaked in sweat. I shook uncontrollably.

"Get up!" he yelled again.

I tried rolling on my side to raise myself to a sitting position, but my arms were too shaky. Every time I tried to move the world swung off its axis more violently.

I must've blacked out before his thick hands came under my armpits, lifted me up, and tossed me through the air like a sack of grain. I floated, weightless for a moment, before crashing onto a pile of hay that was moist and smelled fresh cut.

"Let's go," he said to the horse, snapping the reins. The cart rocked and shook like a boat battered by waves. I felt sick again and dry heaved, then fell unconscious.

WHEN MY EYES OPENED, I WAS INSIDE A SMALL ROOM LYING ON the wood floor next to the stove where a pot of lamb or beef stew simmered. In between waves of nausea, it smelled delicious. I hungered for what was inside that pot.

A woman who I assumed was his wife stood by the stove in a thick brown wool skirt that reached just below her knees. She stirred the delicious-smelling stew with a wooden spoon, tasting it and doling out spoonsful to their little girl. The child watched me curiously while clinging to her mother's muscular calves, milky-white as limestone.

"You sure he's a *Żyd*?" said the woman.

"Yes, Kaja. He's a *Żyd*," said the man sitting down at the table.

"How do you know he's a *Żyd*?"

"I check his *chuj*."

"He looks young. How old is he?"

"I don't know." He turned to face me. "How old are you, *Żyd*?"

I tried to say "seventeen," but my lips and tongue couldn't form the word. My vocal cords would only produce dry, guttural sounds. I tried several more times to speak, straining the muscles around my mouth to form the word, pushing air through my throat to produce a sound, but nothing came out. I didn't know what was happening to me. It was terrifying. I wondered if I'd ever be able to speak again. My mind was a jumbled mess, my memory ruptured, I wasn't even sure what had happened to my family. I only remembered losing track of them when the Germans arrived, being chased by dogs, getting shot in the leg, swimming the river while being shot at, bits and pieces of surviving in the forest.

"He can't hear?" asked the woman.

"I don't know. Maybe he's deaf. Are you deaf?!" yelled the man. He grabbed a pot and banged it next to my ear. My body jumped. "He's not deaf. He must be mute. Are you mute?"

I assumed that was my condition and confirmed with a nod.

"He doesn't look like a Żyd," she said.

He slammed his hand on the table. "He's a Żyd, Kaja! A mute Żyd! I told you—I see his *chuj*! He's a Żyd!" He slammed down his hand again on the table. "You don't believe? Look yourself."

The little girl started crying. Kaja picked her up and rocked her in her arms. "Shhhhh, Lilli. It's okay." Then she turned to her husband. "Why you bring a Żyd here, Stanisław? You know they're bad luck."

"If he don't die, I put him to work and we make more money. He'll help plant more fields, cut more wood, build more fences. Then we go buy more sheep, cow, pigs, geese. He only cost us some food, Kaja!"

"No. I don't want a Żyd here. They worship the devil, put a curse on you—they killed Christ! If he's here bad things will happen to us. I don't want him near Lilli. Not in the house. No, no. Get rid of him."

"I'm not getting rid of him, Kaja. I put him to work."

"What if those Germans cross the river? If they find a Żyd here they'll kill us."

"We get rid of him if they cross river. But they won't. Russians will stop them."

"We can't trust a Żyd. No. They steal and stab you in the back."

"If he's a no-good worker, I get rid of him. I promise."

"What if the person who shot him still looks for him?"

"Ach—Germans across the river shot him. They're not coming here. Is that who shot you?"

I nodded "yes." The room tilted again, and I went from feeling nauseous and chilled into hot waves of sweat. This Kaja woman was going to kill me, or have me killed. I had to escape this place as soon as possible. I wasn't safe here. Maybe she'd kill me at night in my sleep. I wanted to run, but my leg still burned and throbbed. Blood and dirt caked the entire pant leg. It looked like a rotting log dug up from the soil. I wasn't sure if the bone broke. My mouth was dry. I needed water. I pointed to my mouth, grunting, unable to form the word *water*.

"He doesn't look good. What if he dies?" she said, putting Lilli down and returning to stirring the stew, ignoring my pleas. I knew she wanted me to die. Part of me wanted to die, too. I felt so sick within my body that it seemed like it belonged to someone else.

"We bury him in the woods," said her husband matter-of-factly. He filled a cup with water from a bottle and handed it to me. I eagerly drank from it, grateful for his kind gesture. Although she wanted me dead, he clearly didn't.

"And if he's sick for a long time?" She dipped a spoon into the stew and tasted it. I imagined it tasted salty, with chunks of tender meat and potatoes and cabbage covered in sauce. My nausea disappeared for a moment, and I was ravenous. My mouth watered at the thought of chewing on those savory chunks of meat and potatoes, filling my stomach with the rich flavors of that warm stew.

"If he's sick, I take him to town and let the other Żyds deal with him."

She tossed another piece of wood inside the black iron stove. "We give him a week or two to get better and then decide if we keep him."

He noticed me motioning for more water and filled my cup again. "Good. I'll make a bed of hay for him in toolshed."

"First, get alcohol from Muniek and a pair of pants and shirt from the son. His clothes stink like an old dead pig." She handed Stanisław a bottle of milk. "Give this to Muniek."

The room began spinning again, and more queasiness churned in my stomach; a chill gripped my bones, followed by a wave of heat. I blacked out.

When I awakened sometime later, it felt like an icepick was jabbing my thigh. Writhing in pain, I grunted and hollered through gritted teeth, saliva foaming at the corners of my mouth, rolling down my chin. "Settle down!" ordered Stanisław. He pinned my shoulders against the floor with his heavy hands. I realized my pants were off and Kaja had unwrapped the bloody bandage and was swabbing my wound with alcohol. "Żyd is lucky the bullet goes in here and out here," said Stanisław. "I think it misses the bone."

I looked down and saw the two small black holes on each side of my thigh, their edges caked in dirt, blood, and pus, giving them the appearance of small volcanoes that had erupted. The skin surrounding the crusty black openings was a sickly blend of blue, green, and yellow. If not for the scraggly blond hairs sprouting from my thigh, I wouldn't have recognized it as my own.

She rubbed the skin aggressively with the alcohol-soaked cloth. I writhed and moaned as she made the tender skin round the wound burn and sizzle, as if a blowtorch were being held to it. She was torturing me, and I think she enjoyed it.

When she finished cleaning the wound, Stanisław wrapped a dry cloth around it and handed me a fresh pair of pants, under-shorts, and a clean shirt to wear. He told his wife and his little girl to look away. The little girl hid behind her mother's dress and shyly peeked out at me from the sides. I turned my back to her as I lay on the floor, slipping out of my old, filthy undershorts to put on the fresh pair before pulling up my pants.

"You hungry?" Stanisław asked. The pain had eased its grip. I nodded "yes." Although I wasn't sure if I could keep the food down.

He helped me to my feet and sat me at the table, where Kaja slammed down a hot bowl of stew in front of me. Although my stomach was still unsettled, the rich vapors of meat, salt, spices, and butter roused my hunger. I ate the stew, one small spoonful at a time. "You like?" asked Stanisław. I nodded my approval. "You heal quick with Kaja's stew."

They sat down at the other end of the table, as far away from me as possible, and we ate in silence. Kaja had Lilli on her lap, where she helped her eat from a small wood bowl. Lilli had stew smeared on her chin and round cheeks. She pointed at me and smiled, then giggled. Kaja shifted her body so Lilli couldn't easily see me. But Lilli kept turning her head to steal glances of the stranger at her table.

I finished my bowl quickly and hoped for more. Stanisław noticed my empty bowl.

"Fill his bowl, Kaja."

"No. He's had enough!" said Kaja. "He doesn't need more. The Żyd will take and take until you have nothing."

"Be quiet. He's probably not eaten for a long time, and we need him strong for work. Fill his bowl."

Kaja put Lilli down and angrily got up, grabbed my bowl in disgust, filled it halfway, and handed it back to me. Our eyes met for a moment. Behind the disgust she held for me, I thought I saw a flash of curiosity. I nodded to show some appreciation, even though I despised this woman.

My stomach was now full and I could barely keep my eyes open. Through the small grated door on the iron stove, I saw in its black belly the logs and embers glowing copper-red. For a split second, I imagined sitting with Zelda and holding her hand as we gazed at the dancing flames inside her family's wood-burning stove. My heart dropped. I wondered if Zelda had also lost her parents, or was alone and hungry somewhere, or dead. It was too terrible to ponder. A heavy exhaustion swept over me and my head dropped onto my arms as I fell asleep at the table.

Next thing I knew, Stanisław had lifted me to my feet and placed my right arm over his shoulder so my weight was off my right leg. He was maybe an inch taller than me with a bull's neck, his shoulders broad and thick. He cinched me by the waist so tightly it was hard to breathe, and walked me across the yard to the shed.

Inside the shed, he set me down on a pile of hay spread over the dirt floor. Covering the hay were three gunnysacks to lie on. He filled a seed sack with more hay and handed it to me to use as a pillow. I lay down on my side and wrapped my arms across my chest. A cool wind blew through the cracks in the shed and I shivered from fever. Chills coursed through me again. How I longed for the warmth of Zelda.

He went back to the house and returned with a thick wool blanket and tossed it over me. I appreciated this gesture. I pulled the blanket tight around my body and shook, my sweat turning cold. Throughout the night, I went in and out of sleep, wrestling with feverish nightmares. At one point I woke and thought I saw the silhouette of Kaja standing at the door, suspiciously gazing down at me. Or was it a ghost? I didn't know what to do. Her hair was down, its edges glinting in pale moonlight, her bare feet wide and gripping the ground; she wore a loose housecoat, unbuttoned over her nightgown. Then Stanisław came out of the house. "Kaja, what are you doing?" he hollered across the yard.

"Shhhh," said Kaja. She glided away, and I heard her whisper to Stanisław in the yard: "I'm looking for the horns."

"What horns?"

"The horns the *Żyds* grow at night."

"You mean devil's horns?"

"Yes."

"Did you see any?"

"Not yet."

"Leave him alone, Kaja. He's not the devil. Let him sleep."

They returned to the house.

22

THE NEXT DAY, AT FIRST LIGHT, THE ROOSTER'S CROW WAKENED me. My leg continued to throb, but not like the previous day. Splinters of sunlight cut through the cracks of the shed's wood-planked walls. Silk threads of a spider's web in the corner above me glistened as a fly struggled to free itself from its grasp. The spider was nowhere to be seen.

Inside the toolshed, I kept track of the days by cutting lines into the shed's wall with the tip of a sickle. In the beginning, it was excruciatingly painful to walk: every step felt like being stabbed in the leg. But as the days passed, the infection's swelling went down, and the pain receded.

The only time I left the shed was when I needed to relieve myself. Carefully standing up and balancing myself along the shed's outer wall, I'd make my way to the other side, just a meter, and urinate out of view. When I needed to relieve my bowels, I used a single crutch Stanisław had made for me out of an oak branch to help me hobble over to the outhouse at the back of the yard, behind the house, near the tree line. Close to the outhouse was a water pump where I washed my hands and face and filled a glass jar with water that I kept in the shed for drinking.

Stanisław brought me two meals a day, one in the morning before he left to work in the fields or the forest, the other meal in the evening when he returned for dinner. Kaja came in once a day, usually later in the mornings, to drop off alcohol and fresh rags for me to clean and dress my wound. She never said a word and barely looked at me.

They treated me no differently from the chickens, goats, pigs, and ducks. I was like a farm animal kept in its pen where my owners were feeding and healing me before putting me to work. And once they finished working me, I figured they'd send me off to slaughter. In fact, if I didn't heal quickly, I worried they might slaughter me sooner for being more of a burden on their lives than an asset.

Before eating, I'd carefully pick through my food and smell every spoonful before ingesting it, fearing they poisoned it. And I always had by my bed a rock and the hand sickle to use as a weapon in case they came at night to kill me. But Stanisław was strong. It would be hard to fight him off. I debated trying to run away at night, even with a wounded leg. However, there was no place to go. For now, I was being fed and given a place to sleep. So, despite my fears, I decided it was best to stay put, at least until I healed.

During this time of fear and paranoia, I fell into a well of loneliness and despair I'd not thought possible. I missed my family so badly that at night my stomach would twist into knots, doubling me over in agonizing cramps. Sometimes the pain was so bad it felt like ground glass was winding through my guts.

Visions of the past would pry their way into my consciousness, despite my attempts to stop them. I'd see Mama and Bubbe working together in the kitchen making fresh challah and whitefish for Shabbos. Powdery white flour coats Mama's hands and arms as she kneads the dough into two separate ropes. She braids them together and lets the challah sit so it has time to rise before placing it in the oven. Butter stains mark her white apron, flour dusts her hair where she has pulled it back to get it off her face. The honey-sweet buttery aroma of the challah baking in the oven fills the apartment with pure joy. Standing near Mama at the counter,

Bubbe cleans and fillets the fish with the expertise of a fisherman, always saving the fish head for the alley cats.

I'd see Basha in the mornings pounding her little fists on the bathroom door, ordering Sara to get out so she can have her share of time in the bathroom before going to school.

I'd see the two of them race me down Krakowska Street to the bakery after Papa gave each of us twenty kopeks to buy a pastry.

I'd see Papa and me playing chess while Bubbe sits in her plush velvet chair next to us listening to classical music on the radio, sipping her tea and knitting a sweater. Papa gazes at the board in silence, locked in deep concentration, puffing on a cigarette, stroking his mustache, resting his long index finger on a pawn, bishop, rook, or knight as he debates his next move. Sometimes he gets so lost in thought that I find myself fixated on the ash at the end of his cigarette, growing ever longer until it succumbs to the force of gravity, landing on either his pant leg, or the floor, or the chessboard.

It just didn't seem possible that they were now gone.

Grief was now my constant companion. Sometimes it crushed me, but most of the time, it numbed me. I felt like a dead leaf on a river, floating in its current with no sense of direction, no purpose, no control over where I was going. I felt myself being sucked beneath the water by an eddy, pulled down to the muddy riverbed where, over time, I'd eventually disintegrate.

I reached a point where I didn't see any sense in going on.

I picked up the hand sickle and ran its razor-sharp blade lightly along my wrist. But the thought of slicing through my wrists repulsed me. Then I spotted a rope in the shed behind a feed bag. I retrieved it and stretched it out. It was a meter long, a couple of centimeters thick. It seemed strong enough to hold my weight. I ran my fingers along its course fibers, sections of it coated in dirt and grease. I tied a slipknot on one end of it and placed the noose over my head. The shed's weathered rafters looked old and weak. I stood on a tin bucket set on top of a wood crate, balancing myself with the crutch. Reaching for the rafter, I gripped it with both hands, then gradually let my weight hang from it. It bent and almost split. I let go before it broke.

Stepping down from the bucket, I lay back down on my pile of hay, hopeless and weary, watching the dust motes float through blades of light piercing the cracks in the wallboards. I cried like a baby. Nothing seemed to matter anymore.

My fingers reached for where the button was on the waistband of my old pants—I wondered if Zelda was still alive. If so, did she still have the button I gave her? I realized no matter how trapped I felt in my prison of melancholy, she was the one thing worth living for.

I TRIED DISTRACTING MY BROKEN MIND AND HEART BY FOCUSING on the world around me. I watched Kaja work long hours with Lilli nearby wandering around the yard on her small and plump wobbly legs, often falling and crying, then getting up and starting all over again. Kaja wore a blue-and-white babushka most days. Her shiny blond hair, the color of wheat, ended at the top of her shoulders, often tied in a ponytail. She had catlike eyes, set wide apart, stern and icy blue; a short nose with a broad bridge, as if once broken, like a boxer's nose. A small star-shaped scar marked the center of the bridge, and another small crescent-shaped scar was etched in her cheek.

Although disgusted by her ignorant ideas about Jews, I admired her hard work while caring for Lilli. She labored tirelessly milking the cow and goat; throwing feed to the chickens, ducks, and geese; putting out hay and corn for the cow, sheep, goat, and pig; shoveling their shit; carrying buckets of water from the well pump; loading wood into the house; cooking the meals and washing the clothes in a large tin tub and hanging them to dry on a rope stretched between two wood poles planted in the ground beside the house.

When Kaja and Lilli were inside the house, I observed the animals roaming aimlessly around the yard and inside their pens. To entertain myself, I'd given them names and roles. Mendel, the pig, was the mayor of the farm. The chickens, Silvia, Masha, Gola, and Mazal, were his harebrained advisors. Moses the rooster was an arrogant *mamzer*—a wealthy bastard businessman who was always chasing the ladies. Lipa the goat and Bima and Sima the sheep oversaw garbage collection, eating whatever they found, while Esther the cow managed fertilizer and milk supplies. Head of transportation was Zissa, the horse, meaning "sweet one" in Yiddish.

Inside the shed, to occupy my mind, I focused on memorizing Stanisław's tools and their locations. On the wall hung an old ax that he probably used for splitting wood and chopping down small trees, and there was a double-handle saw for cutting down large trees and a single-handle saw for smaller timber. There were two long-handle shovels, three pitchforks, two rusty hoes, a sledgehammer and a pickax, a worn grinding stone for sharpening tools, a rusty hammer and chisel, two double-handle and single-handle scythes, shiny silver and curved like a crescent moon, a leather horse bridle and stirrups, various types of string and rope tied into bundles and scattered about, many grain bags and gunnysacks, a wheel for the cart, a broken axle, oil, and grease. In the very back, a bicycle lay buried beneath piles of gunnysacks. The plow and harrow were outside the shed.

I played a game where I closed my eyes and recounted each tool and its location and gave myself points for the items I remembered and subtracted points for each item I forgot. As I improved, I added more details to the game, like which direction the tool was facing, its precise location, and any distinguishing features it may have had, like rust, scratches, knots in the wood handle, and so on.

One day, I began reciting the names and locations of the tools out loud and realized, to my surprise, that I could speak again. The connection between my brain, tongue, and vocal cords seemed to repair itself magically. However, I continued acting as though I were mute. I didn't trust Kaja for good reason and didn't want anyone to know about my past, nor what had happened to my family in the forest. I didn't even want them knowing my name. Being silent gave me a sense of control over my situation; it was my only form of protection.

23

IN EARLY JULY, AFTER A MONTH AND SIXTEEN DAYS ON THE FARM, I had nearly fully recovered. My thigh still ached from the bullet wound, but the wound itself had almost entirely healed. The black hole had completely closed and the discolored skin around it had returned to normal. I walked with a slight limp but had the energy to work long days with Stanisław, from sunrise to past sundown.

The work was healing in the way it distracted me from my melancholy and grief. Almost every day, I learned something new. Stanisław taught me how to cut down trees with a double saw and split firewood and harrow and plow the fields and plant wheat, oat, flax, and corn and build a stone wall along the edge of a field that divided his field from the neighbor's. I learned how to set fence poles and repair the broken railings, make compost from all the animal shit, milk the cow and goat, sharpen the harrow with metal files and the scythes and sickles with the grinding stone. I was in awe of how much Stanisław knew—how capable, confident, and strong he was. His tenacity and work ethic were admirable. Through the long days of hard work, I sensed we were building a comradery, a respect for each other. Just being in his presence helped elevate my spirits.

One day we were sitting on a fallen tree trunk taking a water break after sawing down several trees when Stanisław told me about how hard his father had worked him on the farm he grew up on. I wanted to know if it was this farm or some other farm. I wrote

the question in the dirt with a stick: *Did you grow up on this farm?*
Stanisław gazed at the ground in befuddlement. I pointed again
to the question, and Stanisław shrugged. "I don't read. Kaja read a
little. But Lilli will go to school and read good!"

I had never known anyone illiterate. Even the poorest Jews
in Kraków learned to read before they were old enough to hold a
book in their hands. But in the countryside, things were different
among the Polish peasants. Maybe they didn't have a tradition of
teaching reading to their children. And yet Stanisław was one of
the most intelligent men I'd ever met. He knew about agriculture,
livestock, carpentry, fishing, and hunting; he could identify what
types of mushrooms and berries were edible, and which were
poisonous. He was one of the best teachers I'd ever had, and I
was starting to trust him.

I wanted to know more about Stanisław—where he came
from, why he farmed, if he had come from a long line of farmers, if
his parents were still alive, if he had any siblings, and how he met
Kaja. I considered breaking my silence to converse and get closer
to him. But I knew this would prove to Kaja her beliefs were
true: Jews couldn't be trusted—we were all liars and spies. If she
ever discovered I really wasn't mute, she'd certainly exile me from
the farm.

I wasn't ready to leave, so I couldn't take the risk.

24

BECAUSE WE WORKED FROM MORNING TILL EVENING, I SAW VERY little of Kaja, and that suited me fine. The less I saw of her, the better it was. Her stern and suspicious glances made me feel as if I was in constant danger. Sometimes I wondered if she didn't like the friendship Stanisław and I were building through work and all the time we spent together. She could be so unpredictable, so moody, distant, and strange. In fact, I didn't understand why Stanisław and Kaja were married. It appeared there was no love, no affection between them. It seemed to be a practical marriage. One of survival.

I saw how Kaja's anger and resentment could quickly explode into hateful arguments and often physical fights. The intensity of her anger frightened me because I knew she could fully turn it on me as well. Kaja would hit Stanisław and then get slapped or kicked, or vice versa. From overhearing their arguments, I learned Kaja despised the farm. "All I do is work like an ox!" she'd yell at Stanisław from across the yard. "I'm sick of this filthy place!" Stanisław, who sometimes drank too much vodka at night, would call her spoiled and threaten to hit her some more if she didn't stop complaining. But Kaja refused to be intimidated. I'd seen her in the yard take the blows and respond with her own. She rarely backed down.

One night, Stanisław and I had returned to the farm late, near midnight. We were both hungry. Stanisław thought Kaja was asleep and so he allowed me into the house, something Kaja forbade. From the pot on the stove, still warm, he doled out a big bowl of borscht with plump pieces of chicken in it and handed it to me, then took out a bottle of vodka and filled two small glasses. He emptied his glass in one gulp. I took a small sip from mine and felt the burn of it going down my throat.

Sitting at the table, we ate in silence at first. "You a good worker," he mumbled. "Maybe you become a farmer, like me. I think you could be a good farmer. You learn fast. From now on I call you Jurek. That will be your name." He poured himself another glass and swilled it. "You're a good boy. Like a son to me."

His words meant the world to me.

"And don't let Kaja bother you. She can be mean as a badger. She's not happy. But she's a good mother to Lilli. And she cooks good and takes care of the animals."

I nodded in agreement, wondering why he was telling me this.

"I tell her you work hard. She knows. I think she starts to be nicer to you now." He poured himself another glass and clinked it against mine. "Now drink!" he said. "Enjoy."

Sitting at Stanisław's table and sharing a meal with him was comforting. I felt his respect and trust, which brought me closer to him. It was clear he was seeing me as an individual person, rather than just a Jew who provided free labor.

He cleaned his bowl of borscht with a piece of bread, poured himself another glass of vodka, and offered me the same. My head felt light from the first drink and now the room started to shift. I declined to have more, but he insisted. He poured me two more glasses, and I lost count of how many he had. A calming sense of numbness spread throughout my mind and body as the table and floor started undulating. And nothing seemed to matter. I'd never been so drunk before.

Stanisław's translucent blue eyes had turned glassy, his words slurred together in sentences that had lost their meanings. He said something about cutting wood tomorrow and going to town before I stood up and tumbled to the floor. He laughed and picked me up and helped me walk to the door. "Go sleep!" I think he said as I stumbled out the door and fell several more times before making it to the shed.

I dropped onto my bed of hay and gazed out the shed's little window where strips of black clouds drifted like smoke past the full moon. Zissa whinnied from her shed and then was quiet.

Lurching through my drunken fog of thoughts, going in and out of consciousness, I wondered if I'd heard Stanisław correctly. Were we going to town tomorrow? If so, it would be my initial visit to Przemyśl. And maybe I'd find Zelda and her family there. While drifting off to sleep, I envisioned seeing Zelda in the market, running to her, clutching her in my arms, smelling rosemary in her coppery-red hair, lavender on her neck, feeling the steady rhythm of her calm, even breaths on my chest, kissing her freckled lips, holding her hands. . . .

I was in a deep sleep when the shed door creaked, jarring my eyes open. Standing at the door, silhouetted in the silvery moonlight, Kaja wore her housecoat with nothing beneath it. She gazed down at me as I stared confusedly back up at her, stunned by her appearance. I wasn't sure if this was a drunken dream or wakefulness. Without saying a word, she straddled me. I froze. Her nakedness pressed against my groin. She grabbed my hands and placed them on her breasts. The room spun. Her face was obscured by shadow, the edges of her blond hair shimmering in the moonlight.

Shocked and utterly bewildered by what was happening, I almost told her to get off me, but caught myself before exposing my mute charade. Instead, I grunted as I tried pushing her away. But she kept me pinned on my back, her calloused hands pressing down on my chest, her muscular thighs squeezing down on my hips. Sweat and smoke emanated from her body; her strength rivaled that of a man.

"Stay still," she whispered harshly. "He's drunk and asleep." She leaned over me, rubbing her naked body against mine, moving in such a way that aroused me despite my inebriated mind telling me this was all so wrong.

I had lost my bearings; the roof was bending; my thoughts jumbled. This wasn't supposed to be happening. It made no sense. I despised this woman, and she despised me. I was the dirty *Żyd*—a curse, a devil in human clothes. And she was nothing to me but a Jew-hating peasant.

I wanted her to stop. Stanisław would kill me. Zelda would never forgive me. Yet my aroused body told me something else, something I didn't understand. Despite feeling shame, it seemed to hunger for the arousal, warmth, and comfort of her naked flesh pressing against mine. It craved to be desired, to be consumed, to be enveloped by this wild woman's naked embrace. She put me inside her and whispered, "If you let go in me, I'll tell Stanisław you rape me, and he will kill you."

Yes, he would certainly kill me. And I would deserve it. This betrayal of him, and of Zelda, was a *shanda*—a curse I might never escape from.

Her words put the fear of God in me. Terrified of losing control, I tried pulling away again, but she kept me clamped between her muscular thighs, pinning my wrists to the ground with remarkable strength. She ordered me to be still as she trembled and rocked more wildly. Her breath quickened; a muffled primal groan arose through her body—her nails dug into my chest, drawing thin lines of blood.

I separated from my body, floated above the scene, gazed down at myself trapped beneath her, feeling nothing.

Finally, she collapsed on top of me. I returned to my body. We lay there for a moment; her thick-boned back slippery with sweat; her blond hair, soft as corn silk, brushing the side of my face; her erratic, heaving breaths slowing down, becoming steady.

Without saying a word, she rolled off me and left.

I lay there, stunned, unable to make sense of what had just happened. I didn't know what to do. Run? I feared facing Stanisław in the morning. Would she tell him? Did he hear her leave the house? If I ran, where would I go? I wouldn't trust another farmer. Nor would I want to be with a Jewish family in Przemyśl. With the Germans just across the river, if they attack, the Jews will be the first to go. That was for certain. For the moment, Stanisław's farm seemed the safest place to be.

However, Kaja now had a secret weapon to get rid of me whenever she wished. Or did she? Maybe he wouldn't believe her. Maybe he'd think she was lying to get rid of me. What proof would she have? I never released myself inside her.

My head throbbed as my mind tumbled in so many directions. The bloody scratches on my chest ached. I cleaned them at the well, then returned to the shed. I tried to sleep, but waves of guilt and shame washed over me as I recalled that day when I proposed to Zelda beneath the willow by the river. We made promises, one being to always tell the truth. We swore to always be truthful, no matter how painful the truth may be, and agreed to never keep secrets from each other, because we believed secrets were a betrayal that would poison the relationship. We declared our utmost trust and vowed to never intentionally harm each other.

Yet now I realized how naïve we both were before the war; and what little we knew about life's complexities. How there are things beyond our control—unpredictable forces and circumstances— that may cause us to behave in ways we never thought possible. And those regressions, those unusual behaviors, are best kept secret.

25

AT FIRST LIGHT, MOSES'S PIERCING CROW CUT THE MORNING
quiet as if proclaiming what had happened last night was evil.
My chest was still sore with three long red scratches, straight as
furrows, raked across it. Proof of the crime. I kept my shirt
buttoned to hide them.

Sitting on my bed of hay, I watched Mendel the pig meandering through the mist drifting across the yard. He grunted
and sniffed while searching for scraps to eat. Lipa the goat was
drinking dirty water from a tin bucket, then dropped a pile of
pellets before moseying away in Mendel's direction. Sima and
Bima wandered the yard, plucking bits of grass and weeds from
the ground, their puffy, oatmeal-colored wool coats carrying in
the fibers some burs and bits of hay. I imagined the four of them
having a secret conversation among themselves about what they
knew had happened last night inside my shed. Mendel was telling
Lipa what a fool I was to allow such a thing to happen. Lipa
responded: "*What was he to do?*"

"*Push her off him!*" responded Mendel. "*Has he not the strength
to do such a thing?*"

"*He was too terrified,*" said Sima. "*You heard what she said. She
would've told Stanisław he raped her. And that would be the end of him.*"

"*You can't back down from threats,*" said Mendel. "*You must
stand up to them. Otherwise, they'll just keep you stuck in a situation
you don't want to be in.*"

"*Oh, shut up, Mendel,*" said Lipa. "*You act like you know every-thing. You don't, you foolish pig!*"

Just then, Stanisław exited the house and crossed the yard, kicking the geese out of the way, holding a cup of tea and a bowl of food. I sensed danger in the way he kicked the geese and was certain he knew something. Mendel concurred.

"*Oh yes,*" he said. "*He seems angry. I think he knows something.*"

"*Shut up,*" said Sima. "*You're being paranoid.*"

Stanisław's eyes appeared downturned with rage. Maybe he awoke from his stupor last night and found her side of the bed empty, or heard her return to the house. Or maybe she had already told him. But then why would he bring me breakfast?

"*That's right,*" said Lipa. "*Why would he bring him breakfast?*" he asked Mendel.

"*To poison him,*" said Mendel.

"*Oh yeah,*" said Sima and Bima in unison. "*Mendel has a point there.*"

Stanisław called me over to the cart and handed me the cup of black tea and a bowl containing a piece of bread covered in butter, two hard-boiled eggs, and a slice of kielbasa. Normally, I'd devour that meal like a hungry dog. But my appetite had left me. Embarrassed and sickened by my actions, I was also terrified he knew what had happened. In my paranoia, I feared Mendel was right. As absurd as it may sound, someone could have poisoned the food. Yet I thought I must eat something; otherwise he'd become suspicious.

I first smelled the egg; its sulfuric odor was unusually pungent. The garlicky-onion smell of the kielbasa was also more potent than I remembered, almost burning the inside of my nostrils. The but-ter on the bread appeared darker, closer to beige than yellow. Men-del stood behind the fence, watching me. "*Be careful,*" he said.

I took a minuscule bite of the egg, chewing it carefully to see if I could detect an abnormal taste. It tasted normal. I did likewise with the kielbasa and bread.

"Well?" said Mendel.

"I don't know yet," I replied. "I've lost my appetite."

Stanisław noticed my unusual behavior and asked what was wrong. I pointed to my stomach and made a face, pretending my stomach was hurting. "Let's go. Eat," he said gruffly. "We have lots of work and we go to the market today to sell firewood." I sipped a small amount of the tea and it seemed okay, and I ate a few more small bites of food. When Stanisław went inside the shed to gather the saws and axes, I quickly tossed the rest of the food behind a bush where it couldn't be seen.

At the horse shed, I secured Zissa's bridle and harnessed her to the wagon. "Be careful," whispered Zissa. "I think he knows something happened last night."

"How do you know?"

"I just sense it," she said as Stanisław loaded the back of the wagon with the saws, some rope, and axes. For a moment, I imagined he might kill me in the forest with the ax or hang me from a tree with the rope. I prepared to run farther east should he come after me.

"Go get a sack of potatoes, a sack of carrots, and a cannister of milk from the shed and load the wagon," he ordered. There was a sharp edge to his voice that made me nervous.

After I stacked everything on the wagon, he arrived from the chicken coop with a case of eggs that he set down on the bench between us. He snapped the reins, and Zissa begrudgingly pulled the wagon out of the yard and onto the dirt road that led to the woods and to town.

As we traveled down the road, I sensed a wall dividing us that had not been there before. His demeanor was uneasy, as if he knew what had happened. He was unusually quiet and stern.

"*What do you think, Zissa? Does he know?*" I asked her. Zissa didn't respond, maybe because she was lost in her own thoughts, or perhaps she hadn't heard me.

Halfway to town, we turned off the main road to a smaller dirt road that led into the forest. We discovered an old fallen oak tree. The wood was dry, better for burning.

Using the double-handle saw, we cut the tree into sections, then split those sections into quarters with our axes. I kept a wary eye on Stanisław as we worked for several hours before sitting down on a log to rest. He drank some water from his canteen and passed it to me. A couple of crows cackled in a nearby tree, possibly warning me of what was to come. Above, an eerie wind rustled the leaves on the oak and maple branches, maybe another sign of danger.

"We have enough wood," said Stanisław. "Let's go."

We loaded the split wood onto the back of the cart as Zissa picked at some blades of grass, waiting patiently to leave. "*What do you think, Zissa? Is this it? Will he kill me in these woods before we leave?*" Zissa didn't respond. Her silence made me even more nervous.

After loading the wood, we collected the saws, axes, and rope and stored them in the wood box beneath the seat. Then Stanisław took out a hunting knife and walked toward me. I stepped back and prepared to run. But he passed right by me and went to a tree where he knelt by its exposed roots. "Look," he said excitedly, "*podgrzybki*—boletes. These are good! See?" He pointed underneath the cap. "Brown or light brown good.

White—no good. They make you sick. I'll give these to Kaja to put in soup. You will like it!" His sudden shift in mood made me think he must not be aware of what happened last night. Cautiously relieved, I helped him pick the mushrooms, filling a small sack with them before leaving.

26

ON THE OUTSKIRTS OF PRZEMYŚL, THE DIRT ROAD TURNED TO gravel, then to cobblestone as we approached the market in the main square. Seeing so many Jews rushing along the street and going about their business surprised me. It felt like I had traveled back in time, to preinvasion Kraków. Despite the presence of Russian soldiers, Jews were moving about freely as they gathered in small groups on street corners and cafés chatting, debating, gossiping, their clothes no longer tagged with the Star of David armbands and patches. There were the Communists and Bundists, Yiddishists, Orthodox, the not so Orthodox, the anti-Orthodox, and of course the Hasidim wearing their black frocks, furry brown and black *shtreimels* shaped like stove pipes, their sidelocks either twisted round their ears or hanging down the sides of their faces like curly ribbons. Some were poor tradesmen, others appeared to still have some means.

Seeing the Jews of Przemyśl living in this state of freedom was disorienting. It didn't seem real, as if I were in a dream that had transported me back in time. And what made it more surreal and disturbing was to know that just across the river, less than one hundred meters wide, on the German side of the border, my fellow Jews were living a miserable existence of daily suffering and human degradation.

Everywhere I looked, in the cafés and bakeries, down the cobblestone streets and corridors between buildings, I searched for a sign of Zelda and her family. But they were nowhere to be seen.

On our way to the square, Stanisław stopped at an abandoned centuries-old synagogue. Shelling and fire had destroyed this one, leaving ruins behind. The large rectangular building, at least four stories tall, was constructed with enormous stone blocks that reminded me of the ones used for building the pyramids in Egypt. Beneath the towering roof, black charcoal scars of smoke and fire framed the tall arched windows.

"Germans bomb this Żyd building when the war started," said Stanisław. "Before Russians pushed them back." He dismounted the cart and led me toward the destroyed synagogue. "They bomb bridges and Pansaz Gansa market and Żyd temple on Jagiellońska Street and set fire to Żyds homes and kill many, many Żyds— many hundreds Żyds killed at Lipowica, Prałkowce, Przekopana near Wiar River. Come—I show you."

I didn't want to go inside the building. It looked haunted, as if it were a monument for murdered Jews. Once a house of God, now it was a house of death and destruction.

Using an iron rod, Stanisław pried open the charred door and insisted I follow him inside.

It was dark and musty, the floor covered in ash, an acrid stench of charred wood permeating the dense air. A dusty white light filtering through the arched windows above illuminated the burnt wood benches leading up to the bimah where the rabbi gave his sermon. I imagined the scene before the bombing, before the flames of hate deformed the benches. I imagined how the Jews of Przemyśl once filled those benches with their families, friends, and neighbors; everyone dressed in their finest Sabbath clothes, freshly washed, and ironed for the service; the parents listening intently to the rabbi's sermon while the children squirmed; the cantor leading the congregation in an ancient song that still echoes through the centuries.

The four massive pillars framing the bimah reached several stories high, each crowned at the top. They reminded me of the pictures I saw in high school of the Greek Temple of Zeus. Despite being covered in dust and soot and scarred black from raging flames, they appeared holy in their majesty, stoic in their permanence.

At the foot of the great columns, the ornately carved wooden ark that once held the sacred Torah scrolls was obliterated. Also missing were the brass and silver lamps, the decorative sconces and candelabras, and the ornate chandeliers that must have adorned the building, like the old synagogue we attended in Kraków, before its destruction.

Stanisław picked up a piece of charred wood and examined it. "Oak," he said, carelessly tossing it back on the ground. I turned to leave, my heart aching from seeing such vicious destruction. But Stanisław stopped me. "You and your family go to *Żyd* temple?" I nodded.

"Where? Warsaw?" I shook my head. "Kraków?" I nodded. "What your father do?" I picked up a piece of wood and drew a picture of an umbrella in the dirt and ash that coated the floor.

"Umbrella?"

I confirmed with a nod.

"He makes umbrellas?"

I nodded again, and Stanisław laughed. "You're an umbrella maker's son? I've never had an umbrella in my life. Only people in the city need umbrellas." He started complaining about how Kaja wanted to live in the city. "She wants to sell the farm and live in a city like Warsaw or Kraków. Can you believe? I say: Are you crazy? What am I going to do in a city? She says: You can work in factory. I laugh—ha! I never will work in a factory. I never will live in a city. Too many people, too much noise, everyone on top of everyone, no air to breathe. I will not even live in a town like Przemyśl. On the farm we live free. This is our life, I tell her."

He continued to complain about Kaja but I lost track of what he was saying. I began thinking about Papa and the umbrella shop, and how terribly I missed him. I walked away from Stanisław while he was still talking. He was getting on my nerves.

"Where are you going?" he called out.

I had to leave the building. It was bringing back too many memories.

"Stop!" he yelled.

I continued walking toward the end of the dark cavern where light spilled through the front door. He came up from behind me and placed his hand gently on my shoulder. "Jurek. Where is your father? Kraków?" I gazed at Stanisław for a moment. From my look, he knew. "Your father is dead?"

I nodded.

"What about mother and brothers and sisters? Everyone dead?"

I nodded again.

His face tightened, and his eyes narrowed and turned dark as he looked at me a long time, longer than ever before. "Germans are evil," he said under his breath. "Worse than the Russians. Worse than animals."

There was a long silence. The air was still. Stanisław breathed heavy, his arms folded across his chest.

"Sorry," he said, placing his heavy hand on my shoulder. His voice was gentle, as if I were a good friend of his, or a member of his family.

My armor cracked as a wave of guilt and grief welled up inside me. Guilt for having survived when my family didn't. Grief over never being able to see them again. Never. My eyes filled with tears. I turned and walked away. I didn't want him to see me as weak.

He followed me out the door into the gray light of the humid afternoon. We mounted the wagon and continued to the market.

27

PEASANTS SELLING FOOD AND WARES FROM THEIR CARTS WERE jammed haphazardly into the square. Rows upon rows of wicker baskets filled with corn, carrots, potatoes, cabbage, oats and brown flour, tomatoes, cucumbers, squash, basil, and thyme; wood boxes packed with eggs, cheeses, butter, and jam; cages stuffed with clucking chickens, ducks, and geese; butchered pig, lamb, goat, and many sausages hung from strings above tables made of wood planks. Wandering amid the bustling chaos were Jews, Poles, and Russian soldiers. A gray marble fountain with a bear inside it occupied the middle of the square.

Stanisław found a space for Zissa and the cart along the perimeter of the market. He was one of the few vendors selling firewood. Customers lined up quickly to buy it.

"You get on the cart and I call out the order and you make a wood bundle and give to me," he said, handing me a ball of twine and a knife. People selected the wood they wanted from the pile. I gathered their pieces, cut the twine, and tied off the wood bundles. I gave them to Stanisław, who first collected the money before handing the wood to the customer. Most often, people tried to haggle with him over the price, which was why he collected the money first before distributing the wood. Like Papa, he had short patience for haggling. But unlike Papa, rather than come to an agreement, he'd tell customers to go to hell if they didn't like his price. Almost always they gave in at the end and paid the price he set.

Once I became adept at filling the orders, my mind wandered. I scanned the market, searching for Zelda and anyone I knew from Kraków. There were faces that looked vaguely familiar, but I wasn't sure if my mind was playing tricks on me. In fact, one person looked like my good friend, Big Izzy. We'd met in cheder when we were studying for our bar mitzvah and we both hated cheder and skipped it more often than we attended. Football was our first love, and Big Izzy was a monster on the field. He was a half foot taller than the rest of us. On offense, rather than dribble the ball around opponents, he'd go right through them. On defense, rather than steal the ball with a tackle, he'd crash into opponents like a tank, throwing a shoulder into them, sending them flying across the field like rag dolls.

Although this young man had the face and brown frizzy hair of Big Izzy, his body looked different. He was hunched over and frail looking, and his clothes hung loose as rags on a scarecrow. Although he was too far away for me to be certain it was him, I noted which building he entered at the end of the square. That's probably his place, I thought.

"Hurry up!" ordered Stanisław as the line grew. I picked up the pace. Then twenty minutes later, while tying off a bundle of wood, I looked across the square again from atop the wagon, peering over the heads of the crowds, and glimpsed a young woman's copper-red hair, shoulder length, flashing in a sliver of late afternoon light. I was taken aback, almost losing my breath. The young redhead was visible for another moment before disappearing round a corner. I swore it was Zelda. The color of her hair and its length, the way she walked and the shape of her body . . . My heart raced.

"Eh!" yelled Stanisław. "Wake up!! People waiting!"

I jumped back to work trying to fill the customers' orders. But I barely heard them as I figured out what to do next. And then my mind went blank.

Without thinking, I jumped off the cart and sprinted in a wild dash toward the street where I saw her turn. Weaving through the market at full tilt, I knocked into people and jumped over squawking chickens and quacking ducks and dodged baskets full of vegetables and grains and whipped past the blacksmith hammering horseshoes and a baby screaming at the top of her lungs. The church bells started clanging, as if sounding an alarm.

At the end of the square, I reached the street she had turned down and ran past three small children playing hopscotch on the sidewalk and an older couple dressed in black walking arm in arm. There was no sign of her. I ran up the street and looked down the next street. It was empty. I ran down a third street, then a fourth. But she was gone. I stood in the middle of the street, turning in circles, perplexed, pondering what to do next. Rounding the corner came two Russian soldiers on foot. I turned and walked away from them, heading back to the market.

When I came to the edge of the square, I saw Stanisław at the other end atop the cart, taking orders and tying off the wood bundles, haggling with customers over the prices of the wood, potatoes, milk, eggs, and turnips he was selling. I realized I was a fool to leave like that and feared what my punishment would be.

For a moment, I contemplated not returning. I again considered running away to the east, into Russia. But mentally I was nowhere near ready to leave the farm. I had food and shelter there. And I owed Stanisław my labor. He had saved me, even if it was to have me work for him. He could've left me on the side of the road to die, but he didn't. Regarding Kaja, I hoped that what had occurred between us was just a strange, onetime event that would never happen again.

I quickly made my way through the market back to Stanisław's cart. He caught sight of me as I sheepishly approached him. His face twisted into a grimace. Jumping down from the cart, he came up and slapped me so hard across the face I hit the street. "Stupid boy! Never do that again!!" he hollered. "Now get up and work!"

From the ground I saw customers pointing at me and laughing. I stood up, dusted myself off, then noticed two of the customers laughing were young Jewish men my age. They mocked me in Yiddish, calling me a stupid Polish peasant, a moron, an imbecile. I exploded into a violent rage. I punched the most offensive one in the face, knocking him to the ground where I jumped on him and blindly continued beating him senselessly. The other Poles cheered me on, entertained by the sight of what they thought was a Polish peasant beating the hell out of a Jew. A sick sense of power consumed me as I continued to pummel him. I'm ashamed to say I felt a disturbing satisfaction in humiliating one of my own, as if I was taking a revenge against my passivity and cowardliness in confronting the Germans' daily humiliations.

Stanisław pulled me off the young man and shoved me back to the cart. The young man had blood around the nose and eyes, his wire-rimmed glasses smashed to pieces. I watched with a twisted sense of pride and shame as he and his friend slipped away.

BY SUNDOWN WE HAD SOLD ALL THE FIREWOOD, THREE-QUARTERS of a bag of potatoes, all the eggs and milk, and half the carrots. The town was turning dark. At the end of the square, a lamplighter used his long wooden pole to ignite the streetlamps, their small golden flames casting an inviting glow beneath the elm trees surrounding the square. I wondered if Biala the lamplighter was still in Kraków, or if he had escaped, or if the Germans had killed him.

Before we left, Stanisław found a vendor selling bottles of vodka and other goods. He dug into his pockets that now bulged with money and told the man to give him three bottles of vodka, four bars of soap, two jars of honey, and five chocolate bars. He paid the man and put all the goods in the toolbox behind our seat except for one bottle of vodka. Uncorking the bottle, he had a swig, then snapped the leather reins and steered Zissa out of town. She took the road at a fast trot, happy to be returning home where she'd find food and the comfort of her shed.

Stanisław shoved the bottle of vodka into my chest. "You stupid running away. Why you do that? What's wrong with you?" I didn't want it and tried pushing it away but he insisted. I had a swig and gave it back to him. "That beating you give the *Żyd*. If I not stop you, I think you'd kill him." He laughed and drank some more and then passed the bottle again. "I once almost beat a man to death," he said. "I caught him trying to steal one of my chickens at the market. If the police not pull me off him, I would've killed him! Never take from a man what's not yours."

I wanted to forget what had happened, and so I drank more. The spirits numbed me, as before, and provided a respite from my troubling thoughts. And as I got drunk, the wagon began floating. The trunks and limbs of the thick trees lining the road formed a wall around us, bending and swaying in the warm wind as if made of rubber; the canopy of stars spreading across the sky appeared to be within reach. Stanisław started humming a song that sounded like the one Zelda would sometimes sing to me. "*Belz, Mayn Shtetele Belz.*"

The song took me back to the day Zelda and I were fishing on the Vistula in late August of '38, a year before the bombs dropped. The day was hot. Smoky storm clouds gathered over the river in the late afternoon; insects swarmed, and the bass were biting as the sky blackened. We caught one fish after another. Then the storm clouds exploded, releasing a massive downpour. We ran beneath the bridge for shelter and sat on a log huddled next to each other, my arm wrapped firmly round her waist. Thick sheets of rain battered the river's surface, making it roil. Zelda began singing "Belz." Her tender voice, slightly raspy and smooth as honey, made my heart melt.

> *Belz, mayn shtetele Belz,*
> *Mayn heymele, vu ich hob*
> *Mayne kindershe yorn farbracht . . .*
> *Mayn heymele vu ich hob*
> *Die Sheine Chalomes a sach.*
> *Belz, my little town of Belz*
> *My home, where my childhood days passed*
> *Belz, my hometown of Belz*
> *In a small and simple room*
> *Where I would sit and laugh with all the children.*
> *I would run with my prayer book every Shabbos*
> *To the banks of the river,*
> *And sit under the green tree.*
> *Belz, my little town of Belz*
> *Belz, my hometown of Belz*
> *My home, where I dreamed so many*
> *Beautiful dreams.*

When the song ended, I knelt before her on the soft grass of the riverbank. Thunder rumbled in the distance. Taking hold of her hands, I told her that in the world, there was no one I loved as much as her. The gentle light reflecting off the water illuminated her deep green eyes, holding me in their tenderness. She kissed my lips and said, "I love you, too."

In that moment, I believed that my life was set in stone—that nothing, no person or event, could ever come between us.

2 8

THAT NIGHT I LAY IN MY SHED FEELING COMPLETELY ALONE AND adrift. I belonged to nothing, and to no one. I had nothing. My heart felt like the ruins of the temple we saw that day, hollow and charred, coated in soot, smelling of old ash and charcoal. I had lost my way.

I left the shed and went to Mendel's pen. He was asleep by the fence. Squatting next to him, I petted his bristly head with its wiry fur and floppy ears. He made a quiet grunt of satisfaction. His flat snout twitched, as he must have been taking in my scent.

Coming from the house were the sounds of Stanisław and Kaja laughing and singing while getting drunk. But then Kaja complained about the soap he bought, telling him it was the wrong kind, and Stanisław blew up. Their argument turned physical. Lilli cried and a plate broke. Kaja screamed at Stanisław to get out, but he refused. Then they stopped fighting and there were only the sounds of Lilli's crying. I felt bad for Lilli. When my parents argued, no one was ever hit. There was never any violence.

As I continued petting Mendel, I closed my eyes and thought about the girl at the market with copper-red hair. "*What do you think, Mendel? Was that Zelda I saw in the market today?*"

"*How should I know?*" said Mendel.

"*Should I take the bicycle out of the shed and ride back there tonight and look for her?*"

"*I wouldn't. If Stanisław or Kaja discover you left, they'll become suspicious and undoubtedly clear you off the farm.*"

Mendel was right. It was too risky to leave. I patted his head and stroked his floppy ears once more before returning to the shed.

While drifting off to sleep, I saw Zelda's face illuminated by the warm flames of the streetlamps when she left Kraków with her family. Her face—so full of sorrow. I wanted to grasp her before she disappeared into the shadows of darkness.

But no sooner had I fallen asleep than the shed door creaked open, awakening me. My heart jumped into my throat. I thought this would never happen again. I feared this woman's unpredictability and was terrified that Stanisław would discover us. Yet some part of me hungered to be enveloped in the heat of her nakedness.

Kaja gently lay next to me, her face softly lit by the moonlight slipping through the cracks in the door. She had a bruise beneath her right eye and her cheek swelled.

"I hate him," she said. "He is a stupid man. A stupid, stupid fool with no sense about him. I should leave him and move to the city." She paused, as if waiting for a response. "I'm sick of the filth here. All I do is feed the animals and shovel their shit. I want to live like the women do in Warsaw and Kraków. I want to have nice clothes and a clean place to live. You understand? And Lilli shouldn't grow up in this disgusting place. She should grow up in a city where she can go to school and find a good husband." She paused and inhaled deeply, as if trying to calm herself down. "I made a mistake. I should've never married him. This is no life."

She held my hand while staring up at the roof, the rugged contours of her face barely visible in the darkness. "You're a *Żyd* from a city. I know you had nice things—a big home with pretty furniture and things. A good school, nice cafés and restaurants. I know you understand what I'm saying. Right?" She looked at me and I nodded. To my surprise, I felt bad for her. Although our situations were entirely different, I understood her feelings of being trapped in a situation she didn't want to be in. I understood her loneliness.

She ran her hands over my body, guiding my hand between her legs to that place where she was moist and inviting. She shifted her body beneath me, wrapping her thick, muscular legs round my waist, tightening them around me, squeezing our naked bodies together. Gripping my arms, her eyes closed and her mouth opened as she took me inside her, our breaths heavy, her earthy scent and warm flesh filling my emptiness as she undulated beneath me.

Then the house door banged open. "Kaja?" Stanisław hollered from across the yard, slurring his words. "Where are you?"

"Oh shit!" whispered Kaja as she scurried out from beneath me and peeked out the door. "He's coming. Pretend you're asleep." She quickly snuck out the door. I listened to her bare footsteps dashing behind the shed.

"Kaja, where are you?" he mumbled again, sounding incoherent.

His uneven footsteps stumbled toward the shed as the sounds of Kaja's feet padded away toward the outhouse between the back of the house and the surrounding forest. In the darkness, and given his drunken state, I thought it was possible he may not see her. As his footsteps approached, I lay on my bed and was about to close my eyes to pretend I was asleep when I noticed she'd left her housecoat near the door. Just as the door opened, I grabbed it and tucked it beneath my hay mattress and pretended to be asleep.

There was a long silence as I waited and prayed for him to leave. His breath was heavy and smelled of vodka. "Kaja?" he mumbled softly. "Kaja?" Then he kicked me. "Eh! Where is Kaja?"

Pretending he awakened me from a deep sleep, I gazed up at him, appearing confused. He could barely stand and leaned against the door for support. I raised my hands in the air, showing I did not know where she was. He stepped over me and peered into the back of the shed. "Huh," he grunted, and left.

As he stumbled across the yard, I heard the door to the outhouse slam shut. "Where were you?" he shouted, thick-tongued.

"What does it look like?" said Kaja.

"I called for you. You didn't answer."

"I did, but you didn't hear me because you're drunk."

"Shut up, woman!"

"Go to hell!" she said before entering the house.

I heard nothing after that except for Mendel, who was now making his usual grunting sounds while slurping some water by the fence. I opened the shed door and looked at him across the yard. He stood by the fence staring at me disapprovingly with his triangular-shaped ears flopped forward like small wings.

"Don't say anything," I told him.

"She'll get you killed," said Mendel. *"You need to stop this."*

"But how? What choice do I have?"

"You need to leave here."

"And go where?"

"Go east, into Russia."

"And what about finding Zelda?"

"Maybe she's there."

"And maybe she isn't. Maybe she's in Przemyśl, or back in Kraków."

Mendel sniffed the air with the flattened pink end of his long snout, examining me with his dark eyes framed by white eyelashes. *"You're playing with fire,"* he said before slowly pivoting his massive body and strolling away.

THROUGH JULY AND AUGUST, THE BARLEY, OAT, FLAX, AND CORN pushed up through the soil. By the beginning of September, the fields were thick and tall, glowing gold and green, rippling in the wind like water. The grains had ripened and were ready for harvest. I realized in early October that my birthday had come and gone in late August without me ever noticing it. I was now eighteen.

During this period Kaja visited me once in July, and once in August. The last time she visited me in August, after having sex, we lay beside each other arm in arm, the salty sweat coating our bodies drying in the cool air. Her calloused hands stroked my hair and caressed my face, treating me with a strange kindness I'd not felt before. It comforted me yet was odd and unsettling at the same time. I didn't trust it but hungered for it even though I still feared Stanisław discovering us. However, Kaja didn't seem afraid. Or if she was afraid, she was good at not showing it. Perhaps she desired capture, or simply disregarded the risk of being caught. I wasn't sure. All I knew was that I wanted her affection, despite the terrible risk involved and the shame I felt for betraying Zelda and Stanisław.

The wind was strong that night, thrashing the trees' branches, banging the shed's door, making it difficult to know if any of those sounds could also be Stanisław leaving the house in search of Kaja. The wind's fury kept me on edge. But Kaja seemed relaxed, uninterested in the dangerous situation we were in. She wanted to stay and tell me about herself.

"My parents once took me to Kraków when I was six, a few months before they died," she said. "Have you been to Kraków?" I nodded and wanted to tell her I grew up there. "I remember busy streets with all kinds of people going to the clothing shops and cafés and bakeries and restaurants. And there was a square. I think it was called Zgody Square."

It was strange to hear her mention Zgody Square, a world away, the place where we had our umbrella shop, and where Zelda and I would always walk after school with our bags full of books. On warm evenings in the summer, we'd often sit on a bench in the tree-lined square and eat ice cream and watch the people passing by. We'd create stories about the people we observed. To know that Kaja as a child had walked the same square with her parents seemed an impossible coincidence.

"At the square I remember the men wore nice suits and hats and the women had pretty dresses," she continued. "My father and mother always dressed nice. They lived the way you're supposed to live. Not like here where we dress in dirty rags and live like animals." She lay on her side next to me, resting her head on my shoulder.

"My father and mother left home one night to go to the theater and never came back. The theater caught fire, and many people died. My aunt and uncle had a farm close to here. They came to get me and they raised me. When I was sixteen, I met Stanisław in the market. He persuaded my uncle to let him marry me. I wanted to leave my aunt and uncle. I hated my uncle. He was a nasty man. So I married Stanisław."

I felt bad for Kaja. Holding her in my arms, I gently stroked her back. She snuggled her body closer to mine. For the first time, I genuinely felt connected to her.

She took a deep breath and made a sigh that was full of regrets, and lay next to me a few moments more, lamenting all she'd lost. Standing up, she gazed out the partially open shed door. "If my parents didn't die, I'd not be here. My life would be so different. So much better." She continued staring across the yard, contemplating her losses. "If I had somewhere to go, I'd leave here tomorrow."

She turned to face me, perhaps seeking a reply, or wanting to say something else, and then departed.

In the weeks that passed, she stopped coming to lie with me. She went back to ignoring me, as though I didn't exist. Sometimes when Stanisław and I returned from working the fields, I'd see her working in the yard or vegetable garden, carrying water from the well or feeding the animals, and she'd never even cast a glance at me.

I suppose the reality of having sex with a Jew now revolted her. Or maybe it was our developing closeness, or a blend of the two. It was also possible that she decided she didn't want to lose what little she had. She realized the danger in her actions, for both her and me. If Stanisław discovered us, he could assume our betrayal was one of mutual desire and blame her as much as me, no matter what kind of lie she might concoct. The consequences could have been fatal for us both.

A part of me was relieved to no longer be living in fear of Stanisław discovering us, nor weighed down by the terrible burden of betrayal. And yet, I'm ashamed to say, another part of me missed being with her.

AT DAWN I SHARPENED THE SCYTHES ON THE GRINDING STONE before going to the fields to cut the grains. Stanisław had taught me to first wet the stone with water, then angle the blade and apply just enough pressure to make it sharp as a razor. I pumped the foot pedal, spinning the stone as the blade licked it, spraying gold sparks that looked like the sparklers we'd wave in the air on Purim. After sharpening the scythes, we loaded them into the wagon and headed out to the oat field.

Silky clouds of mist floated over the fields, which were dewy and still in the windless morning. The oats had turned from a sea of green to a ripened golden yellow reaching up to my waist. Stanisław showed me how to cut the oats down with the double-handle scythe and then gather them in bundles so they had time to ripen some more and dry on the ground. "Three to five days," he said, "then we tie them for threshing." He popped one of the oat kernels off the stalk and bit down on it and handed me a kernel. "Taste," he said. "The sweetness tells you when it's ripe. The harvest will be good."

Rising from the fields in the east, a huge orange sun started slowly burning away the mist. Stanisław walked up and down the fields, swinging his scythe back and forth in a graceful arc and steady rhythm, like the pendulum rod of a metronome. I followed close behind him, gathering the cut oats and laying them in a row. He moved so fast that I struggled to keep pace with him.

By midday, the hot sun beat down on our backs, our clothes soaked in sweat and coated with oat seeds, bits of stalks, and small black field beetles. Half the field was sheared.

My back and legs became sore from bending forward for such long periods of time. I gazed upward to stretch my back and caught sight of a hawk circling above, scanning the fields for rabbits, moles, and field mice. On outspread wings, he glided the hot air currents, ascending toward the sun in a slow spiral, then sailing down to earth before ascending again. Birds I'd seen while fishing on the Vistula—crows, red-winged blackbirds, sparrows, and swifts—whipped past us as we crossed the field, kicking into the air insects and seeds with each swing of the scythe.

In the late afternoon, we took a break and sat beneath an oak tree, where we devoured some bread, sausage, cheese, and apple. We washed everything down with water before returning to work.

By dusk the air was cool and the sun glowed like molten iron as it dipped beneath the horizon, rapidly dimming. Patches of hilly clouds in darker hues of blue and purple drifted peacefully across the evening sky.

We continued working in the darkness when a Russian army truck pulled up to the edge of the field, its cloudy yellow headlights casting an eerie glow across the oat stubble. Over the past few months, we'd seen Russian trucks, tanks, and jeeps crossing the country roads periodically, but never had one stopped at our field.

Stanisław was maybe twenty meters ahead of me with his head down, swinging the scythe, slicing a path through the oats. He was oblivious to their presence until he reached the end of the field, where he turned to cut in the opposite direction. He saw them and paused for a moment, then resumed working, steadily chopping down the oats, crossing the field toward their truck.

Four soldiers with rifles slung over their shoulders waited for us. When we reached the end of the field, the commander held up his hand, motioning for Stanisław to halt. Stanisław ignored the commander and turned to cut down the oats in the opposite direction. I nervously followed him, gathering the oats and laying them in a windrow. I thought Stanisław was putting us in danger. Then the soldier hollered, "Stop!" I stopped, but Stanisław continued working, completely ignoring him. The soldier fired his rifle in the air. Stanisław paused and turned to face the commander, not moving an inch. His face was firm, his blue eyes cold and impenetrable. He waited for the soldiers to approach him. I stood a few steps behind him and feared that maybe these soldiers were looking for Jews, even though they were Russians.

My mind raced and heart thrummed as I considered what the options were. I contemplated making a run across the field to the tree line about two hundred meters away. It was dark and I could probably make it to the forest without getting shot and hide there until they left.

"What's your name?" the commander barked at Stanisław in Polish. He was Stanisław's height and had a walrus mustache and thick black face stubble, like Papa's. A dirty gray wool officer's cap shaded his heavy-lidded eyes.

Stanisław locked eyes with the commander and stared into his dull face with a look of disgust. "Stanisław Zelenski."

The commander pointed at me. "This is your son?"

"Nephew."

"What's your name?" the commander asked me.

"Jurek," said Stanisław. "He doesn't speak. He's mute."

"Is that true?" the commander asked me. "You're a mute?" He grinned mockingly, and the other soldiers chuckled. But Stanisław continued gazing into the commander's face with impassive eyes that were ready for battle. I was grateful for how Stanisław had protected me.

"What do you want?" said Stanisław. He watched the three other soldiers go to the cart and cut open the gunnysacks filled with the potatoes and beets that we harvested the day before and forgot to unload. "Get away from there!" Stanisław yelled at the soldiers. The commander punched him in the face. "Shut up, stupid *pshek!*"

Stanisław took the punch and grinned faintly, then head-butted the commander, knocking him to the ground. Shocked by Stanisław's action, I feared our end was near. Again, I considered running for the woods. But Stanisław displayed a sureness, a resolve, a sense of pride and determination that made me want to stand by him. To run would be cowardly, and I had already felt and acted a coward many times before. This time, I wanted to be like Stanisław. I owed him my allegiance and stood my ground alongside him.

The commander slowly rose to his feet, holding his bloodied nose. He took out his pistol and pressed it against Stanisław's forehead, then punched Stanisław in the face again with his free hand. Stanisław barely flinched as he took the punch, as if his jaw were made of iron. "Go on," said Stanisław, "shoot me."

In silence, the other three soldiers watched, eager to witness their commander's response. A jolt of fear rippled through me, followed by a strange stillness. I felt myself float outside my body and spiral above the treetops, like the hawk, where I looked down upon the scene. Nothing really matters, I thought. Whatever happens will happen. It was all beyond my control.

The commander hesitated, seeming to debate what he should do next. He cocked the trigger while continuing to press the barrel against Stanisław's forehead and held it there to see if Stanisław would flinch. He didn't. Then the commander fired.

The gunshot made me jump and shut my eyes. A terrible ringing echoed in my eardrums. I kept my eyes closed, not wanting to see Stanisław dead on the ground. I'd seen enough death. But when I opened my eyes, Stanisław was still standing in his footprints with the same resolute expression on his face. The commander had fired to the side of his head.

The commander and soldiers laughed, and then he ordered his men to take two gunnysacks of potatoes and beets and load them onto their truck. "The only reason I don't shoot you now is because we need you stupid *psheks* to provide food for our troops. But the next time you touch me or any of my men, I'll kill you." He shoved his pistol into Stanisław's chest, pushing him backward.

The soldiers loaded the gunnysacks into their truck and drove off.

"Russian rats," said Stanisław, spitting on the ground. "They think they better than us. Next time I'll have my gun and will shoot them all." He picked up the scythe and marched back to where he had stopped working. "We finish this field tonight and tomorrow cut wood to sell in town."

Despite Stanisław's many faults, there was much to admire in him. I was in awe of his toughness and courage in the face of danger. While some may have perceived him as reckless, I admired his bravery and fearlessness, as well as his ability to preserve his dignity and honor. I longed to possess those traits myself.

31

THE FOLLOWING DAY AT THE MARKET, I WORKED ON TOP OF THE wagon, tying bundles of wood while keeping an eye out for the young woman I thought was possibly Zelda. But she never appeared.

Although it would be risky, I planned to return to town that night once Kaja and Stanisław were asleep. I thought even if I didn't find Zelda, if I could find someone in town who was from Kraków, and then maybe I'd discover the whereabouts of her and her family.

We arrived at the farm early that evening. I washed my hands and face at the well, then returned to the shed. Stanisław met me there with a bowl of borscht and a thick slice of bread.

"We go to sleep early tonight," he said. "Tomorrow will be a long day harvesting the wheat and flaxseed." He returned to the house and had his dinner with Kaja and Lilli.

Later that night, once their lights were out and the house was quiet, I retrieved the bicycle from the back of the shed. Using a gunnysack, I cleaned off all the grime and oiled its rusty chain. The tires were flat. I searched the shed for a pump and found one buried beneath some hay and a pile of rope. After filling the tires with air, I checked for leaks. There were none. One pedal was broken, leaving only the peg sticking out from the crankshaft. But I could still pedal with my foot on the peg.

Before leaving, I debated once more if I should take the risk. I feared if they discovered my sneaking off, Stanisław would give

me a beating before banishing me from the farm. But my hunger
to find Zelda outweighed the risk.

I nervously walked the bike through the yard and headed to
the road, hoping not to rouse the animals. But Mendel grunted
loudly as I passed by him, and several of the geese squawked. I told
Mendel to be quiet and ordered the geese to do likewise.

"*Where are you going?*" asked Mendel.

"*To town to search for Zelda.*"

"*I wouldn't do that.*"

"*Why?*"

"*What if Kaja comes to visit you at night?*"

"*She hasn't in a while, so I don't think she will tonight.*"

"*You never know.*"

"*True. You never know.*" Mendel's thoughts gave me pause. But
I needed to do what I was doing, no matter the consequences.

"*You better be careful and get back here quickly,*" he warned.

On the road, I pedaled at full speed with my legs pumping up
and down like pistons. My moonlit shadow raced along the dirt
road beneath me. The damp cool air smelling of fresh hay and cut
grains filled my lungs—fear and excitement charged through me
like bolts of electricity. I'd never gone to town alone. For the first
time in many months, I felt free.

To my right stretched rolling farm fields. To my left were thick
woods. A wind rustled the trees. Cutting through the woods were
silhouettes of wolves moving in packs, long branches turned into
snakes. My eyes were playing tricks on me.

Then, in the distance surfaced the yellow headlamps of a Russian military truck barreling toward me. This was real. I swung off
the road and hid in the tallgrass along the embankment, listening
carefully as the truck approached. When the truck passed, drunken
soldiers were singing Russian songs with some women. I kept my
head low in the grass, only raising it when the singing grew distant.

Once again, it was quiet. It seemed safe to return to the road and continue onward.

In town, the streets were mostly empty. Several Russian soldiers patrolled the square. I cycled past a smoky tavern where more Russian soldiers and townspeople were drinking inside. A small-bearded man played the piano while a full-bodied blond-haired woman with a face round as a coin swayed among the men, singing folk songs in Russian, not Polish. Most of the soldiers sang along with her.

I located the street where the young woman resembling Zelda went missing. No one was around. I now realized the foolishness of thinking I could come to town late at night and locate her, or someone who knew where she was.

Across the square, I spotted two young Hasidic Jews sitting on a bench having a smoke and engaged in conversation. Maybe they were from Kraków. I wanted to approach them but felt some apprehension. I worried they'd become suspicious of my questions because of my goy appearance. Even if I spoke to them in Yiddish, they may not believe I'm a Jew. They may think I'm a spy for the Russians.

As I debated what to do, a Russian jeep drove down the street with two soldiers in it. I hid in the arched doorway of a building and watched them pass by. When they were gone, I came back out and saw the two young Hasidic men, one tall, the other short, walking away. I figured since I'd come all this way, I should try to speak to someone.

I rode up beside them, cleared my throat, and said hello in Yiddish. It was strange to hear my voice speaking to another person. It had been six months since I had spoken to anyone. They stopped and looked at me, surprised, as if I'd come from another planet. "Are you from Kraków?" I asked, continuing in Yiddish. They shook their heads. "Where are you from?" They looked at each other and hesitated.

"Why do you want to know?" asked the short one.

"I'm looking for a young woman I knew in Kraków. Zelda Abramovitch. Have you heard of her, or anyone with the family name?"

"No," said the taller one.

"What about Izzy? Izzy Stein?" I asked, remembering I'd seen a young man months ago who I thought might have been him.

"Never heard of him," said the shorter one. "Let's go," he said to his friend, hurrying away.

I rode down several more streets hoping to speak to another Jew. But no one was around. It was too late. Most people were in bed asleep. I sensed it was too risky to spend any more time in town, so I quickly rode back to the farm.

When I arrived, Mendel and the geese were asleep. I set the bicycle in the back of the shed and covered it with several gunny-sacks. Discouraged but not hopeless, I planned on returning to town another night when it wasn't so late.

32

A COUPLE OF DAYS LATER, KAJA AND LILLI RODE OUT TO THE OAT field with us. A warm wind blew in from the east. To the west, an ominous bank of mountainous dark clouds was building rapidly along the horizon. Stanisław worried the storm might damage the fields. "Hurry," he said. "Hail could be coming."

We rushed up and down the oat field, gathering the cut oats into bundles and tying them off with string before stacking them on the cart. Stanisław called them sheaves. Lilli made her own little sheaves and wrestled with the string and then got distracted by the worms she was finding in the dirt. Kaja was at the cart stacking the sheaves and when I handed her one, she gave me a strange look, as if she knew I had left the farm two nights before. Just as she was about to speak, Stanisław shouted for us to work faster. I dashed away and tied off more sheaves and noticed the wind picking up and the dark storm clouds in the west moving closer.

Once we finished the oat field, we moved to the smaller wheat field. Racing against the storm, Stanisław and I rushed up and down the field, whipping our scythes back and forth at double the normal speed. Kaja ran behind us, gathering the wheat into sheaves. She was much faster at it than I was.

The eerie sky above turned a dark gray-green; the winds abruptly shifted from east to west. An angry wall of dust sped toward us from the west as the wind whipped up and turned cool.

I wondered how the flaxseed, barley, and cornfields would survive the storm.

The wind threw dust in our eyes as lightning bolts flashed deep inside the massive black clouds. Heavy booms of thunder, sounding like bombs, echoed around us.

Lilli began crying and ran across the field to Kaja. Stanisław ordered all of us back to the wagon as the first drops of rain fell. From beneath the seat, he retrieved an oiled canvas tarp that we used to cover the sheaves of oats and wheat. We tied down the four corners to the wagon. Kaja and Lilli hid beneath the tarp while I sat next to Stanisław. The rain, winds, and thunder turned vicious.

Stanisław snapped the reins against Zissa's flanks. "Yah, yah!!!" he yelled, getting her to trot back to the yard fast as she could go.

He parked her by the horse shed and we all jumped off the wagon and ran carrying sheaves into the shed. The rain turned into a downpour followed by a rush of colder air, then hail. Frozen white marbles pelted our bodies, stinging our heads and backs as we hurriedly unloaded the last of the sheaves. When the cart was empty, Stanisław unharnessed Zissa and took her inside the shed. Lilli sat by the door collecting the ice balls, some large as wagon ball bearings, piling them into mounds and sucking on them.

We waited inside the shed together as the hail pummeled the roof and beat the ground. I worried the roof might collapse. Kaja helped Lilli sweep a pile of the hail balls into the shed so they could make piles of melting hail balls. Her golden hair was wet and pulled back behind her ears. Her soaked clothes clung to her body, revealing the smooth curves of her full breasts and sturdy hips. Our eyes made sure to never meet. I bit down on my lip while nervously pacing back and forth by the doorway, feeling trapped in such tight quarters with Kaja and Stanisław, the heavy weight of guilt pressing down on me as the hail kept pounding.

"Why are you pacing?" asked Stanisław. "Stop pacing."

I obeyed his command and stood still, crossing my arms tightly over my chest, squeezing my fists, counting the seconds to when we could get out of there.

After a couple of long minutes, the hailstorm's relentless pounding stopped, the winds gradually slowed, the rumbling thunder soon disappeared, and the rain turned to a soft patter.

Stanisław leaned against the edge of the doorframe, anxiously chewing on a wheat stalk, watching the storm slowly move past us, the dark clouds still churning, his face stern from worry about the remaining fields being destroyed by the hail.

Kaja started softly humming a song in a tender voice that soothed and comforted Lilli. Her singing reminded me of Zelda's singing and made me long for her. Kaja's eye caught me looking at her. In the dim light of the shed, her face appeared kind and inviting. Her low, gentle voice was seductive. In that moment when our eyes met, while missing Zelda, I hungered for Kaja, and forgot about Stanisław.

"Let's get to work," said Stanisław. "The rain stopped."

Holding Lilli's hand, Kaja went to the house to prepare dinner.

Stanisław lit a couple of kerosene lamps in the shed and showed me how to thresh the grains. In the warm lamplight, he whacked a bundle of oats against the edge of a large tin bucket, separating the seeds from the shaft. Once the bucket was half full of seed, he stirred them with his thick hands, loosening the chaff from the seeds. He then handed me a fan made of a large piece of cloth stretched between two sticks. As he poured the seeds from one bucket to another, I fanned them, sending clouds of chaff in the air that floated like snow through the lamplight.

He told me a story about what happened one night when he and his father were threshing grains. "We were threshing just like you and me now," he said. "I was eight years old. He told me to wait while he went inside the house to get more gunnysacks and when he left, I took some wheat and put it in the lamp to watch it burn. It caught fire fast and I stumbled backward and knocked over another lamp and it spills kerosene on the floor and catches fire." He started laughing.

"The wheat and hay catch fire and I go running from the shed screaming and my father comes running out the house and calls for my mama and big brother to help him put out the fire. Everyone screams and grabs buckets of water from the well. I know my father is going to beat me for setting the fire. While they're putting out the fire I run to the forest and hide there for two nights. On the third night I come back and sneak into the house because I'm so hungry and thirsty. My father catches me stealing some bread and apples and slaps me. He takes his whip and is about to whip me but Mama comes running out their room and stops him. He had a bad temper. He was crazy. I never will beat my children with a whip. A slap is enough. I apologized to him. He says to repay him for everything that burned, I must thresh the wheat, oats, and flaxseed by myself, without stopping, until it is all finished.

"He and my brother harvested the fields and I threshed all day and all night. If he caught me sleeping, he slaps me awake. Mama gave me meals in the shed. It took a week to finish it all. After, I wanted to leave soon as I was grown enough.

"At twelve, I run away to work on other farms and save money. At twenty, I bought the house and land—four hectares. Now I have eight. With you working, I can soon buy another five hectares."

He poured the bucket of oat seed into a gunnysack that I held open, then grabbed another sheaf of oats and began threshing them on the bucket's rim. "I always hated my papa. Such a mean sonofabitch."

His story made me long for my father. His gentleness, which I so often interpreted as weakness, now seemed more of an asset than a deficit. Yes, Papa compromised too quickly, and physically was not strong. But in his gentleness and sensitivity, in his willingness to sacrifice his own desires and needs to make another person happy, in his kindness toward others, he was one of the strongest men I knew. This was something I never appreciated, nor understood while growing up.

Plus, Papa's other strength was being a mensch, a man of integrity. This was something else I could be proud of and aspire toward, yet something I fell short of achieving. In this time of loneliness and loss, I had traded honesty for deception, integrity for betrayal. Papa would have disapproved and been disappointed in me. And he would be right. In this situation, I was the weak one.

THAT NIGHT I COULDN'T SLEEP AND WANTED TO RETURN TO town. I slipped on my pants and was about to leave when the shed door abruptly creaked opened. Kaja stared at me oddly. I was stunned to see her after thinking it was over.

"Where are you going?" she asked.

"Nowhere," I was about to reply. But I caught my tongue and remained silent. She sat down next to me and removed my pants. I felt myself tumble into another river of confusion. Although this was all wrong, I didn't stop it.

She caressed my face, as if exploring it for the first time, then straddled me and massaged my chest and shoulders with her rough, calloused hands. Whatever thoughts I had for ending our betrayal, whatever fears I had about Stanisław discovering us, I carelessly cast them aside as I immediately fell under the spell of her wanting touch.

She laid her head on my breastbone and listened to my heart-beat as she stroked my face and chest. Her silky hair brushed against my lips. She had washed it. It carried the scent of rose oil. My hands automatically embraced her, freely exploring the land-scape of her body, its smooth curves and folds. I felt like we were lovers reuniting after a lengthy separation.

Her soft lips gently pressed against mine, warm and moist. It was our first kiss. She tasted of tea and sugar. I was aroused and throbbing. Our fingers intertwined. She was so tender it frightened me. The emptiness inside my heart, the melancholy that had made its home inside me, the constant numbness—it was all draining away. I felt alive again. Alive!

She opened her thighs as I caressed her full breasts, her nip-ples hardening beneath my fingertips, and I went inside her. Our bodies merged. She swayed back and forth on top of me like the branches of a willow thrusting in gusts of wind. There was no holding back. She told me to release inside her this time. Her fingernails dug into my shoulders. I let go. Her head whipped back and her body arched. She gasped for air, her fingernails digging deep into my flesh . . . and she let go.

The electrified air swirling around us went still as she slowly lowered herself down and settled beside me. Our breaths fell into a slow, steady rhythm while our tired limbs rested against one another, relaxed. She draped her weighty thigh across my waist and gripped my hand. With her other hand, she turned my face toward her and stared into my eyes. Her soft gaze had turned hard and suspicious, as if she were trying to read my thoughts. Her moist pink lips were now dark and thin, her eye-brows furrowed with questions.

"Where did you go two nights ago?" she asked. "Did you go to town? Maybe you have a girlfriend? Do you have a girlfriend?" I shook my head. "Then where did you go?" I wondered if Stanisław also knew I had left. But if he knew, he would've said something already. "Maybe you spy on us?" I kept shaking my head, looking at her in confusion, thrown off guard by this sudden shift in the mood.

She pulled her hand away as her voice shifted from being warm and tender to cold and angry. She sat up. "Are you lying? You *Żyds* all lie. Are you lying?" I shook my head again and she slapped me. "Don't lie to Kaja!" she whispered. "I will get rid of you if you lie." The slap was a shock, a stinging rejection.

She lay back down next to me and kissed my cheek where she had slapped me. "I'm sorry," she said in a tender tone that sounded sincere. "I didn't mean to hurt you." Now completely confused, unsure of what to trust, I just wanted her to leave. "Please don't go again," she requested. She gently combed her fingers through my hair. "Promise me."

Her pleading words and sudden shift in demeanor sent chills through me. I nodded in agreement to appease her, knowing inside I had promised her nothing. She was seductive and unpredictable. And I was a lonely, lost, desperate fool in need of her affection and sexual desire, no matter how immoral it was, and how dangerous.

But now I truly wanted it to end. It must end. Her impetuousness, and my pathetic weakness, was leading us toward disaster. Stanisław would eventually catch us and kill either me or both of us.

It was now clear; I had to leave the farm as soon as possible, before it was too late. But where to go? I wasn't sure. And winter had arrived. To travel through winter would be reckless, and perilous.

33

FROM NOVEMBER TO FEBRUARY, AS THE YEAR TURNED FROM '40 to '41, winter frosted the land with ice and snow. At night, the bone-chilling winds cut through the shed's walls, penetrating my blankets and clothes. Fortunately, Stanisław and I had sealed most of the walls' cracks and gaps with a mixture of mud, clay, and straw. We did the same for Mendel, Sima, Bima, and Lipa's shed, the chicken shed, and Zissa and Esther's shed.

One night, Lipa the goat and two of the chickens, Silvia and Masha, didn't get back to their sheds in time to protect themselves from the extreme drop in temperature. They all froze to death. Mendel knew how to stay warm inside his shed by burrowing beneath a mountain of hay that Stanisław had given him. Sima and Bima had their thick wool coats to keep them warm.

I kept myself barely warm enough to sleep by heating two tin buckets of rocks on the iron stove inside the house, then placing them next to my hay mattress and beneath my blankets. One bucket was by my feet, the other near my chest. I never complained to Stanisław about the cold. He would've laughed if I had.

Stanisław and I worked hard through the winter. Every morning we went to the forest wearing our heavy wool coats and wool pants and thick leather gloves to protect us from the biting cold. We cut down oaks, elms, and pines with the double saw, trimmed them with the single saws, chopped them into firewood with our axes. Some of the wood we brought back to the farm and the rest we sold in town. "Come spring," he said, "I'll buy more land, another cow, two sheep, and a few pigs."

We hunted deer with his rifles and captured rabbits and squirrels in wood traps he taught me how to build. He showed me how to skin, gut, and cook them on a stick over a wood fire, or fry them in a pan with lard. One day a week we'd go to the frozen pond and pound a hole through the ice with the pickax and drop a line with some worm bait on it and catch brown trout. At night we'd sometimes go to the river where the trees hid us from the Germans on the other side and we'd catch large-mouth bass.

In preparation for planting in the spring, Stanisław showed me how to repair the cracked wooden supports on the plow that attached to Zissa's harness. He taught me how to replace the broken spiked teeth on the harrow, repair the splintered spokes on the wheels of the horse cart, grease the axle and all the ball bearings. He treated me like a son who would one day take over the farm, and I thought of him as a father.

DAY IN AND DAY OUT, A LOW BLANKET OF GRAY SKY HUNG over the snow-covered fields speckled with bare trees stripped of all their color. During these frigid winter months, my inner world mirrored the outer world. It, too, was colorless, stark, and forbidding.

While selling firewood in town, I never saw the young lady with copper-red hair again. In fact, I began questioning if I'd even seen her some months before. I wondered if I had concocted the image from the dire hopes of my imagination. I was giving up on finding Zelda.

I worked, ate, slept, and twice Kaja visited me just before spring arrived. The first time she was drunk. I tried rebuking her advances by pretending I was ill. But she didn't care. She told me Stanisław got so drunk that he passed out and so it was safe. But I no longer wanted her or trusted anything she said. She was too dangerous, too strange, and unpredictable.

Undeterred by my charade of feigning illness, she fondled my sex, trying to arouse me, but nothing happened this time—my body was numb. I had retreated to a shelter deep inside myself.

She sidled next to me, placing my hands on her breasts, whispering in her vodka breath how she longed to have me inside her. I pushed her away. She threatened to scream. I froze. She kissed my cheeks and nipped at my ears, and then gently glided her lips and tongue across my body. My mind protested, yet my body, once again, surrendered to her determined advance. I clenched her shoulders as she drove her hips hard into mine, our knees and toes digging and grinding into the dry hay and dirt. Her smooth back, slick with sweat, shimmered in the dim light as the humid air thickened with the pungent odors of our bodies. A strange, feverish craving, buried deep inside me, unleashed itself. We grunted like animals, moaned from the caverns of our long-buried pain. We got lost in the hollows of our desires, our yearnings and fears, laments and humiliations. . . . Raging through my limbs flowed a bitter loathing for her, for myself, for everything that had transpired between us.

She finally released a last gasp, and I finally let go. Through the anguished longings of our bodies, we had succumbed to each other's aching loneliness. And now, it was finally over.

The second night she came to visit me, I shoved her out of the shed. Kaja was physically strong. But I was stronger. She came at me with her fists. But I caught them and pushed her to the ground. She gazed up at me with bloodshot eyes wet with rage as I stood my ground. When she got to her feet, she called me a dirty Żyd and spat on me. It didn't bother me. I had finally stood my ground, taken control, and put a stop to defiling myself. Whatever the consequences would be, I was ready to face them.

3 4

IN THE FOLLOWING DAYS, I WAITED FOR KAJA'S REVENGE IN response to my rejection of her last advance. But nothing happened. She simply went back to ignoring my existence, as she'd done before. Maybe she needed more time to develop her plan for my demise. Or maybe she simply no longer wanted me, which was hopefully the case. All I knew was that I was eager to leave the farm as soon as possible. I just needed to wait for the weather to change.

In the following weeks, the warm sun and rains of spring melted the ice and snow blanketing the fields, revealing the farmland's rich black soil that awaited plowing and planting.

I wanted to search for Zelda in town one more time, or try to find someone who knew her family's whereabouts. If I came up empty, I'd leave for Kraków in the coming days and search for her there.

The next morning, Zissa dug her hooves into the mushy black soil as she dragged the big iron plow behind her. Stanisław threw his weight and muscles against the plow, pushing and guiding it, wrestling with it to stay upright and run a straight line down the field. The sharp edge of the rusty plow cut through the dense, moist soil like the bow of a ship breaking across the sea. I followed Stanisław up and down the fields, picking up each stone unearthed, working hard to keep pace with him. I tossed stone after stone after stone into the rickety wooden wheelbarrow that Stanisław had built years ago, then piled them into small mounds at the edge of the field. Some would be used for building walls, others would be left behind.

We finished work early and got back to the farm before the blood-orange sun dipped beneath the trees. I was removing Zissa's harness when Stanisław came barreling out of the house with a bottle of vodka and two small glasses. "Good news," he said, slapping me on the back. "Kaja is pregnant. She's sick in bed and I know it's a boy this time from the way she's acting." I feigned a smile and grabbed Stanisław's hand to congratulate him as a wave of nausea went through me. He poured us each a glass and toasted the new baby, clinking his glass against mine, swilling it all down in one gulp before pouring himself another. "Drink!" he said. "In honor of my boy!" Barely able to look him in the eye, I felt my face flush with the shame and guilt that accompanies betrayal. I brought the glass to my lips and guzzled it down. My guts were in knots. I kept telling myself the baby wasn't mine. But in truth, it could've been. Fortunately, I'd be gone by the time of its birth, so I'd never have to know.

35

THAT NIGHT, I RETURNED TO TOWN TO SEARCH FOR ZELDA, OR at least find someone who knew her. With Kaja sick in bed, I knew she wouldn't come to see me. And even though the long day of clearing the fields of stone had taken its toll on me, my renewed sense of determination had rejuvenated me.

I entered town and crossed the square on my bicycle, where people were taking evening walks. Sitting on the bench by the bear fountain, four Russian soldiers smoked cigarettes and played cards. I turned down a side street to avoid them and went to the apartment building where I'd seen the young man who looked like Big Izzy go inside. If it really was him, I thought maybe he'd know something about Zelda and her family.

I moved my bicycle inside the arched doorway and stood at the foot of the stairs, wondering what to do next. There were three floors and four apartments on each floor, which meant there were twelve apartments whose doors I'd have to knock on until I found him. But I wanted to avoid interacting with that many people. I debated what to do. Then an old man entered the building wearing a *shtreimel*, the tall fur hat of the Hasidim. His thick beard was long and white and he carried a small brown paper package tucked beneath his arm. I greeted the man in Yiddish. His heavy white eyebrows, unruly as wild vines, jumped over his wire-rimmed glasses in astonishment. *"Redstu eydish?"* he asked. "Yes," I said, letting him know I speak Yiddish. He leaned in closer to examine my face and looked deep into my eyes, as if he was searching for a sign. *"Du bist a id?"*

"Yes."

The old man looked at me shrewdly. "But you don't look like a Jew."

"Ikh bin a id! Do you want to see my *schmeckle?"* I responded, threatening to unzip my pants.

The old man stepped back, gazing at me suspiciously. *"Fun vanen bistu?"*

"Kraków. Kazimierz, 28 Nowa Street. I went to synagogue and the mikvah on Szeroka Street and the cheder on Józefa. My father, Lev Berkovitz, owned the umbrella shop at Zgody Square. Berkovitz Custom Umbrellas."

His face immediately lit up and his thicket of white eyebrows jumped over his glasses again; his mouth curved into a welcoming grin. "That was your father's store?"

"Yes."

He pointed to his temple. "I know it! Ach—such beautiful umbrellas. The handles. Never I saw such beautifully carved handles. I wanted one of your custom umbrellas but could never afford it. They were for people with money, not a poor man like me." He chuckled to himself. "So, what is your name?"

"Reuven."

"Reuven Berkovitz, the umbrella maker's son. I'm Yitzhak Heschel. And where are you and your family living now?"

I ignored his question. "I'm here looking for Izzy Stein. I knew him from Kraków. Is he living here?"

The old man's thoughts still clung to his question. He gazed deep into my eyes and moved in uncomfortably close to me. I smelled the wool of his black frock and the pickled herring on his breath. Tea stains marked his gray mustache and beard, like

Khone, and Zelda's father. His breath was heavy and labored. "Where is your family?" he repeated.

The man intruded into a private place where he wasn't welcome. A wall of resentment arose inside my chest. "I just need to know if Izzy Stein is here."

The old man nodded, his smile evaporated, his face became solemn. He knew something terrible had happened to my family. "I live right here with my wife," he said, pointing to the door behind me. "Would you like to come in for a bowl of soup?"

"No, thank you. I don't have time. Just tell me if you know Izzy Stein."

The old man stroked his long gray beard. "Stein?"

"Yes, Stein."

"There was a Stein here."

"Izzy?"

"A father and son. I don't know their first names. But they left a few days ago and I don't know where to. I never spoke to them. They kept to themselves. Trust me, I know every family in this building. I know the Mirowitzes, Grinbands, Szlajfers, Adlers, Bergels . . ."

"What about the Abramovitches? Are they here?"

"Yosef and Masha Abramovitch?"

"Yes!"

"Yosef and his wife used to repair and alter our clothes back in Kraków. Such a good family. And Yosef is such a mensch. And their daughter, Zelda, such a beauty and so . . ."

"Yes—but are they here in Przemyśl!?" I was losing my patience.

"I don't believe so. I would know if they were here. The last time I saw them was before the wall was finished. Yosef was very ill and Masha was depressed. Now with the wall . . . it's almost

impossible for people to escape. Especially old people like ourselves. Maybe they left before the wall was finished? I don't know."

"What wall?"

"The ghetto wall. You don't know about the wall?"

"No."

"How long have you been here?"

"A year."

"Ach—a year. So much has happened! You have no idea."

"I've been working on a farm. I know nothing about the war
except it continues."

"They finished building the wall just a few months ago, in
March. It's a *broch*—a *shanda*! A curse and disgrace no one can
comprehend. Not even God. A bloody prison the Germans call
a 'ghetto'—a *Juden Ghetto*.' Just like the one in Warsaw."

"How did you escape?"

"My family was one of the last to leave before they finished
construction. How we escaped is too long of a story for now.
But I can tell you we heard from some people the conditions are
now unbearable. People in the ghetto are going hungry and there's
typhus and because they can't leave, they must buy their food in
the black market inside the ghetto where the costs are three times
higher than the food in the markets outside the ghetto. They say
electricity goes out for long periods and toilets don't flush and garbage doesn't get collected and the Germans have forced Jews to
spy on Jews if they want to survive. They said a council of Jewish
elders called the *Judenrat* work for the Germans spying on people
and reporting resistance activity and it's the same with the Jewish
police force, the *Ordnungsdienst*, they're called. They spy and take
bribes and steal and sometimes even take advantage of women.
This is what I've heard—my hand to God! The Germans have
made the Kraków ghetto a hellish place for the Jews."

"Do you know if the Abramovitch family is still there?"

"It's possible. But I have no idea."

The old man pursed his lips and his heavy-lidded eyes turned grim. "I can see you want to go there to find them. Trust me. Wait. Don't go back there now. It's too dangerous to travel there. And Kraków itself . . . Kraków . . ." His words got stuck in his throat. He looked down and shook his head in disbelief, unable to finish his sentence. His eyes welled with tears. He placed his hand on mine and took a deep breath as he tried to gather himself. "Wait till the end of the war, then go search for them," he said. "Don't go now. Trust me. Don't go now."

I thanked him for speaking to me and turned to leave.

"Please," said the old man, taking hold of my arm, trying to guide me to his door. "Before you go. Come. Come inside for a bowl of soup and meet my wife. You would like her and she would like you."

"I appreciate your offer, but I must get back to the farm before they discover I'm gone." I reached into the gunnysack and offered him three potatoes and three carrots.

"No," said the old man. "I appreciate your mitzvah, but you keep it."

He tried pushing the potatoes and carrots away, but I stuffed them in the pockets of his frock. "They're for you and your wife."

"You're too kind—a mensch, like Yosef. Are you sure you won't come in for a bowl of soup?"

"Thank you, but I must go." I rolled my bicycle out onto the street.

"*Zei gezunt*—be well" were the old man's last words as I rode off.

While heading back down the winding dirt road to the farm, I made my final decision to leave the next evening for Kraków. I'd get there by stowing away on a freight train that headed west through Przemyśl at night.

THE FOLLOWING MORNING, IN THE COOL GLOW OF FIRST LIGHT, Stanisław showed up at my shed holding a long butcher's knife. I thought it was all over. Kaja must have told him I had raped her, as she had threatened to do when she had first forced herself on me. Stanisław towered over me with the knife gripped in his thick hands. "Come on," he said. "Follow me."

I figured he was taking me to a field, or some place in the woods near the farmhouse where he would stab me to death. My legs felt wobbly as we crossed the yard. I prepared to make a run through the forest, hoping the thick brush and dense trees would serve as obstacles to help me escape. But instead of going to the forest, he crossed the yard and headed off to the pen where Mendel was going about his business eating some hay, bits of old corn feed speckling the ground, and new blades of grass. "Tonight, we celebrate the baby with a meal of Kaja's pork stew!"

I immediately felt sick. This couldn't be happening. Mendel looked up and caught the flash of the killer in Stanisław's eyes. "*Run, Mendel!*" I thought. He took off for the farthest end of the pen and started grunting and squealing in terror. Stanisław sprinted after him and tried cornering him against the fence poles, but Mendel made a dash between Stanisław's legs and sprinted to the other end of the pen, in my direction.

"Get in here and stop him!" hollered Stanisław as he chased after him. I stood motionless, ignoring his order. Stanisław continued chasing after Mendel around the pen in circles and was becoming increasingly frustrated. He dove after him twice and came up empty-handed each time. Mud and manure splattered the front of his shirt and pants, and clumps of dirt hung from his chin. "What the hell is wrong with you?!" he yelled at me. "Get in here and cut him off!"

I told Mendel to keep running, but he was tiring out. His grunts and squeals pierced the air like the shrieks of a terrified child. Then Stanisław trapped Mendel in the corner again and this time landed on top of him. He straddled Mendel's ribs with all his weight as Mendel squirmed frantically beneath him, releasing even more horrific high-pitched whines and squeals as his hooves kicked frantically in the air. Stanisław swept the knife across Mendel's throat; blood spurted everywhere. I turned away, gagging, and headed toward the woods. It was too overwhelming.

"Where are you going, Jurek?! He's just a pig! A stupid pig! Now get back here and help put him in the wheelbarrow."

I ignored him and continued to walk away. Suddenly, he came up from behind and shoved me to the ground. "Do what I say, boy!" Something inside me snapped. I wanted to kill him. I didn't care what would happen to me. Jumping to my feet, I tackled Stanisław to the ground and punched him in the face. He grabbed hold of my arms and threw me off him, rolled on top of me, pinned me down between his legs, like he did with Mendel, and landed a punch to my face. I squirmed out from beneath him and tried putting him in a headlock. He stripped my arms off his neck, spun round, and threw a headbutt. Everything went black.

When I awoke, he was already loading Mendel's dead body into the wheelbarrow. My nose felt broken, and I tasted blood in my mouth. Before Stanisław wheeled Mendel away, he turned and looked at me over his shoulder. "Go wash the blood off your face. We're going out to the fields once I put him on the spit."

At the well, I washed the blood and dirt off my face and hands. My head and nose ached terribly from the headbutt and my cheek had swelled from the punch. But the aches and pains were worth it. I mourned the loss of Mendel, yet found some dignity in holding my ground.

When I returned to the shed, Mendel was hanging upside down from a rope tied to one branch of the oak tree. A hook at the end of the rope went through Mendel's right shank. Stanisław was gutting and cleaning him.

I went inside the shed, lay down on my hay mattress, and recited the kaddish for Mendel. I thanked him for his company, then completed my plans for leaving the farm that evening.

About an hour later, the smell of roasting meat filled the air. I stepped out from the shed and spotted Stanisław tending the fire pit behind the house. Mendel turned on a spit suspended over a fire and hot coals. I imagined his spirit spun in the black smoke above him, carried away by the north wind to some other world.

Kaja exited the house and took over roasting Mendel so Stanisław and I could go to the fields and plant. He said something to her that made her laugh and she glanced over at me for a second, appearing cold and malicious, before turning away. He had probably told her about my reaction to Mendel being killed. Then he came to the shed and ordered me to load the cart with gunnysacks of oat, wheat, and flaxseed for planting.

We were silent as Zissa took us to the fields. When we stopped at the edge of the first field, we each grabbed a gunnysack of wheat seed and walked up and down the plowed rows lugging the gunnysacks across our shoulders, sprinkling handfuls of the seed along the furrows. We then covered the seeds with dirt and pressed them down into the soil with our boots, trying to protect them from the crows and blackbirds that took pleasure in poaching them.

By noon, we finished planting and took a break to eat lunch in the shade of an oak. The fields were serene, the sky a clear deep blue. Wrens and swifts swooped past us catching mayflies and gnats. A hawk circled on the air currents high above. Stanisław offered me some bread, sausage, and cheese, but I turned it away. I wasn't hungry. "What? You don't eat?" he said. I nodded. He shrugged. "Suit yourself."

During those moments when we ate in the quiet of the fields, I'd always felt an unspoken comradery with Stanisław that we shared through work. But now I loathed him for killing Mendel. I flashed back on the knife I'd driven through Schlöndorff—a memory that felt as though it belonged to someone else's life. He had deserved it. He had beaten the old man to death and would've killed Papa and me if he had the chance. The stabbing was justified. But Mendel was innocent. He didn't deserve to have his throat slit, even if Stanisław had raised him for slaughter.

Stanisław drank some water and handed me the bottle when, from out of nowhere, three Russian planes blasted over the tree line heading west toward town. We watched them soar over us. Moments later, bombs exploded in the distance. Stanisław pointed east, where furious clouds of brown dust swirled above the dirt road. "Russian army!" he yelled. A convoy of Russian jeeps, trucks, and tanks appeared on the road, also speeding toward town.

"Not good," said Stanisław. "Germans are attacking again." He spat in disgust. "I hope Russians and Germans kill each other."

We continued working the fields, finishing the planting of flaxseed, wheat, and oats. Explosions echoed in the direction of Przemyśl.

By evening, long lines of Russian convoys steadily moving toward the border packed the roads. Hordes of people from town also packed the roads going in the opposite direction, toward the east, with whatever belongings they could carry in their wagons, horse carts, trucks, and cars. It was Kraków all over again. However, the numbers of explosions were much greater than what we experienced in Kraków. I wondered if the Germans were attacking only Przemyśl, or also other towns along the border. I learned later it was the entire border—a massive attack.

During the first two days of the siege, the Russian troops held the Germans from crossing the river. But on the third day, the battle shifted. From the fields we saw the Russian convoys hastily retreating, heading east, back into Russia. The Russian planes flying over us had disappeared, the bombings had stopped, the skies were now empty. Clearly, the Germans were winning the battle. They were now crossing the river in masses while continuing their attack to the east.

From the fields we saw German convoys of trucks, jeeps, tanks, and artillery equipment heading to the Russian border, stretching across the dirt roads like one long, endless freight train. Clouds of yellow dust hung over the roads and fields. Their menacing engines rumbled from day into night and back into day, like a factory that never shuts down. It was terrifying to see the iron crosses again painted on the sides of their vehicles, the black swastikas on their bright red flags. Stanisław said he heard from another farmer that the Germans were overtaking eastern Poland and preparing to conquer Russia.

My plans to leave would have to be postponed until the fighting settled down. To leave now would be suicide. The freight trains had stopped running, and the German army controlled all the roads. I needed to be patient.

37

A FEW DAYS LATER, STANISŁAW AND I HAD BEEN WORKING IN the woods all day cutting firewood when it became clear the German attack was succeeding. Another farmer we met in the woods informed us the Russians had fully retreated from Przemyśl and were now being pushed farther east, into Russia. He told us the attack had been massive, stretching along the entire German-Russian border. He said the roads were clear to the west and the freight trains were running again. In the evening, I would leave.

When Stanisław and I returned to the farm at dusk, we pulled into the yard and noticed the open gate to the sheep and goat pen. Sima and Bima the sheep were missing along with Esther the cow. Mendel was also gone from the spit.

Stanisław had me unhitch Zissa and put her in the horse shed while he went to check on the other animals. As he crossed the yard, Kaja came out of the house, strolling toward him in a trance-like state. Her blue dress was torn open and bloodied, and a large purplish bruise the color of a ripe plum marred the side of her face. She cradled a bloody sheet in her hands that had a small, whitish-blue fleshy object inside it.

Lilli came running out of the house crying uncontrollably and grabbed hold of Kaja's ragged dress. Stanisław ran up to Kaja and held her as she weakly leaned against him. He took the sheet from Kaja and examined the fleshy object and howled in pain like a wounded coyote. Lilli clung to Stanisław's right leg, wailing. He lifted her up and held her in one arm while he placed his other arm round Kaja's shoulders and led her back to the house.

While Stanisław tended to Kaja, I walked in a daze, shocked and confused by the scene, searching for Sima and Bima in their shed. But they were nowhere to be found. In the chicken coop, attached to Sima and Bima's shed, I found Moses lying in a pool of blood with his chopped-off head placed on top of a bucket used for storing grains. The two chickens—Gola and Mazal— were also missing, their blood spattered across the hay and dirt floor, and bloody white feathers scattered everywhere. Smeared across the walls of the chicken coop was a swastika painted with blood.

When I exited the chicken coop and walked to the back of the yard where the well was located, I found Esther lying dead in the grass with her throat and belly slit and guts spilling out. Another swastika painted with her blood marked the wall of the well.

The carnage was agonizing. I returned to my shed and tried to comprehend the horror of what had happened to Kaja. Most likely, they had raped her, which had caused her to miscarry. The thought was horrific. No matter what kinds of misgivings I had about Kaja, to think of her being abused in such a brutal, inhuman way turned my stomach into knots. How terrifying for her. And poor Lilli. God knows what she had witnessed. And yet at the same moment, I also feared Kaja blaming me for this situation. I worried she might try to convince Stanisław that the Germans came to their farm because they knew a Jew was here. Or maybe she believed the baby inside her was mine—another *Żyd* devil with horns—and that the baby, or I, had cast a curse on her that resulted in this tragedy. Or maybe her superstitions led her to believe I had used evil magic to make the Germans punish her. In her twisted thinking about Jews, there were many ways she could point the finger and blame me for this tragedy.

It was time to run. I filled a gunnysack with a bottle of water and some bread and cheese that I had saved. In Zissa's shed, I grabbed some carrots and sausages that were stored in a wood food box submerged beneath the ground and then returned to my shed for the bicycle.

While retrieving the bicycle, the door behind me creaked open. Spinning round, I saw Kaja standing at the door with a pitchfork in her hand and the sharp tines pointed at me. She screamed and lunged, driving the tines toward my chest. I jumped to the side, dodging the tines. She jabbed at me again, trapping me in the corner of the shed. "You did this! You killed my baby!" She stabbed wildly in the darkness and then lunged at me again, but this time I stepped to the side and slid past her. I ran out the door and tripped, falling on the ground. She came after me, thrusting the pitchfork into the dirt centimeters away. I scrambled to my feet and kept running toward the chicken coop. She gave chase but then collapsed by the tree.

Stanisław burst out of the house and collected her in his arms as she sobbed and pointed to where I stood. "He did this! The dirty Żyd brought the Germans here. He killed our baby," she hollered. "Kill him. You must kill him!"

"Stop it!" yelled Stanisław. He motioned for me to return to the shed so I'd be out of her sight. But rather than immediately turn his attention back to Kaja, he held me a moment longer in those knowing, translucent blue eyes of his, appearing to acknowledge that the time had come for me to leave the farm.

From behind the shed door, I watched as he continued talking to Kaja, trying to calm her. She then fell unconscious. He lifted her in his arms and carried her back to the house.

As soon as Stanisław entered the farmhouse and closed the door behind him, I knew he had said goodbye to me for good. He didn't need to look back.

With a heavy heart, I pulled the bicycle out of the shed, threw the gunnysack over my shoulder, and rode away from the farm, now focused on nothing else but finding my Zelda.

3 8

HALFWAY DOWN THE ROAD TO PRZEMYŚL, THE SKY ALONG THE
eastern horizon began glowing a deep blue as daylight approached.
I left the road and snuck deep into the woods. There I would hide
the entire day until darkness fell again.

In the woods I found a small stream running through the
trees where minnows swam between the smooth gray-, brown-,
and copper-colored rocks lining its bed. The water was cold
and clean. Cupping it in my hands, I washed my face and filled
my bottle and then lay down on a bed of pine needles next to the
stream and listened to its steady burbling. Riding over the tall
pines were wisps of golden clouds, shaped like sickles suspended
in the sky. Crows cawed to each other from the treetops, bickering
as if engaged in a debate, reminding me of the Hasidim in Kraków,
who gathered on street corners to discuss and argue Talmudic
interpretations, politics, business—and to gossip. I wondered
how many of the Hasidim were still in Kraków, and if they still
debated on the street corners inside the ghetto. I couldn't fathom
life's current conditions there.

The crows soon dispersed, leaving the forest quiet and
tranquil. The stream burbled softly next to me, and the gentle
wind murmured through the pine branches, calming my frayed
nerves and lulling me to sleep.

Some hours later, in the darkness of night, the low rumble
of a vehicle coming in my direction jarred me awake. I'd lost track

of the time and worried I'd missed the train. I grabbed my bicycle and was about to run it back to the road when I saw a yellow blade of light slicing through the woods. It was the same type of searchlight I'd seen by the river during the massacre. My heart wanted to leap out of my chest as my entire body trembled. It was hard to breathe.

Coming slowly down a small dirt road I hadn't seen, a jeep scanned the woods with its searchlight. I lay flat on the ground as it approached from about twenty-five meters away. They were close enough for me to hear the faint sounds of the soldiers speaking German. The harsh yellow light slowly swung back and forth across the trees like a scythe. I lay flat on my stomach, perfectly still as the light beam swung over me.

When the jeep finally passed and was far enough away, I grabbed my gunnysack and started running through the forest to Przemyśl rather than riding the bicycle. I was certain the road would be too dangerous because of checkpoints.

By the time I got to Przemyśl, it was many hours past midnight and I knew I'd missed the train. The streets were eerily quiet and dark clouds covered the dawn sky, producing a dull gray light that drained the town of all its color. The damage to buildings from the bombs and shootings was sporadic. Some buildings were untouched, while others were pockmarked by bullets and shrapnel, burnt out and half-standing, or reduced to rubble from shelling and bombs. Clothing and furniture lay scattered among the piles of bricks and stones.

German jeeps, trucks, and shiny black sedans with small Nazi flags mounted on their bold, sweeping fenders had parked in various spots along the main street. Nazi flags hung like funeral curtains from many of the government buildings. I turned a corner and almost bumped into two German soldiers on patrol. One of them gave me a kick in the rear and yelled, *"Dummkopf tschusch!*" I put my head down, relieved he identified me as merely a poor Slav peasant, and not a Jew.

I passed the building where the old man who reminded me of Khone lived. Only the front of the building remained, the rest of it destroyed by shelling and fire. I avoided looking at the rubble in fear of seeing the dead bodies of the old man and his wife. It was best to not know their fate.

I WAS CERTAIN THE GERMANS HAD DESTROYED THE OLD SYNA-
gogue, but to my astonishment, it was still standing. Its enormous
limestone walls, already scarred from Germany's attack at the start
of the war, were now further damaged by more shrapnel and bullets.
Its two huge front doors made of oak, tall and arched, were barred
shut with wood beams nailed securely to the doors. I decided to hide
here until night, when I would jump on the next train. At the rear of
the building, I found a broken window to crawl through.

Inside the room were the remnants of charred desks and chairs,
a small oriental wool carpet covered in ash and half-burned. Most
likely, it was the rabbi's office. From there, I wandered into the expansive main hall where the congregants, maybe two to three hundred, came for service. Among the burnt and broken benches was a
wood bench that was still intact. I lay down on it, using my gunnysack as a pillow, and stared up at the ceiling where there was a hole
that a bombshell must've made. A column of gray light beamed down
through the hole, dimly illuminating the inside of the synagogue.

A few hours later thunder rumbled in the distance and rain-
drops began falling through the column of light, forming puddles
on the old wood floor. I went to one of the broken windows that
looked out onto the main square and watched the peasants at
the market hurriedly packing their food baskets as the rainfall
increased. I recognized some peasants. One of them, Muniek,
had a farm near Stanisław's. He looked haggard and scared as he

packed his baskets of potatoes and beets. While loading them onto his wagon, a German soldier walked past him and took a few potatoes without offering to pay. Muniek said nothing.

More German police and soldiers patrolled the market. The Jewish men, women, and children now wore the Star of David armbands again as they walked through the market with weariness and defeat imprinted on their melancholy faces. It was like watching an old newsreel of Kraków after the invasion.

Two German police officers stopped a middle-aged Jewish man walking with his wife and little boy. One officer took the father's umbrella away from him; the other officer demanded identification papers. The father handed the officer his papers and waited while his family stood in the pouring rain getting soaked to the bone. The little boy hid beneath his mother's long crimson coat. The officer asked the father a question. The father responded, seeming to protest. They argued shortly before the officer jabbed him in the stomach with his club and handcuffed him. Other Jews passed by, ignoring the scene, as if it didn't exist. They all knew that to interfere would lead to their own arrest and beating, or worse.

The wife screamed for the police officers to let her husband go as her little boy continued hiding beneath her coat. The officer holding the umbrella slapped her face so hard that the sound seemed to echo through the square. She was stunned into silence for a moment, then screamed again when they shoved her husband into a car. The officer broke the umbrella over his knee and tossed it on the street before driving off. The little boy stayed hidden behind his mother's coat. And like the little boy, I remained hidden behind my broken window, afraid to interfere, afraid to be seen. What was I to do? What could anyone do?

When facing the Germans, we were so weak and so terrified of fighting back. There was no point. We knew we'd lose. At that moment, I thought Kaja could be right. Maybe we, the Jews, were all cursed for some unknown reason. The hatred and abuse we experienced at the hands of the Germans, and throughout our history, for that matter, was incomprehensible.

I retreated from the window and found a dry bench in the dark cavern of the temple. Sitting there in a daze, I watched the rain spilling through the jagged hole in the roof, streaming down the alabaster walls, flowing across the warped and rotting wood floor, and seeping through its black cracks where it flowed into the soil below.

Inside this charred and crumbling sacred house of worship ravaged by the flames of hatred, there was nothing but a decaying skeleton, a hollow shell devoid of life and spirit. I imagined the cantor standing between the bimah's towering marble columns, now glistening with rainwater, singing Kol Nidre on Yom Kippur and asking God to forgive us for our sins.

While gazing up at the ceiling, I envisioned black umbrellas floating like clusters of mushrooms down the river where my family was killed. Some umbrellas disappeared beneath the water, others stayed afloat in the gentle current. Interspersed between the umbrellas were Bubbe, Mama and Papa, Sara and Basha, floating tranquilly down the river on their backs, facing the sky. Their skin, white as pure limestone, lips a purplish-blue, eyelids closed in an eternal sleep, their faces in a state of permanent repose. Zelda emerged from the forest shadows along the riverbank and walked toward me. Thick fog rolled down the river, enveloping her before she vanished.

WHEN NIGHT FELL, THE SYNAGOGUE WAS PITCH-BLACK SAVE for a broken window lit by the yellowish flame of a streetlamp. I carefully walked through the darkness to the window and climbed through it.

On the street, I found my bearings and headed to the bridge with the gunnysack slung over my shoulder. The heavy rain had turned into a light drizzle. Inside a bar across the street, Polish workers and German soldiers drank at tables lit by the flames of oil lamps. There were no Jews on the streets, which meant it must have been past curfew.

Two jeeps passed as I headed toward Sportowa Street, where the freight train crossed the bridge. At the bridge, I made sure no one was watching, then took a few steps down the grassy embankment and hid beneath the bridge's heavy iron struts and girders that were brown and decaying with rust. The ground was wet from the rain.

From my position, I watched the street where a German tank drove past, then several trucks towing anti-artillery equipment, fuel trucks, and transports full of troops. They were all heading east into Russia, the opposite direction of where I was going. I feared Russia was going to be the Germans' next conquest. And after that, maybe they'd try to conquer Asia. For their appetite to conquer and rule seemed limitless.

A couple of hours had gone by when the tracks above my head hummed. I reached up and touched one of the rusty girders and felt a slight vibration. Down the tracks in the distance, two bright headlights emerged like twin full moons, growing brighter as they approached. A long snake of wooden boxcars filled with freight trailed the engine. The train was heading west, toward Kraków.

My pulse sped up as my legs tightened and prepared to spring. The rails and iron bridge trembled and shook as the massive coal-powered engine approached. Clouds of dark gray smoke and steam bellowed from its smokestack. I stayed crouched beneath the bridge, preparing to pounce on a boxcar.

The train's engine slowly chugged by, only a meter above my head, stinking of burnt oil and coal, fiercely hissing and puffing with its pistons pounding like jackhammers while its enormous steel wheels squealed and whined on the iron rails, clacking across the track seams, sounding like gunshots puncturing the smoky air.

The thunderous engine noise vibrated through my entire body, jolting me with an energy fueled by sheer fear.

The engineer leaned out his window as the train crossed the bridge and rang the train bell while keeping a close eye on the tracks. I wondered if he was a Pole or a German and why he was watching the tracks so closely. He was probably searching for mines, or for people like me who were trying to stow away on a boxcar.

I waited anxiously and debated at what moment I should make my attempt to jump on board as the cars passed by me one by one. I watched for German soldiers. Time was running out. With the train nearing its end, a swift decision was necessary. My heart sped up as I sprung from my cover and climbed onto the bridge and ran alongside the train for several meters searching for something to grab on to. A boxcar with a small platform attached to its rear appeared.

While running full speed, trying not to trip, I maneuvered my body between the boxcars. Making one misstep would crush me. Within reach was a metal railing attached to the small platform. I grabbed it and stepped up on a coupler with my right foot and hauled myself onto the platform. It was small, about three-quarters the size of my bed of hay, just wide enough to stand or sit on. Mounted to the boxcar's wood-planked wall were rusty metal rungs leading to the roof.

I wondered if I'd be able to get inside the boxcar through a hatch on the roof. But then I worried about getting locked inside the boxcar and missing my stop at Kraków. Or if the Germans stopped the train and searched it, they would easily trap and discover me. I decided it was best to stay put on the small platform, even though I was more exposed. I sat down on the hard metal floor and pulled my knees against my chest and draped the gunnysack over my head to help shelter me from the rain.

PART THREE

KRAKÓW GHETTO

4 0

THE TRAIN BARRELED WEST TOWARD KRAKÓW, SLICING through dark forests, farmlands, and small villages. The air was cool and wet, thick with the aroma of the fields and manure; the night sky was a starless black void. It was all eerily familiar. The same landscape I'd seen traveling in reverse with my family on that dreadful night we fled eastward from Kraków to Przemyśl. On the train I remembered Bubbe snuggled against me, her warm pillowy body pressed against mine, nervously knitting my scarf, her needles clicking away as they laced the wool yarn into small knots. Sara and Basha found an escape from our sad reality, immersing themselves in their books, while Mama and Papa sat next to each other arm in arm, gazing out the window into the unknown, their eyes straining with trepidation. Mama picked at her nails while Papa anxiously stroked his mustache, contemplating the future. Scared as we were, none of us could have imagined the tragic fate that destroyed us.

If only things had been different. If only Papa hadn't gotten drunk that night and ventured out; if only we hadn't stumbled upon Schlöndorff's brutal savagery; if only we'd left Kraków perhaps a day later or went somewhere other than Przemyśl; if only we had missed the train, or were never picked up by the drosky . . . If only . . .

Chance was a malevolent force that night, immoral and utterly heartless.

Nothing in the world could explain my family's senseless death.

The landscape whipped past my eyes, a blur of trees and fields, wood shacks and barns. After several hours of sitting like a curled-up snail on that hard metal platform with my knees sandwiched against my chin, I ached all over. My back throbbed and my butt was sore. The soaking wet gunnysack clung to my skin. Then the rain stopped. I pulled off the gunnysack and stood up to stretch my legs. My muscles were stiff and cramped. Inhaling deeply, I filled my lungs with the clean moist air of the fields and forests. I felt calm until the train began slowing down just as we passed a sign along the tracks for Bochnia. I knew of this village. We were about forty-five kilometers away from Kraków. I wondered why we were slowing down for Bochnia. Perhaps a boxcar was to be loaded there.

I craned my body over the edge of the platform railing to see round the side of the boxcar. In front of the train, on the south side of the tracks, a German transport truck plus two tanks and a jeep idled.

The train came to a stop and the jeep's large searchlight began scanning the boxcars. Several soldiers leaped out of the truck. A few of them walked with their attack dogs pulling on their leashes, sniffing the tracks and boxcars. The soldiers moved quickly in my direction, shining their flashlights across the boxcars as they investigated the tracks and the boxcars' undersides.

My platform had a clear view of the wet field on the opposite side of the tracks, the north side of the train. Across the field was the vague outline of a forest, maybe two hundred meters away. I considered making a run for it, but didn't know whether more soldiers with dogs were coming down that side of the tracks.

I jumped down from the platform and peered round the side of the boxcar. Two more soldiers with dogs approached from that direction. Trapped and terrified, I wasn't sure where to go next. I wanted to run, but they were too close. I wouldn't make it to the forest with the attack dogs chasing me down through the open field with no trees or thickets to dodge through, no rivers to cross to safety. I felt like a cornered fox with a leg caught in a snare. Then I remembered the ladder rungs.

I jumped back onto the platform, clenched the gunnysack in my teeth, and vaulted up the rungs to the boxcar's roof. Lying flat against the cold metal, a suffocating terror overwhelmed me as the dogs' violent, incessant barking grew louder. A commander yelled orders to search the cars.

My eyes scanned the darkened landscape beyond the train, desperately searching for a way to escape the turmoil. I spotted two soldiers on the north side of the train walking past, followed by three soldiers that stopped at my boxcar. The dogs' bloodthirsty barking rang in my ears. I saw flashes of them nipping at Bubbe's heels, Papa trying to kick them away, a pack of them chasing me down the riverbank, the deathly whites of their eyes and fangs piercing the darkness.

The dogs below must've caught my scent. I tried slowing my breath. The soldiers searched beneath the boxcar and rattled its door latch. The latch released with a clank and the door slid open. One soldier ordered another to search the boxcar. His boots pounded like sledgehammers across the wood floor. The dog's rabid barking came at me from below, and I imagined its teeth tearing through the roof. The soldier searched the boxcar from one end to the other and called out that it was clear. They slammed the door shut and latched it. For a moment, I was relieved.

I peered over the roof's edge to see if they were leaving and noticed a carrot lying on the platform below. It must've fallen out of my bag. Soldiers were walking past it when one dog stopped and barked at the platform. I quickly slid back from the roof's edge so I was out of sight. My mind spun in terror. There was nowhere to hide if they climbed the ladder and checked the roof. I considered jumping but feared I'd break a leg or ankle from such a height. I lay still and listened.

The soldiers below discussed where the carrot could have come from. One of them said it must've come from a stowaway. Another thought the stowaway had escaped through the fields or was farther up the tracks. Then one of them mentioned the ladder rungs and volunteered to check the roof. I had to do something. I assumed a ladder might exist at the boxcar's opposite end. If so, I could try to make a desperate run to the tree line.

Grabbing my gunnysack, I crept to the other end of the boxcar and discovered there was no ladder, only a narrow wood beam running along the roof's edge. There was nowhere else to hide, so I bit down on the gunnysack and slid my body over the roof's edge and hung from the beam perfectly still and listened.

The dogs' barking continued as the thumping of a soldier's boots climbed the metal rungs. I prayed he wouldn't cross to my end of the roof. My grip on the beam was tenuous and slipping. I had to shift my grip to keep my fingers and forearms from cramping. Four to five meters below my dangling feet there was no platform, only iron couplers and the tracks. If I let go, I'd certainly break my legs or back.

The soldier's footsteps crossed the roof in my direction. Breathing hard, I bit down on the gunnysack. If it dropped, the sound would certainly lead them to me. Sweat ran down my back, fingertips sliding—the muscles in my hands and arms now burning to the bone.

The sounds of his footsteps stopped.

My feet frantically searched for a toehold on the boxcar's wall to keep me from falling while I dangled like a marionette on a fraying string.

The soldiers below called to their comrade on the roof. "*Was ist dort!*" they barked out. "*Nicht!*" he answered. His footsteps scurried back to the opposite end of the car.

My hands and forearms couldn't take the pain anymore. Just as I was about to let go, my right foot discovered a bolt protruding from the boxcar wall. I put some weight on the small toehold, momentarily relieving the weight on my hands, and gingerly pressed against it. My eyes peeked above the roof line. It was clear.

Summoning the last shreds of my strength, I pushed off the toehold and hauled myself back up to the roof and lay there dead still, exhausted. My aching fingers had frozen in the shape of claws. I tucked them beneath my armpits, and the warmth of my body helped to unfreeze them and relieve the excruciating pain.

A whistle blew and the train jolted, its massive wheels grinding on the iron tracks, creaking forward slowly, clacking a measured beat. Taken by exhaustion, I clung to the metal rod running down the center of the roof so I wouldn't fall.

While lying there drained of all energy and unable to move, I became terrified of going through more checkpoints and of being trapped on the roof or platform again.

Catalyzed by pure desperation, my body dragged itself along the roof to the ladder rungs. I waited for the train to pass the Germans' transport trucks, tanks, and jeeps. Once we rounded a smooth bend, leaving them behind in the darkness, I climbed down to the platform.

The train had picked up speed and I hesitated to jump, scared of getting injured. But then my body jumped involuntarily, rolling down the gravel embankment where it landed in a moist grassy field. Miraculously uninjured, I slung my gunnysack over my shoulder and sprinted across the field toward the sanctuary of the tree line.

41

IN THE FOREST, I RESTED FOR MAYBE AN HOUR BEFORE HEADING west toward Kraków. The narrow dirt road had fields bordering one side, woods on the other. It was peaceful. Not a soul in sight. I walked and listened to the conversations of crows bickering in the forest and watched starlings and red-winged blackbirds poach seeds from the newly planted fields. To the east, the dawn sky glowed as feather-like clouds drifted aimlessly along the golden horizon, their edges burning brighter as the sun slowly emerged.

An old farmer on a horse cart loaded with rocks rounded a bend in the road and traveled toward me. His ancient face was as lined and craggy as the rocks he transported. He nodded and waved, as if he knew me. I nodded back, as if I knew him, and kept walking. His appearance made me nervous. Traveling through darkness would be safest, I thought. I needed to get off the road and hide in the woods until nightfall.

A path covered in weeds led from the road to an abandoned, dilapidated barn in the woods about thirty meters away. Its cedar-shingled roof was collapsing on one end, windows broken, doors missing from their hinges. The mud-and-stone walls were deteriorating, with parts covered in a thick green moss. Patches of weeds and grass poked up from the dirt floor.

Near a pile of deer droppings there was a shallow fire pit filled with ashes and a few pieces of partially burned wood. Broken green glass, several empty vodka bottles, a few rusty food cans, rags with dried blood, some old chicken bones, eggshells, stripped corncobs, a man's black leather shoe with the sole and shoelaces missing, and pieces of torn gunnysacks were strewn across the ground.

In the corner I found a dirt-coated yarmulke made of velvet, dark navy blue, with embroidered silver threads braided like rope circling its rim. I cradled it in my hands and picked off the chunks of dirt clinging to it, wondering what happened to the man it belonged to. Perhaps he was on the run and accidentally left it behind. Or maybe he was dragged here to be beaten and killed by some antisemites. There was blood on the rags, possibly his blood.

Khone had worn a similar yarmulke, but it was black. I hoped Khone was still alive. I wanted to have tea with him in his sitting room, pet his cat, Nes, and share my grief with him. The blood on the rags reminded me of the blood on his chin and cheeks when the soldiers had sheared away his beard. The memory of the grotesque barbarism turned my stomach.

On the yarmulke, above the threads, were the gold-embroidered Hebrew words *Shema Yisrael*—Hear, O Israel. The beginning of the morning and evening prayer: *Hear, O Israel: The Lord our God, the Lord is One.* We were taught these words in cheder. Such stupid words, I thought. How moronic. How naïve. What fools we were to recite such empty words.

I was tired of being chased, tired of being the prey, the victim, the weak one, the fearful one. I was tired of being a Jew.

I spat on the yarmulke and threw it to the ground and stamped it into the dirt and swore at it. I pounded it with my fist and found a shard of glass and sliced it to pieces. Then suddenly, I wept. I didn't know why, but I cried like a baby. I crawled into a corner of the dilapidated barn and curled up into a ball. A pain ached in the pit of my stomach; inside my heart was a vast hole. How I missed my family, and Zelda, and Khone. How I missed my home, my friends, and the life I had.

I wept unabashedly. There was no stopping it. In that desolate corner of the barn, my weary body and broken mind completely surrendered to my sorrow and grief. I wept until I was completely empty inside, until sleep carried me away.

WHEN I AWAKENED, THE LAST OF THE DAY'S SUNLIGHT CAST ITS reddish glow through the shattered window above me. Spanning broken shards of glass, a lone spiderweb fluttered in the warm breeze, just like the one in Stanisław's toolshed. Its shimmering silky threads caught the last fragments of the sun's fleeting light. I searched for the spider, but he was nowhere to be found.

I sipped some water, conserving it, and ate my last food—a carrot and a few bread morsels.

When the sky faded to darkness, it was time to leave.

The forest floor was a soft carpet of pine needles. The trees' branches rustled strangely in the light wind. The woods felt un-welcoming, haunted with ghosts. My heart pounded as I walked faster. Suddenly, the shapes of dogs and soldiers silently appeared from behind the trees and brambles. I ran, thinking someone was following me. There were footsteps. My body shivered as roots and vines grabbed at my feet, trying to trip me. I kept running and looking back, seeing flashes of shadows. From the quiet emerged the murmurs of rushing water. Sprinting down a ravine through dense brush and fallen trees, I followed the trail of sounds.

The river I came to was wide and its current swift. I walked up and down its pebbly bank, searching for a way to cross. There were no bridges or fallen trees that I could see. Maybe it was shallow enough to walk across. I tossed my shoes in the gunnysack and slowly entered the icy waters.

The current was strong, but manageable. With the water at

my chest, I gradually waded toward the opposite shore, my steps cautious and deliberate. But then the bank abruptly plummeted and I lost my footing. The current swiftly seized my body and dragged it toward the middle where its grip was unyielding. Below my feet was nothing but water. I let go of the gunnysack and attempted to swim across. Yet the fierce current, growing in strength and speed, refused to release its grip. Quickly came the roar of water blasting over the rocks. The darkness obscured whatever was coming.

Moving ever faster, I got sucked beneath the roiling waters and then thrown into the air. A rock appeared from nowhere, slamming into my left shoulder and head. Dizzy and nauseous, I grappled to keep my head above the cold frothy waves. But the wild waters rushed into my mouth and throat, choking me, forcing me to gasp for air.

The river pulled me down into a maze of rocks, scraping my back and arms before throwing me skyward again, only to be sucked back down beneath its surface once more. Disoriented and seemingly adrift, I resigned myself to the river's overpowering turbulence. My ability to survive was grim. But just when I thought my life had reached its end, the river spat me out into a pool of calmer waters at the foot of the rapids.

Drained and battered, I swam to a fallen tree, its length spanning from the shore to midriver. My right hand caught hold of a frail, decaying branch, then swiftly found a sturdier one just as the other broke. I inched along the large branch as the river's current still waged a tug-of-war against my progress.

Frantically reaching out for the trunk, I dug my fingernails into its deep grooves and finally hauled myself out of the water's grasp. I snaked my body across the trunk's expanse and headed for the shore where I collapsed on a bed of smooth river stones.

Lying on my side, I coughed up the rest of the river water

inside me and filled my worn lungs with the cool night air. My head throbbed, as if pummeled with a hammer, my left arm and back bruised from being battered by the rocks.

Above, stars and galaxies speckled the blackness of the moonless sky like wheat seed scattered across a harrowed field. Without rhyme or reason, chance had saved me once again. Yet this time, I felt grateful for being alive. Perhaps because there was a reason—to find my Zelda.

Looking around, I noted the gunnysack carrying my bottle of water and shoes was now gone, stolen by the river. The cold and wet clothes that clung to my body were the only things I had left. When I stood up, a warm liquid flowed down the side of my face. I touched it with my fingertips and saw blood. My fingers searched my forehead and found a large bump, the size of a plum, on the left side where the bleeding came from. I thought of Chaim's head cut and tore off my right shirtsleeve and wrapped it tight around my forehead, stopping the blood from flowing down my face.

Sticks, twigs, rocks, and pebbles bruised and cut my soft bare feet as I hobbled through the forest with no sense of direction. The frigid river water soaked my clothes, making me shiver uncontrollably, as if the cold were trapped inside my skin. I rubbed my arms and torso vigorously to generate some heat inside my body.

After hours of walking, I found a narrow dirt road leading to a small farmhouse, smaller than Stanisław's. The pebbles and sticks I walked across poked at my bleeding feet like sharp nails and broken glass. Stabbing pains shot through them. I'd never make it to Kraków without some shoes.

I crept up to the farmhouse to see if the farmer had stored a pair of boots outside, like Stanisław would do when his boots were full of dirt or manure. There was nothing in front of the house. A chicken coop, a sleeping goat, and a toolshed were in the back. The chickens started clucking when they heard my footsteps on the dry grass. The toolshed's warped door creaked on its rusty hinges as I slowly opened it. I searched for shoes amidst the hay, harrow, pick and shovels, ax and saws. By the plow was a pair of leather boots. A miracle. I also found another gunnysack and a gray wool cap with a short brim, like the one I used to wear on the farm, and a dirty jar I could use for carrying some water after I cleaned it.

The boots were too big on my feet, so I filled them with soft grass and moss to make them fit snugger. At the well behind the shed, I cleaned the jar and filled it with water.

When leaving, I noticed the silhouette of a man standing in the middle of the field staring at me. He was stationary with his right arm eerily swinging back and forth as if he was motioning for me to return. I thought it was the farmer. He must've heard me and followed me to the road. I ran feebly on aching feet and looked back to see if he was giving chase, but he remained planted to the spot where he stood. Then I realized the man was in fact a scarecrow and it was the wind that swung his arm back and forth. I laughed at my confusion.

After walking the dirt road through the night, the first light rising behind the hills to the east greeted me, confirming I'd fortunately been walking west when I lost my sense of direction in the woods.

I rounded a bend in the road and saw the railroad tracks leading to Kraków in the distance. I figured I'd take the day to hide in the forest and sleep and then set out under the cover of night again, hoping to reach Kraków by morning.

I went far into the woods, hidden from the road. Behind a knoll, I lay down in a soft grassy area next to an old gnarled oak. Above me, a sea of foamy clouds, their bellies the color of hot coals, slowly drifted by. Several crows soared overhead in spirals, gliding on the wind's shoulders, cawing to one another as if they were laughing at the absurdity of the world below.

A few hours later, beams of hot sunlight pierced the opening in the tree canopy, drying my clothes and warming my skin. I slept in this peaceful place until nightfall.

42

THE NEXT DAY, BY LATE AFTERNOON, I HAD REACHED THE Podgórze section of Kraków. The streets buzzed with Poles and Germans shopping, lounging in cafés, dining in restaurants, bustling to and from their businesses. The electric trams, packed with passengers, cut through the cobblestone streets, crisscrossing at major intersections on shiny tracks running in gentle curves and hard straight lines. Cars and trucks, horse-drawn droskies and people riding bicycles soared past me. A work detail of Jewish men hauled heavy pushcarts loaded with coal, bricks, and firewood. At the market, horse-drawn wagons from the farmlands were stacked with gunnysacks filled with grains, potatoes, carrots, corn, cabbages and beets, cages of chickens and geese, and cannisters of cow's and goat's milk.

Polish and German policemen casually patrolled the streets, as if everything was back to normal. There were fewer German soldiers in the city compared to the war's beginning. But now many of the signs for businesses, including bakeries and butcher shops, cafés and restaurants, clothing stores and markets, and even some of the street signs, were written in German.

I figured the General Government established in Kraków at the start of the war to serve Nazi Germany and control the Occupied Territories must've imported large numbers of German politicians and administrators, along with their families, to live in the city. It seemed like Kraków would soon be a city that was no longer Polish, but German.

I scurried down Wielicka Street with my head down, avoiding eye contact with all those around me. Although I looked like a simple Polish peasant from the countryside, I feared someone would see me for what I was—a Jew in disguise.

In the window of a shoe store, I stopped to observe my reflection. One sleeve was missing from my soiled shirt; my oily pants had holes and dirt stains; my boots were too large for my body; a bloody head bandage poked out from beneath my cap. I appeared as a disheveled, crazed clown shot from a cannon. After removing the bandage, I saw the cut was no longer bleeding. It was now a bluish-purple bump with a scabby line running through its center. My hair, once colored a light sandy-brown, the same shade as Mama's hair, was now the color of dry leaves, a dull brown matted with dirt. In it were tiny clumps and flecks of dried blood that I removed.

I tore off my other sleeve so my shirt was evenly sleeveless. The body weight and muscle I displayed surprised me. My bones had thickened and my arms, once skinny and shapeless, were now defined by ropy muscles and bulging veins in the forearms and biceps. My shoulders were broader and neck thicker—long days of farm work and cutting trees and hearty meals prepared by Kaja had strengthened me. The patchy brown beard that had once sprouted from my baby face had filled in and was thick along the jawline, cheeks, and chin. This raggedy, unkempt beard of mine had grown fast and made me appear several years older than my eighteen years. I looked weathered and worn, my eyes deep-set in their sockets, darker, older, less innocent and more cunning, with a weary sadness living inside them.

As I walked toward Zgody Square, where the old man said the ghetto was located, I passed a tall Polish policeman who paid no attention to me, and then two young German soldiers standing on a street corner smoking cigarettes and whistling at the young Polish women walking by.

At a busy outdoor market, Poles and Germans, mostly women, shopped among the big woven baskets and wood boxes filled with colorful fruits and vegetables, thick sausages and large loaves of bread, potatoes, and grains. Life appeared surprisingly normal, though there were no Jews at the market. Unless some were in disguise, like me. I wondered if there were markets inside the ghetto.

All the colorful food made me ravenous, and I searched for what I could steal. Within minutes, I spotted an unattended crate of large sausages. The farmer they belonged to had his back to them as he busily tied up his horse. I felt a little guilty stealing from this farmer knowing how hard he must've worked to make those sausages—raising the pigs, growing their feed, shoveling their shit, slaughtering them, butchering their meat, spicing it, stuffing the casings, hanging them to dry. No matter, I needed to eat something. I would take only two sausages. The time for remorse could come later.

I waited for the right moment and made sure no one was watching, then grabbed the two sausages and slipped them into my gunnysack along with a loaf of bread that was beneath his table. I easily ducked out of the market and walked to a small park. Sitting down on a bench, I glanced around, wanting to be certain no one had followed me, then took out the sausages and tore into them, savoring the salty, peppery, garlicky taste of the meat filling my mouth. I broke off a chunk of bread and ate that, too, before leaving.

One more street down, I rounded the corner to Józefińska Street where, like a mirage, the ghetto's main entrance suddenly appeared. I froze in my tracks and gasped. I thought my eyes must be deceiving me. The ghetto gate was a monolithic cement structure with a double arched entryway rising eight to ten meters high. Expanding out from both sides of the archways was a wall, about three meters high, crowned with cruelly designed arches in the shape of Jewish headstones. It was a message from the Germans to the Jews: *Inside these walls is where you will die.* Mounted on the center column between the archways of the gate was a large Star of David. Below it were the Yiddish words *Yidisher Voinbatsirk*— Jewish Residential Area.

The words alone were remarkably benign, and deviously deceptive. Because they were written in Yiddish, it seemed as if the Jews had written them. As though the Jews themselves, and not the Germans and Poles, had ordered this wall, naming it a "Jewish Residential Area" instead of what it really was, the Jewish ghetto.

With this façade in place, I suppose it made it more palatable for the Germans and Poles living outside the ghetto walls to go about their daily lives without grappling with an ounce of guilt or remorse over the grave injustices they had perpetrated upon the Jews.

Yet the armed German soldiers guarding the gate beneath those words, and the barbed wire strung along the upper edges of the brick walls encircling the perimeter, blatantly exposed their deception. A person with even a smidgen of common sense couldn't ignore the reality that this was in fact not a "residential area" for the Jews, but a prison.

My eyes filled with tears as I gazed at the wall in disbelief.

A man driving a horse cart full of coal pulled up to the gate where a soldier checked his ID. He waved him through. Several men on a corner inside the ghetto, all of them tagged with Star of David armbands, paused from their conversation to watch the cart pass by them. A policeman crossed the street and broke up their gathering. He also wore a Star of David. As the old man in Przemyśl had said, Germans enlisted Jews to watch over the Jews.

A woman cradling a baby in her arms came out of the door of her apartment building and stopped on the sidewalk to listen to two young boys, around nine or ten years old, in shorts and tattered shirts, playing their violins, begging for money. She handed one of them a piece of bread and walked on.

4 3

WITH NO IDENTIFICATION PAPERS, I NEEDED TO SNEAK INSIDE. I followed a section of the ghetto wall running close to the Vistula River along Wita Stwosza Street. Buildings, with their windows and doors sealed with mortar and bricks, were now extensions of the wall. When one set of buildings ended, a newly constructed brick wall topped with barbed wire reached to the next building, and so on. Where there were breaks in the wall, wood beams with barbed wire fencing filled the gaps.

At Lwowska Street I made a right turn where a second ghetto gate led to Zgody Square. Mr. Malinowski's Podgórze Pharmacy was near the gate. I figured if anyone knew where Zelda and her family were it would be Mr. Malinowski. It was his pharmacy that had always provided Mr. Abramovitch with his blood pressure medication.

Along Lwowska Street ran the trams entering and exiting the ghetto gate. Cars, trucks, and horse carts also passed through these gates. Four police guards armed with pistols stopped each vehicle and checked the driver's identification papers, and randomly searched the wagons carrying coal, wood, and sacks of food. At first, I considered hiding inside a wagon carrying firewood that was covered by a tarp, but then realized if it was searched, there'd be no way of escaping. Also, I'd be putting the innocent driver in danger.

A tram pulled up to the gate and stopped. The tram had a sign with arrows pointing to the section for Jews. Two police guards marched onto the tram and inspected the identity papers of the passengers. The third guard stayed by the gate to check the people entering and exiting the ghetto on foot. I didn't see a place to slip through the gates undetected.

I continued following the perimeter to see if there were other ways to slip inside. By the river, I came across a group of eight Jewish women shoveling gravel along its bank in the blazing afternoon heat, their arms and faces glistening with sweat and coated in dirt. Five cocky German guards smoking cigarettes paced among the women, joking with one another as they grabbed the women's buttocks and breasts, making the women recoil in fear. While walking past, I examined the pitiful, defenseless group of women to see if Zelda was among them. But she wasn't there.

Across the river was Kazimierz, my old neighborhood. I tried to imagine what my street must look like now with all the Jews gone. I thought about how many were dead, how many escaped to the east, how many were locked inside the ghetto. Khone immediately came to mind. I hoped he had escaped the ghetto and was somewhere alive and safe. I longed to sit next to him in the shop and smoke a cigarette, have a cup of tea, and listen to his stories. I thought of my childhood friends—Big Izzy, Mo, Isaac, Adam, Roman, Naftali, and Chubby Fischel—and our workers—Icek, Pinie, and Hersch—and the people from the neighborhood—Big Ziggy the coal man, Smelly Meyer the fishmonger, Avrom the water carrier, Old Schmuel the street sweeper, Biala the lamplighter, Moishe the baker, Jakov the shoemaker . . . How many of them were still alive?

I kept going, taking Kaçik Street to Wielicka Street where the trams used two other gates for entering and exiting the ghetto.

When a tram passed through one gate, I noticed a small gap between the gate and the side of the tram that I could slip through. It was on the east side of the tram where no soldiers stood, and no doors existed for entering and exiting the tram. With the guards positioned on the opposite side of the tram, I'd be able to steal inside the ghetto without being seen.

44

WITHIN EYESIGHT OF THE GATE, I HID IN THE ENTRYWAY OF A shuttered clothing store and waited for nightfall. When it finally came, three German soldiers guarded the gate beneath a yellowish umbrella of light, pacing, smoking cigarettes, and looking bored. A tram leaving the ghetto approached. Two of them boarded the tram and inspected it while the third watched the gate. To slip through the gate undetected, I needed to wait for a tram that was entering the ghetto, not leaving it.

For over an hour, no more trams entered or exited the ghetto. It seemed they had stopped running. Losing patience, I searched for another way in. But just then, in the distance, a tram's headlight cut through the darkness as it approached. My body tensed as I prepared to dash across the street and hide behind a vacant German army truck parked next to the tracks.

The sidewalks and streets were clear. I sprinted to the truck and waited nervously as the tram pulled up to the gate and stopped. Then I bolted across the tracks to the other side of the tram where I crouched behind it.

Two German soldiers on the opposite side of the tram boarded and ordered the Jews to hand them their *kennkartes* as they searched the passengers for contraband. Glancing up at the window above my head, a Jewish woman stared down at me, looking confused. She was middle-aged, the age of my mother, with coal-black hair and dull, weary eyes. I brought my fingers to my lips, motioning for her to not say anything. She turned away and handed a soldier her *kennkarte*. I waited and listened. The soldier ordered her to open her bag. She was silent as he examined it before moving on to the next person.

When the soldiers exited the tram, the metal gates opened for it to pass through. I glanced up one more time at the woman as the tram moved, still worried she might report me. But she sternly stared straight ahead, ignoring my presence.

My body trembled as I squeezed past the gates, hidden from the soldiers on the other side of the tram. Once inside the ghetto, I rushed along Lwowska Street toward Zgody Square, where the Podgórze Pharmacy was located. I hoped the Germans hadn't shut it down, or taken it over, and that I'd find Mr. Malinowski there.

THE AIR INSIDE THE GHETTO WAS PUTRID, STINKING OF GARBAGE and sewage. Yet the people on the streets seemed oblivious to the stench. Some were taking evening walks, others gathered in small groups, just like in the old neighborhood. They were probably talking business, debating politics, the war, sharing their stories of woe, spreading rumors, gossiping about the neighbors. There were some men dressed in business suits and women in fine dresses, others wore work clothes. The ultra-Orthodox men wore their long black gaberdines with their furry *shtreimels* mounted on their heads like stovepipes covered in fur. The ultra-Orthodox women wore their long black dresses reaching their ankles, their hair covered by dark wraps or wigs. But then there were people in the street, young and old, children and the elderly, dressed in dirty, tattered rags, feet wrapped in newspapers, open sores on their arms and faces, their wild hair matted, thick as straw.

A few of the children with big sad eyes, small and bony, sickly with skin covered in sores, walked up to people or stood beside them holding out their dirty, desperate little hands with palms splayed open, facing up toward the stars. They begged for something—anything—a morsel of food, or even a few kopeks. Some people gave them a little of whatever they had. But others who had become numb to the daily suffering told the children to go away, or shoved them to the side and reprimanded them.

Lurking beneath the faces of those who appeared to still have some means, beneath all their banter and occasional laughter, I saw reflected in their anxious, bewildered eyes a sense of fatigue, a fear and uncertainty of what tomorrow might bring. In the well-dressed, there were cracks in their façades—the stains on their expensive clothes, the little tears and loose threads on the men's fine trousers, shirts, suit jackets, and coats. And on the women's dresses, skirts, blouses, and jackets there were the frayed hems, broken zippers, missing buttons, and stains. Their finely tailored clothes needed to be cleaned and repaired. I supposed they could no longer afford such things. Obviously, no one, not even the wealthy, was impervious to the degrading conditions of this night-marish place.

Inside the ghetto, I felt light-headed and off-balance. The over-crowding and compression of so many people in such a small area, packed tight as chickens in a cage, confused and overwhelmed my senses. Then I noticed people looking at me oddly, perhaps because I wasn't wearing a Star of David armband or a yellow star on my shirt, or perhaps because I looked like a Polish peasant who had lost his way. Paranoia consumed me again as I worried someone would report me, or that a German or Polish policeman would arrest and interrogate me. Or worse, torture me.

I quickened my pace, hurrying past a building that used to be a clothing store and was now the office for the Jewish Ghetto Police, marked *Jüdischer Ordnungsdienst*. I never imagined the Germans would create a Jewish police force. But it made sense. Who better to keep watch of the Jews than those slimy, pathetic, soulless Jews willing to collaborate with the Germans to save their own skin.

It appeared nothing was as it had been. The old courthouse was now a prison. Businesses and stores had disappeared. Jakov's shoemaker shop, Mr. Levy's candy store across the street, the hardware store on the corner, the bakery next to it where Mama would occasionally buy our challah when she was too tired to make it—they were all gone. Even the street signs had changed from Polish to Hebrew. I suppose the Germans did this to reinforce the sense of isolation inside the ghetto, and to send the message: *This is the only place where Jews belong.*

A hand grabbed my arm from behind, its fierce claw spinning me around. A short, wiry policeman wearing a Star of David armband on his jacket stood before me, his little mouse ears poking out the sides of his police cap. He sported a waxy black mustache the width of a rat's tail.

"Where's your armband?!" yelled the little policeman in Polish.

"I lost it," I answered in Yiddish, disgusted by the sight of this traitor.

"*Kennkarte!*" he demanded.

"I lost that, too."

"Bullshit!" he barked back in a guttural Yiddish, as though he was trying to sound like a Nazi. "No armband, no ID. I'm taking you in."

From my gunnysack, I retrieved the last of my stolen sausages and offered it to him while pleading with the little man to give me a break. He snatched it in his greedy paws and stuffed it in his bag. "Get your *kennkarte* tomorrow at the *Arbeitsamt!*" he warned. "If I catch you again without your ID, I'll toss you in jail. Understand? Now get out of here."

45

WHEN I ARRIVED AT MR. MALINOWSKI'S PHARMACY IT WAS LATE in the evening and I expected it to be closed. However, to my surprise, the lights were on, and upon entering, I discovered the place bustling with people, the room abuzz with social activity. It was an entirely different energy from what I'd just experienced on the street. Five Hasidic men wearing their black frocks and brown fur *shtreimels* huddled together near the counter debating where to find kosher meats on the black market. Stroking their long gray beards, they grabbed one another's forearms, pointed crooked fingers, threw their hands up in the air as if swatting gnats. Steps away three middle-aged women laughed and giggled while whispering secrets in one another's ears. In the next room over, at the back of the pharmacy, several men sat in the shadows furtively scanning newspapers and magazines, showing one another articles while monitoring the front door. Their strange behavior made me realize it must still be illegal for Jews to read newspapers and magazines. Yet Mr. Malinowski was obviously willing to take the risk of providing a refuge where they could feed their hunger to stay connected to the outside world. But where was Mr. Malinowski?

Three Polish-looking women filled prescriptions and worked the cash register behind the long glass-and-wood counter that stretched the length of the room. I scanned the room for Mr. Malinowski, but couldn't find him. I noticed people staring at me, pointing and whispering, making me so uncomfortable that I considered leaving. But then, to my relief, Mr. Malinowski suddenly emerged from the storage room with a small box that he handed to a woman working behind the counter.

Appearing precisely the same as when I worked for him over a year ago, he was still trim, neat, and handsome—the picture of perfect health. His meticulously trimmed mustache accented his high cheekbones; his face tanned from mountain hiking, fishing, or hunting. He still stood ramrod straight and square shouldered with his shiny, fine brown hair combed and oiled straight back, not a hair out of place, his prominent jaw clean shaven, his perfectly clean and pressed white pharmacist jacket fitted neatly over his white shirt and forest-green tie. It struck me that Mr. Malinowski looked the same, while the world around him had dramatically changed.

He spotted me and at first looked confused, then surprised. A subtle grin broke across his face as he waved me over to the counter. Relieved to be recognized, I squeezed past the groups of people still staring at me and shook his hand.

"It's so good to see you, Reuven."

"And it's good to see you, Mr. Malinowski."

"I didn't recognize you at first."

He appeared taken aback by my dirty, ragged appearance, and probably my odorous smell as well.

"Are you and your family all right? I heard that all of you had left for the east some time ago."

"That's correct. We went to Przemyśl."

"I'm assuming after the Germans invaded the east, they transported you and your family back here."

"Yes." I didn't want to tell him the truth until we could speak in private.

"Thank God you're all still together. I know so many other families that weren't so fortunate."

I looked away and nodded in agreement, trying to hide my anguish.

One of his assistants tapped him on the shoulder and asked if a customer could pay for their medication with a piece of jewelry—a pearl necklace.

"Just give them the medication now and tell them they can pay us later," he replied. Turning back to me, he asked, "Do you have time to visit?"

"Yes! I would like that very much."

"Go upstairs to my apartment and wait for me there. We'll have a cup of tea and catch up before you go back to your family. I'll be up in fifteen minutes."

At the back of the shop, a narrow wooden staircase led to his apartment above. Inside was a small front room sparsely furnished with a small dark cherrywood table and four matching chairs, a wood-burning stove, a blue velvet couch on a red oriental carpet. Off the main room was a small bathroom with a bathtub, and in the back a bedroom just large enough for a double bed and dresser. On the dresser was a picture of a boy, Mr. Malinowski I presumed, maybe nine or ten years old, standing in front of the pharmacy between his parents, who were tenderly holding his hands. I remembered he told me his father was also a pharmacist and had opened the pharmacy in 1910. Because there were no other children in the picture, I assumed he was an only child.

Next to that photograph was another picture with him and a friend, both my age, standing next to a river with a forest and mountains behind them, wearing rucksacks and holding fishing rods in one hand, their other hands resting on the other's shoulder. Mr. Malinowski and his friend had a few days' beard growth and wore bright smiles on their tanned faces.

Two French windows in the front room faced the square. Below, halfway across the square, I spotted three German soldiers sitting on a bench casually smoking cigarettes and talking while a Jewish police officer patrolled the far end of the square. Two SS officers strolled past him. One of the SS men reminded me of Schlöndorff. He was tall and trim and seemed to glide across the ground like Schlöndorff. I searched for signs of the small hump on his shoulder, but he was too far away for me to see him clearly. If he had somehow survived the stabbing, I needed to stay on guard, making sure our paths would never cross.

I sat down on the couch and closed my eyes to rest while waiting for Mr. Malinowski, and immediately fell asleep.

When I wakened, Mr. Malinowski was at the stove pouring hot water from the kettle into a teapot. "Forgive me, I couldn't stay awake," I said, sitting up on the couch.

"You must be very tired."

"Yes, a bit."

He handed me a cup and poured the tea. "One sugar or two?"

"Two, please."

"Come, sit down." He pulled out two chairs from the small table. "Are you hungry?"

"A little." In fact, I was ravenous. I used a small silver teaspoon to stir the hot black tea with the melted sugar and took a sip. The sweet black tea was delicious, its flavor the same as the tea we drank at home. My chest suddenly tightened with an ache full of such deep sadness. I took a breath and tried shoving the feeling back down into the dark place it came from before it consumed me.

"Are you okay?" asked Mr. Malinowski, noticing the shift in my demeanor that I had tried to conceal.

"Yes," I replied. "I'm fine."

He sliced a loaf of dark rye bread and set it on a plate before me with some soft cheese, sausage, and apple. "The sausage isn't kosher."

"That's okay," I said, now ravenous for the food. The delicious scents of the fresh bread, aged cheese, and spiced sausage made my mouth salivate. I wanted to tear into the food but restrained myself by sitting on my hands. Trying to show good manners, I wanted to wait for him to sit down before eating. But he must've noticed me staring hungrily at the food. "Go ahead—eat," he said.

I eagerly took a slice of bread, slathered the soft cheese across it, then layered several pieces of sausage over the cheese and bit into it. It was delectable and I devoured it in seconds.

"You're quite hungry," he said as he slowly sipped his tea, appearing amused by my voracious appetite.

"Yes, a bit."

"You must have more."

"Thank you." I quickly prepared another piece of bread with sausage and cheese, devoured it, and washed it down with the tea.

"Does your family not have enough food?"

Although I still didn't want to talk about what had happened to my family, I trusted Mr. Malinowski, and didn't want to continue withholding the truth from him.

I paused from eating and gathered myself. "They're gone," I said flatly, trying to keep a lid on my emotions.

"What do you mean? They left the ghetto?"

"No. I mean they died." My words sounded matter-of-fact, as if they'd come from someone else's mouth.

He looked down and shook his head in that way when a person doesn't want to believe what they've just heard, or when they're wrestling with a fact that they know is true, but don't want to accept it as such.

When he looked up, his sad eyes held me in their gaze. "I'm so sorry, Reuven. Can you talk about it? If you don't want to talk about it, I understand."

I wasn't sure if I wanted to talk about it. It was confusing. I had told no one about what had happened, not even that old man I'd met in Przemyśl, Yitzhak. A part of me wanted to tell some of the story to Mr. Malinowski. Yet I feared going back to the memories. I wanted to lock them away in a black box forever, fearing that remembering the past would make me relive it, summoning feelings of anguish so unbearable that I'd fall to pieces, and not be able to put myself back together again. And yet a part of me wanted to tell someone. A part of me needed to get it out of my body, while another part of me wanted to bury it.

Cautiously, I started telling him the story, starting with our escape to Przemyśl. I didn't want Mr. Malinowski to know about the stabbing of Schlöndorff. I was afraid he might lose respect for me, or worse, it could put him in danger, or compromise him if he had that information. When he asked why we left, I told him Papa had decided our family would be safest in Przemyśl, which was the truth, just not the entire truth.

I described bribing our way to the train, and how we found the forest. I described the tragic events that unraveled by the river in the simplest of terms, avoiding any details that would bring me back to that place. And he knew not to ask for details.

His jaw slackened, his eyes locked on me the entire time, welling with tears, his head shaking in disbelief. When I finished explaining what happened to my family, he had to excuse himself from the table and go into his room for a few minutes. When he returned, he apologized for having to leave, explaining he needed a moment to gather himself.

I went on with the story, describing to him how I escaped and survived in the forest, and how Stanisław had found me lying on the side of a road and saved me. He wanted to know how I survived in the forest, what I ate, where there was water, how I dealt with the wound, and how I navigated the woods. We went through one pot of tea after another. His deep blue eyes, always kind and inquisitive, completely attentive, soaking up my words and never straying from me as I shared my story. It felt strange, and good, to be conversing again after being silent for so long. To have someone I trusted deeply listen to me was comforting.

Mr. Malinowski asked a lot of questions about Stanisław and expressed his admiration for how Stanisław had formed a bond with me, despite being aware of my Jewish identity. Of course, I didn't mention Kaja. No one would ever know about Kaja. That was a secret I'd carry to my grave.

"Once the Germans launched their attack on the Russians, why take the risk of coming back here?" he asked. "It doesn't make sense. Didn't you know there was a ghetto here?"

"I did."

"Then why not go further east, deeper into Russia where it would be safer for you?"

"I came back to search for Zelda Abramovitch. I don't think you knew, but we were engaged."

"My God, I did not know that."

"Do you know if she and her family are here?"

"I know they were here at one point. Zelda would come here to pick up their medications. Mr. Abramovitch had very high blood pressure and his wife was taking phenobarbital for her anxiety."

"Do you think they're still here?"

"I'm not sure. I haven't seen or heard from them in maybe a couple of months. You lose track of time here." He got up from the table and headed for the door leading downstairs. "Follow me. I can give you the last address I had for them."

It had been two years—eight long seasons since I'd last seen my Zelda, and so much had happened. I couldn't believe that now, finally, I might see her, squeeze her in my arms, kiss her freckled lips, listen to her tell me stories in her soft raspy voice once again.

It seemed impossible to be so close to finally finding her. I felt as if I were in a dream.

Mr. Malinowski led us downstairs to the pharmacy where it was dark and quiet. He turned on the light and went through the filing cabinet that had the names and addresses of his customers with last names beginning with the letter "A." He quickly found the Abramovitches' card and gave me their last address on 10 Krakusa Street, apartment 6.

"This is incredible, Mr. Malinowski! Thank you! Thank you! I'll go there right now!" I started to head for the door.

"No—no! It's too late for that now. It's past curfew and you have no papers. If you're caught, they'll toss you in prison and interrogate you and possibly torture you or even kill you if they think you're part of the resistance. No, you need to be patient. Tomorrow we'll go to the *Arbeitsamt* and get your *kennkarte* ID, and they'll assign you work. The ghetto also has a Jewish council now, the *Judenrat*, which carries out German orders. You can get an armband there and then go find Zelda and her family. As for a place to stay, you'll sleep on my couch tonight and stay with me until I find you another place to stay. I'd let you stay here as long as you like, but it's not safe for you, me, or the pharmacy. If the Germans, Polish, or Jewish police ever find out I'm housing a Jew, they'll arrest both of us. And they'll shut down the pharmacy— the only pharmacy in the ghetto. That would be a disaster for everyone. So, you must be careful to not let anyone know you're staying here. Not even the Abramovitch family."

I promised to not tell a soul and thanked him again for all his help. Before leaving, he had a look at the bump on my forehead, swabbed it with some alcohol, and placed a small bandage over it.

When we returned upstairs, he gave me a set of clean clothes. "These pants will be a bit long on you. But take them for now, along with this shirt. Tomorrow, we'll find you some clothes that will fit better." He handed me a pillow and blanket along with a pair of navy blue silk pajamas, the same color as the scarf Bubbe was knitting. "The couch is yours and you can draw a bath and clean up. But it'll be a cold one since we didn't have time to heat the water."

"Don't worry, I'm used to cold water," I said.

"You can use my razor and scissors for that scraggly beard of yours," he said as he handed me a towel and toothbrush.

I insisted he use the bathroom first, but he declined. "You go first," he said, leaving the room. "Believe me. You need a bath right now a lot more than me." He rolled his eyes and held his nose, making me laugh.

I ran the bath and trimmed my scraggly beard with the scissors and then shaved. The skin beneath my beard was pale compared to the rest of my grimy face weathered by the sun and wind. I slipped into the cold bath, not nearly as cold as the pond water on the farm, and scrubbed the layers of dirt off my body. The water quickly turned from clear to a shade of muddy brown.

After drying off, I put on the pair of silky pajamas. They were freshly ironed and smelled clean, like the clothes Mama had sent out for washing. It had been over a year since I'd worn clean clothes. The silky fabric was soft and comfortable. Yet it felt strange to wear such luxurious nightclothes. Kaja would've envied me, while Stanisław would've laughed at the absurdity of such things. Just as he laughed at the thought of people in towns and cities using umbrellas.

I said goodnight to Mr. Malinowski and lay down on his blue velvet couch where I slipped beneath the fresh cotton sheets and rested my head on a puffy down-filled pillow. I appreciated the comfort even though some strange part of me missed the firm prickliness of my hay mattress, the earthy scent of the fields, the pungent odor of the farm animals and their fecund manure, the brush of the warm wind of the summer months blowing over me as I slept inside the toolshed. Why I missed such things, I could not say. Perhaps because that was what had become familiar to me.

As I lay there trying to fall asleep, my anxious thoughts latched on to searching for Zelda the next day. I wondered what she would look like now, and how she would act. Her personality could be different now. Who knew what she'd think when she saw me, or if we'd still get along. I debated if she had remained true, or had cheated as I had. I'd never ask. I'd never want to know. Maybe she was even engaged to someone else by now. Anything was possible.

But I just wanted to have good thoughts about finding her. So, I let go of the bad. She now seemed so close, almost within reach. I could feel her soft cotton dress in my hands, smell the lavender scent on her neck, see her deep green eyes, the color of oak leaves, studying my face, peering inside me. I believed wherever she was living, she was waiting for me.

IN THE MORNING WE HAD FRESHLY BREWED COFFEE, WARM
bread slathered in butter and blueberry jam, and hard-boiled
eggs. As we ate, Mr. Malinowski updated me on the war. So
many things had happened that I wasn't aware of. In April of last
year, 1940, Germany had invaded Denmark and Norway. Denmark
surrendered within hours, but the Norwegians fought on until May
before being conquered. That same month, the Germans invaded
Holland, Belgium, Luxembourg, and France, and Churchill became
the new prime minister of Britain. In June of '40 Italy declared
itself an ally to Germany, and Paris fell. In July, the Germans
established the Vichy government in France and attacked Britain.
Bulgaria, Hungary, Yugoslavia, and Greece had become Hitler's
allies. The world was caving in to the Nazis. And America, dis-
appointingly, still hadn't entered the war.

We finished our meal and went downstairs where Mr.
Malinowski's three assistants were already at work preparing
medications before the pharmacy opened. He told them he was
taking me to the *Arbeitsamt*, the labor office, and would be back
soon.

While walking down Targowa Street we passed the ghetto
prison again, and the *Jüdischer Ordnungsdienst*—the Jewish police
building. On Józefińska Street he pointed out the Jewish Aid Agency
where people dressed in rags stood in a long line hoping to receive
some food.

"I'm sorry to say the living conditions here are getting worse by the day," he said, crossing the street. "Before the walls there were approximately three thousand people living in this area. Recently, one German officer I know estimated about fifteen thousand are now crammed inside here. You've never seen apartments so crowded with people. Fifteen people—adults and children—living in a two-bedroom apartment. Everyone on top of everyone with hardly enough room to move an inch, let alone breathe."

"Are there people trying to escape?" I whispered.

"Yes. Not many, but some," he replied. He glanced around us to be certain no one was within earshot. "If you find Zelda and her family, I'll do what I can to help all of you escape. If you don't find them, then I have a way for you to escape on your own. But you must not wait too long. Life could suddenly become even worse here at any moment."

We entered the *Arbeitsamt* and walked down a long hallway to an office where Mr. Malinowski greeted a short, plump German man sitting behind his desk, the scattered strands of his oily black hair stretched across his bald pate, his breath smelling of garlic.

"Good morning, Mr. Kraus."

"Good morning, Mr. Malinowski. What can I do for you?"

Mr. Malinowski turned on his charm and concocted a story about how I never received a *kennkarte* and armband when they transported me to the ghetto from Tarnów the day before. "That's not possible," said Mr. Kraus. "All of the transports are processed at the time of arrival."

"Well, somehow it happened," replied Mr. Malinowski as he reached into his pocket and secretly slipped Mr. Kraus a small bottle of pills. I don't know what kinds of pills they were, but whatever they were, Mr. Kraus clearly wanted them. He eagerly pocketed the bottle without making eye contact, opened his desk drawer, and handed me a Star of David armband and a blank *kennkarte*.

I printed my family name on the first line, first name on the second line, and signed at the bottom. In another room, they took my picture to attach to the card with a small brass grommet. They stamped a black number, 051495, in the right corner of the card, and once they printed the photograph, they would stamp in the left corner a red circular General Government and Kraków Labor Office seal.

"Come back in three hours to pick up your card and show up here tomorrow at seven o'clock for your work assignment. Understand?" said Mr. Kraus while shuffling some papers on his desk.

"Yes, sir," I replied.

"Here is a temporary card to keep until the other one is ready." He handed me a small white card with my name printed on it, the 051495 number stamp at the bottom, along with the red General Government and Kraków Labor Office seal in the right corner.

"Thank you, Mr. Kraus," said Mr. Malinowski, reaching for Mr. Kraus's hand and shaking it. Mr. Kraus's glassy eyes darted about, still trying to avoid Mr. Malinowski's gaze.

Before leaving the building, I slipped on the armband with disgust, feeling the refuge of my Polish peasant identity instantly stripped away. Now, tagged like an animal, I was once again nothing more than a despicable Jew to the Germans and their Polish collaborators.

On the street, I thanked Mr. Malinowski for his help and was about to leave when the thought of Schlöndorff pricked my mind. "By the way, Mr. Malinowski, have you heard of an SS captain by the name of Schlöndorff?" Even though my grown body and beard had changed my appearance from the time he last saw me, I still feared being identified by him should he be alive.

"No. Why?"

"He was the man who shut down Papa's umbrella shop and searched our home. He didn't like us. I wanted to be sure to avoid him if he was possibly in the ghetto."

"I've not heard of him. But I will inquire into his whereabouts and let you know." He reached into his pocket and handed me some money. "Here's a few zloty."

"I don't need it."

"Take it, please. And be careful. And make sure you get back here in three hours to pick up your *kennkarte* and return to the pharmacy before curfew."

"Thank you, I will."

"Good luck. See you tonight." He shook my hand and walked away.

I nervously took Limanowskiego Street to Krakusa Street where I found Zelda's building, number 10. As I stood before its thick wood door a restlessness ran through me, making my limbs wobbly. I entered the doorway and dashed up three flights of stairs filled with wild children yelling and screaming, chasing one another up and down the stairwell and through the hallways, their clothes tattered and soiled, their hands and faces gritty with dirt. Several boys and girls had their heads shaved for lice.

I reached apartment 6 on the third floor and knocked on the door and waited, but no one answered. I knocked again. My legs shook with a mixture of fear and excitement; a nervous queasiness stirred inside my belly.

I put my ear to the door and heard faint voices. I knocked again and again, refusing to leave until someone answered. Then a woman's voice answered from behind the door.

"What is it!" she hollered, sounding like Zelda's mother.

"Mrs. Abramovitch? It's me, Reuven Berkovitz."

"I'm not Mrs. Abramovitch."

"Can you open the door, please?"

"No. Go away."

"Please! I beg you. I'm searching for the Abramovitch family. I was engaged to their daughter, Zelda. I need to find her."

"What did you say your name was?"

"Reuven Berkovitz."

The door slowly opened and before me stood a small elderly woman in a black dress and black stockings, her salt-and-pepper hair pulled back tightly in a bun, her crinkly crow-like face studying me suspiciously. Behind her were families packed in the hallway and sitting room. Some lay across the floors sleeping, others eating; one man paced in a small circle, as if trapped in a cage. The pungent odors of cooked food, dirty diapers, sweaty and un-washed bodies emerged from the apartment. A rope hung across the hallway with wet clothes draped over it, forming small puddles on the floor.

"Does the Abramovitch family live here?" I asked.

"Not now."

"They did at one time?"

"Yes."

"When did they leave?"

"About a month ago."

"Do you know where they went?"

"Who knows? The father was sick—a very sick man. I think heart problems. And the mother was having problems up here." She pointed to her head. "The girl—she was a good girl, such a good girl."

"You mean Zelda?"

"Yes, yes. Zelda was her name. She took good care of them and worked at the Madritsch factory sewing—repairing German uniforms. Poor girl. She had her hands full."

"And you don't know where they went?"

"No."

"And no one else in the apartment knows?"

"I knew them better than anyone. They said they were mov-ing in with a relative. But I don't know where. They wouldn't say.

They could be somewhere in the ghetto. Or maybe they made it out of the ghetto—you know—hiding. I don't know. Who knows where anyone is now? People are here one minute, gone the next, deported by the Germans—disappeared! Or they somehow escape." She started to close the door, but I held it open.

"Should you see them again, please tell Zelda that Reuven Berkovitz is looking for her. She should go to the pharmacy and ask Mr. Malinowski where I am. He will know."

She nodded and shut the door, appearing to not give much thought to what I had just requested.

On the street I contemplated what to do next. I decided to search for Zelda by going from street to street, building to building, apartment to apartment, knocking on doors and asking anyone I came across if they knew of Zelda and her family's whereabouts.

I went to the building next door, then the next building. When I exited and was about to enter a third building, a Gestapo dressed in plainclothes stopped me. Maybe he'd been watching me. He demanded to see my *kennkarte*, and I gave him my temporary card. He looked at it suspiciously, then pointed to the transport truck parked across the street and ordered me to load into it. I feared he was arresting me.

47

INSIDE THE TRUCK BED, AMID PILES OF SHOVELS AND SLEDGE-
hammers, dirt and straw, were eight other Jewish men, the youngest
about fourteen, the oldest maybe sixty. Several were engaged in
conversation. I interrupted and asked if we were being arrested.
They laughed at my question and informed me we were being
taken to a worksite. I asked if anyone knew the Abramovitch family.
Nobody had heard of them.

The truck drove for maybe twenty minutes before it stopped
and we were ordered to get out. To our dismay, we found ourselves
in a Jewish cemetery. We couldn't imagine why they brought us
here. I looked around at the headstones and black iron fence
surrounding the perimeter. Elm trees and oaks, bushes and wide
swaths of thick green grass divided sections of the cemetery. It
all looked familiar to me. Then I realized this was the cemetery
where Grandpa Eliyohu was buried but had no memory of where
his headstone was.

I'd been to this cemetery only once before with my family
when I was very young, maybe ten years old. We had laid pebbles
on Grandpa's brown granite headstone, marking the anniversary of his death. It was a warm day and Bubbe knelt on the
ground picking the tall blades of grass around the edges of his
stone, grooming it like a gardener, making sure it looked clean
and well cared for. Engraved at the top was the Star of David,
and beneath the star were the Hebrew words *Po Nikbar*—Here

lies . . . I don't remember what his epitaph said. All I remember is he died 16 August 1924.

We all recited the kaddish and Bubbe lit a yahrzeit candle placed at the base of his headstone. Bubbe kept talking about how much she missed her Eliyohu and how she'd see him soon. She patted down the grass where her resting place was reserved next to him.

When we had left Kraków, I never even considered we were leaving Grandpa Eliyohu's grave behind. But I'm sure Bubbe had thought about it. She must have realized there was a strong possibility of never being buried next to her husband, that she'd die somewhere far from Kraków, a place where we'd have to bury her in a strange cemetery where she knew no one. Would it even be a Jewish cemetery? The thought must've tormented her. But she never mentioned it. Or maybe she had told herself a different story, the same story we all told ourselves at the time to maintain our sanity and keep going forward—that our situation was temporary, that life would go back to normal once the war ended with the Germans defeated.

Two German soldiers reached into the back of the truck and tossed shovels and sledgehammers at each man, ordering us to dig up the headstones and break them into quarters.

We looked at one another, confused. Why would the Germans have us destroy the headstones of the dead? For what purpose? To humiliate us some more? To defile our dead ancestors as a punishment for being Jewish? Maybe their plan was not only to kill us all off, but also to erase any records of our existence. This way they could ensure we would never be remembered.

Like slaves, we obediently followed their orders. We paired off in twos, one man with a shovel and the other with a sledgehammer, and began digging up the headstones and breaking them into quarters. But one man, a Hasidic, tall and bony, stork-like, with a dense black beard and *peis* curled round his ear, stood in his place gazing down at the ground in a state of terror. While clutching his cap with hands that shook uncontrollably, his head nodded in disbelief as he wept and whispered solemn prayers to Adonai, his God.

A soldier walked up to the man and punched him hard in the jaw. His yarmulke flew off his head as he dropped to the ground. The soldier then swiftly kicked him with his heavy leather boots square in the middle of the back, giving him a jolt that made him arch backward, writhing in agony. He ordered the Hasidic to get up and work. "*Schnell! Schnell!*" the soldier barked, burying his boot in the man's ribs again as he tried crawling away. Gasping for air, he cowered and apologized to the soldier, pleading for God's forgiveness through mumbling, beseeching prayers.

The rest of us pressed on, unearthing stones, eyes fixed on the soil beneath our feet, determined to evade the harrowing sight of the brutal pummeling nearby. I flashed on the three monkeys Khone had carved into the ivory of Papa's umbrella handle—hear no evil, see no evil, speak no evil. Yes, we were the monkeys now, so terrified of this evil, hoping it would magically disappear if we averted our eyes and closed off our ears and pretended it wasn't there.

At first, I pitied the man. He had done nothing wrong. But eventually my pity turned into a sense of frustration, and then anger, followed by disgust. I wanted the man to stand up and stop groveling on the ground while stammering and whining for God's help. Get up! I thought. God damn it, get up! Pull yourself together, *mamzer*! To my surprise, his weakness suddenly filled me with such a rage. His frailty was a stinging embarrassment to us all, a humiliation that confirmed our failings, our weaknesses, our fears of fighting back. Under my breath I said to the man working next to me: "He needs to stand up, for God's sake." The man nodded.

The Hasidic man finally crawled away from the soldier and used a headstone to pull himself up to his feet. He grabbed a shovel, now ranting to himself like a madman, and began digging. The soldier stood there watching him, as if the man had become a curiosity. The soldier took out a cigarette, casually lit it, and took a few drags while watching the babbling, crazed Hasidic a moment longer, before walking away.

Using our shovels and sledgehammers, we hacked and pried and ripped the stones out from the soil and roots that clung to them. I swung my sledgehammer high over my head in a looping arc, crushing the headstones into pieces. We all tried to avoid reading the names on the headstones by placing them in the dirt face down. But one name I accidentally read—Dr. Lipa Melamed. Melamed meant "teacher" in Hebrew. The epitaph read: "In loving memory of Dr. Lipa Melamed, a healer, devoted husband, loving father, and trusted friend. May his soul find eternal rest under the wings of God."

A guard watched over me as I swung my sledgehammer against the headstone again, and again, destroying the record of Dr. Melamed's birth and death, crushing his loving epitaph, annihilating his proud name, turning it all into nothing more than broken chunks of rock and dust.

My stomach turned. I wanted to vomit.

We worked through the day and into the night smashing the headstones of the dead. Although most of us were numb from all the loss and degradation we'd experienced, the destruction of the headstones seemed to sweep away and discard whatever fragments of humanity we still had left inside us. We were all falling into a bottomless chasm of emptiness and numbness. Even the sensations of sorrow, sadness, humiliation, and shame were dissipating, because to feel those emotions, you'd have to be alive inside. And we were all becoming as dead to the world as the people buried in the soil beneath us.

When we finished that night, the Germans ordered us to collect all the pieces of broken headstones in wheelbarrows and pile them near the truck. I rolled my wheelbarrow from one end of the cemetery to the other, collecting broken headstones. And then it happened. I picked up a headstone fragment with a part of my grandpa's first name engraved on it: Eli . . . The rest of the name was severed. The name may have been someone else's full name, Eli, in Hebrew meaning "my God" or "ascended." Or it may have been a fragment of another name beginning with Eli, such as Eliana, Eliezer, Elior, Elisheva, Elitzur, Eliram, Elishua. But I chose to believe it was his name on that stone—Eliyohu.

I coddled it in my hands, brushing my fingertips over its jagged edges, before a soldier ordered me to keep moving. I then gently placed it on the pile of headstones in my wheelbarrow and for a moment considered trying to sneak it back into the ghetto. But I knew if the Germans found it, that would be the end of me and possibly the other men I was working with as well. So I tossed the fragment of Grandpa's headstone into the woods on the other side of the cemetery fence, returning it to the earth from which it came, hoping no one would ever find it.

48

EVERY DAY AFTER WORKING FOR THE GERMANS, EVEN IF IT WAS past curfew, I searched at least one building for Zelda and her family before returning to Mr. Malinowski's apartment. The hope of finding her was the sole force driving me forward. Yet, despite my efforts, I encountered no one who knew of their whereabouts. Mr. Malinowski, however, remained steadfast in his encouragement, reminding me that people were constantly being transported in and out of the ghetto. He urged me to never give up hope and to persist in my daily search.

A couple of weeks later, I moved out of Mr. Malinowski's apartment. The timing couldn't have been better. The Germans had spiked their number of random searches of apartments and businesses for weapons and those suspected of forming a resistance.

A fellow I had worked with, Aaron Schmeltzer, offered me a mattress in the apartment that he and his family shared with three other families. Mr. Malinowski was grateful that I'd found another place so quickly. He said he would miss our evening and morning conversations and told me to come by as often as possible to share a meal or cup of tea so we could stay in touch. I told him I'd also miss our conversations and would visit him soon. I gave him the address of where I was staying so he could find me in case he heard anything about the Abramovitch family, or simply needed to reach me.

The new apartment was noisy and chaotic. Families were packed in so tightly that every square inch was occupied. Sleep was scarce, and the emotional distress caused by overcrowding was an unyielding force that quickly wore people down, frayed the nerves, and caused constant friction. Every night there were at least several children who were up late sick and crying. Often the parents got into arguments over food and space. One time, two of the mothers got into a fight over whose turn it was to use the stove. One of them grabbed a knife and threatened the other. Fortunately, her husband stepped in and disarmed her.

People dealt with the relentless stress in different ways. Some withdrew into themselves, pulling away and trying to disappear. Others took on a larger presence, taking up more emotional space, becoming more aggressive and power hungry and more volatile. And still others seemed to have the fortitude, the focus and discipline of the mind to maintain a centeredness inside themselves, a levelheadedness, acting as counterweights to those who were succumbing to the overwhelming emotional pressures. These very stable people reminded me of Mr. Malinowski, Khone, and Zelda.

I had always been impressed by Zelda's innate ability to sustain her concentration and balance during times of intense stress. I witnessed this trait of hers five years ago when her father had fallen down the stairs and injured his back so badly that he couldn't work for nearly seven months. During this time, her mother fell ill with pneumonia. Money became so tight that Zelda had to work two sewing jobs after school and full-time on the weekends, plus shop for food and watch her younger brothers.

Living under this extreme stress, she somehow kept up with her studies while supporting her family. She rarely lost her composure. I was in awe of her inner strength, her mental and physical endurance. From what I could see, she never lost her focus on what needed to be done, what all the priorities were. She maintained a firm patience with her little brothers and always remembered that while her troubles were challenging, they were also temporary. "Nothing in the world is permanent," she'd always say. "Permanence is only an illusion."

THREE MORE WEEKS PASSED AND STILL THERE WAS NO SIGN of Zelda and her family. I had covered all the apartments on Krakusa Street and was now working my way down Józefińska Street. Several people I encountered along the way had known the family from the neighborhood in Kazimierz, but did not know where they were now. Another person provided me with an address for a building they thought they were living in. But that was a dead end. Two other people I met thought they heard someone say the Abramovitch family left Kraków just before the completion of the wall. I asked who they got this information from. They had no recollection of who the person was that said it.

IN THE LAST WEEK OF AUGUST, THE GERMANS TRANSPORTED US back to the cemetery where we had destroyed all the headstones and ordered us to build a road. For what purpose, or where it was going, we didn't know.

We cleared all the trees in the searing heat with clouds of mosquitos and gnats swarming us. We leveled the black soil and dug up the decaying caskets, moldy and worm infested, weighted with their contents of human remains adorned in suits, dresses, and gowns.

The Germans ordered us to pile the caskets and the dead into a mound, douse it all in gasoline, and set it aflame. Plumes of black smoke swirled around us, appearing as though the ghosts of the dead were being unleashed. When the wood caskets burned away, the naked bones—skulls, spines, ribs, and femurs—revealed themselves. Some men recited the kaddish beneath their breath.

Others spoke to God and the dead in sacred words of desperation, begging for forgiveness. And there were those of us who were silent.

THE NEXT DAY THE GERMANS ORDERED US TO USE THE BROKEN headstones for paving the road we had cleared and leveled. One by one, we laid the headstones flat, face down in the dirt, hoping to protect the identity of the person to whom that headstone belonged. This was our last attempt to guard the dignity of the person who died. But the Germans, never ones to miss an opportunity to humiliate us, forced us to flip the stones so their inscriptions faced upward. Yet another way to desecrate the dead and demean the living. Yet another way to remind us—extinction was our destiny.

It took weeks to finish the road. Afterward German guards forced us to clear a forest and construct barracks for what seemed like some type of camp. In the forest we cut down oaks, pines, and birches that were then sawed into planks and beams. At the camp, we cut and hammered the planks and beams together to construct walls, roofs, doors, and floors. The days were long and scorching hot—our bodies coated in a thick, syrupy sweat composed of pine pitch, sawdust, dead gnats, and mosquitoes. They never told us what the barracks at Płaszów would be used for. But Mr. Malinowski said he'd heard that Płaszów was going to be a labor camp for Jews and political prisoners. A contact of his said the Germans were planning to move all the Jews out of the ghetto and into the camp so there'd be no more Jews living inside Kraków's city limits.

49

WHEN FALL ARRIVED IN OCTOBER, THE LEAVES ON THE MAPLES, oaks, and elms filling the parks and lining the streets of Kraków began turning from deep greens to pomegranate reds, fiery oranges, bronzes, and golden yellows. The cool winds plucked them from their branches and scattered them, like vibrant paint splotches, across sidewalks and streets, parks and the riverbank.

For a week, the Germans forced us to rake the city clean of the beautiful leaves before their rich colors faded away, leaving them brown and mottled. We gathered them into piles and shoveled them into trucks that transported them to a spot by the river where they burned. Floating along the river's current heading north were the leaves that had fallen from trees overhanging the water, or had escaped the burning mounds by catching the blast of a cool fall wind. Patches of leaves colorfully carpeted the water's surface. I imagined some would float all the way to Gdynia before flowing into the Baltic Sea. But most wouldn't make it that far. Most would sink to the bottom of the river where they'd disintegrate over time and become a part of the river's basin. And some would land on the banks where they might live through the winter frozen and preserved, suspended in time while encased in sheets of ice until the warm spring sun would shine on them and melt the ice, releasing them once again into the river where they'd float on its current before disintegrating and disappearing forever.

During these fall months, I searched for Zelda in the moments I had between work and sleep. There were still many more buildings to go. And I thought even if she and her family were not here because they were hiding in the countryside, there was the strong possibility the Germans would find them soon and transport them to the ghetto, like so many others.

50

ROSH HASHANAH AND YOM KIPPUR CAME AND WENT; SUKKOT came and went. By the start of December, the northern winter winds and snows blasted across the farm fields and valleys, over rivers and lakes, through the forests and down the mountains.

During this time there were people on the ghetto streets—men, women, children, and the elderly—freezing in layers of soiled rags and dying from hunger, covered in sores and sick with typhus and TB, scratching themselves until they bled from lice. As I passed them, they would hold out their desperate bony hands, dirt-stained and long-nailed, begging for food. Dead bodies, some naked and scabby, had a bluish-white sheet of skin, thin as parchment, barely covering their bones. They lay in the gutters for days until workers with wooden carts picked them up and stacked them on top of one another like pieces of wood. The workers piled some of the bodies into mounds and set them aflame; other bodies were buried in the trenches we dug.

In these dark and cold days of winter, my searches for Zelda diminished. I questioned how much longer I could endure trying to find a person who seemed to no longer exist. I figured Zelda either was still hiding on her uncle's farm or was some place in the world where I'd never find her. Perhaps transported to another ghetto. Or something else may have happened—a thought I tried to avoid.

Shamefully, I had to admit to myself that I was gradually losing the mental and emotional stamina to keep going. I was physically depleted from the long hours of labor digging trenches and laying railroad track in the frigid temperatures; I was sleep deprived and beaten down by the ghetto's unrelenting despair. People were going mad with their interminable sorrow and suffering. The sense of being trapped and suffocated by these wretched conditions was overwhelming. I was unsure of how much longer I could survive in the ghetto before I, too, would go mad.

I met with Mr. Malinowski one day after work and shared my disturbing thoughts. He said if I didn't find Zelda and her parents soon, then I needed to escape and save myself. "A German I know told me things will only get worse for the Jews in the coming months," he said. "Once the winter thaws, you must leave before it's too late."

He knew a truck driver who could hide me inside his vehicle and transport me north to the port of Gdynia. There, Mr. Malinowski knew of another man who would help me stow away on a Swedish iron ore freighter returning to Sweden. Strangely, even though Sweden was a neutral country, they were still trading iron ore with the Germans while also providing refuge for their Jews. Mr. Malinowski's words reinvigorated my drive to continue searching for my Zelda in the limited time that was left.

A WEEK LATER, THE KIND AND GENEROUS MR. MALINOWSKI invited me over for a Hanukkah dinner. It was Sunday, 14 December 1941, the first day of Hanukkah. After working all day shoveling a foot of fresh snow off the streets and sidewalks, I sat down at his table and warmed my body by the wood-burning stove. Set on the table was an abundance of food, including a pot of matza ball soup, fresh challah and latkes, and a roasted chicken. "Where did you get all this food?" I asked.

"Several customers came by and insisted I take it. I refused, but they wouldn't listen. They said they'd be offended if I didn't accept their offering as they put it all down on the counter and left, just like that. Such kind people. They had no business leaving me this food when they have so little." He handed me a bowl of soup. "Such acts of kindness help restore one's faith in humanity. Don't you agree?"

"I do."

"It's very humbling."

"And so are your mitzvahs, Mr. Malinowski. Your good deeds and selflessness are also humbling."

"Oh, please," he said, sweeping away the compliment with a wave of his hand.

"Seriously. You risk your life every day to help those who come to you in need of assistance. There are very few people like you in the world. At least I haven't met many. So, thank you, Mr. Malinowski. The Jews of the Kraków ghetto are indebted to you."

"Enough," he said, unfurling his napkin with the snap of his wrists, spreading it across his lap. "I'm just a pharmacist doing what any man in my position should do."

"You're more than that. Most men wouldn't have the courage to do what you do."

"When I was twelve years old, my father once told me the purpose of being a pharmacist is to heal and relieve the suffering of others through medicines. He made me take an oath that I would always follow that principle should I ever become a pharmacist. It's an oath I made to my father, myself, and the good Lord upstairs. I try, to the best of my abilities, to uphold that oath. And yet I feel

I'm not doing enough here. In this dark place, one can never do enough to help those who are suffering."

He placed a white candle in its silver candle holder at the center of the table and handed me a pack of matches. "Now I don't have a menorah, but will this candle do?"

"Of course."

I struck a match and moved the flame toward the wick while reciting the same words my family recited for countless generations. "*Baruch atah Adonai Eloheinu Melech ha-olam, asher kid'shanu b-mitzvotsav, v-tzivanu l'hadlik ner, shel Hanukkah. Amen.*"

"Amen," said Mr. Malinowski. "Now translate the words of the prayer for me."

"Blessed are you, our God, Ruler of the Universe, who makes us holy through Your commandments, and commands us to light the Hanukkah lights."

"Beautiful," said Mr. Malinowski. He poured us each a glass of wine and I blessed the wine before we drank. Then I blessed the challah, ending the blessing by breaking off a piece of bread for each of us to eat. I chewed it slowly, savoring each bite of its sweet, buttery flavor. I thought of Mama's fresh challah, its honeyed aroma wafting through the apartment, filling me with a sense of security and belonging—a memory now braided, like the bread, with love and grief.

"Dig in," said Mr. Malinowski. "We have enough here to feed a family of ten. And I have a special gift for you at the end of the meal. So, eat up."

I figured the surprise would be a dessert he had hidden away. Maybe rugelach or lekach, honey cake.

Over his shoulder, I glanced at the picture of Mr. Malinowski with his parents. As close as I felt to Mr. Malinowski, I knew so little about his past. He seemed to avoid speaking about it and I never wanted to pry. But having Hanukkah dinner and drinking wine with him made me more comfortable in asking some questions.

"Do you have any siblings?" I asked.

"No. I was an only child, and my father died when I was fifteen. So, from then on, my family consisted of my mother and myself, and a couple of cousins from my father's side."

"Where does your mother live?"

"She passed away years ago."

"You must miss her."

"I do. We were very close."

"Did you ever want to have a family of your own?"

"No. Not really. I knew I wouldn't be a good husband or father because of my commitment to my work and outdoor adventures. Having a family was never a priority of mine." He finished his glass of wine and refilled my glass before pouring himself another.

"Were you ever in love?" I suddenly asked, surprised and embarrassed that a question like that had just leaped from my mouth. There was a long pause. His eyes tensed, as he contemplated the question. He took a large gulp of his wine.

"I apologize, Mr. Malinowski. That was a very personal question."

"It's okay," he said, gazing across the room as though seeing someone he knew. "We're good friends, and I trust you." Pausing a moment longer, he seemed to struggle with how to articulate his thoughts, then took another sip of wine. "Yes," he said, shifting his eyes back to me. "Yes—I was in love once. But circumstances made it impossible for us to be together." He paused again, as if debating whether he should go into more detail. His face appeared to wrestle with the weight of something unresolved. "Suffice to say, it just wasn't meant to be."

"Do you miss her?"

"Her? Yes . . . I do."

There was a long silence after he said that, and I wasn't sure how to respond. He continued to stare across the room. I realized he was possibly looking at the picture of him and his friend on the mountain posing for the camera with their arms draped over each other's shoulders. He seemed deep in thought, still trying to wrestle with whatever had happened to his love.

"I'm sorry it didn't work out," I said.

"Oh, there's nothing to be sorry about." He forced his lips into the shape of a painful grin that tried to disguise his sorrow.

I wanted to change the subject and went over to the side table to look at the photograph of him with the mountain climbing friend. I picked it up and handed it to him. "Who was this friend of yours?" I asked. "You look like best friends."

Mr. Malinowski's expression shifted to one of bewilderment. "Why, that's Pavel. He was my closest and dearest friend. We grew up together and both loved the outdoors. We camped and fished, hunted, and climbed mountains." He drank some more wine and topped our glasses again. "He died ten years ago, just two months after that picture was taken. We were climbing a granite crevasse when he slipped off the edge and fell."

"That's horrific. I'm so sorry."

"Thank you. I miss him dearly. And although it's been many years, I still feel his presence always right here, beside me. Those who you love deeply never really leave you. As you know very well." He gently put the picture down beside him and abruptly stood up from the table. "Now, enough about me. Let's get back to you. First, would you like some tea?"

"Of course."

He had hot tea already prepared on the stove and poured my glass, and then filled his. In the center of the table, he set down a small plate filled with walnut, raspberry, and apricot rugelach. I ate a piece and the pastry was so delicious I practically melted into the floor.

Mr. Malinowski took his seat again and gave me an odd look as he smiled and reached into his breast pocket and handed me a blue envelope. "Happy Hanukkah," he said. The warm candlelight flickered brightly in his watery blue eyes.

After carefully unsealing the envelope, I read the contents of the note and felt my breath taken away as I absorbed the words. "Is this real?" I asked, gazing up at Mr. Malinowski in complete astonishment and disbelief.

His eyebrows arched with enthusiasm as he nodded, answering my question with a beguiling grin. I read the note over and over. The handwriting was unquestionably Zelda's. It was a request for phenobarbital for her mother, Masha Abramovitch, and it included their address.

Mr. Malinowski's face gleamed. "I received the note late this afternoon. Yosef's neighbor brought it in."

"And you waited this long to give it to me?"

He laughed. "I wanted to make sure you first ate your dinner!"

I jumped up from the table, almost knocking over the wineglasses, and shook Mr. Malinowski's hand and then hugged him and kissed his cheeks. He smiled and looked slightly taken aback by my outpouring of physical affection. "I must go," I said.

"Hurry," he said. "You still have some time before curfew."

I threw on my coat and shoes and was about to leave. "Wait," he said. "You need to give them this." He quickly wrapped some chicken, brisket, challah, latkes, and rugelach in brown paper and a cloth and handed it to me. "Tell them I say hello and that I wish them a happy Hanukkah."

We went downstairs and he walked me to the door. I was about to leave when he grabbed my sleeve. "My God! I almost forgot. She needs this more than anything." He ran back to the counter and returned with a bag containing the medication. "The directions for taking the phenobarbital are on the bottle. But remind Mrs. Abramovitch, it's one pill a day, preferably in the evening. Good luck, and let me know how it goes with Zelda."

"Of course," I said as I dashed out the door.

51

INSIDE HER BUILDING, THE ICY STAIRS WERE DIRTY AND littered with garbage—breadcrumbs, empty tin cans, broken bottles, jars, and pieces of paper. Several rats scampered off into the holes of the walls and stairs.

On the second floor, I knocked on the door to apartment number 4. The celebratory sounds of people laughing and singing Hanukkah songs flowed from a unit down the hallway. Children's voices called out the letters on the sides of their dreidels as they spun and landed. *"Nun! Gimel! Hei! Shin!"*—meaning: *Nes Gadol Hayah Sham*, a great miracle occurred here. Despite the irony of hearing such words of joy and celebration amid the decay and desperation of the ghetto, the words also resonated profoundly for me. How true, I thought; to find Zelda was a miracle.

Again, I knocked on the door to apartment number 4 and put my ear against the wood and listened. Amid the murmurs of conversations, coughing and hacking and babies crying, a man sang accompanied by an accordion. I tried to open the door, but it was locked. I pounded on it again, even harder this time. Finally, a small boy of maybe six opened the door, his large round eyes sunken, skin sallow; he had a cough with a runny nose and a deep red rash on his cheeks.

"Does the Abramovitch family live here? Zelda and her parents?"

The child nodded, scratching the small pink bumps crusted with scabs on his head and arms from lice.

"I have some things I must give them, so I'm going to come in, okay?"

The boy nodded again and led me down the dark hall. The electricity was out, and the stench of unclean bodies and urine hung in the frigid air. From the bedrooms came more coughing and wheezing, and people talking.

I stepped over two bodies covered in blankets lying in the hallway, the vapors of their breath the only signs they were alive. In the first bedroom, more people lay on the floor huddled beneath layers of blankets and carpets, their bodies sandwiched together for warmth. I searched for signs of Zelda but didn't see her. A family of four sat packed together in a corner, clustered round the light of an oil lamp as they shared bread and scraps of food from a plate they passed around. In the second bedroom was the accordion player, a young man with a patchy black beard sitting on the floor with his back against the wall. More oil lamps lit the room. I searched through the darkness, yet still no sign of Zelda or her parents. A group of children sat around the accordion player, leaning against his legs, gazing up at him in awe. His eyes were closed as he wistfully sang a nostalgic Yiddish song, "Mamele," a song Zelda would sometimes sing to me on our walks to work, or picnicking by the river.

"Mamele, mamele." Mother, dear Mother. "Mit libshaft vel ikh rufn dikh Mamele." With love, do I call you mother. "Ogyn mid, shvakh dayn hant." Tired eyes, your hand is frail. "A golden harts hostu, un yeder kind farshteys." You have a golden heart, and every child understands this.

The apartment lights suddenly came on; the accordion player's eyes sprung open. "A Hanukkah miracle!" he shouted. The surrounding children laughed and repeated his words and got up and danced while shouting "A Hanukkah miracle! A Hanukkah miracle!" Then the lights went out again, and the children fell quiet.

"Where are they?" I asked the boy. He looked confused, then led me to the sitting room where even more people lay scattered across the floor. Several people sat on wood chairs. On the one couch, an elderly couple lay next to each other, smoking cigarettes and talking, wrapped in blankets and heavy winter coats. Near them, on a table in the center of the room, a menorah burned brightly with the first candle and center candle, the *shammash*, lit, marking the first night of Hanukkah.

The boy pointed to a corner of the sitting room before returning to the bedroom with the accordion player. In the corner, two dressers stood side by side, making a four-foot-high wall, creating a separate space in the shape of a shoebox. Three people sat together round their oil lamp inside the small space, wrapped in blankets and coats, sharing some bread, and sipping their soup, the contours of their faces obscured by shadows. At first, I wasn't certain if they were Zelda and her parents.

Nervously, I shifted to another angle to see their faces more clearly. The silhouette of the young woman's face illuminated by the warm glow of the oil lamp's flame came into focus. The edges of her thick, curly hair glowed copper-red. She delicately dipped her spoon in the soup and brought it to her lips with her pinky raised in the air—I knew it was Zelda. Yet she had changed, appearing older than her years, spindly with dark shadows looming beneath her tired eyes, the sharp bones of her face and hands suggesting she was gaunt beneath her thick layers of clothing. Her posture, which had always been straight as a ballerina's, had rounded slightly; her shoulders curved protectively inward. She was engaged in conversation with her parents who hunched forward, appearing fragile and at least ten years older than when I last saw them two years ago. Whereas Zelda had always spoken emphatically with her hands, often dramatically whipping them through the air like an orchestra conductor, they now rested quietly on her lap, almost listless. A cloud of grief appeared to hang over them. I wondered where her brothers were.

My heart sank. An uneasy restlessness enveloped me. I didn't move save for my hands that trembled slightly as they gripped the packages of food and medicines. I needed a moment to comprehend what I was seeing. Then her mother looked up and spotted me standing in the shadows a short distance away.

Her thick black hair was now threaded with gray. She stared at me as if she were observing a hallucination. Zelda turned to see what had captured her mom's attention and cast a similar look of bafflement and disbelief. She stood up and cautiously walked toward me. My legs trembled with nervousness. She wore a heavy moss-colored sweater over layers of shirts, a black skirt with dark red wool leggings beneath it, her shoes made of faded brown leather. She seemed to float across the floor as her long arms and delicate fingers drifted by her side, like the stringy branches of a willow swaying in a breeze.

"Reuven? Is that really you?" Her voice was demure, and raspier than before.

"Yes," I said. "And is it really you?"

She hesitated, looking at me oddly from some remote place that seemed worlds away. "Yes . . . mostly . . . I don't know."

At that moment it seemed everything had changed between us. My stomach got twisted into a knot of sadness. She didn't reach out to touch me, and I hesitated to touch her. I was afraid to touch her. Afraid! Why? Why was she so distant? Or was it me that was distant? We looked at each other as if we were standing on opposite sides of a canyon with a wide gully between us. Here we were, finally together after so much time had passed, yet so separate, so shy of each other. This was the woman I had longed for, the woman I had planned to marry, to have children with, to build a life with—and now we seemed to be strangers. I didn't understand it.

I nervously placed the package of food and medications on the ground by our feet and timidly moved to embrace her. Awkwardly wrapping my arms round her sparrowlike body, I gently pressed my hands against the thick layers of her clothing, my fingertips tracing the sharp bones of her ribs and shoulder blades.

She immediately stiffened at my touch. Her breath quickened. She pulled back. Apparently, I'd done something she didn't want me to do. I had crossed a line I should've seen, moved toward a physical closeness she wasn't ready for. I felt like such a fool.

After the brief embrace, I noticed her once lustrous copper-red hair was now a dull brownish-red, oily and unkempt, no longer carrying the scent of rose oil. Her long and slender neck, having always smelled of lavender soap, now smelled of sweat and wool, an odor that filled me with sorrow. Her arms hung rigid by her sides. My mind raced through a maze of thoughts and uncertainties. Maybe there was someone else in her life. Or maybe something horrible had happened to her. Or maybe a couple experiences this when they have been separated for a long time and have gone through many terrible things during that period—when two people have lost too much, endured too many traumas, witnessed too many tragedies. Maybe all the sadness and suffering had built a towering brick wall around each of us, like the ghetto, isolating us from each other, making each of us a prisoner inside our own walls.

Such a profound loneliness I felt in this moment gazing at Zelda, whom for so long I loved and yearned for. In this moment of confusion, I tried to clarify if what I had felt before was real, or just imagined.

"I missed you," I said, hoping to break down the wall to reconnect.

She hesitated. "I missed you, too."

But her words sounded tremulous, hollow, insincere, a polite response full of ambiguity.

"Are you sure?"

She nodded "yes" while looking down, avoiding my eyes.

"Do you still have the button I gave you?"

"I do."

"Where is it?"

"Right here." She pointed to where my black button secured her sweater over her heart. "I had lost a button and used yours to replace it."

I was encouraged to see she still had it.

"Well, at least you put it to good use."

She grinned shyly and there was a long silence. "I was afraid I'd never find you," I said.

She didn't reply.

I was scared and nervous, unsure of what else to say. Naïvely, I thought we'd pick up where we had left off. I thought if we ever found each other again, we'd fall into the other's arms and feel that same deep, mad, passionate love and commitment we'd had for each other before the war broke us apart. That insatiable hunger to be together, believing nothing could tear us apart— just like the movies. But how wrong I was. The war had not only physically separated us, but seemed to have broken our hearts apart.

We stood there for a long moment in an uncomfortable silence. I wasn't sure if she even wanted me to say hello to her parents. I bent down and picked up the package and tried handing it to her. "This is from Mr. Malinowski. There's some food in here and a medication for your mother."

"You give it to them," she said. "They'll be so happy to see you." She led me to where they patiently sat waiting for us. They started struggling to get up. "No need to stand," I said, as I bent down to give each of them a hug.

"Where have you been, Reuven?" asked Mr. Abramovitch, his voice gravelly and breathy. Next to him was his old leather-bound Talmudic prayer book that I remembered him packing the day they first left Kraków. He leaned into the light of the oil lamp to see me more clearly, his small wire-rimmed glasses resting at the tip of a long sloping nose, his black yarmulke barely capping the dome of his sizeable bald head. He placed his hand on mine, once plump, now bony. "Tell me what has happened to you and your family since we last saw you?"

"That's a long story, Mr. Abramovitch. I promise to tell you later when we have more time."

"Is your family with you? Are they okay?" asked Mrs. Abramovitch. "We'd like to see them." She was thin and pallid; dark shadows framed her weary eyes; her index finger nervously picked at the corners of her thumbs, just like Mama used to do.

"Yes, they're here," I replied, deciding they'd learn the truth later.

"Zelda never stopped talking about you," said Mrs. Abramovitch. "My hand to God—she never gave up on hoping to find you. And I knew you'd eventually find each other. I knew. I read it one day in the tea leaves, a year ago. Isn't that right, Zelda?"

"Yes, Mama." Her reply sounded obligatory and made me wonder how much of what Mrs. Abramovitch just said was exaggerated, or even true at all. She either didn't know what Zelda was really feeling, or knew and was saying what she could to keep us together. Mr. Abramovitch was quiet, occasionally sipping from his cup of tea, his bulging eyes swollen and sickly, full of doubt.

"You two finding each other is our Hanukkah miracle. It's *bashert*! You two were always meant to be together, forever," said

Mrs. Abramovitch, patting me on the hands, then pinching my cheek. "I still can't believe it's you."

I looked over at Zelda. She was staring across the room, occupied by other thoughts, maybe not even registering what her mother had just said. Mr. Abramovitch suddenly grabbed my hand and moved his face closer to mine, his eyes pleading with me. "Take her with you, Reuven. Please."

"What do you mean?" I asked.

"Yes, take her with you," repeated Mrs. Abramovitch. "You and your family must try to escape this wretched place, and you must take Zelda with you. We beg you."

"Stop it," said Zelda.

"Our two boys are missing and we can't leave until we find out where they are. But we can't lose our Zelda, too," said Mr. Abramovitch, huffing. "You and Zelda must survive. Promise us you will take her with you."

Before I could respond, Zelda cut in. "I'm not leaving you," she said vehemently. "We stay together, no matter what."

"But you must," said Mrs. Abramovitch.

"Drop it," said Zelda firmly.

"This is from Mr. Malinowski," I said, quickly changing the subject. I handed Mrs. Abramovitch the packages of food and medication. "Mr. Malinowski said you need to take one pill every day, in the evening."

"Such a mitzvah," said Mrs. Abramovitch. "Please thank him for us."

"How do you know Mr. Malinowski?" asked Mr. Abramovitch.

"I've known him a long time. He was a good friend to my father, and I worked for him part-time after the Germans took our shop. He knew I was looking for your family and so when he received the note for Mrs. Abramovitch's medication, he told me where to find you."

Mr. Abramovitch began coughing and wheezing. "Such a mensch," he said between coughs. "The kindest man."

Zelda jumped up and ran to get him a glass of water. His chest sounded thick with congestion, and he seemed in pain. I wondered if he had typhus.

She handed him the glass of water while Mrs. Abramovitch patted him on the back.

"Are you okay, Papa?" asked Zelda. He sipped some water between coughs, then settled down.

"Yes—I'll be fine now," he murmured.

Zelda stood up and told her parents that she wanted to speak to me privately on the stairwell.

"Go and talk," said Mrs. Abramovitch. "You have a lot to catch up on. But don't be long. We have food here that you need to eat."

"We won't be long," said Zelda.

ZELDA LED ME OUT OF THE APARTMENT AND INTO THE DARK stairwell where it was cold and damp. A couple of children burst out the door of the next apartment, giggling and chasing each other downstairs where they entered another apartment. Then it was quiet. Zelda wrapped her arms round her chest and shook from the cold. I took off my coat and offered it to her. "Thank you, but I don't need it. You should go, Reuven. Please."

"What do you mean?"

"I'm not the right person for you anymore. So please, just go."

I gazed at her, dumbfounded, and was speechless for a long moment before finding my words. "What do you mean? I don't understand what you're saying. We haven't seen each other in two years. A lot has happened . . ."

"I've changed. I'm not the person I was. And I'm sure you've changed as well. So please, find someone else and forget about me, Reuven. It'll be better for you." She opened the apartment door and was about to close it behind her, but I caught it and held it open.

"Wait. Please. What you say is true. We aren't the same people as before. How could we be? So please, give us some time to know each other again. Why can't you do that?"

She looked at me with such sadness filling her eyes.

"Is there someone else?" I asked.

"No. There is no one else."

"Then try."

"I'm sorry," she said, slowly backing away, and then closing the door.

I stood there for a long time staring at the door. Tears filled my eyes, my heart was crushed and aching, my sense of self broken into meaningless fragments. Nothing seemed to matter anymore.

I stood there frozen on the landing, waiting for her to open the door again to invite me back inside and tell me how much she missed me, and that she really didn't mean what she'd just said. But the door remained shut.

Slowly, I plodded down the stairs, feeling off-balance, gripping the railing to steady myself, winded, as if kicked in the gut.

52

THAT NIGHT I STAYED AWAKE UNTIL MORNING, TURNING OVER in my head what Zelda had said, trying to understand why she was so convinced she was no longer the right person for me; why she wasn't willing to even give us a chance.

The next morning, I wanted to go back and see her immediately but had to report to work duty. Before the first light, I met at the *Arbeitsamt* sixteen bedraggled and exhausted men waiting in the freezing cold for the truck to arrive. The sky was a dreary, smoky gray canopy; the wind gusts from the north added another layer of misery. We were all bundled in every scrap of clothing we owned. Some wore so many layers they looked like stuffed pillows with their heads, arms, and legs poking out. We wrapped scarves like huge bandages round our heads and necks for added warmth, and covered our hands with whatever gloves, mittens, or rags we could find. On my feet layers of socks and rags filled my oversized boots.

All day long we worked in the farmlands with the cold winter winds howling like a pack of wolves as they clawed through our clothes and froze our skin. Our fingers and toes turned numb while prying up old railroad track and ties and replacing them with new ones. We sledgehammered rail spikes, shoveled and filled wheelbarrows with gravel and dirt. The one thing that took my mind off the relentless work and freezing cold was thinking about Zelda and what she had said last night.

Maybe something had happened to her in the countryside. I had to know why she was so distant and hardened—why she wasn't willing to get to know me again. If it were true that there wasn't another man in her life, then it made no sense that she wouldn't at least want to give us a chance. Even though the war had changed us, I still believed that those parts inside us that had loved each other were still alive. But perhaps I was just being foolishly naïve.

AS WE WORKED ON THE TRACKS INTO THE NIGHT, THE RELENT-less winds drove thick snowfall horizontally across the earth, icy flecks stinging our cheeks and eyes like needles.

The German soldiers guarding us stayed warm and cozy inside their trucks while keeping watch. They'd step outside only to give orders, or to beat a man to the ground who they decided wasn't working hard enough, or to have a smoke and stretch their legs. They drank whiskey from their small silver flasks and ate copious amounts of bread, cheese, and sausage while we watched like hungry, sad-eyed hounds, hoping they might toss us a scrap.

When we finished replacing all the tracks, ties, and ballast, we marched back to the truck in a single file and returned to the ghetto an hour past curfew.

I was light-headed and ravenous from the cold and having little to eat all day, but went to see Zelda again before returning to my apartment for some food and sleep. Even if it was for just five minutes, I had to try to talk to her again.

The fresh snowfall blanketing the streets and sidewalks sparkled like sugar crystals in the moonlight. The wind was now still. Nobody was out. It was serenely quiet. The ghetto appeared almost magical, as if time had reversed itself, becoming the quaint neighborhood it once was before the war. Everything was clean and peaceful in its pure whiteness. A thick layer of foamy snow now covered the dirt and garbage and coated like frosting the window-sills, door stoops, rooftops, and streetlamps.

A man with a long black beard steered his horse-drawn cart down the center of the street, the shoulders of his muddy brown coat dusted with snow, the muffled sound of the horse's hooves clopping steadily, the wheels of his cart softly crunching across snow crystals, the golden flame of his kerosene lamp glowing brightly by his side. In that fleeting moment, all the sorrow and pity of the ghetto, all the death and disease, all the misery and hopelessness, seemed to have vanished.

I knocked on Zelda's apartment door lightly because I was afraid of waking people up. No one answered. I turned the knob and the door opened. Upon entering the apartment, I quietly made my way down the hallway and found Zelda huddled by the stove, wrapped in an old wool blanket frayed along the edges, sipping a cup of tea. Her parents and almost everyone else in the apartment were asleep. It was later than I thought. When I approached her, she politely asked me to leave. I politely said I wouldn't before we talked, then sat down next to her.

"It's past curfew. Why are you here?" she asked.

"I wanted to see you."

"What do you want from me?"

"You," I said. "I want you."

She sipped her tea and gazed into the belly of the stove where the embers glowed red beneath the gray ash, casting a warm light over her troubled face. "I don't know. . . ."

I opened the stove's door and turned the pieces of firewood inside and set another small log on top. The flame grew. "Why?" she asked. "Why are you being so insistent?"

"Because I love you. That's why I came back to the ghetto. To search for you. You're all I have in the world."

"What are you talking about? You have your family."

"My family is gone."

"I don't understand."

I hadn't planned on it, but I began telling her the story of what happened to my family. As she listened, the wall she'd built around herself slowly crumbled. Her demeanor shifted from being distant to warm and embracing. She took my hand and tenderly cradled it in hers, holding me in her eyes with the kindness and compassion I remembered from our past. She wept as I spoke, as did I. She whispered in her gentle, raspy voice: "I'm sorry, Reuven. I'm so sorry. . . ."

When my story concluded, she wrapped her arms around me, enveloping us in a tender silence that rekindled the loving bond I had shared with her since childhood. This was my Zelda, the young woman I had known before the war.

"Ever since coming here, I've looked everywhere for you," I said. "How long have you been here?"

"Just two weeks. The Germans found us on my uncle's farm in Dębica and forced us back here along with hundreds of other Jews."

"Isn't that where you went when you first left Kraków?"

"Yes."

"I never heard from you after that."

"And now I know why I never heard from you. I wrote you almost every day and couldn't understand why you never responded."

"Your letters never came, and I didn't have an address for your uncle. I kept looking for you, expecting you'd return when so many others had. But when another family took over your apartment, I thought I might never see you again."

"Mama, Papa, and I first came back to Kraków in June of '40. I looked for you but you were gone by then."

"We had left for Przemyśl the month before. Why weren't your brothers with you?"

"Joshua and Eli stayed on the farm to help my aunt and uncle. And then when they built the wall, Mama, Papa, and I left Kraków again and returned to the farm. But when we arrived, my brothers, aunt, and uncle had disappeared. We don't know where they are, or what's happened to them."

"I'm so sorry, sweetheart. Maybe they made it into Russia."

"I pray. It's been torturous to not know where they are. Especially for Mama and Papa."

The room was quiet save for the sounds of people sleeping, heavy breaths, soft groans, muffled coughs. I opened the stove's little iron door and fed it another piece of wood. The logs inside glowed and crackled. The scent of burning wood filled the room. Zelda took another sip of tea and watched the flames dance across the logs, their warm light flickering across her sad face. I noticed a scar running horizontal across her wrist and reached for it. "What happened?" I asked.

"Nothing," she said, pulling her sleeve down to cover it. Her demeanor had suddenly shifted, and I knew not to pry further.

"It's way past curfew, Reuven. You should go now." She abruptly stood up and led me to the door. "Be careful returning to your building this late."

I didn't want to leave her. "When can I see you again?"

She stood before me holding her cup of tea against her chest, searching my eyes for possibly some kind of reassurance. "Come when you can," she said before giving me a small kiss on the cheek.

"Goodnight," I said. "I'm so glad I found you."

"I am, too. Goodnight."

THE NEXT DAY I WORKED AT THE BRICK FACTORY STACKING CLAY bricks until dark. When I came back to Zelda's apartment that evening, German army trucks, jeeps, and police cars had parked in front of the buildings. At first, I thought they must be conducting a search for weapons and people they suspected of organizing a resistance. They did that from time to time in the ghetto. Without warning, they'd conduct raids and round up innocent people and bring them in for questioning. They killed some right on the spot; they killed others after their interrogations or sent them away to Płaszów to be worked to death in the limestone quarry. But this was something different.

Terrified residents spilled out of the doors handing soldiers and officers all their furs, including their coats, shawls, hats, gloves, rugs, and blankets. I didn't understand what was happening. Then, a black car appeared, slowly cruising down the street with small Nazi flags mounted on its front fender and a loudspeaker secured to its roof. It announced that everyone must immediately surrender all their furs, warning that those who violate the order will face imprisonment or death.

At Zelda's building, Jewish and Polish police officers guarded the front doors while anxious residents ran out of the building with their furs clutched in their hands. One of the Jewish police officers looked familiar to me. The one with the small mouse ears who first stopped me when I stole into the ghetto. He caught sight of me and grabbed my collar, pulling me to the side. "I know your face," he said, speaking under his breath. "Aren't you the umbrella maker's son?"

"Yes."

"Don't be stupid and go in there just yet. Let the soldiers and SS finish their business."

"But I have family in there. They need me."

"They're beating and arresting people and there's nothing you can do for them now. I'm warning you, wait for this to end."

"I can't."

He shrugged and shoved me off. "Suit yourself."

Stair by stair, I squeezed past the frenzy of residents, soldiers, and policemen running up and down the stairwell. One feeble old man tripped and fell on the first landing, spilling his armful of furs and bloodying his face. His son helped him get to his feet and collected his furs.

When I reached Zelda's floor, the door to the apartment was open and I went inside. Frightened parents, grandparents, and children lined up along the walls of the hallway, holding hands, crying, attempting to console one another. One mother was trying to breastfeed her screaming baby. Next to her a father held the hand of his little girl who sucked her thumb while clenching her teddy bear that was missing a foot.

In the first bedroom, two soldiers plunged their bayonets into the mattresses, slicing them to pieces, sending their cotton stuffing flying up in the air; in the second bedroom, another two soldiers recklessly scattered the contents of valises, trunks, and dressers across the floor as they searched for more furs, money, and jewelry.

Zelda and her parents huddled together in their corner of the sitting room, clinging to one another, their eyes watching the mayhem in horror. I joined them, wrapping my arms round Zelda, her breath shallow and rapid as her body shook uncontrollably.

Mr. Abramovitch started having a coughing fit. Mrs. Abramovitch immediately tried giving him water while patting his back.

We watched helplessly as one SS officer threw open the cabinets in the kitchen area and swept everything inside them onto the floor; pots and pans went crashing and clanging; glasses, plates, and cups, smashed into hundreds of pieces on the floor. Two other SS men pounded the wood floor around the stove using the heels of their black leather boots until they heard a hollow sound in the floorboards. One of them, young with cherublike cheeks and ice-blue eyes, used his knife to pry open the floorboards. Three of them came up easily. He reached inside and extracted a roll of cash tied with a string, plus a cloth bag full of jewelry and a mink wrap. A devilish grin broke across his boyish face, as if he'd discovered a long-lost treasure. His partner, older and more weathered looking with dark leathery skin, yelled out in German, "Who does this belong to?" Nobody answered. He walked through the room holding the mink fur in the air as if it were evidence of some terrible crime. He repeated the question again. Still, no one responded. Then he came to our corner and asked us whom it belonged to and I answered him in German, "It's not ours, sir."

"Then whose is it?"

"We don't know."

He pointed to Mr. Abramovitch's prayer book. "Give me that." Mr. Abramovitch handed it to him, still trying to control his coughing. He flipped through the pages. "A prayer book?"

Mr. Abramovitch nodded. "Yes," he said, his voice dry and hoarse, barely perceptible.

"Do you want to keep it?"

"Yes."

"I can't hear you."

"Yes. I said yes."

"Then tell us who this fur and jewelry belongs to."

"I honestly don't know, sir." He struggled to breathe while coughing. Mrs. Abramovitch kept rubbing his back and Zelda was telling him to calm down.

He handed the book to the younger officer. "Throw this garbage into the stove." The young officer opened the door to the stove and tossed the book inside it. The flames inside brightened.

"I'll ask one more time," said the SS man. "Who does this belong to?"

"We honestly don't know, sir," I replied.

"I think you do." He turned to the younger officer. "Take the girl."

I stood up between Zelda and the young officer and begged the older officer in broken German to not take her. I said she had nothing to do with what they found and made up that she was ill and had a heart condition, hoping they'd somehow take pity on her and let her go. He grinned and shoved me to the side, then grabbed Zelda by the hair and yanked her out from the corner. She completely snapped and fought him off, scratching his face, screaming for him to let her go. My mind went blank as I lunged at him, knocking him to the ground, punching him rapidly when suddenly something hard as metal smashed into the back of my head, knocking me out cold.

When I opened my eyes, I found myself tied to a chair, with the ropes so tight that my hands had gone numb. My head was foggy and throbbed from the strike. I felt disoriented, then realized I was inside one bedroom. The young SS officer was on top of Zelda, struggling on the floor in front of me. Another soldier attempted to hold down her legs as they desperately squirmed and tried kicking him away. One of her shoes was off. The other soldier pinned her arms. Something muffled her screams. My mind snapped and I went mad, crying out some primal sound, whipping my head back and forth, begging them to stop, pleading with them to let her go, writhing and twisting in the chair, straining to pull my arms and legs free from the ropes locking them down, shrieking for someone to help. "Shut him up!" yelled the young Nazi on top of her. The soldier holding down her legs jumped up and punched me repeatedly in the face and stomach, laughing, calling me a *Jude* rat. I vomited on myself as I continued pleading for them to stop. The soldier grabbed some stuffing from one of the ripped mattresses and jammed it in my mouth, gagging me, then tied a stocking over my mouth so I couldn't spit out the stuffing. Zelda's legs kept kicking and flailing. I struggled to breathe, to suck in air through my nose. The room spun and tilted as it went in and out of focus. My chair fell over. I hit the ground on my side. The young Nazi finished, pulled up his pants, buckled his belt, spat on Zelda, called her a *Juden* whore. "That was fun," he said to one soldier. "Your turn."

While lying on the floor, I rocked in my chair, squirming and twisting, trying to free my wrists and ankles from the ropes so I could reach Zelda. The young Nazi walked toward me, removed his club from his belt, and cracked me again on the head.

When I regained consciousness, I couldn't move. The room was off-kilter. I was still on my side and tied to the chair with my mind and body paralyzed. The soldiers were gone. Zelda stood up in a daze, put on her torn undergarments, buttoned her dress, ran her fingers through her hair, wiped away the blood that had flowed from her nose and the cut on her cheek. She calmly untied me from the chair and helped me stand up, and stared at me with the dull, traumatized eyes of a human being who was not of this world. They'd taken everything from her—stolen her soul, ripped her insides. There seemed to be nothing left of her. And now, nothing left of me.

THE LIGHTS WENT OUT IN THE APARTMENT AGAIN AND PEOPLE lit their oil lamps. We found her parents in their corner, weeping in the darkness, grateful to see both of us still alive. One look at Zelda and they knew what had happened to her. We sat down with them and lit the oil lamp. Zelda laid her head on her mother's lap. Mrs. Abramovitch caressed her, gently stroking her hair. Mr. Abramovitch placed his hand on Zelda's shoulder and spoke to God in Hebrew, praying to him, thanking him for saving our lives.

His prayers angered me. How could anyone thank a God for anything when their daughter had just been raped? The prayers were meaningless, just empty words strung together to create lies for people to blindly believe in, lies to give hope and reason where none existed.

Zelda got up and went to the bathroom to wash herself. The minute she left the room Mrs. Abramovitch frantically grabbed my arm and pleaded with me. "You and Zelda must leave here immediately. Please, please promise us you will take her away. I beg of you. What happened tonight can't ever happen to her again. She won't survive it. She'll try to kill herself."

Mr. Abramovitch took my other hand and clasped it in his. "They're going to kill us all at some point. Everyone knows it inside here," he said, pointing to his heart, "but no one says it. You know we are too old and sick to escape. You and Zelda must live. God wants this for you. Please, leave us. You must. Will you promise me this?"

"I will try," I said.

Zelda reappeared wearing a dark blue dress, black stockings, and a heavy black sweater. The other clothes she took to the stove and fed to the fire.

When she finished, she sat down next to me and her parents. They told her what they'd just told me. "No," said Zelda. "I'll never leave you here. Never! So, don't mention it again." They tried to reason with her, but she was steadfast in her decision.

She couldn't be still, so she set to work loading the stove with some wood, stoking the fire, then setting a pot of water on it to boil for tea. While waiting for the water to boil, Zelda and I picked up and organized the drawers ripped out of the two dressers that formed their little corner space. Her parents helped fold the clothes we had collected off the floor. Then we assisted another family with gathering their belongings and picking up the pieces of their broken plates and chairs.

When the water boiled we sat together and drank our tea with some bread and jam. Mrs. Abramovitch told Zelda she should see a doctor and asked me if Mr. Malinowski could help find one. I said he could. But Zelda refused her mother's suggestion, telling her she had no need for a doctor. "But just to be safe, Zelda. Please, see one," implored her mother. Zelda still refused, and there seemed to be no way to change her mind.

It was late when we finished our tea, and I needed to get back to my apartment before curfew. But I didn't want to leave Zelda and her parents alone. I took Zelda to the side and asked her privately, "Would you want me to stay here tonight?"

"Yes," she said, without hesitation.

Mr. and Mrs. Abramovitch were also pleased I was staying. "You are family," said Mr. Abramovitch. "You must move in and stay here with us from now on." Mrs. Abramovitch created a space for me on the old Persian carpet next to Zelda's mattress. I remembered that carpet used to be in the sitting room of their apartment in Kazimierz. Mr. Abramovitch had his sewing machine on a section near the window. He was so nearsighted that even with eyeglasses he sometimes had to lean in centimeters away from the fabric to see where it needed to be stitched. Working with fingers that seemed too thick for doing the delicate work of sewing, he would pump the machine's pedal with his feet as he carefully pulled the two pieces of fabric past the needle, driving up and down like a piston. When finished with the stitch, he'd cut the thread and tie it off, then tug on the two pieces of fabric, making sure he had sewn them together securely.

I blew out the oil lamp and lay on the carpet next to Zelda's mattress wrapped in my coat and using a sack of clothes for a pillow. But then Zelda tugged on me, motioning for me to move onto her narrow mattress. I squeezed next to her, both of us on our sides, my chest pressed against her back, my arm stretched across her. She placed my hand over her heart, where my button kept her sweater closed. Our bodies felt joined, conforming to each other, like two pieces of fabric sewn together.

5 4

THE NEXT DAY, I WENT TO SEE MR. MALINOWSKI AFTER WORK and reported all that had happened in Zelda's apartment. The news sickened him, but he was not surprised. He'd already heard many other stories from last night of the SS and German soldiers committing depraved acts of physical and sexual violence. He said they had also killed some people and took others to prison where they would most likely be tortured.

I begged him to help us escape the ghetto immediately, including her elderly parents.

"You remember the truck driver I told you about who is transporting some people to Gdynia?"

"Yes."

"I can get in touch with him in a few days and arrange a time. But you must let me know if they're really committed to going before I speak to him."

"I will."

That evening I told Zelda and her parents of the plan to escape, but again, her parents refused to go and pleaded with us to go ourselves.

"We can't leave without knowing where Joshua and Eli are," said Mrs. Abramovitch. "They may come here anytime, and we must be here for them."

"Please, Mama and Papa. We should leave here now and search for Eli and Joshua when we're in a safer place. We will die here."

"That is why you two must go. And we will stay," said Mr. Abramovitch. He began coughing again. Mrs. Abramovitch gave him some tea. She stared at me like a frightened cat, her index finger picking at her thumbnail, just like Mama used to do.

I asked Zelda to follow me out to the hallway. There, in the strongest terms, I pleaded with her to honor her parents' demand. It was clear they were adamant about waiting for her brothers to reappear and wanting us to leave without them.

"I agree with you about my brothers. There's no point in staying here any longer to wait for them. And I would go with you, but you know I can't. I'd never be able to live with the guilt of that. Would you have left your parents behind?"

"Of course not. But this situation is different. Here, your parents are begging us to leave because the most important thing to them is that you're safe, and that you survive. God forbid, if you're abused again, or something even worse occurs, they'd never be able to live with themselves."

"I know. And I feel the same about them. So, I'm stuck here, Reuven. However, you aren't."

"Yes, I am. I can never leave here without you."

IN THE WEEKS THAT FOLLOWED, ZELDA WAS QUIET AND WITH-drawn. She went to work during the day repairing German soldiers' uniforms at the Madritsch factory, and at night took care of her ailing parents. Every evening when I returned from work, we all sat together in their little corner by the light of the oil lamp and shared a small meal of stale bread and soup. Sometimes there was a little sausage or cheese, or a half chicken or piece of fish that Zelda purchased on the black market with her meager earnings from the Madritsch factory.

Mr. Madritsch was like Mr. Malinowski in that he was a Catholic Pole who was a friend to the Jews. Unlike the Germans, he paid his workers either with a few German marks a week or a loaf of bread they could take home to eat or sell on the black market. He treated them better than anyone else, and Zelda knew how fortunate she was to be assigned to work at his factory.

Mr. and Mrs. Abramovitch and I would make small talk over the meal while Zelda withdrew into a shelter of silence—a place I was familiar with and understood all too well. We worried about her mental health and did everything we could to draw her out of her burrow of protection. I'd ask her questions about what she did at work that day, what the latest gossip was. Amid all the despair, there were still people having affairs, breaking up, getting pregnant outside of marriage, stories of stealing money and jewelry from one another. I tried entertaining her with my own stories about the men I worked with on the various jobsites. One man had such a strong gambling addiction he had to make a bet on anything possible. He'd bet on when a bird was going to take flight from a branch, when a German soldier guarding us would put down his rifle or take out a cigarette, or what side of a flipped coin would show in five tosses, or how many times a rock would skip across the water on the first, second, and third throw.

At night, I'd curl up next to Zelda, my chest to her back, and she'd pull my arm across her waist and hold my hand, lacing her long fingers with mine. Although she was quiet, it was clear she wanted me close to her as she tended to her wounds, those parts of her soul that were broken. I wondered if she might become pregnant from the rape, but then remembered her telling me she hadn't had her period in months. She said it was from stress and lack of nutrition. Sometimes she'd have nightmares, waking me with a kicking leg or an arm flailing. Sometimes she yelped or mumbled incoherent words, her body hot and moist with sweat.

Before going to sleep, I'd try to soothe her by massaging her neck and shoulders, which were sore from sewing all day. She'd sometimes hum one of her Yiddish songs softly or ask me if I remembered something from our childhood, like the sword swallower we saw together at the circus that came to Kraków one year, or the time she caught a catfish that was so large it pulled her into the river.

Even though she was hurting, she softened toward me. One night she even apologized for having pushed me away when I first found her. "Why did you do that?" I asked.

"I was so ashamed."

"Of what?"

"A Polish peasant had molested me when I was at my uncle's farm. I blamed myself for what had happened—telling myself how stupid I was for going to the market alone. Mama and Papa had warned me not to go, but I insisted. It made me feel so dirty and worthless inside. I tried hurting myself by cutting my wrist. That's the scar you saw that first night that I tried to hide. I didn't think I deserved to be loved after being abused."

"I'll always love you," I said. "No matter what has happened to you."

"Thank you, Reuven," she whispered. "I will always love you, too."

IN THE MORNINGS, BEFORE LEAVING FOR WORK, SHE'D READ A few pages of her book about Kabbalah, *The Tree of Life*, and meditate briefly. Unlike her father's prayer book, she had hidden *The Tree of Life* beneath her mattress, saving it from being destroyed. When I asked her what it was about Kabbalah that was helping her, she told me about a concept in Kabbalah called tikkun. She said tikkun spoke of ways to mend the world, such as repairing the imbalances of the universe, or restoring universal morals and ethics to repair the world's injustices. She said tikkun also suggested that by working to repair the world through acts of moral justice, compassion, and kindness, people could even repair their own broken souls.

I appreciated the concept of tikkun theoretically. However, in the reality we lived in, trying to change the world through individual deeds that were compassionate and morally just seemed not only impossible, but absurd to me.

The living conditions inside the ghetto were collapsing into a primal existence of increased desperation and misery. Food on the black market was scarce, and most could not afford whatever was available. In the decrepit, filthy apartment buildings, the electricity, plumbing, and water services were breaking down more frequently; the numbers of swarming rats, mice, lice, and roaches were multiplying. Dysentery, influenza, typhoid, and typhus were taking more lives, and medical care was more difficult to come by. People were malnourished, especially children and the elderly, and many of them were sleeping and dying on the streets.

Most of us averted our gaze when we came across starving children on the street, covered in scabs and dirt and infested with lice, their heads large and out of proportion with their fragile, withering bodies. They'd hold open their tiny hands, begging for a morsel of food. You'd give them what you had, but it was never enough. And there were always more along the way.

And yet outside the ghetto, on the other side of barbed wire fences and brick and cement walls that were approximately three and a half meters high and thirty centimeters thick, was a world completely different from ours. A normal, civilized world where clean and healthy, well-dressed Poles and Germans filled the sidewalks and streets, some making their way to work in offices and shops, others going to cafés where they'd stop to have breakfast. Cheerful Polish nannies working for the high-ranking German officials rolled their little German babies in prams down the sidewalks with their colorful shin-length dresses and skirts fluttering like flags in the wind. The Polish and German children carried their leather bookbags on their way to school, laughing and teasing one another and playing tag, kicking footballs, and playing hopscotch, as the Jewish children once did. Their markets were abundant with colorful fruits and vegetables, chickens, geese, ducks, meats and fish, baskets full of grains and spices.

They knew we existed. They saw us every day cleaning their streets, cutting their wood, shoveling their snow, carrying their bricks and garbage, building their roads, digging into their sewers. Yet our suffering was invisible to them because of its acceptance as being "normal" and "deserved."

Inside the ghetto, it seemed civilization was nearing its end. Besides the desperate hunger and illness, there was the constant, pummeling fear of being snatched off the street at any moment by the Germans and thrown into prison or deported to Płaszów to be worked to death in the stone quarries, or sent to some unknown destination to face some unknown fate.

In the preceding months, they deported hundreds, causing parents, grandparents, teens, and children to disappear, or to be beaten or shot without provocation. Many people were breaking down mentally, vanishing into the shadows of despair. Some went completely mad.

I watched one young woman, bony and frail, dressed in rags roaming the streets and sidewalks cradling a dirty baby doll in her arms, talking nonsensically about Nazi dybbuks—menacing spirits—that had killed her husband and child and were now casting evil spells on all the Jews of the world. She walked up and down the street in a trance state, pounding on her chest, calling out to the lost souls of her loved ones, begging them to return. On another day a slight, middle-aged man unshaven and scabby, dressed in a soiled black suit ripped and full of holes, his red tie backward and one lens in his wire-rimmed eyeglasses shattered, announced to those he passed that the Germans were aliens from outer space sent to earth to rule the world. He danced and laughed wildly, thrusting his pelvis back and forth as if humping the air, crazed, lost in a stream of unsettling hallucinations.

Where we lived people were constantly on edge, some of them instantly snapping and verbally attacking one another, or even breaking into fistfights over a scrap of bread, or an apple, or if a sock was stolen, or whose turn it was to use the stove to cook a meal, or whose children were too loud and too much of a nuisance.

Some had become paranoid, accusing one another of spying for the Germans, or poisoning the water or food, like what happened at the start of the war. Others had become listless, like Mr. and Mrs. Abramovitch, lost in a sleepless melancholy, always exhausted, struggling with physical illness and depression, unable to get out of bed, showing no interest in eating, hopeless, often just wanting to die. There were only two things that kept them going: One, Zelda's insistence they not give up. Two, their desire to see their sons, Eli and Joshua, again.

WINTER'S ICY GRIP LOOSENED, MAKING WAY FOR SPRING'S warmer winds and rains. The fields were a deep brown again, ready for tilling and planting after having spent months buried beneath snow and ice.

On Monday, 27 May, after transporting bricks all day in an unusually stifling heat for that time of year, I went to the pharmacy to pick up Mr. and Mrs. Abramovitch's medications. Mr. Malinowski said he had something urgent to tell me and requested I go upstairs and wait for him. I thought he might have some information about Zelda's brothers.

While waiting in his apartment, I went to the kitchen sink and washed away the patches of crusty brick dust off my hands, arms, and face, shedding it like a second skin, turning the water into a muddy red clay.

When Mr. Malinowski arrived, he made a pot of tea and offered me a seat at his table. He said the word was out that the Germans were planning some type of mass deportation action in the ghetto within a week, maybe two. His contacts weren't certain of the exact day. "Some people may be sent to Płaszów," he said. "Others may be deported to camps like Belzec and Mauthausen. Many may be killed. We just don't know exactly what they've planned. But I believe it's something terrible. Possibly an entire liquidation of the ghetto." He fidgeted with the cap on the small blue porcelain sugar cube container decorated with white cherry blossoms. "You and Zelda and her parents must escape from here immediately. There's no more time to delay."

"When should we go?"

"Day after tomorrow. It's already arranged."

"But what if Mr. and Mrs. Abramovitch still refuse to leave?"

"If they don't save themselves, then they'll certainly never see their sons again."

"They don't see it that way."

"Then I say this against my beliefs and better judgment: Lie to them. There is no more time now. The end is coming. Tell them I heard their sons were transported to Treblinka. And so now they need to save themselves so that if their sons survive, they'll be alive to see them. Tell them that."

The kettle boiled and whistled and he poured the hot water into the teapot containing the dried flecks of black tea. "There are two sewers leading out of the ghetto, one at the intersection of Józefińska Street and Krakusa Street, the other at the intersection of Józefińska and Węgierska Street. These sewer lines run beneath the streets leading to an outlet that empties into the Vistula River near the railway bridge." He lifted the cap to the sugar jar and put one sugar cube into each of our glasses. "I've paid a Jewish policeman to meet the four of you the day after tomorrow at their address at eleven thirty p.m. He'll take you to the intersection of Józefińska Street and Krakusa Street and show you where to enter the sewer line that will lead you to the outlet at the river where there will be a man with a delivery truck waiting for you. He'll smuggle the four of you fifty kilometers north along the river to a place where a barge will pick you up and take you north to Gdynia. At the port in Gdynia, you'll meet a man, Mr. Markarski. He'll help you stow away on a Swedish iron ore freighter returning to its port in Sweden."

The entire plan sounded unbelievably risky. But Mr. Malinowski said he was certain it was a better option than staying in the ghetto. He handed me Mr. Abramovitch's medications. "Promise me you'll come back here and see me after the war is over."

I embraced him. "I'm forever indebted to you, Mr. Malinowski. I'll certainly come see you after the war."

AT ZELDA'S APARTMENT, I FOUND HER IN THEIR LITTLE CORNER feeding her mother some clear soup in the warm flickering light of the oil lamp. Mrs. Abramovitch looked feverish, her face pallid and damp, dark circles rimming her sallow eyes. She complained of a severe headache and nausea.

"What's wrong?" I asked.

"The doctor thinks she has typhoid," said Mr. Abramovitch in a raspy exhalation. "He saw her earlier today."

"But she'll get better soon," said Zelda, holding the spoon up to her mother's dry, cracked lips. "Won't you, Mama?" Mrs. Abramovitch appeared too tired to respond. Zelda brushed back the moist strands of hair pasted to her mother's forehead and encouraged her to have a sip of soup. I had had serious doubts about Mr. Abramovitch being able to physically make an escape, but now, with Mrs. Abramovitch so ill, the entire plan seemed unfeasible. Yet we had no choice. I agreed with Mr. Malinowski. No matter how dangerous, or how ill they were, trying to escape was better than waiting to be slaughtered.

I told Zelda and her parents what Mr. Malinowski reported to me regarding the Germans' plans to liquidate the ghetto. And then I forced myself to tell them the lie about their sons. Their faces fell into grief. Zelda gasped and clenched her mother's arms. It was so painful to watch that I wanted to run. I could barely look any of them in the eyes.

"Treblinka concentration camp? This can't be true," said Mrs. Abramovitch.

"Who said they transported them there?" asked Mr. Abramovitch. "Who reported it? Show me the report on paper. I don't believe it."

"How does he know this?" asked Zelda. "Is he certain?"

The questions were overwhelming. My chest ached with guilt.

"He spoke to a German he knows, Mr. Kraus, who works in the *Arbeitsamt* office. He provided the information."

"I don't believe it!" said Mr. Abramovitch harshly, sending himself into a coughing fit.

"Nor do I," said Mrs. Abramovitch, handing her husband some water. "Why should we believe anything the Germans tell us? They're all liars. Show us proof, Reuven. Bring us the report! We'll not leave here until we see proof."

For the next hour I continued pressing my point, begging them to believe me and leave, and they continued to plead for Zelda and me to escape without them. During this time, Zelda's eyes watched me closely, examining my face as if it were under a microscope. She knew me better than anyone. She could tell by watching the movement of my eyes, my facial expressions, even the slightest shift in tone of voice, whether I spoke the truth. It was obvious she was unconvinced. But she remained silent.

Caught in a stalemate, we all realized there was nothing else anyone could say to change the other's mind. Zelda and I went to the stairwell to speak in private.

We sat down on the stairs in silence and held hands. We were both mentally exhausted by the conversation that had taken place. A sliver of moonlight penetrated the stairwell window, illuminating Zelda's face. Her green eyes, now softer, less suspicious, projected a sense of clarity and resolve.

"Was it all a lie? Or just the part about my brothers being in Treblinka?"

I hesitated, not ready to cave in. "Everything I said is what Mr. Malinowski told me."

"It's okay. I understand what you were trying to do. I want them to agree to leave as well. But just tell me the truth."

I couldn't hold out any longer. It was impossible to look Zelda square in the face and continue to lie. "The part about the ghetto is true. Mr. Malinowski received word that the Germans are planning a mass deportation, possibly an entire liquidation of the ghetto. But yes; the part about your brothers was fabricated. He has no information on where they are."

She kissed my cheek. "You've lost everyone, my love. Please— go save yourself. I'll stay here with Mama and Papa and we'll somehow survive. And once the war is over, we'll find each other again. I'm sure of it. And we'll build a life together then. But for now, you must go."

I encircled her bony waist with my arm and cradled her head against my chest. "You're being absurd," I said. "You know I can't leave you." She tried to convince me otherwise, but like her and her parents, I stubbornly stood my ground, unyielding.

56

FIVE DAYS LATER, ON MONDAY, I JUNE, JUST BEFORE SUNRISE, A
group of us were leaving the ghetto on a transport truck to go
work in Płaszów when we noticed something strange occurring
along the ghetto perimeter. Groups of *Sonderdienst* and SS had
assembled along the ghetto wall and military trucks and horse-
mounted soldiers were moving in formation down the street. It
was happening. This was what Mr. Malinowski had referred to.
"Not good," whispered the man beside me. "What should we do?"
murmured another man. "Nothing we can do now but try to
remain calm," replied the other man.

I investigated the other men's faces and saw mirrored in them
the contorted expressions of my own unmitigated terror. Trapped
inside the truck, a suffocating sense of helplessness overwhelmed
us. We couldn't shake the dread of our loved ones trapped inside
the ghetto walls, unaware of the horror they were about to confront.
Several of the men began praying for God's help. Although I didn't
believe in such things, I shut my eyes and joined them in their
prayers.

A pit grew inside my stomach as I debated what, if anything,
I could do to go back and help Mr. and Mrs. Abramovitch hide.
Zelda, I knew, was already at work at the Madritsch factory. I
prayed she'd be safe there.

I contemplated jumping off the truck and running back to
the ghetto. But the *Sonderdienst* and SS surrounded the gate. It

would've been impossible to get past them without being killed. Then a man leaped off the truck and ran a couple of meters before a gunshot sounded. He dropped dead to the ground. No one said a word.

When we arrived at Płaszów, the truck's headlights cast a murky glow through the heavy fog blanketing the stone road we had constructed with our ancestors' headstones. "This is such a *broch*," said one man, breaking the silence. A curse on us, it was.

We passed the main gate and came to a stop where we unloaded. Guards handed us shovels and ordered us to dig a drainage reservoir three meters deep. Twine and wooden stakes marked the perimeter of the reservoir. A hundred meters away, on the tracks a freight train waited for its cargo to be loaded. No one knew if the cargo was going to be animals, coal, grains, timber, military supplies, or something else.

Over the next few hours, the sun made its ascent and its warm rays burned away the fog. By noon, the scorching sun beat down on us, sucking oxygen from the air, our clothes soaked in sweat. Overhead a red-tailed hawk circled effortlessly in the infinite blueness of the naked sky, gazing down upon us hopeless, pathetic slaves with our feet glued to the earth as we shoveled dirt in a fearful silence. The only sounds were those of our heavy breaths, occasional grunts, the ring of metal spades slicing into earth, thumps of dirt landing in a pile. The German guards commanded us to move faster. "*Schnell! Schnell!*" They cracked their whips.

All we thought about was what kind of mayhem could be unraveling in the ghetto. I prayed repeatedly that Zelda was safe at the Madritsch factory. Mr. Madritsch would want to protect his workers, I told myself.

A whip cracked inches away from my ears and the man working next to me wrenched backward in pain as if a bolt of electricity went through him. He yelped like an injured dog. The SS officer ordered him to dig faster. We all picked up the pace, working relentlessly in the blistering heat for hours. There were no breaks, and very little water to relieve our mouths that were parched and dusty.

In the late afternoon, another transport truck pulled into the worksite and unloaded more men from the ghetto. They joined us in digging the reservoir. I searched for someone I may have known. Swiftly a whip cracked against my back, stealing my breath, sending a stabbing, burning pain across my spine and ribs that lasted for minutes that felt like hours. The SS man holding the whip dressed down from the heat to a crisp white undershirt, his jacket and button-down shirt carefully folded over the branch of an oak tree. A cigarette dangled from his lips beaded with sweat. I watched in disgust as he randomly lashed the other men, ordering them to work harder. He was a pure sadist. I wanted to take my shovel and crush his head with it.

"Are you okay?" whispered a man behind me. I looked over my shoulder while continuing to shovel the dirt furiously. The young man looked familiar, but I wasn't certain. Then I thought this was the same young man I had seen in Przemyśl.

"Big Izzy?" I said under my breath. I wasn't sure if it was him because he looked so different. When we were young, he was the largest kid I knew, a monster on the football field. Now he was thin and stooped over like an old man, his skin pallid, his shoulders rounded and bony.

"Who do you think?" he whispered.

"Where've you been? Were you in Przemyśl?"

"I was there briefly with my father. Then we got transported back here when the Germans invaded the east."

A guard approached and we stopped our conversation. When he passed, I whispered: "Did you just come from the ghetto?"

"Yes. It's a nightmare."

"Tell me."

He told me everything he knew while we monitored the guards. He said the *Sonderdienst*, SS, Gestapo, and Jewish and German police were going from building to building notifying people whose names were on a deportation list that they had until ten o'clock to get to Józefińska Street to be processed for what they were calling a "resettlement." They were selecting all the people without work stamps, the old and very young, the weak and disabled, those without skills. Izzy said they were allowing each person only one piece of luggage weighing no more than twenty kilos, and that anyone on the list who didn't report by ten o'clock in the morning would be shot on sight. No one knew where they were being resettled. People suspected they'd be killed or sent to prison, so they attempted to conceal themselves in places like closets, pantries, cellars, attics, and rooftops. But most were following orders.

He saw hundreds of people carrying their luggage down Józefińska Street while the *Sonderdienst* and SS were going building to building, bashing down doors and searching for the people in hiding. He saw them shooting people in the streets who weren't walking fast enough and heard they even went to the hospital on Józefińska Street to shoot people in their beds— old people and disabled people, even children. He said at the orphanage they threw children out the window, and at a home for the elderly they made them jump up and down in the yard crowing like birds before shooting them.

A guard slowly strolled past us and tossed his cigarette stub on Izzy, ordering him to shut up and pick up the pace. We dug faster and then witnessed the first group of deportees being herded through the gates like cattle.

There were men, women, children, and the elderly, each carrying a single valise or rucksack, utter confusion and terror etched in their faces, some in shock, others engulfed by despair, eyes vacant, hands, knees, and faces bloodied and bruised. Many of them appeared to sense something ominous was in store for them. They walked tentatively, glancing about in confusion. The small children gripped their parents' hands, white-knuckled, smelling and tasting the danger. One small boy tearfully clutched a little red firetruck in the crook of his arm while his father grasped his other hand. Near him an old woman dressed in black, walking as if in a trance, dropped her valise and left it behind. A young Hasidic man picked it up and tried giving it back to her, but she waved him off, seeming to know there was no point in carrying the extra weight to a place she'd never return from.

While digging, we kept a sharp watch on the stream of desperate people arriving, hoping and praying to not see our loved ones among them.

The German guards and SS were deceptive in the way they herded people onto the cattle cars, making it appear as if they were going on a train ride that would transport them to a better life, perhaps a new future similar to the one they had before the war. Those who believed in this charade probably imagined having their own homes where they'd lived with their family in a clean apartment with running cold and hot water, heat and electricity, a stove for cooking, a bathroom for bathing. Some of the people's faces were filled with longing, others carried fear and disillusionment.

The Germans were doing what they could to keep the droves of people calm. If things got out of control, God knew what they'd do. Everyone seemed to cooperate out of a terror informed by the merciless violence they'd witnessed the Germans inflicting on others, and for some, themselves. Every so often someone would get a boot in his back, a club to the head, a rifle butt to the chest for speaking out, or stepping out of line, or calling out for a loved one, or collapsing from exhaustion.

One woman had clearly reached the end of her wits. Sinewy and raven-haired, she wore a bright yellow summer dress and cradled a tiny baby wrapped in a dirty white blanket pressed against her breast. She begged an SS officer to release her from being deported. The SS officer slapped her so hard across the face that she stumbled to the ground, barely keeping hold of her baby. When she stood up, her nose and mouth were bleeding. Still clutching her baby, to my surprise, she ran after the SS officer, grabbing hold of his hand, dropping to her knees, pleading with him to let her go back to the ghetto. He punched her this time, knocking her unconscious. She dropped the baby on the ground. A *Sonderdienst* officer carelessly grabbed the baby by its foot, holding it upside down like a rag doll, and with his other hand dragged the frail mother by her arm back to the masses of people who were being loaded onto the train. Leaving the mother in a heap on the ground, he tossed the baby on top of her, and walked away.

"This is unbearable," I murmured to Izzy.

"Don't watch any of it," he whispered back. "Just dig."

The pandemonium distracted even the guards. Then they noticed our work had slowed down as we continued to search the crowds for loved ones. They began whipping us again, ordering us back to work.

I started catching glimpses of more people I'd known since childhood. While being shoved into the boxcar, Mrs. Lefkovitz, my elementary school teacher, grasped her husband's hand. Smelly Meyer the fishmonger hugged his valise against his chest like a shield while Avrom the water carrier was weeping, calling out for his parents. Big Ziggy the coal man tried to protect his wife and keep track of his children who were straying in different directions.

Then Khone appeared. Dear Khone. Where had he been hiding? Why hadn't I seen him in the ghetto? He was being herded toward the boxcar. His black cap tilted back, his body hunched forward and leaning heavily on an umbrella he used as a cane. Another man helped him walk by supporting his free arm. Khone's leathery face was swollen and bruised from a beating, or falling on the ground. Bloodstains spotted his white shirt. A German guard beat his back with a club as he laboriously climbed the boxcar steps. When Khone reached the top of the stairs, he entered the boxcar and turned round to look back, as if he'd lost someone in the crowd. For a moment, I thought our eyes met. Khone appeared completely resigned to whatever fate awaited him. That bright mischievous twinkle that once glimmered in his vivacious eyes was now gone, the flame extinguished, as if his soul had already departed. I thought: As long as I live, I'll never forget you, Khone. I love you like a grandpa. The greatest wood and ivory carver in Kraków, probably all of Poland. That's what I'd tell my children, should that day ever come. The guards shoved another man in front of Khone, forcing him farther back into the darkness of the boxcar where he disappeared in the masses of human cargo.

Using all their tools of punishment—cattle prods, sticks, clubs, whips, and rifle butts—the SS continued to cram so many people into the boxcars that everyone had to stand. With the temperature outside so brutally hot and heavy with humidity, I couldn't imagine how suffocating the heat must have been inside those containers meant for supplies and cattle.

Near the roofs of the boxcars, people frantically tried to pull themselves up to the small rectangular openings with bars running across them to fill their lungs with some oxygen. I imagined other people were pressing their mouths against the wood-planked walls, hoping to suck some air through the cracks and holes.

When the guards and SS could no longer crush more people into the boxcars, they slammed the doors shut, throwing down the steel latches and securing them so no one could escape. Several SS blew their whistles and motioned for the locomotive to pull away.

Hundreds more Jews from the ghetto still waited in the yard in the pummeling heat, horrified by what they'd just witnessed and terrified of what would come next. Some were so exhausted they passed out; others prayed to God in silence while others cried out for his mercy.

As the blue haze of dusk settled, the hot and humid air continued to oppress. Dirt caked our clothes and coated our sweat-soaked skin; our backs, shoulders, hands, and legs ached from the endless digging. They gave us one break in the evening to drink some dirty water dribbling from a decaying black rubber hose attached to a rusty tank on a water truck. I felt guilty drinking the water when no water was offered to the people waiting for what we all assumed was the next train.

Several hours passed and still no train had arrived. I estimated the drainage reservoir was now about fifty meters long and twenty meters wide and maybe three meters deep. The long wait for the next train confused all of us.

The people filling the yard sat on the ground packed together in small groups. I continued searching the crowd for Zelda and her parents, hoping never to find them. Then suddenly Izzy called out to his father who he spotted wandering aimlessly on the perimeter of the yard along the tracks. He threw down his shovel and ran to him, calling out his name. His father saw him and held his hands up in the air, motioning for him to stop, but Izzy kept going. A guard ordered Izzy to halt, and I yelled at him to come back, but he continued running to his father. Several shots rang out and Izzy fell to the ground in a heap. We all watched in silence as his father instinctively ran to him. Then several more gunshots punctured the air, and the father dropped near his son.

The people filling the yard jumped to their feet and exploded into a pandemonium of pure hysteria. Everyone ran in different directions, screaming wildly as more shots rang out. People fell to the ground, some from being shot, others trying not to be shot. Some hid behind scattered trees while others huddled together, hoping to escape the blast of bullets coming at them. Over the course of I don't know how many minutes, every single Jew in the yard—women, children, men, the elderly—were slaughtered, one by one. A few of the men digging saw loved ones killed. Several of them passed out. A few others went mad, throwing their shovels at the Germans and running to their loved ones before being shot and killed in their tracks.

With no one left standing, the SS officers and German guards casually strolled through the yard of scattered bodies, as if they were taking a walk through a park. They searched for survivors by tracking the sounds of their moans of pain, cries for help, and gasps for air. When found, the Germans shot them one by one.

They chatted and joked and laughed with one another as they ransacked the dead for their money and jewelry, tearing their clothes to pieces, stripping out the linings of coats, pants, dresses, and skirts; rifling through valises, satchels, gunnysacks, rucksacks, and shoulder bags; searching inside hats, shoes, wigs, and hair wraps. Several guards walked across the yard, going from body to body, prying open the mouths of the dead and using their pliers to extract teeth capped in gold. They pocketed what they found and made sure to leave nothing behind.

5 7

AROUND MIDNIGHT, AFTER WE FINISHED DIGGING THE DRAIN-age reservoir, the Germans ordered us to load all the bodies in wheelbarrows, along with all the personal effects littered across the yard, and transport them to the reservoir. We realized what we had dug was not a reservoir, but a pit to serve as a mass grave.

The guards forced us to toss the bodies into the pit and pile their personal effects onto a mound at the end of the pit. There, they soaked them in petrol and set them aflame. The smoke-filled air was thick and acrid, a suffocating stench of burning cotton, wool, and leather. The smoke and fumes burned our throats and scorched our lungs. Our pathetic, vacant, bloodshot eyes and blackened faces, covered in sweat, soil, soot, and misery, flickered in the menacing light of the raging flames.

I crossed the yard with a wheelbarrow and came across the bodies of an old man and a little boy, maybe grandfather and grandson, half-naked and bloodstained, lying next to each other, holding hands. Before loading them into the wheelbarrow, I gently separated their hands. Although I'd seen death before, my stomach turned and my legs buckled. I dropped to my knees and vomited. A rifle butt came down on my back, knocking out my breath while sending a sharp pain through my spine. "*Mach schnell!*" the guard towering over me hollered. I jumped to my feet, loaded the grandfather and grandson into the wheelbarrow and pushed their dead bodies across the dirt yard toward the pit.

The old man's feet were shoeless, his undershirt covered in fresh blood from a gunshot, his pockets turned inside out, his pants torn to shreds by a soldier's bayonet. The boy wore black knee socks with brown leather boots and black laces, a bloody blue button-down shirt tucked into gray wool shorts. A wooden kangaroo poked out of his pocket.

As I approached the pit, the whisperings of a hoarse voice, parched and barely perceptible, came from somewhere nearby. I stopped and turned in all directions to see where it came from and for a moment, I thought it must be a dybbuk or a ghost, or some voice inside my head. Like the other men, I felt I must be going mad. While pushing the wheelbarrow toward the pit, I heard the dry whisper yet again and realized it was coming from my wheelbarrow. I inspected the bodies and noticed the old man's thin lips scarcely moving behind the hairs of his long gray beard and mustache. His eyes were closed, his skin a deathly blueish-white, his limp body motionless, save for his crusty, trembling thin lips. I moved in closer to hear what he mumbled. "*Hineni Hashem. Hineni Hashem*—Here I am, God."

I didn't know what to do. A soldier saw me standing still and ordered me to move, pointing his rifle at me. "*Mach schnell, schweinhund Jude!*" I lifted the wheelbarrow and continued to the pit. When I passed him, he jabbed me with the point of the rifle and kicked me in the ass and had a laugh. There was little I could feel. A part of me had left my body by this time.

When I reached the rim of the pit, it was clear I'd found hell. Bathed in the deathly firelight of the raging flames, a tangle of arms and legs, naked feet and torsos jutted out at odd and disturbing angles from the growing piles of dead bodies. *Hineni Hashem.*

Hineni Hashem. I kept hearing the old man's dry whisper growing louder. Heads with jaws agape drooped sideways and upside down on the mound. A woman's frozen hand poked out from the top of one heap, as if reaching for a rope from the heavens. *Hineni Hashem. Hineni Hashem.* The old man's call for God grew louder inside my head.

An SS captain standing by the pit ordered me to dump the old man and little boy into it. He gazed at me through the darkness, our faces flickering in the warm light and black shadows cast by the fire burning beside the pit. The way his eyes clung to me made me think he knew me. He slowly strolled toward me, gliding like a ghost along the edge of the pit. When he reached me, he poked the old man with the tip of his rifle. The old man's hand made a slight twitch; a gasp of air and a groan emerged from his mouth. "*Hineni Hashem*," he mumbled. "*Hineni Hashem*." I thought if the SS officer had an ounce of humanity in him, he'd shoot the old man before having me toss him into the pit. The thought of the old man's last moments on earth being spent buried alive beneath a pile of dead bodies was unbearable. The SS officer gazed down at the old man with a vacant stare, then ordered me to dump the old man and the little boy into the pit.

As I bent down to lift the old man from the wheelbarrow, I whispered into his ear, "God sees you." I then dropped him into the pit and picked up the little boy and dropped him near the old man.

Avoiding the SS officer's gaze, I turned and grabbed the wheelbarrow's wood handles and pushed it away. While walking back to the dead, I continued to hear the old man's murmurs: *Hineni Hashem, Hineni Hashem* . . . Then from behind came the sharp crack of a gunshot splitting the air. I did not look back. I prayed the officer shot the old man dead, and that every Nazi would burn in hell for eternity.

FROM THE NIGHTMARE IN PŁASZÓW, WE ARRIVED AT THE *Arbeitsamt* at first light. No one spoke as we looked at one another with the same thoughts: Who was taken? Who was in hiding? Who escaped? Who survived? Who died?

The SS officer banged his club against the side of the truck and gave orders to return to the *Arbeitsamt* in six hours, noon sharp. We all assumed it would be to return to Płaszów to relive the same nightmare we just suffered through. One man next to me said to his friend, "I can't do this again." His friend replied: "If you want to live, you'll do it."

I took off and started running toward Zelda's building, but slowed down when I saw what was unfolding. Another deportation was already underway. Droves of terrified residents streamed out of the apartment buildings hauling overstuffed valises tied with rope to keep them from bursting open, heaving on their shoulders gunnysacks and enormous satchels of sheets packed with clothes, lugging rucksacks strapped to their backs; heavy bags and purses dangled from women's elbows and shoulders.

Some men wore black and brown fedoras, like Papa used to wear, with their wrinkled and stained suits, as if they were heading into the businesses they once owned or had worked for. Others wore short-brimmed caps, like what Khone used to wear. Most were unshaven from being roused so early. Many of the women wore brightly colored spring coats in shades of reds, blues, greens, yellows, and oranges. Some sported wide-brimmed hats decorated with white lace, pink and purple ribbons, silk flowers, carnations, and roses. Others covered their hair in head wraps and babushkas. Mothers and fathers, their pinched faces distraught, clutched their children's tender little hands, dragging them along, some crying, others cooperating while carrying small bags and sacks of their own. An elderly couple, the man bowlegged, hobbled down the street, supporting each other with their arms interlocked as they strained to carry their valises.

German soldiers, SS, the Jewish police, and *Sonderdienst* ordered the beleaguered residents to walk swiftly toward Zgody Square in an orderly column. Fortunately, the *Arbeitsamt* was only a few streets over from Zelda's building, and the flow of people was going in her direction.

On Krakusa Street, where Zelda lived, an elderly lady tripped and fell on the rough cobblestones; an SS officer jabbed her in the ribs with his club, barking at her to get up and keep moving. I tucked myself inside the steady stream of anxious residents, walking with them until I reached Zelda's building where I ducked inside the entryway.

Bolting up the staircase, I squeezed past the droves of families being herded out, dodging the huge satchels of clothes they dragged behind them. At Zelda's landing, she and her parents were leaving the apartment. "We're on the list," said Mr. Abramovitch, dragging his valise to the staircase. "You and Zelda must escape from here now!" he said breathlessly. "Leave us, damn it. You have work stamps. Please, I beg you. Take my daughter, Reuven. Save yourselves. She won't listen to us."

"Stop it, Papa," said Zelda, her arm cinched round her mother's waist, holding her upright. Mrs. Abramovitch was coughing, arms dangling feebly by her sides, barely able to walk. Zelda turned to me and said calmly and quietly: "Go, Reuven. It's okay."

It was beyond my comprehension how she was so damn fearless, so collected and focused while facing complete bedlam. There was a centeredness to her, some kind of core sense of purpose that gave her a clarity and precision in her thinking that I admired immensely, and envied.

I took Mr. Abramovitch's luggage, grabbed his arm, and guided him down the stairs one step at a time. From behind, people hollered at us to move faster. Soldiers were beating people at the top of the stairs for not walking fast enough. More people shoved their way past us, their elbows sticking in our sides, their luggage banging into us, nearly knocking us down the stairs.

We reached the street and entered the seemingly endless column of residents heading toward Zgody Square, where the military trucks waited to transport everyone to Płaszów. As we walked in silence, my mind raced to figure out a way to escape. Several people broke from the line to hide inside a building. German guards shot them immediately and warned others to not try the same. It was absurd to think of Mr. and Mrs. Abramovitch running anywhere when they could barely walk.

AT THE SQUARE, PEOPLE WERE PACKED TOGETHER, DESPERATELY clinging to their belongings and one another. *Sonderdienst*, SS, and more soldiers strolled through the crowd, some with attack dogs, others threatening to club anyone who sat down. People had already been standing for a few hours waiting for the transport trucks to arrive.

The air was scorching, thick with humidity, the noon sun blasting its burning heat on our exposed bodies. People searched for shade and water, but there was none to be had. Children cried out from hunger and fear. With nowhere to relieve themselves, people were soiling their clothes. Some were falling unconscious.

From where we stood, I realized the pharmacy was maybe one

hundred meters away, a distance that Mr. and Mrs. Abramovitch could walk with Zelda and me supporting them. I thought if we could make it to the pharmacy, then maybe Mr. Malinowski could persuade a guard to allow us inside. Then we could try to make our escape through the sewers at night, once the transport was over. I told Zelda and her parents about the plan. Her parents resisted and again ordered Zelda and me to leave them behind. But we both refused their request and insisted they try to make it.

I grasped Mr. Abramovitch by the arm and towed him through the masses, step-by-step, pressing past the bodies of people waiting for directions on what to do next. With my free hand, I carried his valise. Zelda and her mother, arms interconnected, followed closely behind us. Unfortunately, Mr. and Mrs. Abramovitch had to keep stopping to catch their breath. Despite Zelda and me pushing and pulling them along, supporting as much of their weight as possible, they were reaching a point of complete exhaustion. "You must keep going," we kept telling them. "We're almost there."

With just another fifty meters to go, Zelda and I had to leave her parents' valises behind so we could put all our strength into supporting them. Then the trucks arrived at the opposite end of the square and the soldiers, *Sonderdienst*, and Jewish police went to work directing people with their clubs and rifle butts. Chaos ensued. The SS threatened us with their attack dogs, compressing us into a tighter group as they ordered everyone to walk toward the trucks, which were in the opposite direction of the pharmacy. As if trying to swim against a surging current, we were pushed backward, away from the pharmacy, losing the ground we had gained. The only way to maneuver through the dense crowd, fighting against its flow, was to walk in single file with our hands linked, forming a human chain. I took the lead with Zelda bringing up the rear.

We shoved our way through the hordes of people pushing against us. At one point Mr. Abramovitch fell and I lost his grip.

"Get up!" I yelled. As the crowd swarmed around us, I struggled to lift him to his feet. Mrs. Abramovitch, in a daze and on the verge of collapsing, pleaded with Zelda to let them go. But Zelda refused. "Keep going, Mama!" I heard her yell from the back. "Keep going. You can't give up!"

Slowly we progressed, taking baby steps, and eventually the crowd thinned as we got closer to the pharmacy. We saw Mr. Malinowski standing behind the door's glass, anxiously looking out. Miraculously, we were now within just ten meters of the front door. He spotted us and threw open the door and started running toward us when an SS officer physically blocked him in his tracks, ordering him back inside. Mr. Malinowski tried negotiating with the SS officer who appeared to take no interest in what he was saying. Then Mr. Malinowski reached into his pocket and handed the officer a roll of money. The officer took the money, pocketed it, drew his black Luger from his holster, and pointed it at Mr. Malinowski's forehead, ordering him back inside. Mr. Malinowski hesitated, then tried again to negotiate but was silenced when the SS officer cocked the gun. Raising his hands, Mr. Malinowski slowly backed away and retreated to the pharmacy. Looking out the window again, he watched us helplessly.

The SS officer demanded our *kennkartes*. We handed them over. Then two other soldiers joined him. He examined our cards, saw the work stamps, shoved Zelda and me back a few steps, and ordered the two soldiers to take her parents away. Zelda released a terrifying, high-pitched shriek and tried to bolt after them. But I caught her arm, wrestled her to the ground, and placed my hand over her mouth to muffle her screams. I was terrified that she would get shot or beaten. She bit down on my hand, threw it off her, and dug her nails into my face while writhing on the ground. Screaming in a wild madness, she kicked my legs, scratched and bit my arms as if possessed by a demon. Despite her small size, her strength was shocking. She shoved me off her and almost got to her feet before I wrestled her back to the ground, pinning her arms against her body and immobilizing her. She writhed in distress, unleashing primal screams that pierced the air with unbearable despair, pleading for her mama and papa, wailing with insufferable grief.

The SS officer stood over us and laughed, then walked away, disappearing into the crowd. I looked over to the pharmacy and saw Mr. Malinowski cautiously open the door, checking to make sure the area was clear of soldiers and SS. He sprinted to us and grabbed one of Zelda's arms as I clenched the other, dragging her into the pharmacy as she continued to kick and scream.

One of Mr. Malinowski's assistants, Ewa, a sturdy young woman with short blond hair, helped us restrain Zelda on the wood floor as she continued to struggle while frantically calling out for her parents, imploring them not to leave without her, promising them she would find them. She lost herself in another world, completely consumed by her torment.

The young assistant kept talking to Zelda, trying to soothe her by telling her not to worry, that her parents would survive. But Zelda could not hear her words of comfort. She continued to fight and writhe, kick and holler, twist her arms so she could escape and chase down her parents.

Mr. Malinowski said it would be best to give her a sedative to help calm her. He had Ewa prepare a syringe of phenobarbital and then ordered Ewa and me to hold Zelda still.

"This will help you relax," he told Zelda as he quickly inserted the needle in her arm. "You'll feel better when you wake up. Just try to rest. You'll be okay now. Just breathe slowly."

I held her hand and stroked her hair and face, wet with tears and sweat. She fell into a drowsy state within seconds and no longer struggled. Her speech slurred and her voice dropped to a mere whisper as she mumbled broken words to her mama and papa. And then she fell asleep.

Mr. Malinowski used some iodine to clean the scrape on her forehead that she must've gotten from me wrestling her to the ground. There was also a bruise on her cheek. Tearing her away from her parents left me with the gnawing guilt that I'd done something terribly wrong. Even when I rationalized my actions by telling myself I had saved her, and in the process had fulfilled her parents' wishes, the guilt still burned inside me. My biggest worry was that she'd never forgive me, and therefore, never escape with me. I was uncertain of what I'd do then.

Mr. Malinowski helped me carry her upstairs to his apartment, where we laid her down on his bed. "Hopefully when she wakes up, she'll be calmer and more rational and you'll be able to explain to her why you did what you did." Mr. Malinowski looked at me and paused. He recognized the guilty confusion in my eyes. "You did the right thing, Reuven. Don't doubt yourself. You needed to save Zelda. And now you need to persuade her to escape tonight because it's too dangerous for you to be here. The Germans will liquidate the entire ghetto. If they raid the pharmacy and find you here, they'll kill all of us."

In the closet, he opened a trapdoor in the ceiling and pulled down a ladder. "In the event they come search here before Zelda wakes up, you'll need to carry her to the attic. Once you get up there, pull the ladder inside and shut the door. Now try to get some rest so you'll have the strength to leave tonight."

When he left the room, I sat down on the bed in a daze, exhausted and bewildered by all that had happened. I lay next to Zelda and held her hand and closed my eyes. But the sounds of the deportation filtered through the apartment's windows, making it impossible to rest.

I left the bedroom and went to the window in the sitting room that looked down on the square. Peering from behind the curtains, I saw families shoved into the backs of the transport trucks, and an old woman shot in the head when she refused to get out of her wheelchair. Dead bodies and pools of blood splattered the cobblestones. A little boy, maybe five, wandered in circles, crying for his parents.

Scattered across the square were abandoned valises, satchels, hats, scarves, pushcarts, toy cars and trucks, stuffed teddy bears, crushed eyeglasses, broken plates and cups, books, belts, linens, bras and pantyhose, men's undershirts and shorts, a crushed violin case—a black umbrella, its canopy open, tumbled in the wind.

Feeling numb inside, I returned to the bed and tried lying next to Zelda again. I stuck my fingers in my ears so I wouldn't hear more gunshots and screams, more orders yelled in German, more cries of people calling out for missing family members. I tried shutting out the roar of the trucks coming and going as they transported hundreds of innocent people to destinations they'd never return from.

WHEN I WOKE, IT WAS PITCH-BLACK OUTSIDE, AND ZELDA WAS having a dream. Her body twitched as her mouth mumbled incoherent words. I waited until she settled, then got up and went to the sitting room where I found Mr. Malinowski at his small table having a cup of tea and feeding a few small pieces of wood into the stove that had a pot of borscht cooking on top of it.

The room smelled of chicken and cabbage, thyme, rosemary, and garlic. He looked up at me and saw I was hungry. He picked out a bowl from the wood cabinet above the sink and ladled some borscht into it before handing it to me with a thick piece of bread. I sat down at the table across from him. "Between yesterday and today, they've deported thousands," he said, sipping his tea and gazing at the fire burning inside the small black stove. "Were you in Płaszów the night before?"

"I was."

"I heard they killed hundreds there after loading the trains."

"They did."

He shook his head and rubbed his temples, lamenting the incomprehensible loss.

"Do you know where the trains were going?" I asked.

"A German told me they were all taken to the Belzec death camp."

We sat in the quiet for a short time. The wrenching sounds of the forced deportation had dissipated in the lull before the next deportation. But then the mournful sounds of Zelda weeping seeped into the room.

Mr. Malinowski and I looked at each other helplessly and listened. Guilt constricted my throat and I lost my appetite, terrified of how she'd react to what I'd done. I feared she'd hate me for it, and never agree to escape with me.

Mr. Malinowski looked at his watch. "You need to leave in an hour. I think you should go speak to her."

"I don't know what to say."

He opened the stove's door, stirred its ashes, loaded some new logs, and stoked the fire with his breath. The red-hot coals ignited the new wood.

"Start with an apology, and then listen to her," he said. "Speak and listen with your heart, not your head. And be honest with her."

I CAUTIOUSLY ENTERED THE BEDROOM. IT WAS DARK. ZELDA LAY on the bed curled up in the fetal position, her legs tucked against her chest, her arms wrapped tightly round her legs. I sat next to her and turned on the small bedside lamp. She turned away from the light and didn't look up. The bruise on the side of her cheek had grown slightly wider and was deep purple in the middle and bluish green along its edges. To look at it filled me with shame. I gently placed my hand on her hip. She swiped it off. "Don't touch me," she said. "Just go away!"

"I'm so sorry," I said. "I'm so sorry about your mama and papa . . . and for tackling you the way I did. I tried doing the right thing, Zelda. . . . I wanted to—"

"Shut up," she said. "You had no right to do what you did. Now they're all alone because of you. They have no one to help them. Imagine that. Imagine how they feel!"

I was about to respond but remembered what Mr. Malinowski had told me. Just listen.

"It was my choice to make, not yours!" she said. Tears ran down her face, which was contorted with anger and torment.

I didn't know how to bridge the chasm between us. My mind was a jumble as I searched desperately for the right words.

"More than anything in the world, they wanted you to live, Zelda," I said cautiously. "They made that abundantly clear."

"But they didn't want to be abandoned, either," she responded quickly. "They never said it, but I know that's how they felt. You of all people should know that." She picked at the corners of her thumbs with her index fingers, just like our mothers used to do. "The thought of them on a transport train . . . with no one to help them . . ."

A pit formed in my stomach as I envisioned them in Płaszów being herded onto the trains and crammed into those boxcars like animals.

A heavy silence enveloped the room as she sat up on the edge of the bed. With her back turned to me, she faced the wall where a painting of a sailboat caught in a storm hung. Her head drooped forward as she folded her arms across her abdomen, as if cradling her sorrow, then gathered herself and turned to face me. Her bloodshot eyes, filled with anguish and grief, were beseeching. I carefully reached for her hand and she allowed me to hold it. I kissed it and embraced it firmly between both of mine. "I'm sorry for everything that happened," I whispered. "And I love you more than anything in the world. Nothing can change that."

Her face softened and her eyes closed as she leaned her head against my shoulder. Taking a deep breath, she sighed.

At that moment Mr. Malinowski knocked on the bedroom door and told us it was time to leave. We kissed and wiped away our tears, and then joined him at his table where he laid out his plan for us.

We'd enter the sewer at the intersection of Józefińska Street and Krakusa Street and make our way through the tunnel to where it emptied into the Vistula. There, we'd find a delivery truck waiting for us at a turnoff about five hundred meters north along the river. The Polish driver who did deliveries for Mr. Malinowski had agreed to transport escapees for one hundred

Reichsmarks each. He'd take us fifty kilometers north and drop us off in a forest where we'd wait for a barge that would smuggle us all the way to Gdynia, where the Vistula River emptied into the Baltic Sea. Mr. Malinowski had also paid the captain of the barge.

At the port in Gdynia there was a café, Das Nacht Café, run by a Pole, Mr. Markarski. He'd help us stow away on a Swedish iron ore freighter that was returning to its port in Oxelösund, Sweden. Mr. Malinowski explained that when we landed at the port in Oxelösund, we'd need to pay a trucker to transport us to Stockholm. There we'd find a refugee center that would provide us with food and shelter and help us find work.

Mr. Malinowski packed a rucksack with bread, cheese, sausage, a few cans of herring and sardines, a bottle of water, one hundred fifty Reichsmarks, and some rags to wrap around our noses and mouths when inside the tunnel. "Take these," he said, handing us some clothes. "After going through that sewage you'll need to wash off in the river and get into something clean. Oh— and take this." He handed me a battery-powered lamp that was shaped like a box the size of my hand. "Use this in the sewer. And when you see the barge, you must signal it to stop by turning the lamp on and off. Don't forget."

"But how will we know if it's the right barge to be signaling?"

"You'll see two yellow lights in the bow and on the side of the hull will be the name *M/S Kraków*. A Polish flag is painted next to the name. You can't miss it."

Zelda and I thanked Mr. Malinowski profusely. "One day, when this war ends," I said. "We will come back and somehow repay you, Mr. Malinowski. You're the kindest, most generous man I've ever known in my life."

"The only thing I ask is for you both to be safe and keep your promise to come back and see me when all of this is over."

Zelda hugged Mr. Malinowski and he held her in his arms like a daughter. "I'm so sorry for all that has happened to you. I will pray for your parents' survival, Zelda. And I hope one day you will find your brothers, Joshua and Eli. They will also be in my prayers."

We started to leave when Mr. Malinowski stopped me. "Here," he said, handing me his umbrella. "It's raining outside. Don't lose it. It's irreplaceable." I ran my finger along the shiny, smooth walnut handle, examining the fine detail of the turtles Khone had masterfully carved into it. Engraved in the silver handle cap were the initials T. M., Tadeusz Malinowski.

"I can't take this," I said.

"No, you must."

"Are you sure?"

"One hundred percent," he replied as he patted me on the back and ushered me out the door. "Just remember to bring it back when you're finished using it."

I smiled. "I won't forget."

60

JUST PAST MIDNIGHT, WE LIFTED THE SEWER CAP AT THE corner of Józefińska Street and Krakusa Street and lowered ourselves into the tunnel's humid stench. Mr. Malinowski's battery-powered hand lamp cast a narrow beam of light through the pitch-black darkness. We tied rags around our faces to shield ourselves from the fetid vapors, which made us gag, but they offered little relief.

Following the sewage flow, we slowly waded through the swampy sludge of human waste, which reached our upper thighs. We dodged black tree roots poking through the wet, decaying brick walls, moving cautiously to avoid tripping and falling into the muck. Rats dropped from the walls and roots, swimming past us, while clouds of black flies swarmed around our heads. Zelda was behind me, holding my hand, silent. "Are you okay?" I asked.

"Yes," she whispered. "Just keep going."

The tunnel led to a Y-intersection where we had to go left or right. Since the sewage flowed down both branches of the tunnel, we knew that either would eventually lead to the river. But we needed to choose the one that would exit near the train bridge where the driver would wait for us. I'd completely lost my sense of direction, and so had Zelda. We retraced in our minds the direction we faced when we lowered ourselves into the tunnel at Józefińska Street and Krakusa Street. Zelda guessed that taking the left branch would lead us to the train bridge. I agreed.

As we continued, the sewage slowly descended from our knees to our ankles. The stench dissipated as fresh air now flowed into the tunnel. We rounded a bend and found the opening. It was arch shaped, like the doors to the old synagogue in Przemyśl.

When we exited from the tunnel, we saw looming over us, as if suspended from the sky, a massive iron train bridge. Its girders resembled the bones of a giant prehistoric creature. The trees and tallgrass along the bank rustled in a wind filled with the marshy odors of the river.

I shut off the lamp, and we walked in darkness north along the riverbank. Once we were far away from the sewer outlet, where the water appeared relatively clean, we stripped off our clothes and sent them downriver.

We immersed ourselves in the cold, dark waters, vigorously rubbing our hands over our bodies, scrubbing each other's backs, Afterward, we hastily put on fresh clothes and proceeded north-ward about another two hundred meters. There we found a truck waiting with its engine idling and lights off.

The driver jumped out of the cab nervously puffing on a cig-arette, not much older than us, maybe midtwenties, with blond hair and anxious eyes. He wore a brown cap and a dirty white shirt with suspenders holding up baggy gray trousers frayed at the hem. He was thin as a wheat stalk, twitching and lurching like a chicken.

"Quick, in the back," he said, checking the road behind him, throwing open the rear gate and jumping onto the truck bed. It had wood planks standing a meter high framing the sides of the truck bed. Inside was firewood stacked high. "Help me with moving these logs," he said. Beneath the logs we found a wood crate the size of two coffins.

He pried open the lid and ordered us to get inside. I hesitated, suddenly terrified of being trapped in such a small space. "Let's go," said Zelda, boldly stepping into the crate. She grabbed my hand as I nervously climbed inside with her. My palms and back broke into a sweat; my breath quickened. I feared suffocating in such a small space. We lay down facing each other, her head on my arm, our backs squeezed against the wall, the rucksack pressing against our feet.

"The ride will take about an hour," said the driver. "If we're stopped, you stay quiet, no matter what. Understand? Stay perfectly still. If not, you get us all killed."

He flicked his cigarette away, lowered the lid on the crate, hammered some nails into it, then stacked all the firewood on top. Sealed inside our coffin, my entire body trembled. I tried slowing down my rapid breath. Zelda stroked my hair and kept telling me everything would be okay.

The road was uneven, tossing us from side to side; exhaust fumes penetrated the crate, making me feel dizzy and sick. With the walls and ceiling pressing in on us, I worried about vomiting inside the small black box. To help pull me out of my panic, Zelda held my hands and quietly hummed "Mamele," the same song the accordion player sang when I first found her and her parents in their apartment. I hummed along with her, remembering the first time she sang it to me while we picnicked on a hot summer day by the river.

"*Mamele, mamele.*" Mother, dear Mother. "*Mit libshaft vel ikh rufn dikh Mamele.*" With love do I call you mother. "*Ogyn mid, shvakh dayn hant.*" Tired eyes, your hand is frail. "*A golden harts hostu, un yeder kind farshteys.*" You have a golden heart, and every child understands this.

Her soft, raspy voice soothed my nerves. "Can a song be a form of tikkun olam?" I asked.

"Of course," she said. "Songs and music are one of the best forms of tikkun olam."

"You have the most beautiful voice, Zelda. Sing some more."

She was about to continue singing the rest of "Mamele" when the truck slowed down and came to a stop. German soldiers barked orders at the driver to get out of the cab. We'd hit a checkpoint. The soldiers wanted to know where he was going. He told them he was taking firewood to the market at Opatowiec. They'd not heard of the town. He said it was twenty kilometers north. They wanted to know where he was coming from and why he was out delivering wood so late. He said he was from a few towns back, Księże Kopacze, and needed to deliver the wood so he could get home early in the morning.

They boarded the truck bed and poked through the firewood just centimeters away from us. We heard their every breath and smelled the old tobacco and mildew on their wool uniforms. The heels of their heavy boots pounded the wood floor in search of loose boards, like the SS did at Zelda's apartment when they raided it. Zelda squeezed my hand and pressed her head into my shoulder. She was praying.

The soldiers asked the driver if he had any liquor or food in the truck. He gave them what food he had and said there was no liquor. They exited the truck bed and searched the cab but found nothing. Then they demanded money. He paid them something, and they let him go.

Once he pulled away, Zelda stopped praying and loosened her tight grip on my hand. "I hope we get there soon," I said.

She said nothing. I knew she was thinking about her parents. I wanted to say something to comfort her, but I had no words.

We traveled about another twenty minutes before we finally reached our destination. The driver unloaded the firewood, pried open the top of the crate, and pointed us toward the river. He looked at his watch. "Barge should be here in an hour. Wait by the river and flash your light when you see it. Good luck," he said before driving off.

* * *

THE FOREST WAS PITCH DARK AND STRANGELY QUIET, LIKE THE forest I was in with my family. Oak and elm trees surrounded us. The air carried the fecund scent of the river. I thought I saw a shadow darting between the trees, then another through the thicket. Maybe they were German soldiers? "Did you see that?" I asked Zelda.

"What?"

"Something moving between the trees and those bushes."

"No. Are you sure you saw something?"

I said I wasn't sure, and that we should keep going. I sensed my mind was playing tricks on me.

As we headed toward the river through the thicket of brush and brambles, I kept a tight clasp of Zelda's hand, seeing more shadows appear and disappear. Ghosts from the past. What looked like Papa's hat in a tree turned out to be a nest; Basha crouched on the forest floor was a tree stump; Bubbe's arm coming up from the ground was actually a shrub.

I thought about where my family's bodies ended up. Perhaps at the bottom of the Vistula River, where they'd rot and then return to the soil, like the leaves. Or maybe they had made it out to the Baltic Sea where they'd disintegrate in the currents of the oceans. Wherever their bodies were, I felt their spirits were here, living amid the shadows and forest plants.

We soon arrived at a clearing revealing the Vistula snaking between two grassy banks, glinting seductively in the bright silver moonlight. The tension in my body drained away. Zelda found a weeping willow with a clear view of the river. We sat down and leaned against its trunk, concealed beneath its curtain of long, stringy branches. From there, we monitored the river and had our light ready for signaling the barge.

Time sifted away slowly. The moon made its arc across the sky, from east to west, shadowing the path of its sister, the sun. Then the eastern sky began glowing fiery red at first light, silhouetting the bumpy edges of the treetops across the river.

"Maybe we missed the barge," I said to Zelda. "Or maybe it got delayed at port in Kraków or needed to refuel."

"Let's go down to the river for a better view," said Zelda.

We left our spot beneath the willow and walked through the tallgrass to the riverbank. There we could see farther upriver toward Kraków. Three white egrets glided past us, riding the wind north toward Gdynia, our destination.

"Maybe that's a good omen," said Zelda.

We sat down on a weathered log and waited. The water lapped at our feet while the hum of crickets chirped in the marsh grass. Ripples ran across the river's surface, reflecting the dawn's golden light blooming behind the trees.

Soon the light made us too visible on the riverbank. We returned to the willow, hiding behind its stringy branches, keeping an eye on the river. Since we were both exhausted, I suggested we take turns sleeping so one of us was always on watch.

"We'll do two hours each," said Zelda. "You start."

"No, ladies first."

"Can you stay awake?"

"If I can't keep my eyes open, I'll wake you."

She lay down on her side and snuggled next to me, resting her head on my leg. Warm sunlight sparkled behind the trees. Emerging from the bulrushes and cattails along the riverbank came the growing song-chatter of blackbirds and wrens.

I gently combed my fingers through her thick, coppery-red hair, tracing the smooth contours of her skull down to the delicate curve of her slender neck and across her freckled shoulders. Her eyes closed as she eased into a state of relaxation. Before long she was adrift in a sea of slumber, appearing as an angel descended from the heavens.

Gazing down at her, I thought: Should I ever lose her again, I'll die without her.

61

THROUGHOUT THE DAY, ZELDA AND I TOOK TURNS KEEPING
watch for the barge, but it never appeared. And it was impossible
for me to sleep. Every time I closed my eyes the images of my
family being murdered by the river, and Zelda's parents being torn
away from her, flashed before me.

The sounds of the woods—a squirrel scurrying up a tree, leaves
rustling in the breeze, the snap of a branch, the cawing of crows—
were alarming. The haunting wind carried the dry whispers of the
old man at Płaszów praying *Hineni Hashem, Hineni Hashem. . . .*
My mind felt as if it were balancing on the edge of a razor. Minutes
felt like hours. The day seemed to never end. Waiting and waiting
was rapidly whittling down my patience. We urgently needed to
escape this place.

We contemplated trying to walk to Gdynia, or stowing away
on a train or truck. But Gdynia was almost six hundred kilometers away, and all those options had their own set of dangers
that seemed more ominous than the danger we were already in.
We would wait one more night, hoping the barge would soon
appear.

Hunger gnawed at us. We shared a can of sardines along with
some bread and cheese and a few slices of apple. When we finished,
we explored what was beyond the small outcropping just fifty
meters north along the riverbank. Maybe that would be a safer
place to wait for the barge.

On the other side of the outcropping, we discovered a large wooden rowboat pulled up on shore and tied to a tree. We wondered if it belonged to someone living in the forest. But around the boat there were no signs of trails. "Maybe it belongs to someone who is in the forest hunting," said Zelda. "We should be careful."

We quietly made our way down to the riverbank keeping a close watch on the woods while listening for any unusual sounds of movement. When we reached the boat we inspected it, searching for clues to why someone had tied it to a tree in the middle of nowhere.

The boat was in good shape, about six meters long with four benches, cedar bottom boards, the oars made of solid oak with a thick metal pin securing them to the iron oarlocks. Beneath the stern seat was a fishing rod and reel and a small wooden tackle box with various feathered gold and silver lures. There were two metal traps for squirrel and rabbit, like the ones I'd used on the farm. Brass rifle shells were scattered along the floorboards, and someone had tucked a canvas tarp, possibly used for shelter, beneath the stern seat. Afraid of being discovered, we ran back through the woods to our hiding place beneath the willow.

By early evening, at sunset, mountains of towering white thunderheads, their edges burning red and bronze, amassed in the east. Looming beneath them were lines of charcoal-gray clouds with flashes of lightning crackling inside them. The gnats and mosquitoes bit ferociously. Then the wind picked up, abruptly shifting from the south to the northeast. A rush of cool air pushed out the warm air and the voracious insects disappeared. The churning sky rapidly turned a dark gray-green.

In the growing darkness, the storm's headwinds began howling, whipping the trees, bending them like twigs from side to side, the older branches and limbs cracking and breaking, dropping to the ground in broken pieces. The rain poured down on us in a torrent. Beneath the willow, I opened Mr. Malinowski's umbrella before we became drenched. "Let's find better cover," I said to Zelda. We ran from the willow to the river where we spotted along the upper bank a huge downed oak tree lying on its side. Much of its trunk had rotted out. We made it to the oak and huddled beneath its roof.

From there we saw the river's surface roiling and pockmarked by the pounding rains. Violent winds wailed and lashed the trees as thunder rumbled and then exploded directly over us. The gusts were so strong that foamy white waves broke across the river's surface. I closed the umbrella canopy to prevent it from tearing and breaking as the reckless winds tried ripping it away.

We kept our eyes focused on the river, watching and listening for any sign of the barge. Then, magically, through the white flashes of lightning and heavy sheets of rain, coming toward us, piercing the darkness, two tiny golden stars floated just above the river. As it approached, we realized they were the bow lights of the barge. Two of them, just as Mr. Malinowski described.

I grabbed the lamp and ran to the river's edge through the deluge, hollering at the top of my lungs while madly waving my light at the barge. Painted on its hull near the bow was M/S KRAKÓW and a Polish flag. Without question, this was the barge Mr. Malinowski had told us to signal. But the barge slowly cruised past us, seemingly oblivious to our existence. The low rumble of its coal-powered motor, muffled by the howling wind and rain, soon faded in the distance. I stood there dumbfounded, watching in dismay as it rounded the bend before disappearing into the darkness.

Soaked to the bone, I returned to Zelda. "Now what do we do?"

"I don't know," she said, gazing at the river, searching its dark waters for an answer.

The lightning soon ceased and the winds settled; the downpour diminished to a light drizzle and then stopped. Above, a bright full moon, like a faithful companion, surfaced from the clouds, splashing its silver light across the water.

Zelda took my hand. "I think we should keep moving," she said.

"I do too. I can't stay here one more minute."

"Let's see if the boat is still there. And if it is, then let's take it to Gdynia."

Although the journey would be incredibly risky, I agreed with Zelda. I thought so long as we traveled by night, the boat might be our best bet for reaching Gdynia.

We walked back through the wet forest and found the boat still tied to the tree. The rainwater had filled it up to the bottom of the seats. Fearful that the owner might appear at any moment, we swiftly untied the boat from the tree and started rocking it from side to side. Gradually, we gained enough momentum to flip it and drain the water out.

Sounds of branches snapping suddenly drew our attention to the forest. At first, I thought it could be a deer. But then I thought I saw a flash of metal.

"Let's go!" whispered Zelda. She jumped inside the boat with the rucksack and umbrella as I shoved it stern first into the river. I climbed in, took the center seat, and grabbed the oars. The rains had made the current swift. I rowed hard with the current, making the boat go even faster.

"Did you see someone?" she asked.

"Yes. It could've been the hunter. I thought I saw the metal of his rifle's barrel."

"Me too. Thank God we got away."

Although we were unaware of the challenges awaiting us downstream, I experienced an exhilarating sense of freedom that had eluded me since the start of the war. For here I was with my Zelda, moving swiftly on a current toward a destination full of promise. A burden lifted from my shoulders as I drew in the fresh air, and the shore swiftly glided past us. Glancing at Zelda, seated within arm's reach, I was in awe of her presence. She looked past me, her gaze fixed on the river ahead, a pained expression etched on her face, her deep green eyes holding within them the profound grief of her loss. "Are you okay?" I asked her.

She dipped her hand into the water, watching the smooth ripples enveloping it. "Do you think my mama and papa are alive?"

I didn't have the heart to tell her what I'd seen at Płaszów, nor what Mr. Malinowski had told me. I wanted to forget about the past and only focus on the future. Pulling hard on the oars, I rowed in silence.

"Please, tell me."

"I don't know," I said, wanting her to drop the question.

"But I think you do. You were in Płaszów You saw what happened there."

Slowing down on the oars, I used them primarily to guide the boat as we drifted inside the current. I tried to avoid looking into her imploring eyes.

"I think you know what happened to them," she continued. "Tell me . . . please. It's worse to not know, like with my brothers."

I thought about what to say, and how to say it. Then a gunshot cracked the air.

Zelda fell forward.

Someone fired another shot.

The bullet pocked the water to the right of the bow.

I pulled on the oars with everything I had.

In the distance upstream, at the edge of the shore, a silhouetted man held a rifle pointed at us. He fired off a final shot just as we rounded a bend and escaped his view.

Zelda lay at my feet groaning with a bullet wound in her chest. Blood dribbled from her mouth. I thought my mind had snapped—

what I saw couldn't possibly be real. It seemed to be a hallucination, like in the woods, or perhaps I was caught in a nightmare.

"Keep breathing, Zelda. Just keep breathing," I pleaded as I maneuvered the boat to the opposite side of the river and shored it beneath the cover of two trees.

She was unconscious. I removed my shirt and rolled her onto her side to cover the hole in her left upper back. She coughed up more blood. Her breathing slowed. I begged her not to die, ordering her to keep breathing, to keep fighting. "You can't go!" I insisted. "Please don't leave me. . . . I beg you. . . ." But she couldn't hear my pleas as she slowly slipped away.

I SPENT THE REST OF THE NIGHT INSIDE THE BOAT CRADLING Zelda in my arms, weeping, combing my fingers through her thick locks, talking tenderly to her. In the wisps of wind murmuring mournfully across the willows and tallgrasses lining the riverbank, I heard her raspy, gentle voice singing to me. It was the same song she often sang to me in Kraków beneath the willows by the river as we lay on the soft grass in the warm sun, cuddled in each other's arms. The same song Mama sang when putting us to bed, "Belz, Mayn Shtetele Belz."

I closed my eyes and listened.

> *Belz, mayn shtetele Belz,*
> *Mayn heymele, vu ich hob*
> *Mayne kindershe yorn farbracht . . .*
> *Mayn heymele vu ich hob*
> *Die Sheine Chalomes a sach.*
> *Belz, my little town of Belz*
> *My home, where my childhood days passed*
> *Belz, my hometown of Belz*
> *In a small and simple room*

Where I would sit and laugh with all the children.
I would run with my prayer book every Shabbos
To the banks of the river,
And sit under the green tree.
Belz, my little town of Belz
Belz, my hometown of Belz
My home, where I dreamed so many
Beautiful dreams.

Zelda's sweet raspy voice, soothing as warm milk and honey, flowed through me, cupping my heart in its raw tenderness, filling me with a sense of bewilderment, unbearable loss, and longing.

62

AT FIRST LIGHT I AWAKENED TO THE SOUND OF THE RAVENS cawing from the willow branches above. Zelda was cold and limp in my hands; her freckled arms and face were now a chalky whitish-blue. Blood covered my clothes and pooled at the bottom of the boat. I still couldn't let her body go. I wanted to return to sleep with her in my arms, and never awaken again.

Closing my eyes, I listened to the ravens bickering until they flew off. The woods fell silent, save for the soft lapping of water on the rocks lining the edge of the riverbank. From the distance, the hum of a boat's motor filtered through the woods, growing louder as it approached. It wasn't the thumping sound of a barge's coal-fired engine. Rather, it was the smooth hum of a smaller boat's outboard motor, perhaps a fishing boat.

Peering over the stern, I viewed the river through the stringy willow branches camouflaging my boat. As the motor-boat passed, painted on the bow was the German army's iron cross. A soldier stood in the open cockpit manning the steering wheel. Two more soldiers sat near the stern as they patrolled the river.

I lay back down in the boat and cuddled Zelda in my arms. The woods were quiet again. Bright splinters of sunlight cut through the curtain of green branches as they swayed in the gentle breeze. I fell asleep embracing her.

* * *

HOURS LATER, THE RAVENS RETURNED, THEIR FRENETIC CAWS waking me from nightmares I couldn't remember. Their silhouettes dotted the branches above like splotches of black ink, behind them the sky bathed in the deep blue of dusk.

I gathered Zelda's limp body in my arms and lifted her out of the boat before gently setting her down on the soft grass beneath the willow.

At the river's edge, I removed my shirt, rinsed the blood from it, then carefully used it to clean the bloodstains around Zelda's mouth, slender neck, her palms, and long, delicate fingers. I combed her coppery-red hair with my fingers for the last time, and carefully folded her limp arms across her chest, placing her right hand over the button I'd given her.

"Don't lose it," I said. "I'll come back for it."

From the bottom of her sweater, I removed a button and placed it in my pocket. "And when I join you, I'll give your button back to you."

I wrapped her like a mummy in the canvas tarp that was stored in the boat, tied a rope around its center and at each end to keep it closed.

Carefully setting her body back down inside the boat, I knotted the ends of each rope around a large river rock. I didn't want her body to float along the surface for anyone to see, like what happened to my family. She needed to be hidden beneath the waters, shielded from the chaos of the world above. She needed to be in a place where she could rest peacefully.

When dusk turned to night, I set out to the middle of the river, where it was deepest. The current wasn't as strong as the night before. I drew in the oars and drifted quietly. The night was moonless, and above me, a dome of stars covered every inch of the sky spanning from horizon to horizon.

I cradled Zelda's body in my lap, my heart aching with a crushing, interminable grief. I felt as though I no longer belonged to this world. The thought of letting her go, of living without her, was incomprehensible—unbearable. Tears streamed down my face as I whispered how much I loved her, how deeply I missed her. I promised to uncover the truth of what happened to her parents and brothers. I begged her for forgiveness, apologized for not being able to save her or her parents.

I recited the kaddish: *"Yitgadal v'yitkadash sh'mei raba b'alma di v'ra chirutei. . . ."*

After the prayer, I gently lifted her body onto the boat's gunnel and carefully lowered her into the dark waters, glinting with pearls of starlight. She floated momentarily on the surface until I released the rocks into the river, one by one. The heavy stones swiftly drew her body into the depths, where she'd vanish into eternity, taking a part of my soul with her.

6 3

OVER THE COURSE OF THE NEXT THREE DAYS, I ROWED AT NIGHT and tried to sleep during the day in the swaths of woods that stretched between the small towns and villages nestled along the river. But sleep was hard to come by. Nightmares haunted me frequently, jolting me awake. I'd often find myself gasping for air, my forehead wet with sweat, my limbs weak and quivering with tremors. I never remembered the dreams, only the fragments of terrifying images.

At night, I used the fishing rod and tackle left inside the boat to troll the river as I rowed north. I caught mostly zander, pike, and perch-pike. I did not hide from the boats and barges that passed by me. After nearly a year of living and working in the countryside, I was confident in my ability to pass as a Pole and not a Jew. Also, my melancholy had rendered me fearless. I no longer cared about what could happen to me.

On the fourth night, a German patrol boat spotted me and pulled up alongside my rowboat, blasting their spotlight down on me. The only things visible in the blinding light were three ominous German soldier silhouettes pointing rifles in my direction. They didn't frighten me because I didn't care what they planned to do. Nothing mattered anymore.

One of them spoke to me in Polish and asked what I was doing out so late fishing. I told him this is the time I like to fish.

Then I pulled up the line tied to the boat's gunnel and showed him the two zander and two pike tied at the end. He told me to go stand in the stern so they'd have a better view of what was beneath the seats. He saw the tackle box and ordered me to open it. I held it up and unlatched the lid. He peered inside and saw a pack of cigarettes the hunter had left behind. He ordered me to toss him the pack. I followed his orders. They called me a stupid Pole and left.

On the fifth night, I passed through the demolished city of Warsaw. Building after building lining the river was in ruin, crushed by bombs and artillery. Chunks of brick walls with blasted-out windows stood like ancient ruins amid the collapsed buildings and mountains of bricks. Fires burned where people huddled in small groups staying warm in the cool night. Ominous clouds of black smoke drifted like specters over the devastated city.

I rowed past a bridge that had sections of it missing, giving it the appearance of a giant dinosaur's spine split into pieces. I wondered if there was still a ghetto in Warsaw, or if the Germans had annihilated it along with everything else. As terrible as the Kraków ghetto was, at least the Germans left the city intact. Warsaw, from what I could see from the river, was reduced to rubble, as if a massive earthquake had leveled it.

I rowed through the port to the locks the Germans had destroyed. As I passed through them, I noticed the distorted shapes of several bodies caught in their broken doors. One body had a dislocated leg wrapped around its neck, another body's arm was twisted around a tree limb, the angles of its bones all wrong.

For the next six days, I rowed between ten to twelve hours a night, often through rain. I cooked the fish over an open fire, drank rainwater from a bucket stored in the boat and well water from the war-damaged villages speckling the riverbank. I never interacted with a soul. I mastered hiding from people, making myself invisible, passing through the days and nights as nothing more than a shadow, a ghost, a soulless human being floating through the ether of war, through the stench of dead bodies rotting in the fields and floating down the river, through the noxious fumes of petrol and burned villages. Charred trees stripped of their branches and leaves, broken limbed, roots unearthed, dying or already dead, stood naked and alone in the abandoned fields.

I had conversations with Zelda, speaking aloud to her, sharing my day, telling her what kinds of fish I caught, what types of boats I saw, what the weather was like, the names of the villages I passed—Wyszogród, Ciechocinek, Chełmno, Nowe, Gniew. . . . She sang Yiddish songs and made-up songs about how she missed me. I told her I missed her more. She said at least now she was with her parents. But she still didn't know where her brothers were. I asked her to never leave my heart. She promised me she wouldn't.

On the seventh day of travel, I reached the mouth of the Vistula where it emptied into a bay that connected to the Baltic Sea. The dark, charcoal-colored clouds above cracked open for a moment, allowing a curtain of sunlight to spill down. The brilliant light shimmered along the surface of the calm blue bay, warming my back briefly before disappearing behind the clouds again.

I rowed along the industrial coast lined by factories and freight trains, and past several large freighters heading into the port of Gdańsk. Unlike the small harbors I had passed through, Gdańsk was a huge shipyard that appeared to be left untouched by the war. I assumed it must have been a strategic port for the Germans' supply chain of foods, goods, fuels, and military supplies.

Inside the harbor, a ship was dry-docked and under construction. It stood about nine to twelve meters tall, the height of a three- to four-story building in Kraków. The ship's unfinished hull resembled a massive steel skeleton. Men dangled from its sides like spiders, working from ropes and scaffolding. Across the hull, sparks danced in the air where they welded and riveted steel plates onto its bare frame.

I rowed past Gdańsk and several hours later, in the dimness of dusk, entered the port of Gdynia. It was even larger than Gdańsk. Silhouetted against the muted sky, giant cranes spanned the port, standing tall and angular atop their massive iron-beamed platforms. Their long booms, at least five stories tall, pointed toward the heavens. Behind them a huge factory chimney bellowed thick columns of smoke, swirling across the sky like black veils, floating out to sea.

At the end of the harbor, I discovered a small dock for skiffs and rowboats. I tied up my boat there and went on land.

The port buzzed at a frenetic pace. Droves of men heaving sacks of grains, cement, heavy metal pipes, and timber on their backs and shoulders loaded and unloaded the ships, trucks, and boxcars stationed in the port. Other men pushed carts stacked with crates, coal, and iron ore.

Traversing like ants in an endless flow, lines of men lugged their cargo up and down the ship's ramps that reached from their decks down to the dock. Above the men loomed the colossal cranes, sweeping their long angular arms through the air with clamshell buckets dangling like giant pendulums from the ends of their cables.

Three ships moored to the dock flew their country's flags from their sterns. One ship was German, the other Finnish, and the third came from Sweden. The ship from Sweden had a crane next to it unloading what must have been iron ore from its hold. I remembered Mr. Malinowski telling me it was iron ore that Sweden was still trading with the Germans. He said the Germans heavily depended on mass quantities of iron ore to make the steel used for producing their tanks, aircraft, weapons, ammunition, bridges, railways, factories.

Next to the ship, a line of men unloaded gunnysacks of grain from a boxcar and carried them up the ship's ramp to the deck where they unloaded them. I noticed coming down the dock toward me were several soldiers patrolling the port. Rather than hide, I joined the line of workers loading the gunnysacks onto the ship. Once on deck, I planned to slip away to find a place to hide aboard the vessel.

64

DARKNESS HAD FALLEN WHEN I JOINED THE LINE OF MEN LOADing the gunnysacks onto the ship. The men looked tired from working all day and took little notice of me. They appeared to all be Poles, except for one. He had a scraggly, wiry rusty-brown beard and sorrowful green eyes that looked familiar to me. He was around my age, maybe a bit younger, bony as a scarecrow but strong. Glancing nervously back at me for a moment, he also seemed to recognize something in me. I sensed he was like me—a Jew in search of a way to escape to Sweden.

Carrying my gunnysack up the ramp, I followed the man in front of me to the hold where the cargo was unloaded. He led me down a set of metal stairs and into a dark steel cave dimly lit by yellow lights mounted on the metal ceiling. The musty odor of mildew, seawater, engine oil, and cigarette and pipe tobacco smoke permeated the air. Several Swedish sailors directed us to where they wanted the gunnysacks stacked. An older officer with a thick white goatee, broad shoulders, and a bulbous nose puffed on his pipe while leaning against one of the rusting steel-beam supports. He observed us and gave orders to the sailors.

After unloading our gunnysacks, we climbed a steep metal staircase at the opposite end of the hold that led to the deck. I glanced across the ship looking for a place to stow away before going back down the ramp. At the stern were two lifeboats stationed with canvas tarps covering them. I figured if I could get to one of those boats without being seen, it would be the perfect place to stow away

Once the hold containing the iron ore was empty, a crane mounted to the ship's deck gently lowered from its cables a huge metal hatch-cover to seal the hold. Several sailors on deck carefully guided the hatch-cover to its position, and then bolted it down.

Many of the dockworkers had already left after working all day. I needed to make a move. After loading my last gunnysack into the hold, I shot up the metal stairs to the deck and saw it was clear of sailors between where I stood and the lifeboats stationed at the stern.

In the cover of darkness, I sprinted to the lifeboat on the starboard side and found a small space to squeeze myself into between its hull and the deck. I lay there quietly and listened. A train engine hissed in the port below and trucks drove by. Toward the bow, where the bridge was located, a small group of sailors were yelling orders in Swedish. Then a whistle cut through the air, followed by the long blast of a horn. A rattling sound indicated the ramp was being retracted. The ship's engines now rumbled beneath me, making the metal deck pressed against my chest vibrate. A column of black smoke bellowed from the smokestack, curling in the wind. It reminded me of the smoke we saw rising from the airport on that clear and beautiful, warm sunny morning on 1 September 1939, the day the war began.

I emerged from beneath the lifeboat to climb inside it. Small brass rings running along the gunnels secured its canvas tarp cover. I quickly opened a section of the tarp just wide enough for me to slip through.

Inside the lifeboat, lying across its wooden planks, I stared into the abyss of darkness as the deep rumble of the ship's engines powered us through the harbor and into the vast expanse of the open sea. I felt safe inside the lifeboat, yet completely lost and untethered. I was leaving my homeland for the first time. And although it was a relief to escape the horrors of the German occupation, a wave of longing for my loved ones and my old life consumed me. And then other strange feelings emerged. Although Zelda and my family were dead, I felt as if I were abandoning them. I felt guilty for still being alive while they had perished. Why them and not me?

In that dimly lit space, surrounded by the rhythmic pulse of the sea, I grappled with the question of why I should go on living when they were gone, especially Zelda. She was my last hope.

Although I was fleeing to freedom, it all seemed terribly wrong, and meaningless.

THE SHARP BLARE OF THE SHIP'S HORN AWOKE ME THE FOLLOWING
day. We had entered a harbor at dusk and there was a ship docked
in the port with a crane looming over it, emptying buckets of iron
ore into its hold. I realized I had slept through the entire trip. My
parched mouth craved water and my belly ached with hunger. But
it was too early to leave my hiding place and sneak away. I needed
to wait for the ship to dock.

Peering through a slit in the canvas cover, I watched a group
of sailors uncoiling the mooring line before dropping it down to
the dock below. They secured a ramp to the port side of the ship
near the door where we had loaded the gunnysacks of grain. I
worried workers would soon board to unload the grain, trapping
me inside the boat through the night. But then the engines shut
down and the sailors began leaving the ship with their big duffel
bags slung over their shoulders. I assumed they were going home.

Standing atop the ramp was the officer I saw in the hold with
the thick white goatee and bulbous nose. He smoked his pipe and
was speaking to the sailors as they left, perhaps giving them orders
for the next day. He waited for all of them to leave. Then another
man wearing a crisp blue uniform and an officer's hat approached
the pipe-smoking officer, had a few words with him, and then also
headed down the ramp.

I was so thirsty that I didn't think it was possible for me to
wait for this last officer to leave. Plus, I needed to urinate. I didn't

understand why he was lagging when it appeared the entire ship's crew had departed. He remained on the ramp, casually puffing on his pipe, peering down at the dock in what looked like deep contemplation. Then he strolled toward the stern, scanning the ship from port to starboard as if he was giving it a last inspection. When he reached the lifeboat opposite mine, on the port side, he knocked on its bow. Nothing happened. He knocked again and said in Polish, "Let's go. Come out." He lifted the canvas cover and to my surprise, a person climbed out of the boat carrying a small sack. "Don't worry," said the officer to the person in broken Polish. "I help you."

He then walked toward my boat. I should've been scared, but I wasn't. Nothing mattered with Zelda gone. I was dead inside, vacuous and numb. I lifted the canvas cover and stepped out of the boat and met him on the deck face-to-face. This man seemed different from all the others. I remembered the curious kindness in his moist eyes when I passed him in the hold where we had unloaded the gunnysacks of grain. The warmth and intelligence emanating from his leathery, weather-beaten face reminded me of Khone.

"Żyds?" he asked us with a heavy Swedish accent. I looked at the other person and could now see in the soft light of the full moon he was the worker with the rusty-brown beard I had taken notice of. He studied me, as though he was trying to figure out if he knew me. "Yes," said the young man.

"And you?" he asked me.

I nodded, sensing this man wanted to help us from the compassionate way he spoke to us; the way his eyes, framed by deep wrinkles, settled on us with a sense of concern rather than disdain. He seemed trustworthy.

"Tomorrow, unload grain and load ore," said the officer in more broken Polish. "Then night we leave. New York." He took a few quick puffs from his pipe. "America better for you than Sweden. I know," he said, pointing to his forehead with the mouthpiece of his pipe. "I help you go to America. Like I help others."

The reality of suddenly going to America seemed unbelievable to me. I remembered lying in bed before going to sleep, dreamily gazing at my poster of Benny Goodman wailing on his clarinet. I imagined what it must be like to cross the vast Atlantic and see the Statue of Liberty emerge in the distance, and then be inside a New York City jazz club listening to Benny Goodman's orchestra. Papa and Bubbe also liked Benny Goodman's music and we'd sometimes sit together on Friday nights, after Shabbos dinner, and listen to his band. Papa and I would sit on the couch while Bubbe rested in her plush red velvet reading chair, lightly tapping her black leather shoes against the wood floor in rhythm to the music.

The officer took us to the bridge and down a set of metal stairs that led to a narrow hallway barely wide enough for two people to slide past one another. Each side of the hallway had several wood doors. He opened one of them and ushered us inside a cabin. "You stay here. My cabin safe." He showed us a tap with running water, a closet with a toilet, and a drawer containing some apples, sausages, bread, and hard cheeses. I immediately put my mouth to the tap and guzzled down a long stream of water, relieving the dry, chalky taste in my mouth.

"I come back in morning," he said, stepping outside the door. "You stay here. Don't go anywhere in ship. Just stay here. My cabin safe," he repeated, in case we didn't understand. He showed us how to lock the door, and then left.

I quickly used the toilet to finally relieve my full bladder. When I returned, the young man and I immediately took the food out of the drawer and sat down on two small wooden chairs positioned around a short and narrow table that dropped from the wall. Without saying a word, we sliced the bread, cheeses, apples, and sausages and began eating. I filled two glasses of water and handed one to him. I drank one glass of water after another, as did he, trying to quench my insatiable thirst.

"Did you know that man?" I asked the young man in Yiddish, rather than Polish. I wanted to know if he was really a Jew.

"I met him just like you," he replied in Yiddish. "He must've seen us get into the lifeboats. You look familiar. Where are you from?"

"Kraków. And you?"

"The same."

"You also look familiar."

"My name's Joshua Abramovitch. What's yours?"

I stared at him in awe, utterly speechless. Yes, that's whose face it was, now four years older than when I last saw him in September of '39. The oldest of Zelda's brothers. I reached across the table and grabbed hold of his hand. "Who do you think I am?"

His eyes filled with tears as he gazed at me incredulously. "Reuven?" I nodded affirmingly. We both jumped to our feet and embraced, wrapping our arms round each other so tightly we could barely breathe. We desperately clung to each other as if holding the other person would somehow bring back the people we had lost. Joshua was Zelda's flesh and blood and embracing him was as close as I'd ever get to embracing Zelda again. I didn't want to let him go.

When we finally sat down and wiped away our tears, we talked. I told Joshua all that had happened to his family, and mine. He told me what had happened to him and his brother, Eli, when German soldiers kidnapped them from the farm.

The German soldiers had sent them to Treblinka, where they endured endless work in a gravel pit, near starvation, beatings, primitive latrines, freezing temperatures while wearing only threadbare clothes and tattered old shoes with holes in the soles—horrific living conditions that no human or animal should ever have to experience. Tragically, Eli caught typhoid and died there in the fifth month. Afterward, Joshua made a daring escape with two other men. As they ran for the woods, German guards shot and killed both men. Joshua escaped and traveled through the forests on his own for a month before stowing away on a boxcar train, which was how he made it to Gdynia.

We talked and cried until morning. And when our minds and bodies were drained of every last ounce of strength and emotion inside us, we lowered the two bunks mounted to the walls and lay down upon them to rest.

Next to me, I opened the small round porthole and gazed across the calm and expansive Baltic Sea. Fresh sea air smelling of brine filled the cabin. The first light appeared in the distance, washing across the horizon in warm hues of copper, the color of Zelda's hair. On the sea's teal surface, flat and clear as glass, reflections of white, puffy clouds floated westward, toward America. A flock of seagulls riding the winds silently glided past us.

"What do you want to do when we get to America?" he asked.

I contemplated the question, and my mind went blank. I suddenly felt alone again. The future was impossible to imagine, and the past was mostly a ravaged wasteland of loss and ruin that I wanted to forget. Our only refuge was the present.

I listened to the steady rhythm of Joshua's long and deep breaths, the sea lapping against the ship's hull, the low thrum of the ship's engine, and closed my eyes, seeking solace in the depths of sleep.

ACKNOWLEDGMENTS

WHILE THIS BOOK IS A WORK OF FICTION, WITH ITS CHARACTERS and storylines imagined, many events and details are drawn from or inspired by the historical facts of the time and place in which the novel is set. Personal memories of survivors, the journals and diaries that recorded the events of that period, and various historical writings found in books and verified internet sources provided important historical information that is woven into the novel's story.

I owe the title of the book and the umbrella maker storyline to my great-grandfather, Raphael Lending, who was an umbrella maker in Warsaw in the late 1800s. According to family lore, one day he came across a Polish police officer beating a Jewish man. He intervened, hoping to stop the altercation, but ended up stabbing the police officer with a dagger concealed in the stem of his umbrella. Fearing imprisonment for life or execution, he immediately abandoned his business, uprooted his family, and escaped to America. They arrived at Ellis Island on December 24, 1909. A version of this incident is a key turning point for the Berkovitz family in the novel.

Saul Dreier and Ruby Sosnowicz, both Holocaust survivors from Poland and the subjects of a documentary I made over the course of three years, were invaluable sources, providing me with an intimate emotional and psychological understanding of what it was like to live through the Holocaust, and how their traumas affected them in later years. When we returned to Poland and walked the streets where they grew up—Saul in Kraków, Ruby in Warsaw—

their recollections offered me deeper insights into what it was like to grow up in these places: the sights, smells, and sounds of the neighborhood, the rhythms of life, and how it all changed dramatically after the Germans invaded. I am deeply indebted to Saul and Ruby for sharing their lives and trusting me with their personal stories.

I'm also indebted to Julius Feldman (1923–1943), the nineteen-year-old author of *The Kraków Diary*. Written over two months in the spring of 1943, he risked his life to provide a detailed account of what happened to his family and city from the time the Germans invaded Kraków on September 1, 1939, up to his last entry on April 11, 1943. At the time, Feldman was interned at Płaszów as a forced laborer. His diary abruptly ends mid-sentence and remained hidden until the end of the war when it was discovered inside the walls of a barrack at Płaszów. Numerous events and descriptions in *The Umbrella Maker's Son* are inspired by Feldman's diary, such as the evictions of Jews from their homes, the collection of their furs, the forced labor they endured, the painful loss of their civil rights, the construction and conditions of the ghetto, the mass deportations, and the atrocities that occurred at the Płaszów labor camp. Historians assume Feldman perished in Płaszów. The diary he left behind is a miraculous gift to the world.

The Kraków Ghetto Pharmacy by Tadeusz Pankiewicz was another essential historical source for writing this novel. Pankiewicz, a remarkable Catholic pharmacist who risked his life running the only pharmacy in the Kraków ghetto and who is responsible for saving many Jewish lives, inspired the creation of the pharmacist in the novel, Mr. Malinowski. I'm deeply grateful for his highly detailed, first-person account of the horrific events that unfolded when the Germans occupied Kraków, specifically documenting the nightmarish conditions and events inside the ghetto.

Isaac Bashevis Singer's book, *A Day of Pleasure*, with photographs by Roman Vishniac, was another important source that provided background and detailed descriptions of what Poland was like for the Jewish people in the early 1900s. This period is when the mother and father in the novel, Rachel and Lev, were growing up, and when the grandmother, Bubbe, was raising her children. Additionally, two photographic books, *Image Before My Eyes: A Photographic History of Jewish Life in Poland, 1864–1939*, by LucJan Dobroszycki and Barbara Kirshenblatt-Gimblett and *Polyn: Jewish Life in the Old Country* by Alter Kacyzne, were excellent sources for detailed images of the towns, cities, and countryside where Jewish people lived before and up to the time of the war. Pinned on the walls of my writing studio were portraits of tailors, farmers, the markets, apartment buildings, and stores lining the streets. Surrounding myself with these powerful images catalyzed my imagination, providing a sense of what life was like for the Jews of Poland before the German occupation, deepening my understanding of what it meant to lose everything they once had.

Photographs from the United States Holocaust Memorial Museum that captured the horrors of being a Jew during the German occupation made their sufferings even more palpable. Historical articles from this museum and from other internet sources, including Yad Vashem, the Smithsonian, the Holocaust Encyclopedia, the Holocaust Research Project, the Jewish Virtual Library, verified articles on Wikipedia, and others, were also valuable sources for research.

Part II of the book, the section when Reuven works on Stanisław's farm, is inspired by my own experience of working on a farm at the age of sixteen in the North Platte area of Nebraska. Elements of Stanisław's character and descriptions of the farm work were drawn from the extraordinary farm experience I had while working for Joe Hertje, a complicated man full of paradoxes, who served as a father figure and mentor to me. Like Stanisław, Joe was illiterate, yet he was one of the smartest men I had ever met, possessing a vast knowledge of agriculture, mechanics, and construction. Despite his racist and anti-Semitic opinions—stemming from ignorance rather than hatred—he opened my eyes to the complexities of human beings at a very young age. I am deeply grateful for the life lessons I learned while working for him.

Most important, I want to thank all of those people along the way—family, friends, and colleagues—who provided invaluable support in various ways.

My first editor, Peternelle Van Arsdale (her magical name is real, not imagined), was not only a phenomenal editor but also an outstanding teacher for someone like me who was coming to novel writing for the first time. When I sat down to write, I did not know how long it would take (thirty months), and how demanding it would be (more gray hairs). I'm deeply grateful for Peternelle's insights and guidance in the writing of this novel, as well as her detailed notes and keen sense of how to develop the inner world of characters.

Jeannie De Vita, my second editor, was also an extraordinary teacher. Her mastery of fiction writing and its many genres, her understanding of language, composition, plot structure, and character development, along with her unsparingly honest critiques, took my work to the next level. Without Jeannie's guidance and limitless generosity, this novel would've never seen the light of day.

My deep appreciation also goes to author Renée Rosen for generously providing guidance on navigating the publishing world, finding editors, securing an agent, and inspiring me to continue writing. I want to thank Gwen Macsai and Danielle Amerian for taking time out of their busy schedules to read a draft of the novel and provide valuable, insightful feedback. A huge thank-you also goes to Michael Berenbaum for reviewing the book for historical accuracy despite his busy schedule.

My heartfelt thanks and appreciation for unconditionally supporting my pivot to writing go out to my close friend and spiritual brother, Jacob Karni, my mother and sister, Jill and Robyn, and my close and trusted friends, Anne Ream and David Monk. I deeply thank my partner in crime, Darcy Goldfarb, for reviewing and providing comments on the book, bringing love, laughter, and exploration into my life, and inspiring me with her commitment to helping the underserved and making this world a better place.

Finally, I want to thank my neighbor and friend, Tony Armour, who was extremely generous in offering to send my novel to his good friend, Sara Nelson, the senior vice president of Editorial at HarperCollins. Sara was kind enough to review the manuscript and afterward expressed an interest in possibly publishing it once I secured an agent. To assist in this endeavor, she graciously allowed me to use her highly respected name in the business when approaching agents, which no doubt helped me secure one of the best in the business, Harvey Klinger. Harvey provided important, incisive comments that shaped the final draft, which he then submitted to Sara. The deal was made, Sara provided additional comments that further improved the book, and the rest is history. I thank Sara and Harvey with all my heart for bringing this novel to the world.

ABOUT THE AUTHOR

TOD LENDING is an Academy Award–nominated and Emmy-winning documentary producer, director, writer, and cinematographer whose work has been broadcast nationally on ABC, CBS, NBC, PBS, and HBO, among others; has been screened theatrically and awarded at national and international festivals; and has been televised internationally in Europe and Asia. He is the president and founder of Nomadic Pictures, a documentary film production company based in Chicago. *The Umbrella Maker's Son* is his debut novel.